"I was riveted from start to finish by this excellent novel. Action, intrigue, dirty tricks, and humor combine to make this a great addition to the world of fantasy."

~Barry Tighe, The Spawater Chronicles, and Gieves to the Fore.

✤ ✤ ✤ ✤ ✤

"The characters are convincing, the settings realistic and the action scenes gripping. Cas Peace's competent prose makes the reading effortless. This series will be a great hit with lovers of fantasy and adventure."

~Judith Arnopp, Peaceweaver, The Forest Dwellers, and The Song of Heledd.

✤ ✤ ✤ ✤ ✤

"Cas Peace weaves her story with the skill of the most accomplished Artesan. If imagination was an element, she'd be a Master-elite."

~Steven D Jackson, Shifter.

Published by Albia Publishing 2013

Second American Paperback Edition

Visit Cas Peace at her author website: www.caspeace.com

ISBN-10: 1939993261

ISBN-13: 978-1-939993-26-7

Dedication

For my wonderful husband, Dave. What would I do without you, my rock, my soul-mate, my one true love? Not forgetting, all-round fantastic PR guy!

Also for a cherished and much-missed friend, Gerry Dailey. May you dance with the angels until we meet again, dear heart.

Artesans of Albia Trilogy

King's Envoy: Artesans of Albia, Book 1

King's Champion: Artesans of Albia, Book 2

King's Artesan: Artesans of Albia, Book 3

Acknowledgements

I'm constantly amazed when I look back over the time since *King's Envoy* was originally published. So much has happened, so many wonderful things I feared might never happen. And here we are with *King's Champion*, and it is my greatest pleasure to thank and acknowledge all those who have helped make this ongoing journey such a fantastic experience. And if I've left anyone out, I sincerely beg your pardon!

First, for constant encouragement and interest, and also invaluable help at my book launch, heartfelt thanks must go to my husband Dave and my family; Mum and Dad, my brother David, my aunt Pat. Deepest thanks also to my brother and his song-writing partner David Shepherd for their fabulous help with the *King's Envoy* song, The Wheel Will Turn, and also the song from *King's Champion*, The Ballad of Tallimore. It was great fun working, playing, and singing with you. Also to my friends and fans in the village – you helped make the day a wonderful experience for me.

To Sarah Gray and Becky Feetham at the Basingstoke Discovery Centre; thanks so much for that fabulous book launch! Thanks also to the staff of Waterstones in Basingstoke for helping with sales.

To Rhett and Emmaline Hoffmeister, for showing faith in my work. To Diane Dalton, for her understanding over all the UK and US grammar and spelling differences.

And lastly, to all those readers who enjoy *King's Envoy* and leave me such uplifting reviews. You are the ones who matter. You are the reason I write. Thank you all for reading my work and for getting so deeply involved in the lives of Taran, Rienne, Cal, Sullyan, Robin, and Bull. They live because of you. I hope you enjoy *King's Champion* as much, and that you will continue to follow the series. There is so much more to come!

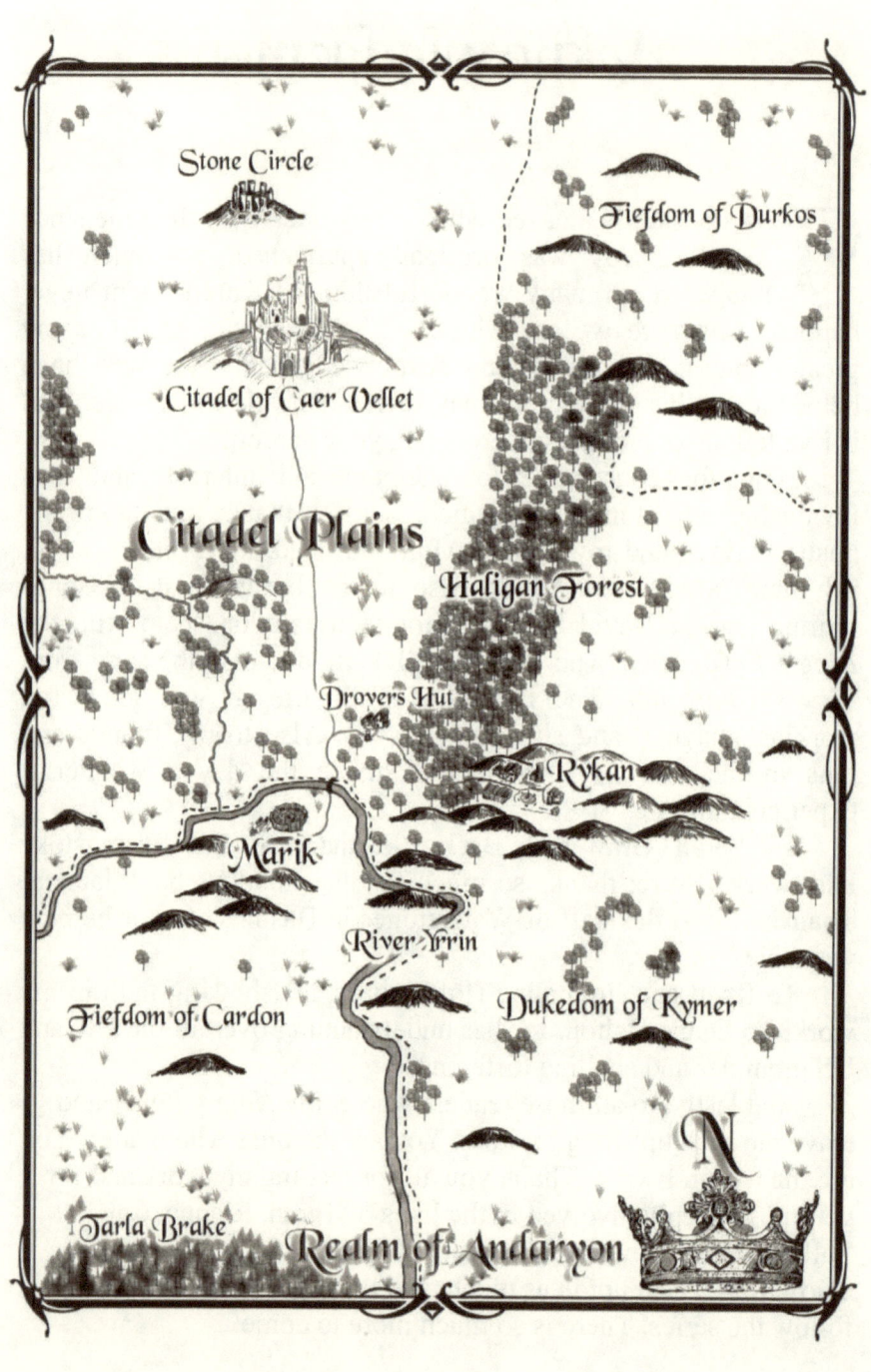

Stone Circle

Fiefdom of Durkos

Citadel of Caer Vellet

Citadel Plains

Haligan Forest

Drovers Hut

Rykan

Marik

River Yrrin

Fiefdom of Cardon

Dukedom of Kymer

Tarla Brake

Realm of Andaryon

Realm of Andaryon

King's Champion

Artesans of Albia

Book Two

Cas Peace

Albia Publishing

Chapter One

Branches whipped past Rienne's face as she clung to the horse's neck. The darkness and the wind of their speed were unremitting. Horse sweat slicked her fingers. Her arms and legs ached fiercely with the effort of staying on the galloping beast, and neither the wiry arms circling her waist nor the unfamiliar chest pressed into her back were helping. She wasn't used to riding this fast and certainly not riding double.

A quick glance to her left showed Cal, his horse weaving its own hectic path through the trees. Taran should be just behind him, Robin and Bull even further back. At least she hoped they were there. She couldn't hear them, couldn't hear anything above the rasping breath of her horse and the rough slap of branches. She felt rather than heard the pounding hoof beats as they jarred up through her thighs and into her protesting back.

Would this ride never end?

Her laboring horse kept trying to slow, but the thin man seated behind her repeatedly dug his heels into its lathered flanks. Rienne heard the poor beast grunt as it plunged on through the trees. She grimaced in sympathy. How much more could it take? Neither she nor the Count were heavy, but even the stoutest horse would struggle to maintain this pace while carrying two riders. Rienne didn't like to think what might happen if it foundered.

How long had it been since she, Count Marik, and Robin had brought the gravely injured and unconscious Major Sullyan out of those dreadful dungeons? How long since they had fled Rykan's palace and the patrols sent to hunt them? Rienne shuddered, trying not to think of Sullyan's unresponsive face as Robin took her onto his horse. Marik had kicked their shared mount ahead of Robin, desperate to lead them far away from Rykan's palace. As she passed him, Rienne saw tears glistening in Robin's indigo eyes. Since then, she hadn't had an opportunity to gauge the Major's condition. Was she still alive or had she, as Rienne privately feared, already died? Her injuries were severe; this wild, panic-stricken flight through an unfamiliar forest might be one ordeal too many.

The lack of light forced them to use the main forest trails, but Rykan's patrols had been coming and going over the previous weeks, as had Marik's men, obeying the Duke's call to arms. Rienne prayed that the tracks they were making would be lost among all the others. If they could get far enough away by dawn, surely they would be safe?

She shied at shadows, her heart lurching at each unusual shape that loomed through the trees. Marik seemed in mortal fear of his life and rode hunched behind her in silence. She could almost feel him listening for the sound of pursuit and guessed he was thinking about his fate should Rykan's men catch them. Only once so far had Bull sensed someone close on their tail. He had urged them on to greater speed, and Rienne prayed hard that her horse would find the strength to endure.

Abruptly, she felt Marik's body tense. She gasped as a dark shape arrowed toward her. She grabbed for the reins, trying to turn the horse's head, but unaccountably, Marik fought her.

"Let go!" she yelled, driving an elbow into his ribs. He whooshed out a breath and let go the rein, but it was too late. A large hand had already clamped onto her horse's cheek strap and was hauling on it, slowing the frightened beast.

"It's me, Rienne! It's alright, we can stop now."

Bull's deep bass voice, harsh with strain, calmed Rienne's shuddering heart. She managed to turn her head and smile as he brought her lathered horse to a walk.

"Are we safe? Have we lost them?" She cursed the tremor in her voice.

Bull frowned. "For the moment. I haven't sensed anyone behind us for a while. Taran and I have dropped the shield. We're too tired to maintain it right now. We still need to be cautious, but I think we can give the horses a rest. Killing them won't help us."

He left her and dropped back, presumably to continue scanning the woods. Cal took his place, nudging his horse alongside hers. "Share with me for a bit?"

Rienne nodded and awkwardly made the transition from her own mount to Cal's. She ached in every bone and moving was both difficult and painful. Once she was sitting behind her lover, however, with her arms wrapped about his waist and her face buried in the back of his neck, she felt much better.

After a few minutes she recovered enough to look behind her. "Cal, slow up a bit more, please."

Cal complied and they drew level with Robin's plodding horse. Rienne glanced at the Captain, then at the limp form cradled in his arms. Sullyan lay unmoving, her head bowed against his chest.

"Any change?"

Robin raised red-rimmed eyes and she realized he had been weeping.

"None."

She nudged Cal's horse with her foot, edging it closer. "Let me see." Reaching across, she drew down a corner of the velvet cloak the Major was wrapped in and put her hand to Sullyan's neck above the silver collar, feeling for a pulse. Her fingers came away bloody. Robin's eyes never left hers.

"It's difficult to tell," she murmured. "The movement of the horse interferes. But I think she's still with us. She's terribly cold."

"I'm doing my best."

Robin's voice choked. Rienne was shocked by his anguish. "Oh, Robin, I know you are. If not for you, she'd still be in that cell and almost certainly dead by now. At least she's among friends, even if ...." She couldn't continue.

Robin closed his eyes. "That's no comfort, Rienne."

She felt an uncharacteristic surge of anger and dug her heels into Cal's horse, urging it alongside Marik's. "Count, have we come far enough to think about stopping yet? We've been riding for hours. Your help in this rescue will count for nothing unless I can assess the Major's injuries and give her some treatment."

"If we're caught by Rykan's men, no treatment in the world will save her," Marik snapped. "We've a long way to go yet."

Bull heard the remark and brought his own horse closer. "Do you have a destination in mind, then?"

"No," snarled the Count, "I thought we'd just ride around in aimless circles until we disappear up our own backsides. What do you bloody take me for? Of course I have a destination in mind!"

Muttering curses, he kicked his horse so hard that it lumbered into a canter again, forcing the others to follow.

Rienne heard Cal's murmur. "I wonder what's eating him."

She glared at him. "I imagine you'd be tetchy too if you lost everything you ever had!"

Wisely, Cal stayed silent.

A couple of hours later Marik drew rein, letting them all catch up. The horses were lathered, their heads hanging low. Their riders were in no better shape. Lack of sleep and too much adrenaline had taken a hefty toll. Rienne could just make out their faces in the false light of dawn that was stealing across the sky.

Marik stopped on the edge of a rise. Exhaustion had erased his foul mood. "We've come a little more north than west now. I'm not completely sure, but I think we're about an hour away from an old drovers' hut I know of, somewhere over that way." He waved a hand vaguely to the left. "Has anyone sensed any patrols lately?"

Bull shook his head. Rienne glanced at Robin, but he didn't respond, preoccupied with his own worries. Taran must have realized this, for he offered to link with Bull to search a wider area. After a few minutes, Bull reported, "The nearest people are a good few hours away, and they seem to be asleep. I think we've shaken them off."

Marik nodded. "Right, let's see if my memory serves me and I can find this hut. It isn't much, but it should give us shelter and the opportunity for a fire and hot water." He glanced at Rienne. "I take it that's what you'll want?"

She gave a small smile. "Among other things, Count."

Rolling his eyes, he led them over the ridge.

By the time they finally found the drovers' hut, it was full daylight. Rienne, still sitting behind Cal, saw a low building with two windows, snugly nestled against a hillside. Its sod-covered roof glittered with hoarfrost, but it looked in good repair. To one side was a small corral with a drinking pool for the horses. There was a lean-to barn attached to the wall of the hut. Rienne wondered whether there would be fodder for the exhausted animals. They carried a small amount of grain in their saddlebags, but what the horses really needed was a warm mash and some decent hay.

Bull rode cautiously up to the hut. There didn't seem to be any recent tracks and the place appeared deserted. He swung down stiffly from his saddle and steadied himself against his horse. Then he passed his reins to the Count, pushed open the door, and disappeared inside.

A few moments later, he re-emerged. "All clear. There's wood for a fire and it's relatively clean and dry. It's even stocked with some supplies." He turned to the Captain. "Robin, give her to me and I'll take her inside."

He stopped short, making Rienne glance quickly at Robin. The Captain didn't appear to have heard Bull. He was staring at the limp form cradled in his arms. Rienne felt herself go cold. There was horror in Robin's dark eyes. Suddenly, he looked at her, his face white with shock. "Rienne, where's all this blood come from?"

She kicked Cal's tired horse closer and Robin showed her his arm where the Major's body had been held against him. His sleeve was soaked with blood, as was the velvet of the Count's cloak. Rienne could feel waves of anguish flowing from him.

Reaching out, she drew back a fold of the ruined cloak. The slim, bruised legs beneath were covered in bright red blood.

The Captain gasped.

"Alright, Robin," soothed Rienne, trying to stay calm though her panic was rising. She was very afraid she knew the cause of the bleeding. "It's just possible that it's … natural, you know?" Sure that it wasn't, she had to offer him something.

"Oh!" Robin colored.

Rienne let the cloak fall. "Let's get her inside, get a fire and some warm water going, and then we can see what we're dealing with."

Rienne felt half relieved, for the bleeding showed that Sullyan was still alive. However, losing more blood—even should it prove to be moon cycle blood—meant danger to the wounded Major. Hastily, Rienne slithered off the sweaty horse and stumbled after Bull.

Wood lay ready in the hut's large fireplace. Bull kneeled before it to coax it into life, while Rienne took in the rude surroundings. A solid wooden table and a few stools occupied one end of the simple room, and a trestle bed with a few folded blankets stood against the wall at the other. There were shelves over the fireplace stacked with wooden bowls and plates, and piled in a heap at one end were battered pots and pans. Crocks of preserves and dried herbs sat there too. Hard-beaten earth served as a floor, and the two windows, one either side of the door, were grimy with dust. Yet the place smelled clean and dry, and when the first crackle of fire lit the gloomy interior, a measure of cheer came to the place.

Bull went back outside to help Robin while Rienne dragged the bed nearer the fire. She placed the folded blankets on the hearth to warm them. When Robin came in with Sullyan, she asked him to sit on the bed and hold the unconscious woman against him. The others stayed outside, presumably caring for the horses.

Bull appeared, carrying a large pail of fresh water drawn from the drinking pool in the paddock. Rienne asked him to boil some, both for washing and for sterilizing her medical kit. Wordlessly, he obeyed her.

She laid her medical bag on the bed and rummaged in it for clean cloths. Delicately, she pulled back the blood-sodden cloak, exposing the poor, battered body beneath. Robin averted his eyes, but she heard Bull's gasp of shock. She grimaced. Of course, he hadn't seen Sullyan in the cell and she knew she ought to have warned him. He would have to get over it, she had more pressing concerns.

Gently, she moved Sullyan's left leg and bent the knee. Her uncontrolled gasp of outrage at the torn and abused flesh between the slim legs clearly told Robin all he needed to know.

"It's not … natural … is it?" he whispered.

She stared up at his pinched, grey face, her horror matching his. She felt sick.

"Dear gods, Robin. No, it's not."

✠ ✠ ✠ ✠ ✠

The door opened, admitting a waft of icy air, and the others came in, smelling of horse sweat, grain, and hay. Rienne turned and beckoned to Cal, who dumped his pack on the table. She was using cloths to stem the worst of the bleeding, muttering as she worked. Sullyan's injuries had clearly been aggravated by the roughness of their ride. She heard Cal's exclamation as he saw what she was doing. The others glanced over but stayed out of the way, giving her room to work. They could surely tell by the look on Robin's face that the news wasn't good.

"Cal, I need to do some stitching. Will you be able to assist me?" He had helped her back at the Manor and was the nearest she had to a trained assistant. He nodded a tad reluctantly and started to lay out what she would need.

She turned to the Captain, but he seemed lost in his grief and she had to speak his name twice. He started and glanced at her. The pain in his eyes nearly overset her professional calm and she had to breathe deeply. "I want you to stay alert," she said. "Sullyan needs our help right now. We can deal with our grief and anger later. Alright?"

For a moment, she thought he might snap at her, but then he nodded. Looking over her shoulder, she spoke to the Count. He was sitting by himself with his head in his hands. Like a kicked dog, he startled at hearing his title.

"Count. Do you still have the jailor's keys? Is there one for these manacles?"

He searched his jacket. Producing the bunch, he indicated a small silver key. "I think it's this one."

Covering Sullyan once more, Rienne said, "Robin, can you turn her without disturbing those cloths?"

Robin helped her bring Sullyan's arms out from under the cloak, exposing the silver manacles. She took the keys from Marik, using another cloth to hold the one he had shown her. Without touching the spelled metal cuffs, she managed to insert the key in each and release them. They fell to the floor. Marik kicked them viciously, sending them tumbling toward the door.

Rienne clicked her tongue in dismay when she saw the burns inflicted by the spellsilver. The injuries were bad but not life threatening. They could wait. Turning her attention to the collar, she was about to try the key in its lock when Marik suddenly grabbed her arm. Panic showed on his face.

Robin frowned. "What is it, man?"

The Count's eyes shifted warily.

"Tell us," urged Rienne.

He pulled back and his voice was hoarse. "Do you remember me saying she wasn't completely sane the last time I spoke with her? She'd lost all hope of rescue by then and knew she couldn't hold out against Rykan any longer. She said … she told me that … when he came to her again"—there was a catch in his voice and Robin's eyes narrowed—"she was going to feign surrender. If Rykan wanted access to her metaforce, he'd have to remove the spellsilver. She told me that when she felt it go … as soon as she felt him in her mind …." He stopped and licked his lips.

Robin glared. "What?"

The Count closed his eyes. "She said she'd destroy herself and take him with her."

Robin gasped. "No!"

The Count flung up his hands as if to ward off Robin's fury. "It was her one last defense. She had nothing left!"

Bull lowered his head to his hands and groaned. Rienne stared at the frightened Count. "Are you saying that when I remove this collar, she'll kill herself?"

Marik nodded miserably. Rienne rounded on Robin. "Can she do that?"

The Captain had his eyes closed, his face pressed to Sullyan's hair. Rienne only just heard his whisper.

"Masters have that power."

"Then what can we do?" she cried. "How can we tell her she's safe? There has to be something!"

Bull rose from his seat by the fire. He put out a hand, tenderly stroking the matted, tawny hair. "We can try preventing her." He cocked his head at Robin. "I know we're all tired, but if you can reach her, lad, she'll recognize you. I'm sure of it. Even like this. We have to try. We can't leave that thing on her. It's killing her anyway."

Robin nodded and blinked his tears away. "I'll need help," he said hoarsely. "Even then I'm not sure we'll have the strength to stop her. I might not be able to reach her in time ...."

"You will," said Bull. "You have to."

"What can I do?" said Rienne.

Bull patted her arm. "Just leave this to us, dear heart. She'll need your strength in other ways, and so will we. This will be very draining. Taran, Cal, can you gather round? If we all sit close together, it'll be easier on Robin. Marik, what about you?"

The Count looked startled, frightened even. He backed up a pace. "Don't think I don't want to, but I'd better not." He ducked his head, hiding his expression. "She might associate me with that place, with pain. I don't think it would be helpful."

His manner and his refusal gave birth to a dreadful suspicion in Rienne. She was about to speak, but Robin cut her off.

"You saw it, didn't you? You watched him!"

Horror spread over the Count's face. He began to perspire. "He forced me. There were two guards with swords at my back. What could I do?"

Robin's body shook. There was murder in his eyes. "You stood there? You stood and watched him rape her, and you did nothing?"

Everyone stared at the Count except Rienne. She dropped her

face to her hands, sobs burning her throat.

The Count was shouting. "There was nothing I could do! I couldn't stop him! I swear I wanted to, but I'd have been killed out of hand, and what use would I have been to her then?"

"Use?" Robin yelled the word. "You've been no bloody use all along! It was your stupid, spineless behavior that let all this happen. If you'd only warned us at that bloody banquet, we never would have left her there. I can't believe she looked on you as a friend! You're nothing but a bloody traitor!"

The Count gasped. Rienne looked up through her tears, seeing his shocked, white face.

"Get out of here!" Robin sounded dangerously close to hysteria. "Go on, before I run you through. Haven't you done enough damage? GET OUT!"

Marik bolted from the hut, the door slamming shut behind him. Robin buried his face in Sullyan's hair, sobs wracking his body.

There was shocked silence, broken only by the sound of Robin's grief.

Bull sighed and placed his hand on the Captain's shoulder. "Come on, lad, we need you. You can't let go now. Sullyan needs you. Don't let her down."

Robin raised his face, his indigo eyes deep pools of guilt. "I've already done that, Bull. I should never have left her at the mansion. I knew it was wrong."

Rienne wiped her tears and took a deep breath, her healing skills and practical good sense coming to the fore. "Done is done and can't be undone. We have to concentrate on now. Sullyan's still alive, Robin. She needs you to fight for her. We all need to fight for her. There'll be time for recriminations later."

With a visible effort, Robin composed himself. "You're right, of course, we have to try. Cal, Taran, bring three stools over, will you? Right, if you'll all lay a hand on me and open your minds, I won't have to reach for the power. Ready?"

Unable to participate, Rienne watched as the three men each laid a hand on Robin's arm or shoulder and closed their eyes. She didn't feel anything when they linked, but her skin tingled into gooseflesh as Robin formed what she presumed was a Powersink. The air seemed to hum, and she vaguely felt him take hold of the power and weave it around himself and Sullyan. Fascinated, she sensed his revulsion as he met the vast blankness of the spellsilver field that encased Sullyan's mind. Rienne knew she couldn't experience its full effects, but even so, a revolting metallic taste had entered her mouth. She couldn't begin to imagine how it was affecting Sullyan.

Robin's eyes were vacant as he murmured, "The shield is in place. Rienne, I want you to unlock the collar, but don't remove it until I tell you. Hold it so that just one end is touching her skin. Maybe then I can slip past it to reach her. When I say, you can take it off, but not before. Alright?"

Rienne grabbed a cloth and wrapped it tightly around the collar. With her other hand, she placed the key in the lock. "I'm ready."

"Go ahead."

She turned the key and removed it. Holding the awful collar by the cloth in one hand, she lifted it, letting just the very end of the silver arc touch the raw skin of Sullyan's throat.

Immediately, a blinding flash of pure metaphysical energy pulsed into the room as Sullyan's powerful but tormented mind made a frantic leap for freedom. Rienne gasped. She had never felt such pain and desperation. She was caught in Sullyan's turmoil, whirled and buffeted by a cyclone of tortured emotions. Confused, wracked by pain, she nearly released the collar. She caught herself just in time.

A moan escaped her as she sensed Robin rushing to block Sullyan's escape. He was calling her name, over and over. The other three men gripped his arm and held onto each other, steeling themselves against the drain of their powers as Robin wrestled with Sullyan's insane desire to die.

Rienne was shocked, afraid, realizing they hadn't reckoned on the depths of the Major's despair. Robin's hold was failing, she could feel it. He was an Adept-elite, but despite the energies contained in the Powersink, he couldn't possibly hope to breach the impenetrable defenses Sullyan had raised against the agony and violation she had suffered. She was two full levels above his skill and had walled herself away behind an unbreakable shield. Rienne sensed his fear as he realized he could never breach it. Sullyan's puissance overwhelmed him, and his soul despaired.

She felt his flash of insight as he understood why he was doomed to failure. Rienne nodded sadly. He was a man, and although Sullyan loved him intensely, a man had betrayed her, abused her trust and her love. A man had brutally violated her body. She would never submit to a man in this extremity, no matter how deeply she loved him.

Robin knew it too, Rienne could feel it. Despite his frantic care, his deep and abiding love and desire, he knew he couldn't put Sullyan through any more pain, not even to bring her back to him. She was too damaged for him to heal, and what she needed, he couldn't give. His soul was an aching well of grief and pain as Rienne sensed him preparing to let her go.

He pulled back, and even Rienne could feel the others' frantic resistance. She thought she heard Bull shouting. The Powersink was failing, fading, and Sullyan's screaming psyche barreled through it. Rienne felt the tortured spirit brush past Robin and sensed Sullyan's recognition, her loving, anguished farewell. Robin called her name, his throat raw with grief and desperation, but Sullyan didn't slow. She was intent on annihilation.

Rienne felt her heart would burst and pressure built behind her eyes. She couldn't bear it, couldn't stand the thought that Sullyan would die despite being surrounded by friends who could save her. A savage feeling of injustice surged through her soul, the emotion too powerful to contain. She wanted to scream her rage and desperation, but before she could open her mouth, Sullyan's escaping psyche exploded through her mind.

Rage met rage in a maelstrom of emotion. Robin was flung violently out of the Powersink, and Rienne heard his cry of loss and pain. His heartbroken torment burst something within her. The incredible pressure behind her eyes disappeared, replaced by warmth. Strength and power flooded the substrate around her, capturing Sullyan's psyche, calming the frantic whirl of violent emotion. She watched it in wonderment. It felt so different, almost alien. It had a color and vibrancy all its own, although Rienne could never have described it. It was insubstantial, even capricious, but it spoke to Sullyan's essence as if to a kindred spirit and drew a response from her that Robin could not.

Tentatively, almost fearfully, the healer gathered this new power to her. Gentle in her hands, it obeyed her slightest whim. Still not quite believing what was happening, Rienne directed it to envelop Sullyan's damaged soul, tenderly but firmly drawing it back from the abyss. The annealing power was soft, unobtrusive, yet immensely strong. It surrounded the Major's tortured psyche like a mother's womb, sealing Sullyan away from harm.

Rienne had forgotten the others around her, and so the moment of the collar's removal came as a physical shock. Within the substrate, she saw Robin start toward the place where Sullyan's essence now slept, peaceful at last and at rest. There was no leap for freedom now. All was quiet and still. Yet he couldn't reach through that warm and gentle barrier any more than he could through the spellsilver field, and she saw him draw back, puzzled, amazed, even hurt.

As they each emerged from the metalink, Rienne looked round at their faces, seeing the same exhausted astonishment in everyone. Then Bull beamed a huge smile and gathered her into a warm, enveloping hug.

"Well done, lass," he breathed, "you did it!"

Robin gaped at her, dumbfounded.

"That was you? But how …?"

She glanced up at him. Her whole body was trembling, both from the effects of her emotions and also the shock of what had just happened.

"I don't really know, Robin. I could feel your despair and I knew we were going to lose her. I got so angry I just had to do something, so I did. But please don't ask me how!"

Chapter Two

Robin helped Rienne wash Sullyan's wasted body, using warm water steeped with herbs. At the Captain's insistence, Rienne also washed Sullyan's hair. He was adamant that no dirt should be left to infect any of the open wounds.

She understood. Dirt was inimical to her healing instincts anyway, but during her time in the Manor's infirmary she had learned how vital cleanliness was beyond the Veils. She used a salve on Sullyan's wounds, pleased to see there was no obvious sign of infection. Most of the injuries were not life threatening; loss of blood and shock were her main concerns.

A couple of the deeper whip cuts on Sullyan's back needed stitching, and Rienne closed them neatly. There was nothing she could do about the broken ribs except to salve the bruised area and apply a supporting bandage. She also cleaned and wrapped the raw sores around Sullyan's throat and wrists where the skin had been burned by the spellsilver.

She left the worst job until last. The torn and bloodied flesh where Rykan's brutality had left its most obvious mark needed a delicate touch. Robin turned white when he finally summoned the courage to look, but he made no comment. Cal assisted Rienne by handing her the implements she needed, but he avoided looking at Sullyan. The wounds were still weeping, re-opened by the roughness of their ride, but when Rienne began cleaning she found that the damage was not quite as bad as she had feared. Cal handed her the needle and suture thread and Rienne took a stitch.

She heard the sound first in the back of her mind and wasn't at all sure it was real. Shaking her head, she put it down to the effects of exhaustion. Their daring rescue and panicked flight had taken its toll on everyone. Focusing her weary eyes on her work, she passed the needle through the torn flesh once more.

This time there was no mistaking it. Her head snapped up. "Can't you hear it?"

Robin frowned uneasily. "Hear what?"

She studied Sullyan's unresponsive face. "I'm sure I heard her voice. As if she was crying out in pain."

Robin shook his head. Rienne began her work again, and this time the noise in her mind was so loud that she dropped the needle. Clamping her hands to her ears, she tried to block out the screams of terror and pain.

"Robin, surely you can hear her? You have to help her, deaden the pain or something. I have to do this, but with all the abuse she's suffered, she just can't bear it."

Robin closed his eyes, still shaken by his inability to prevent Sullyan's rush to suicide. His failure to sense what Rienne could hear only sapped his confidence further.

"I don't think I can reach her, Rienne. I couldn't before."

"Try again. I think you'll find you can now."

Somehow, Rienne knew this would work. She didn't fully understand it, but it felt right, and Robin's power slipped easily through the annealing cocoon she had wrapped around the Major. She knew it when he touched the familiar, strong presence of Sullyan's spirit, stilled the panic he found there, and flooded the half-aware consciousness with soothing sleep. They both watched Sullyan sink into blessed oblivion.

Robin nodded briefly at Rienne. "Go ahead. She won't feel you now."

Her work was delicate and took some time. Afterwards,

Rienne straightened her aching back and wearily rubbed her eyes. Lack of sleep, too much adrenaline, and hours of concentration had left her feeling worn. Exhausted, she watched Cal pack her things, leaving some of the implements still in the boiling water.

She moved aside as Bull helped Robin wrap Sullyan in the clean, warm blankets. They laid stones heated in the fire alongside her. Once the unconscious woman was resting peacefully on the bed, they made a quick meal. Rienne thought it must be noon, judging by the light outside. They had been awake now for around thirty hours, most of it spent either in fear or in flight.

Once they had eaten, Robin lay down alongside Sullyan and wrapped his arms around her. He fell almost instantly asleep. Taran cleared away the remnants of their meal and rolled himself in his blanket. Cal did the same, beckoning Rienne to join him. She glanced at Bull, who was also showing signs of the strain and emotion of the last few days. They all had dark rings under their eyes and unhealthily pale skin.

"Is it safe for us all to sleep?"

He nodded. "I think so. I've had a brief scout round. There's no one for miles, so we should be safe enough. Get some rest."

"I will. I just want to check on Marik. He shouldn't be on his own."

The big man shrugged. Rienne cast an apologetic glance at Cal, opened the door, and stepped outside.

The air was chill and Rienne hugged herself as she glanced around for the Count. She felt sorry for the Andaryan in the face of Robin's fury. The man had obviously given Sullyan what care he could under the circumstances, and he had put himself at considerable risk to help them free her. In fact, she thought, without his help they probably couldn't have done it.

She eventually found him in the barn, moodily cleaning grime from one of the horses' bits. He glanced up fearfully when she entered, then relaxed. Rienne noticed that the rest of the horses' gear was also clean and that the animals themselves had been tended and curried.

She sat on a bale of hay beside him and indicated the gear. "Thank you. You needn't have done all this by yourself. I'm sure the others would have helped."

He didn't look at her, but rubbed vigorously at a stubborn spot on the metal bit in his hands. "I wasn't doing much good anywhere else." After a pause, he asked, "How is she?"

"I think she'll live." Rienne glanced at the Count, noting the sudden tears in his alien eyes. "Don't take what Robin said to heart. He was distraught, feeling guilty about not being there when she needed him. He'll realize he was wrong, you'll see."

"But he wasn't." Marik looked up, the bit lying forgotten in his hands. "He was quite right. Had I stood up to Rykan, not been so spineless, none of this would have happened."

Rienne sighed. "From what I understand, you didn't have any choice in the matter. You didn't know what Rykan had planned when he ordered you not to warn her, did you?"

"Of course not. Rykan's never trusted me, and anyway, he'd never tell a lowly Count his plans. He was at my house when her request came through and I just thought it was coincidence. He's heard me mention her before. I just thought he wanted to meet her. He can't resist beautiful women …."

She smiled gently. "Then the blame doesn't rest with you, does it? From what you've said, you managed to help Sullyan when you could. Would she blame you, do you think, or be grateful?"

"Oh, I don't know." Marik's head drooped. "She knew I was there, of course. She knew I couldn't do anything. Rykan would've killed me if I'd interfered. And the few times I managed to get food and water to her, she never mentioned it." Abruptly, he flung the bit out the door and it landed with a clang, startling the horses. "Gods, but she didn't deserve to suffer like that! What he did to her was brutal! He's worse than an animal. I swear he actually enjoyed torturing her and hearing her scream. She was very strong, but I'll be surprised if she can ever speak again, the amount of screaming she did."

Rienne's eyes filled with tears. Trying to keep her voice level, she said, "I heard her once or twice."

Marik nodded. "That's how she knew someone would eventually come. She was sure she'd managed to reach one of you, though how she got round the spellsilver, I'll never know. She told me she'd used her pain and panic to lend her strength, but she was afraid that whoever she'd reached would just assume they were having nightmares."

Rienne inhaled sharply. That was exactly what she had thought.

"That's why she made me promise to free her horse." Marik shook his head. "She said it would find its own way back, but I just thought she was raving. I was glad to do it, though. Rykan was taking his anger out on it. He was as determined to break the horse as he was Sullyan." He turned to Rienne. "Was she right? Did it get back by itself?"

Rienne nodded. "Robin said it was badly injured. I don't know if it survived."

He sighed. "Don't tell her that, if she asks. She was more concerned for the horse's welfare than her own."

Rienne's heart suddenly faltered and she bowed her head. She only just heard the Count's soft murmur.

"Is there any one of you who isn't in love with her?"

She raised her head in surprise, but when she saw the look on his face, she smiled. "Ah, you too?"

He paled visibly, and she laid a soothing hand on his arm. "It's alright. Bull says she has that effect on most people. He says it's her generous spirit. Most of the men in her company are in love with her one way or another, so I've heard, and I suppose it's no surprise. How many people with that much power can be as selfless as she is? Bull says she'd give everything she had to any one of her command, even the rawest of new cadets, just because he was her responsibility. As long as they're loyal, he says, she'll forgive them anything. So, Count, how much more readily would she forgive her friends?"

Marik stared at her. "But am I still her friend?"

She stood, smiling down at him. "You're here, aren't you?"

He rose and walked out of the barn. Rienne followed him back to the hut and gazed round at the sleeping bodies. She stepped over to the bed, relieved to see that Sullyan's breathing seemed stronger and her face had a little color in it under the bruises.

Marik touched her shoulder. "Get some sleep. I'll watch."

She smiled gratefully. "Thanks. If there's any change in her, anything at all, wake me or Bull. Leave Robin to sleep. He's completely exhausted."

Marik nodded and turned to settle on a stool. Rienne lay down next to Cal, who didn't even stir when she snuggled under the blanket and wrapped her arms around him.

The sound of movement roused Rienne and she reluctantly opened her eyes. When her bleary sight cleared, she realized it was evening again. The windows were darkening, but someone had stoked the fire. Its heat and flickering light filled the hut.

Beside her, Cal was still soundly asleep. She frowned. He wasn't the reason she had woken. She raised her head and glanced around. The dark mound that was Taran lay still, his breathing deep and regular. It wasn't until she turned toward the fire that she saw what had roused her. Count Marik's hand was on Bull's shoulder and the big man had just woken. Rienne saw him frown and glance up. Marik made a gesture, and Rienne followed the line of his fingers. She gasped. Sullyan's eyes were open and her pupils were enormous, like two black holes in her ashen face.

Rienne shivered. The whites and irises of Sullyan's beautiful eyes had disappeared entirely, swallowed by the vast pupils. Her face had taken on an alien cast, and with a sinking sense of shock, Rienne recalled Marik's comments about her sanity. Watching her, it was impossible to tell if Sullyan's eyes were focused, where her gaze lay, or if she saw anything at all. She made no movement, and Robin still slept deeply in the same position behind her.

Rienne kept completely still as Bull sat up, slowly raising his head to a level with Sullyan's. She could hear the Major's breathing and knew she wasn't asleep. Tentatively, almost fearfully, the big man reached forward, one finger brushing Sullyan's cheek.

"Sully?"

Rienne held her breath, barely noticing as Marik withdrew to one of the stools by the table. Sullyan's eyes, those deep, ebony pools, contracted very slightly, showing some of the dark gold iris. She was trying to focus on Bull's face, and her fine brows knit in concentration. Then she gave a tiny gasp.

"Bulldog?"

It was the hoarsest of whispers, but it made Rienne smile with relief. Bull's pent up breath released audibly as he said, "I'm here, love, it's alright. You're safe now."

Sullyan seemed to struggle with consciousness, and Rienne thought she might slip away again. Then she stirred, one small hand creeping out from the blankets, seeking Bull. At once, the big man grasped it, and Rienne saw the stark white of the bandage standing out against Sullyan's bruised skin. Her eyes were more normal now and she was focusing on Bull's face. She took a breath, almost a sob, and her voice was husky.

"I am so very thirsty, Hal. Is there any fellan?"

This simple question seemed to completely overwhelm Bull. He bowed his head over her hand, and Rienne watched his shoulders shake with muffled sobs. Sullyan's hand tightened briefly on his and he pulled himself together with a visible effort. Sullyan smiled at him, although Rienne could tell that it hurt her. When she spoke again, Rienne had to strain to hear her words.

"Hold me, Hal."

There was such need, such desperation in her voice that Rienne felt her heart clench. There was an answering catch in Bull's breath, and Rienne felt like an intruder, watching such an intimate reunion. Neither of them had noticed her, and she didn't want to disturb them. Clearly, Sullyan was recovering. That was Rienne's main concern.

Gently moving Robin's arm without waking him, Bull stood and bent to gather Sullyan up. He hesitated, probably remembering her injuries. "I don't want to hurt you, love."

As the Major looked up at him, Rienne saw her naked, damaged soul plain in her eyes. "You could never hurt me," she whispered, and the depth of love and trust in her tone ripped at Rienne's heart.

Bull put his strong arms around her. She hadn't weighed much before, but her days of deprivation had so reduced her that Rienne doubted she was a burden to Bull. He moved back to the fire and lowered himself down, cradling Sullyan in his lap. As he did so, Rienne felt a faint brush of cold air and turned toward the door. The Count's stool was vacant. He had taken himself off again.

When Rienne turned back to the pair by the fire, Sullyan's head rested on Bull's chest while he gently stroked her hair. Rienne thought she knew what was coming, and it only took a few moments. Sullyan's whole body began to shudder violently as she gave way to her terror, shock, and pain. Bull sat silently, letting the storm of grief run its course, and Rienne was glad. This release was essential. It was the first step toward recovery.

Soon—sooner than Rienne would have thought—she heard Sullyan give a vast, shuddering sigh. Bull raised her chin with a tender hand.

"Better, love?"

She gave a wan smile and swallowed awkwardly. "I could really use that fellan."

Her voice was a rasp, and Rienne grieved for her lilting tones. Bull said, "Then you shall have it," and reached toward the kettle Taran had left hanging over the fire. Rienne was about to rise, thinking he might need help, but it soon became apparent that Bull had done this before. Using his free hand, he made a pot of steaming brew. He put a little honey in Sullyan's mug, even though Rienne knew she normally took her fellan strong and bitter. Bull was right, though, and Rienne approved. Sullyan's body would need the energy. The Major made no comment.

Bull passed her the mug, but when she brought her hands up for it, they were so weak and shaking so badly that she just couldn't hold it.

"I am sorry, Hal," she whispered.

He frowned. "You've nothing to be sorry for, dear heart. We've been here before. We know how to do this. Remember that time in Rothrick when you took that slash that became infected? You were ill with wound fever for days, despite your powers. I did everything for you then, and a lot worse tasks than holding a cup for you!"

Rienne saw Sullyan's gentle smile, and her heart lurched. There was clearly a deep bond of love between these two, even deeper, she thought, than the one Sullyan shared with Robin.

Still unnoticed, Rienne watched while Sullyan drank three

mugs of fellan. She would have preferred the Major to have taken water, but was happy for the moment to allow Sullyan her preference. It wouldn't hurt, and she could have water later. Once the fellan was gone, the Major and Bull sat together staring into the fire. Rienne thought Sullyan had fallen asleep again, but then she stirred. "Where are we, Bull? Is Robin here? Is Marik safe?"

In a low voice, so as not to disturb the others, Bull told her the story of her rescue. She listened in silence until he had finished. Then she drew a shaky breath.

"Did Rykan"—she stumbled over the name—"issue his challenge to the Hierarch?"

Rienne gave a small start and Bull frowned. "You don't have to worry about any of that now."

Desperation was plain in Sullyan's scratchy voice. "I have to know, it is important. Has he challenged the Hierarch or not?"

"We believe so," said Bull. "Marik says he did."

Rienne saw some of the tension leave the Major's body. "Good. One more thing, Bull, and then I must sleep. I asked Marik to free Mandias for me. Did he do it? Did he get home safely?"

Rienne held her breath, willing Bull not to mention how injured the horse was, but she needn't have worried. There was such a plaintive note to Sullyan's voice that she knew Bull would have lied to her even if the horse hadn't made it. As it was, he told the simple truth.

"Yes, he did as you asked. Mandias made it home, and that's what brought us all running—as you knew it would!"

Sullyan's relief was plain, and Rienne had a fleeting vision of them all dashing to her rescue. Had it come from Bull's mind, or Sullyan's? She didn't know, but wherever it came from, it distracted Sullyan from asking after the horse's condition. Sighing, the Major settled back into Bull's arms. He sat unmoving while she fell asleep.

✣ ✣ ✣ ✣ ✣

Screaming—harsh, ragged screaming—ripped through Rienne's mind, jolting her awake. There was movement all around her, men scrambling to their feet, drawing swords and swearing. She staggered upright and grabbed Cal's arm. Taran bumped into her from behind. The fire was low. It was night outside, shadows dancing frantically over the walls. A sharp gasp caught Rienne's attention. Robin was kneeling by Bull's side, staring at Sullyan. The Major's body was shuddering violently. Rienne rushed over.

"What on earth's the matter?"

Robin didn't reply. He was stunned by the appearance of Sullyan's eyes, which were open but unseeing, once more huge and black. The sub-vocal screaming went on, forcing Rienne to cover her ears.

The Major was convulsing, and no amount of calling her name had any effect. Robin took her shoulders, shook her gently, and stroked her face, but there was no response. Rienne felt him probing for her psyche, hoping to calm her as he had done before, but the terrible screaming went on. Frustrated by this second failure, the Captain exchanged a despairing glance with Bull.

"She was alright when she woke a few hours ago," the big man said. "She drank some fellan ...."

Robin glared at him. "She was awake? Why didn't you tell me?"

Bull was about to reply when the door burst open. Marik ran in, staring wildly at Sullyan's writhing form. "Dear gods," he breathed. "Not again."

"What do you mean?" said Rienne. "Has this happened before?"

The Count crossed the room and looked down at the Major, pity and fear in his eyes. "Yes, she had two attacks like this that I know of after Rykan started ... abusing her." He looked round at

26

them. "Can't any of you reach her?"

Robin refused to meet his gaze. "No. She won't hear us."

Marik glanced at Rienne then shuffled his feet, looking uncomfortable. "Would you … I mean … shall I try?"

He was clearly expecting a refusal, and Robin didn't disappoint him. "What on earth makes you think you can help her when we can't?"

His rough tone lashed at Marik and the Count's shoulders slumped. He turned away. Rienne laid a hand on Robin's arm. "Count," she said, "were you able to help her before?"

Marik turned back, eyes moist with unshed tears. "I had to try. There was no one else. She did seem to respond …."

Rienne turned to Robin. "Then you have no choice. What harm can it do to let him try?" Seeing the young Captain's anguish, she squeezed his arm, trying to show her understanding. "She's not hearing any of us, Robin. Don't deny her this chance of comfort."

Robin's anger faded and he stepped slowly back. The Count came forward, holding out his arms. Bull lifted Sullyan to him and stood, stretching stiffly.

Marik sat on the bed, cradling Sullyan in his arms. With a hand to her cheek, he turned her unseeing gaze to his. He stared into her eyes, his own alien pupils wide, and Rienne vaguely sensed him trying to link with her psyche. Softly, he began crooning in a tongue she didn't understand.

For a long while nothing changed, and the sharp, splintering scream continued to ring in Rienne's mind. Gradually, Marik's murmuring voice grew louder, and she realized the screams were abating. They finally ceased, and Rienne gave a sigh. Marik's soothing voice continued as he removed his hand from Sullyan's face. He held her close, rocking her like a child. Her shuddering slowly diminished until she was still again. Her eyes remained open and huge, unfocused. She seemed completely unaware.

Marik ceased murmuring and looked into her face. Satisfied by what he saw, he beckoned to Robin and the young Captain came forward.

"Take her," whispered Marik. "It would be better if she sees you when she wakes rather than me."

Rienne wondered if anyone else had caught his note of wistfulness.

Carefully, Robin took the Count's place. Marik backed away, then turned and walked out of the hut. Rienne let him go. The Captain called Sullyan's name softly. Eventually, she stirred, life returning to her eyes. The pupils contracted, transforming her face from something unrecognizable back to the familiar. She looked up at Robin and frowned, and a sudden fear gripped Rienne that maybe she wouldn't know him. Then the frown became a weary smile.

She whispered, "Robin," her cracked and husky voice completely strange.

He murmured back, "Oh, Sullyan."

Sighing deeply, she said, "I missed you," and then he let the tears fall, unable to hold his emotion.

Chapter Three

There was nothing more she could do for the moment, so Rienne left the hut. Taran and Cal were busy preparing food and Bull was brewing fresh fellan. The smells called to Rienne's exhausted body and wrung-out nerves, but her professional curiosity was piqued and she wanted to talk to the Count.

Cloud rack kept veiling the moon and a chill wind blew from the east, carrying the faint tang of rain. Rienne's eyes took a moment to adjust after the firelight and she could see no sign of the Count.

Once accustomed to the darkness, she walked round the end of the hut toward the barn and corral. She could hear the soft chewing of the horses and smell the grain and hay. Entering the barn, she saw a shadowy figure seated on a pile of straw.

The Count glanced at her but didn't speak as she sat beside him. A moonbeam lanced into the barn, lighting his alien eyes. Rienne shuddered. If she ignored those catlike pupils she could deal with him as she would an Albian, but if she dwelled on them too long, his differences became an almost physical barrier.

He sensed her unease and ducked his head. "I'm sorry if my appearance frightens you."

"Oh, it's not that." She was annoyed she had betrayed her discomfort. "It's just that I'm not used to all this. I'm only a healer. I'm not gifted like the others, and I've never done anything like this before. I'm a bit out of my depth."

He smiled. "I'd never have known."

It was her turn to feel awkward. She picked at a piece of straw, wondering how to ask her question. "Have you ever been to Albia?"

He raised an eyebrow. "Once. That was when I first met Sullyan."

"What happened? That is … I don't mean to pry. You don't have to tell me if you don't want to."

The Count looked down at his hands. In the uncertain moonlight she could see they were strong and long-fingered, a swordsman's hands, brown from the sun and nicked by old sword cuts.

He sighed. "It was six or seven years ago, just after I inherited my father's lands. I was young, naïve, eager to begin my life as a noble. But my father wasn't wealthy and my Artesan gift is weak, so the only options for improving my fortune or status were to either marry into a wealthy family or win power by conquest.

"The first was out of the question, because no noble Andaryan family would look at a lowly Count with such feeble Artesan talents." He snorted. "Lords want to marry their daughters to men who will strengthen their bloodline, not weaken it. So I thought that if I could gain a reputation for good generalship by organizing successful raids beyond the Veils, some high-born noble might offer me a military position which would increase my status."

He shook his head. "I should have known better. I should at least have chosen another realm to raid. But I was cocky then— before I realized how hopeless it all was—and I thought Albia was the best place to start. And so it might have been, had I not run straight into that unique young woman in there."

Rienne was fascinated and smiled, encouraging him to continue. He stared out the barn door and she could almost taste the embarrassment and frustration of the younger man he had been, so keen to prove himself.

"It was sheer bad luck, really, because I don't have anything like the power necessary to direct a portway. I only just managed to keep it open long enough to get all my men through. Of all the places we could have emerged, fate had to pick an area patrolled by Sullyan's company. Later, I learned that it was her first time out as company leader, and that she'd just recently become a Master Artesan. Anyone else and I might have achieved the result I was after. Why did fate throw me into her path?

"Anyway, her scouts saw us and she gave chase, quickly blocking my way back through the Veils. I wasn't too worried by that. I might not have much Artesan power, but I am a capable swordsman. Our numbers were about equal and her men were led by a woman. What did I have to fear?"

Seeing Rienne's raised brows, he said, "You may have heard that Andaryan women don't bear arms, and neither can they influence their metaforce. I'd never met anyone like Sullyan. What was I supposed to think? Naturally, I ordered my men to fight. None of them would engage her because she was only a girl, but she wasn't interested in them. No, she came straight for me. All I saw was a slim young woman holding a ridiculously large sword and—as I thought—an ego to match. My men thought I was mad accepting her challenge, but I intended to disarm her, show off my skill, and teach her the price of her folly. Hah, folly!"

He pursed his lips. "The folly was mine. I barely had time to raise my sword before she sent it spinning from my hand. She even had the gall to offer it back again, saying it wasn't a fair duel as I obviously wasn't ready. But there was no point me trying again. I'd already lost face with my men. It was clearly hopeless, so I surrendered."

Staring at the ground, he sighed again. "Another company had arrived by then, drawn by the noise of combat. Their commander wanted to kill us all for breaking the Pact, but Sullyan said we were free to return. I was bound by the terms of my surrender, and she plainly knew our customs. She knew I couldn't challenge her again. She spared our lives, but I was forced to endure the laughter of my men for being defeated by a woman.

"A few days after, I received a message requesting safe passage for the Albian King's ambassador. To my amazement, it was Sullyan who arrived at my door, and that was the beginning of our friendship."

He fell silent. Rienne said nothing, digesting the story, thinking what an extraordinary life Sullyan had led. She only belatedly remembered the younger woman's earlier pain and panic. "So what was all that about in there, just now?"

Marik started as if he had forgotten she was there. "Oh. I ... I don't really know."

The lie was plain. "Come now, Count. I'm not stupid, but I am a healer, remember? It's something Rykan has done to her, isn't it? Tell me. I really need to know if I'm going to be able to help her."

He shook his head. "You can't—"

Cal's voice cut across the Count's and Rienne jumped. She heard the note of fear as Cal called her name again, and hurried out of the barn. "I'm here."

"There you are," he said. "Sullyan's asking for you. You too, Count."

"Me?" Marik frowned. "What does she want me for?"

Cal shrugged. "You'd better come and see."

Rienne entered the hut, followed by Marik. As she blinked in the firelight, the smells of food and fellan hit her like a delicious wave, making her abruptly aware of how hungry she was. The fear and exertion of the last two days had thrown her body rhythms completely out. It must have been getting on for midnight, but she was ravenous.

The others had already started on the food. Bull passed her a mug of fellan and she sipped the scalding liquid gratefully. He also passed one to Marik, who seemed startled at being included. From his place on the bed, Sullyan cradled against him, Robin watched the Count suspiciously.

Rienne approached the bed and kneeled on the floor. Placing her mug beside her, she took one of Sullyan's cold hands. The Major stirred and glanced at her, smiling faintly.

"Ah, Rienne, there you are. I wanted to thank you for what you have done. You put your life at risk to save me."

Rienne shook her head. "I don't need your thanks. I'm just relieved you're still with us. I don't think I'd have survived what you've been through."

A brief flicker of pain crossed Sullyan's face. "You have done so much already. I hesitate to ask more of you. I know how tired you must be."

Rienne squeezed her hand. "What do you need? Is it to do with what afflicted you earlier? You were in such pain …."

Sullyan shook her head, her tumbled hair rippling over Robin's arms. "Rienne, I have to be able to ride. We cannot stay here much longer. We are too vulnerable this close to Rykan's palace. But it will take me too long to recover my strength naturally. I am far too weak."

Robin interrupted. "We just need to get you strong enough to cross the Veils. Once we get you home, you can rest and recover properly."

The anguish that filled Sullyan's face dismayed Rienne. Tears welled in her eyes, and she was about to say something when the Major glanced warningly at her. Then Sullyan took a deep breath.

"Robin, I need you to take control of a Powersink. Everyone is drained and exhausted, so you must take over my powers too."

Robin gasped and Bull sucked in a sharp breath. Rienne saw

his amazed expression.

Sullyan ignored both. "Will you be strong enough?" she asked.

Robin seemed stunned and answered haltingly. "I'll be strong enough, trust me."

Confused, Rienne glanced at Bull, who shook his head and smiled at her. "She's just casually handed Robin what she nearly killed herself denying Rykan," he explained.

Sullyan frowned. "This is quite different, Bulldog, as well you know. And Robin would never ask."

The Captain was actually trembling. "Are you quite sure?"

She looked up into his indigo eyes. "I trust you with my life and all that I have. You should know that." Robin briefly closed his eyes, and Rienne felt as if her heart would burst. Sullyan's next words jolted her. "But I want Rienne to do the healing."

"What? But how …? I can't …."

Sullyan squeezed her hand. "You can. Just think of the power as a medical instrument or a potent salve. I will guide you. Just open your mind and think of what needs to be done. Robin, you must go very gently with the power. This will feel very strange to Rienne."

She glanced over to where Marik was loitering by the door, looking distinctly uncomfortable. Her voice was husky as she asked, "Count, will you join us? I need your power too."

His melancholy expression brightened and he took a step forward.

Robin's face flushed. "What do you want him for?" he spat, and Marik fell back as if slapped.

Sullyan's raspy reply was barely audible. "Oh, Robin. I owe my life to Marik as much as I do to you. I can never repay him for his care, and he has lost his livelihood because of me. If you love me, then you owe him your gratitude at the very least, not this jealous and angry suspicion."

Robin's color deepened and Rienne knew the charge of jealousy was very near the mark. His anger at Marik had its roots in his guilt at not being there when Sullyan needed him most.

"But it was his fault that you were taken in the first place!" he said. "He stood by and watched what that ... that animal ... was doing to you and made never a move to stop him."

Sullyan's face, grey as it was, paled further. Rienne could see her gathering nonexistent strength to lash out at Robin, but Bull put a hand on her shoulder.

"Enough," he said. "Leave it, Robin. Isn't it enough that Marik saved her life? If Sully doesn't blame him, how can you? You weren't there, you don't know what happened. Make your peace, lad."

"Thank you, Bull," murmured Sullyan. Rienne was relieved. Fighting with Robin was an exertion the Major could do without.

Robin looked silently between Sullyan and Marik before letting his breath out in a huge sigh. "I'm sorry, Marik. I'm upset and jealous and I shouldn't have said what I did. Of course I'm grateful that you helped Sullyan, and I know we probably wouldn't have got her out without you. Please accept my apology."

The Count waved an awkward hand. "No need," he said, but he didn't sound convinced.

Sullyan lay back in Robin's arms. "Can you concentrate now?" she asked, closing her eyes. "I need to clear my mind. Can I trust you to accept Marik's place in the structure?"

"Yes," soothed Robin. "I'm sorry. I'm ready now."

Rienne couldn't help feeling apprehensive. The extraordinary experience of being able to comfort Sullyan's damaged spirit had seemed so natural. It wasn't something she had planned to do or even thought about, it had just happened; she had instinctively known what to do. This was completely different. She didn't have the faintest idea how it would work, and she didn't want to let Sullyan down.

"What do you want me to do?" she asked.

Eyes still closed, the younger woman said, "Take my hand and hold it fast. I will not be able to reach you if you let go. Just close your eyes and let me guide you."

Rienne did so. Without the distraction of sight, her other senses came alive, heightened beyond anything she had ever known. She felt the others as they came into the structure Robin was forming, even recognizing Marik's alien psyche. She felt as if she was floating above herself, cushioned on a swirling cloud of ever-changing colors. And then she heard Sullyan's voice in her mind, surprised that the mental tones were as warm and lilting as her physical voice had been before her ordeal.

Rienne? Concentrate on me now. You know where the worst hurts are. You cannot completely heal them, but you can close the flesh and strengthen muscles and tendons. Begin with the lesser wounds.

Suddenly, Rienne could sense the various places where she had stitched Sullyan's skin. Without even thinking, she used the deep amber power Robin held out to her to meld the flesh and make it strong. Energy seemed to flow over and around Sullyan's body, doing whatever Rienne commanded, and she felt vaguely intoxicated, as if she could heal the world.

Robin, warned Sullyan, *hold back. You are giving her too much. Remember whose power you are handling.*

Rienne felt some of the force draining away and could almost have cried for the loss. Sullyan's voice brought her attention back. *Rienne, I need you to deal with the ribs now. Can you see, two are broken and one is cracked? Seal the cracked one first, it needs no moving.*

Rienne did so, sealing the cracked bone easily before turning her attention to the broken ones. She felt Robin preparing to use the power to dull the inevitable pain, but Sullyan stopped him.

No, Robin, I need to feel where the ends are to ensure they align correctly. Go ahead, Rienne.

Rienne could sense the sweat standing out on Sullyan's face as she fought not to cry out at the pain of the broken bones being set. She was gasping for breath when Rienne finished. These physical hurts attended to, Rienne was about to open her eyes when something caught her attention. Deep within Sullyan's soul she sensed a site of great damage and poison. She yearned toward it, eager to cauterize and cleanse. Reaching once again for the power in Robin's hands, she felt him release it as she approached this vast darkness. The Major had relaxed her vigil in the aftermath of the pain and didn't immediately react to what Rienne was doing. Suddenly, the healer felt a backlash of refusal and rejection so strong and violent it hurt. The irresistible force flung her away from the area.

Don't stop me, Sullyan, she pleaded. *I can heal you of that. It will kill you otherwise.*

There was pain and panic in Sullyan's tone. *No, Rienne. You cannot heal there. You will destroy us both if you try. Rienne, HEAR ME!*

The healer fought, desperate to follow her instincts, but Sullyan was too strong. Once again, Rienne was forced away. She heard the Major calling on Marik and watched while the Count's power, weak though it was, enveloped the terrible area, walling it off.

Puzzled and hurt, she opened her eyes. "Why did you stop me? Don't you know that it will—?"

Painfully, Sullyan gripped her hands, preventing her from finishing her sentence. "Leave it, Rienne." Exhausted, she lay back in Robin's arms. "Let me sleep now. Robin, wake me at dawn, do you hear? Time is pressing, and there are things that must be done. Bulldog, make sure he obeys me."

Robin glared. "You don't need to set Bull on me. I'll do as you ask."

"See that you do," she murmured, smiling.

Rienne watched as the younger woman fell almost instantly asleep. She was deeply unhappy about what Sullyan had prevented her from doing. When Marik left the hut, she once more followed him into the night. He seemed unable to stay with them, probably realizing how much pain his presence caused Robin. Rienne knew he didn't believe the Captain's forced apology.

Before he could reach the sanctuary of the barn, Rienne caught his arm. Staring up at him, ignoring his alien eyes, she said, "That poison is killing her. Why wouldn't she let me deal with it?"

He tried to turn away, but she held him. Unwilling to free himself by force, he said, "Rienne, this is not something I can speak of. Ask Sullyan if you must. But if I were you, I'd leave it as she asked you."

She could hear the pain in his tone. "It's something to do with what Rykan did to her, isn't it? That's why she had you seal it off instead of me."

He scowled. "It has to do with Andaryan blood, yes. More than that, I can't say. I respect you, Rienne. Please do me the same courtesy. It really isn't my place to tell you."

She let him go then and he marched stiffly into the barn.

Chapter Four

Rienne woke to the sound of someone calling her name. She had been deeply asleep, safe within the circle of Cal's arms and dreaming of the power she had held in her hands just hours before. She sat up without waking him and looked around the dimly lit hut. She could see the slumbering forms of Taran, Bull, and Robin, but there was no sign of either Sullyan or Marik.

Slipping from the blankets, she shrugged into her jacket. Her boots were by the fire, and she took them with her to the door. On a sudden impulse, she picked up her medical bag and slung it over her shoulder. Quickly lacing her boots, she cracked the door and stepped outside.

It was barely dawn. A pale peach light was just seeping into the eastern sky. The ground was damp. It must have rained during the night, and that purple bank of clouds Rienne could see on the horizon threatened more. A pale, watery sun was rising, its first rays glinting in the rain droplets on the roof.

Rienne glanced around, finally seeing Sullyan over by the corral. The Major was stroking the nose of Robin's chestnut warhorse, Torka. She was wearing her spare shirt and breeches from the pack they had found at Marik's mansion, and her glorious hair was partially braided, the weight of it falling like a ripple of amber down her back. Despite the potency of that wonderful whirl of healing power earlier in the night, Rienne was amazed to see her on her feet.

Sullyan didn't stir as Rienne approached and leaned on the

railing beside her. The horse turned to her in hopes of a tidbit, but lost interest when it smelled she had nothing to offer. It moved off to crop the wet grass, and Sullyan watched it with unreadable eyes. Rienne thought the younger woman's face looked sad under the fading pattern of bruises. The dark circles under her eyes had all but gone and the healthy skin was regaining its tawny glow.

The healer kept her voice soft. "I thought I heard you call me."

The woman at her side turned from her contemplation of the grazing warhorse. "I did."

"How was I able to hear you?" This speaking and hearing without words was new to Rienne.

Sullyan flicked a glance at her and Rienne had a sudden impression of great sadness before the Major schooled her expression.

"First, it has to do with your being an empath. And then with how you helped me when you removed the spellsilver."

"I still don't understand that," said Rienne. "I don't know how it happened. I could somehow see what Robin was trying to do, and I knew he was going about it the wrong way. I was getting so frustrated and I just wanted to shove him aside and help you. I guess that's just what I did."

"Poor Robin," murmured Sullyan. "He tries so hard, but despite my teaching, he still sometimes fails to understand."

Rienne knew how he felt. "Why did you call me?"

Sullyan shook herself and looked up with a more normal expression. "I need your medical skills, if you will. We are not safe here, and I must be able to travel. Your healing last night accomplished much and the flesh you stitched has knitted. I need you to remove the sutures."

Rienne smiled. "Of course. Where shall we go?"

Sullyan led her into the barn. The morning light shone full through the door, illuminating the hay bales lying on the ground.

Easing herself onto one, Sullyan removed her shirt. Rienne unwound the bandages she had used to support the broken ribs, seeing that the whip cuts on the Major's back had already faded to pink lines.

Deftly, she slipped out the sutures. Sullyan's skin was sleek, her back defined by muscle honed with weapons training. It was marked here and there with the faint, white lines of other, older scars, but also by ribs and spine made prominent by her recent starvation. She stood before pulling on her shirt, allowing Rienne to examine the damaged area beneath the right breast where the ribs had been driven in. It appeared much improved, but Sullyan winced slightly when Rienne touched it.

"Sorry," she murmured. "You'll have to be careful of that for the next few days. Do you want the bandages put back?"

Sullyan shook her head. "I can cope with it now the other hurts have gone." She unbuckled the belt of her breeches, preparing to remove them so Rienne could deal with the other, more intimate, sutures. A sudden rustle startled Rienne. Looking over her shoulder, she saw the Count rising hastily from where he had slept among the bales. He was red faced, acutely embarrassed, and wouldn't meet Sullyan's eyes.

He hurried past them, muttering, "I'll … um … just go and … um, check on the horses."

"Ty," called the Major softly. Rienne frowned; it was the first time she had heard anyone use his given name. Judging by the way he jolted to a halt, the Count wasn't used to it either. Half turning, he looked back.

Sullyan smiled. "I have not yet thanked you for what you did."

Marik took a backward step, reminding Rienne of a nervous horse. "There's no need. You're very welcome."

"I will not forget the dangers you braved, Ty. I know what you sacrificed by befriending me. I intend to repay you for that."

His flush deepened and he turned away. "There's no way you can. Just forget it."

Sullyan watched him go before turning back to Rienne. "So much pain," she sighed. Rienne heard a depth of despair in her voice that had its roots deep in her soul. She had the impression it was not just for Marik's troubles.

The Major removed her breeches and lay down in the straw with a hay bale at her back. Rienne knelt before her and reached for her little suture knife. On examining the area, she was amazed at how well the flesh had healed, considering the ruin Rykan's abuse had left.

Delicately, she removed the first few stitches, but then stopped and looked up at Sullyan, catching the younger woman's eye. Firmly she said, "I want you to tell me about the poison inside you."

Surprise showed on Sullyan's face and Rienne experienced brief satisfaction. Clearly the younger woman was unaccustomed to being caught so unprepared.

"I want to know why you sealed it away rather than letting me deal with it. You do know it will kill you, don't you?"

Sullyan regarded her narrowly. "Rienne, I never had you down as the devious type."

Hearing the sarcasm, the healer grinned. "It comes of having four older brothers. Now, are you going to tell me, or do you want to walk bow legged all day?"

Sullyan looked down at herself, half naked, exposed, and completely at Rienne's mercy. She gave a hard smile. "You do seem to have me at a disadvantage."

Abruptly, her whole face changed and her golden eyes held such an expression of sorrow that Rienne regretted her question.

"Ah, Rienne, I do believe this is going to be the saddest day of my life. Today I must shatter the hopes and dreams of the one person I love above everyone else."

Sullyan closed her eyes and drew a shuddering breath. Then she motioned for Rienne to continue her work.

"Yes, of course I am aware that the poison will eventually kill me. Unfortunately, there is nothing that I, or anyone else, to my knowledge, can do about it. You must have learned during your time at the Manor that even a minor infection contracted beyond the Veils could prove lethal to Albians?"

Trying to concentrate on two things at once, Rienne said, "Yes, but we were very careful to clean all the wounds and disinfect them thoroughly. Robin was very insistent about it. There's no residual infection."

Sullyan's face paled at the mention of her Captain's name. "Perhaps I used the wrong word. Substitute 'contamination' for 'infection'."

Rienne stopped working, her expression slowly changing into horror. "Are you saying you might be … pregnant?"

The Major shook her head. "No, Rienne. Appalling as that would be, conception is not the problem. It is simpler than that. If an Andaryan and an Albian couple together, they cannot create life between them. Only death. Our two species are not at all compatible, and the Andaryan seed acts like a poison, a corrosive infection which cannot be removed. With Rykan's seed inside me, I cannot cross the Veils. The pain would kill me if I tried. Neither can I speak through them without pain in excess of what I could bear." Pausing, she glanced down. "I am trapped here, Rienne. Even if the poison was not lethal, I could survive here only a few months before my body began to fail. Within a year, maybe less, I would die."

Rienne stared, her mouth open. She could barely take it in. "And Rykan knew this?"

Sullyan nodded. "So what he did was …" Rienne trailed off,

too appalled and upset to carry on.

"Brutal enough," said Sullyan. "But also deliberately and callously calculated to force me into a corner from which there is no escape. He did not rape me out of lust, at least, not entirely. He did it to show me how little my resistance mattered. The fact that it made me all the more determined amused him, I think. He knew he had already destroyed me. So even though he did not gain what he wanted, Rykan still has the victory."

Rienne covered her face with her hands, her body trembling. She heard Sullyan's soft murmur.

"You were right that evening in my rooms. You said I should not let duty interfere with my one chance of happiness. Do you remember?"

Rienne didn't want to be reminded of that happy evening now. It was too cruel in the light of what she had learned.

"And now it is too late."

The healer could barely complete her work; her sight was so blurred by tears. Sullyan herself said nothing more, only watched her sadly. Rienne could feel her sympathy and could scarcely bear it. Eventually, packing away her instruments while the Major dressed, Rienne summoned the courage to speak.

"How long?"

"I have no way of knowing." Sullyan was unwinding the dressing on her wrist to inspect the half-healed skin beneath. "The power Ty provided to seal off the poison will alleviate the symptoms for a while. But the seal is not strong, and soon the poison will eat through it and start leaching away my strength. I only pray I will be granted enough time."

"To do what?"

Rienne already knew the answer. In the light of what she had heard, there could only be one thing driving Sullyan now. The Major's harsh words confirmed it.

"Prevent Rykan from taking the throne. Destroy him. Preferably by my own hand."

✤ ✤ ✤ ✤ ✤

Sullyan watched in silence as Rienne left the barn. The healer walked with slumped shoulders, a clear sign of the pain she felt. Sullyan had asked her to send Robin out to the barn, and as she waited she took some deep breaths, trying to find the strength and courage she knew she would need. Her heart was pounding, and one phrase kept repeating in her mind.

Robin, I have something to tell you ....

Too soon, she heard his footsteps. He walked briskly into the barn, her combat jacket slung over his arm. There was a look of innocent enquiry on his handsome face and her heart lurched painfully. She forced herself to approach him, and he held her jacket open. Shrugging into it for warmth, she failed to suppress a shiver.

"Walk with me, Robin," she said, suddenly desperate for sunlight on her face. He turned and paced beside her, his easy acceptance making her feel like a traitor. They moved away from the barn, but the damp earth smell and the faint warmth of the sun were too much for Sullyan. It was all too normal, when nothing in her life would ever be normal again.

She stopped and turned to Robin. When she took hold of his hands, he frowned, startled by the intimacy. She began speaking, her voice as level as she could make it, her eyes never leaving her lover's face. Not even when her words made him try to wrench away.

"Robin, I ...." The words that had echoed in her head refused to come, and she had to clear her throat. "There's something I need you to understand, and I want you to listen and not interrupt. I cannot come back with you to Albia. What Rykan did to me means that my life there has ended. His actions left a poison within me,

45

and that poison will kill me if I try to cross the Veils."

His hands jerked within hers but she gripped them all the tighter, desperate now to say what must be said.

"There is nothing you can do to help me. I must stay here and live out what time I have left. But you must return to Albia—I will not see you suffer because of me."

"I will never leave you—"

Desolate anger surged within her. "You have to! I could not bear seeing you sicken. You must understand, Robin, it is over! Our time together is over."

Robin's face went grey and tears pricked Sullyan's eyes. Grief had made her harsh, but he did not deserve such betrayal. Not from her. She could barely meet his stricken gaze, but forced herself to witness the final moment, the moment Robin was forced to face the ruin of his every hope and dream. His body slumped and she thought he might fall, but her grip on his hands kept him upright. Her heart nearly broke when she realized he would not lean totally on her. Even in his extreme pain, he was aware of her weakness.

He straightened abruptly. Without a word, he pulled his hands away, his strength too great for her to resist. She could sense the pool of tears welling within him, yet he was too numb, too stunned, to shed them.

Helpless, she could only stand and watch as Robin moved away. She didn't call to him. She knew he needed solitude to come to terms with what he had heard. Gentle as she had been, there was no easy way to hear that the love of your life, your one true soul mate, was leaving before your lives together had even begun. She could almost taste his desolation as she walked back to the barn. Collapsing onto a bale of hay, she buried her face in her hands.

She didn't know how long it was—only a few minutes, she thought—before she heard light footsteps approaching. Lifting her face, she met Robin's red-rimmed eyes. She began to rise, but he made a negative gesture and stepped back. Hurt, she gazed at him. He wouldn't meet her eyes and stared instead toward the horizon, where dark rain clouds were massing again. In silence, she waited for him to speak.

"Will you answer me a simple question? Will you give me a straight and honest answer?"

She nodded. "If I can."

His voice was hoarse and she was taken aback by his phrasing, but the need in his question was clear.

Wind from the approaching rain clouds stirred the Captain's short, dark hair. He paused a moment more, considering his words. Sullyan waited with her hands in her lap and her eyes on his pinched, white face.

Muscles jumped along his jawline. He took a deep breath and looked her full in the eyes. She began to tremble. This, she thought, would be the most important question he had ever asked in his entire life.

"Sullyan, do you love me?"

Her indrawn breath was almost a sob. She stood and approached him. Placing her hand on his arm, preparing to bare her soul more deeply than she had ever done before, she said, "How could you doubt me, Robin? Yes, I love you. With all my heart and soul."

She meant for him to sense the depth of her feelings. This was no time to hold back. Touching the edges of his psyche with her powers, she heard the breath catch in his throat. As he stared deeply into her eyes, captured by what she revealed, she knew he finally understood how deeply she had always loved him. How hard it had been for her to maintain her professional position and carry out her duties while containing such powerful emotions. Now he understood why she had contained them.

Contrition flooded his heart, and she sensed his regret for all the hurt he had given her, the trouble he had caused her, the adolescent way he had sometimes behaved while trying to impress her. She forgave him, and felt his heart lift. He was, he suddenly realized, the only one who could help her now. No one else was in a position to do so.

Despite this new knowledge, Robin had one last question. He gripped her hands tightly while pent-up breath sighed out of his lungs.

"Sullyan, are you absolutely sure there's no way out of this? No one who might know of a solution, a cure?"

She dropped her gaze, unwilling to show him her pain. Looking past him into the morning sky, she said, "I wonder if you know, *really* know, what my life means to me? The work I do, the Manor, the position I hold? They have been everything I have ever wanted. They feel right … necessary. I belong there. It is what I was born for.

"I have been in many battles, as you know. Often, I have been in peril of my life. On two occasions, only the skill and care of those who loved me saved me from death. You know me, Robin. You know I am not fey. I do not seek death, in battle or otherwise. So I tell you now, and hear me well. If there was any way in all the Five Realms to avert what is to happen, I would take it gladly."

She turned her full gaze on him. The tears welling once more in his dark blue eyes told her that he had accepted what was to come.

She feared he might take her in his arms, and she knew she could not cope with that right now. Her small store of strength was fading. She sincerely hoped Rienne had told the others, she could not bear to go through it all again. Bulldog had guessed, she was fairly sure, she had seen it in the big man's eyes. She would need his solid, dependable strength very soon, she thought, as would Robin in the weeks to come.

"What will you do now?"

His question was a welcome distraction. Robin was trying to be practical and that was good. It was something she could deal with.

"Under normal circumstances, I would say we had no business interfering in the political struggles of another realm. But I am in a unique position to know exactly what Rykan intends, and I know that if he gains the Andaryan throne, Albia will also be in jeopardy. Rykan will not honor the Pact. So, I will go to Caer Vellet, Robin, to the Hierarch's Citadel, and I will offer my sword and services in defense of his crown for as long as my strength lasts. I have valuable information concerning Rykan's battle plans, and I am probably the only person in a position to thwart him. Especially as he does not have the extra power he planned on."

She smiled, but the Captain looked troubled.

"I have to try, Robin. I have nothing to lose. I also owe a debt to Marik, and if I can persuade the Hierarch to accept him, not only will I rob Rykan of some of his forces, but maybe I can restore Marik's pride and manor as well."

The troubled look didn't leave Robin's face, and Sullyan knew he still harbored doubts about Marik. She had neither the time nor the energy to deal with his mistrust. A few cold spots of rain landed on her face and she glanced up at the darkening sky. Rain-bearing clouds were running in, and the wind was strengthening.

"We have much to arrange today, Robin, and I fear I will need your power again very soon. I am still too weak to manage on my own just yet. We should go in to the others, we have much to discuss."

Chapter Five

Sullyan re-entered the hut with Robin beside her. Every face turned her way, and she could tell from their expressions that they knew. Rienne must have told them. A cold sickness churned deep in her stomach, and she knew she couldn't bear their horror and sympathy. She was hanging on to her sanity by a thread as it was. Any show of emotion—no matter how well intended—might just sever it.

Unable to run from her friends, although she wished with all her heart she could do so, she did the only other thing she could think of. Placing her hands firmly on her hips, feet slightly apart, she faced them squarely. In a startlingly accurate imitation of Bull's deep bass rumble, she gave them his favorite phrase.

"For the gods' sake, let us not have the wake before the bloody funeral!"

A strangled laugh—or maybe a sob—from Bull broke the stillness. Sullyan smiled round at them, trying to convey her gratitude without inviting pity. Then, crossing to the bed and collapsing gently onto it, she said, "I hope you have some fellan brewing, Bulldog. I could really use some just now."

Shaking his head, Bull poured the requested drink. Her hands were trembling as she accepted it and he frowned. She smiled up at him.

"I will rest soon, Bull, but there are things we need to discuss right now."

Marik entered the hut as she outlined her plan. When she mentioned returning to the mansion to enable Marik to collect what he would need in order to accompany her to the Hierarch's Citadel, the Count protested.

"There's no point in me coming with you, Sullyan. I appreciate what you're trying to do, but they'll shoot me on sight. Even if they don't, my presence won't help your cause. I'm a traitor, and you'll be accused along with me."

"I will not leave you behind, my friend. You are no traitor, and my testimony will convince the Hierarch of your loyalty."

Marik shook his head. "Why should he listen to you? I've been Rykan's subject since I took my father's lands. The word of an Albian—and a woman at that—isn't going to carry any weight in Caer Vellet."

"Maybe not, but the word of a Master-elite Artesan surely will."

Marik fell silent, but his troubled eyes clearly betrayed his misgivings. Sullyan sighed. Her strength was fast disappearing.

"Do you not see?" she said, willing him to understand. "Placing yourself under my protection and throwing yourself on the Hierarch's mercy is your only sane course of action. The alternatives are exile and death, neither of which I will countenance."

Marik threw up his hands. "Oh, very well. At least the Hierarch isn't known for torturing traitors. Death at his hands should be quick."

His acceptance relieved her, despite her annoyance at his attitude. Rienne was watching her with concern, and when she suggested another healing session, Sullyan didn't refuse. She knew how close she was to collapse. When it was over, Rienne pressed some food on her and then insisted she sleep for an hour or so. Once again, Sullyan obeyed, retreating to the bed by the fire.

✣ ✣ ✣ ✣ ✣

Sullyan quickly fell asleep and Rienne tried to calm her fears for the Major's health. She knew how deeply Marik's resistance had drained her, and the younger woman's prediction regarding the seal on Rykan's poison was weighing on Rienne's mind. So it was a welcome distraction when Robin drew her, along with the others, to the far end of the hut. Bull served everyone fellan, and while they sat at the small table savoring the brew, the Captain asked Marik for an account of Sullyan's imprisonment.

Clearly, the Count wasn't happy, and Rienne suspected he didn't trust Robin's earlier forced apology. If the young Captain still held Marik responsible for Sullyan's capture, then telling the tale could easily result in another confrontation. Rienne felt sure the Count would refuse. Then Bull added his weight to Robin's request.

"Count, we need to know. I understand it won't be easy to hear or to tell, so I'll ask you to be brief. Just tell us what you can."

The Count looked down at his hands, anywhere but at the taut faces around him. "Brief?" He took a steadying breath. "Rykan came back after you left. He never intended to return to Kymer. He simply went far enough to ensure the council session was well underway. I didn't know it then, but he'd brought his own servants with him, and they must have put something in the food we ate. The first I knew was when I woke in one of Rykan's carriages, along with three other members of my court. We were taken to Rykan's palace and confined to our rooms. No one would tell us what was going on, and the palace was in uproar. From what we heard through the door, it was clear that Rykan was in a frighteningly violent rage. His people seemed in mortal fear of their lives, and with good reason as it turned out, because I heard later that he actually killed some of them. It wasn't until the terror died down that I discovered he had also abducted Sullyan.

"He held a feast, which we were all required to attend. There was no sign of his earlier rage. When Sullyan was brought into the room, he fawned over her as if she was an honored guest rather than a prisoner in spellsilver. I learned then that his 'invasion' of Albia was nothing more than a ruse to get Sullyan sent to my manor as an envoy from your king.

"The spellsilver had affected Sullyan badly, and she hardly had the strength to speak. Rykan kept trying to wheedle his way round her, trying to get her to agree to some kind of alliance between them. She refused, but the strain was evident. I managed to catch her eye, to let her know I would help where I could, but I don't know if she understood."

Rienne glanced over at the sleeping form on the bed, wondering where Sullyan's reserves of strength came from. Marik's low voice continued and she turned her attention back to his narrative.

"I next saw her about three days later. I think Rykan was beginning to realize just how strong she was, even without her Artesan powers. He has a well-deserved reputation as a brutal womanizer, and I doubt he's ever dealt with a female as stubborn as her. He would never have tolerated such resistance from an Andaryan woman. Any female who dared to show such spirit would be killed."

Robin gave a skeptical grunt and Marik glared at him. "Believe me, he's done it before! But it was different with Sullyan. He coveted her powers, and as you know, no Artesan can take another's powers by force. He had to 'persuade' her to give them up, torment her and wear her down until she gave in. He had to endure her obstinacy, and I can only imagine how it infuriated him."

He dropped his eyes, his face pale. "Then he tried another tactic. He told her, in front of us all, that if she continued to refuse him, he would treat her the same way he was treating her horse. He showed her a whip which still bore traces of blood and black hairs. I think that was the first time she reacted to anything he said to her. She didn't know he was abusing her horse. He saw her anger and laughed in her face. Then he ordered his guards to strip her naked, and he used that horsewhip on her until she fell to her knees."

Robin made a strangled sound and Rienne covered her face. She felt sick. Some of those lashes had cut to the bone.

Marik's voice wavered. "She hardly made a sound except right at the end. I think that's what Rykan was waiting for, to hear her acknowledge him. She was virtually unconscious by the time he stopped and ordered his guards to throw her in the cells. That's when I made my first mistake."

He stopped and they all stared at him, horror in their eyes. Outside, rain was drumming on the roof but Rienne barely noticed.

Marik shook his head. "I didn't realize I had risen to my feet. What did I think I was going to do? Surrounded by the Duke's men, there was nothing I could do, even if I was armed, which of course I wasn't. All I did was draw attention to the fact that I didn't agree with what Rykan was doing. I remember the look he gave me when he realized I might have feelings for her. I wish now—" He broke off and heaved a huge sigh.

"I managed to get into her cell. I overheard one of the jailors saying it was a shame the way Rykan had used her, and I played on his feelings. She was barely conscious when I went in, but I managed to get her to drink some water. I cleaned her wounds as best I could and covered her with straw. Before I left, she made me promise to try to release her horse. It wasn't easy, but, as you know, I eventually succeeded. Rykan's horse master received a flogging, but he deserved it for the way the poor brute had been treated."

Marik paused to take a sip of cold fellan. Bull rose and fetched more. Rienne curled her hands gratefully around the cup, the warm liquid helping to dispel the chill brought on by listening to the Count's dreadful tale. She didn't really want to hear any more, but they were locked into it now. She sat helpless, hardly able to imagine the horrors Sullyan had suffered.

Marik glanced plaintively at Bull. "I don't suppose you have anything to fortify this fellan with?"

Bull fetched his bottle of firewater and passed it round. They all took some of the burning liquid, even Rienne. After a long swallow, Marik went on.

"The day after I released the horse, Rykan shut himself away with his generals. I don't know if his next move was his own idea, or theirs. He might have intended it all along, or maybe he was just indulging his brutal nature. That night, after the evening meal, he was in a better mood. I was very frightened because I thought he must finally have defeated her. But I was wrong."

He sounded strained. "He followed me when I went back to my rooms. He never spoke, just gave me a mean look and ordered his guards to bring me. When I realized he was taking me to the cells, I was certain of a sword through my guts. But he had something even worse in mind. He went to Sullyan's cell and opened the door."

Marik's alien eyes were unfocused, dilated with remembered fear. Sweat beaded his face. To stop his hands from shaking, he clasped them so tightly round his cup that the knuckles turned white.

"Sullyan raised her head as Rykan entered, and she saw me standing behind him. I fully believe, in that moment, she was more afraid for me than herself. Rykan stood over her, asking if she had reconsidered his offer. She didn't speak, maybe she couldn't, but when he saw the defiance in her eyes, he smiled.

"I swear—I *swear*—I had no idea what he intended until I saw him unbuckle his sword belt. Either he sensed my horror, or maybe

I made a noise, for he ordered the guards to hold me. They already had swords at my back, but one of them took hold of my arms as well. If he hadn't, I think I would have tried to stop Rykan, even though I would have lost my life."

He stopped, unable to continue. Tears welled in his eyes as he stared down at his trembling hands. Rienne waited for him to compose himself, but he sat unmoving. Then a husky voice sounded behind him.

"Go on, Ty."

He started like a frightened rabbit and spun round to meet Sullyan's gaze. None of them had noticed her rouse. Rienne felt certain she had heard every word, despite appearing to be deeply asleep.

The Count looked mortified, but Sullyan smiled gently. "You are doing very well, Ty. Tell them the rest."

She closed her eyes again. Marik swallowed awkwardly and resumed his narrative, using a detached tone.

"Rykan forced himself on her in that filthy cell, cruelly and with no remorse. She cried out when he took her, but then made no sound until he was nearly done, which I think inflamed him even more. I could see how hard she fought to stay silent, although he was being deliberately brutal. When he finally pushed himself from her, he stood looking down at her with a self-satisfied smile on his face. He told her that it didn't matter now whether she surrendered her power or not. He would continue taking his pleasure on her for as long as he wished. He knew, and more importantly, made sure she knew, what the consequences of his ravishment were.

"He left then, smiling as he fastened his breeches, striding past me like I didn't exist. He even took the guards with him. He just left me there, knowing there was nothing I could do to harm him, or help her."

Tears rolled down his face, but he didn't notice. Rienne gulped back her own sorrow while the others sat with stunned expressions on frozen faces.

"I sat holding her," said the Count, "and that was the only time I saw her give way to what she was feeling. Then the jailor threw me out and I had to return to my rooms. From then on I was watched, and Rykan forced me to witness his abuse twice more. I think he got as much pleasure from my horror as he did from hers. Hearing her scream seemed to encourage his brutality. He always left me with her afterward, possibly hoping I would try to persuade her to surrender. He judged me rightly, for I wanted to. Short of killing her, it was the only way I could think of to help her."

He finally fell silent, his head in his hands, his whole body trembling.

Sullyan cast aside the blanket, rose from the bed, and crossed to where the Count sat. Gathering him into her arms, she held him, tears glistening in her eyes.

"Rykan did not judge you rightly, my friend," she murmured, "for you did not seek to weaken my resolve. On the contrary, your comfort gave me the strength to hold out as long as I did. But let me tell you this. If he had threatened *your* life instead of brutalizing me, I would have given him what he wanted. So he can blame his own lustful nature for the failure of his plan."

This declaration of affection rendered Marik incapable of speech, so Sullyan raised her head and took up the tale herself.

"I knew by then you would be trying to reach me, and I was desperate to slip past the effects of the spellsilver. That was when I thought of using the pain and horror of Rykan's abuse to lend strength to my efforts. I especially thought of you, Rienne, because of your experience with Parren's corporal that day at the Manor. I thought you might recognize the feelings for what they were."

Rienne gasped. "I never even thought of that! I knew the

nightmares were something to do with you. I just didn't consider that I might be able to 'hear' you. I wish now I'd paid more attention to what I was feeling."

Sullyan smiled gently. "Do not reproach yourself. I was not even certain that my call had gone further than the walls of my own skull. As the days passed and Rykan kept up his abuse, I knew I could hold out no longer. He knew it too, and on the final occasion he took great delight in telling me, at the height of his pleasure, that he was bound the next day for Caer Vellet, to issue his formal challenge to the Hierarch. In doing so, he made a fatal mistake. By telling me his plan, he gave me courage to form my own, although I did not want to use it. When next I saw Marik, I told him I intended to feign defeat when Rykan returned. It would not be much of a feint, my resistance was almost gone. I think my sanity was not what it should have been. I believe I frightened you, Ty."

From the circle of her arms, Marik smiled. "I don't mind admitting it."

She carried on. "I had lost all hope that you would reach me in time. I never doubted you would come eventually, but I was so weak that I knew I could let go of life if Rykan pushed me further. My only concern was whether I could convince him to drop his guard long enough for me to catch his mind, and hold on while I destroyed us both. In the event, of course, I did not have to, for you did come in time, and I am very grateful. You put yourselves in grave danger, and I can never repay you."

There was an awkward silence. To end it, Rienne rose from her chair and gave Sullyan a brief but fierce hug, mindful of her sore ribs. She then did the same to Marik, adding a kiss on the cheek for good measure. He colored and ducked his head.

Robin also stood. He held out his hand to Marik, who took it with a bashful grin. The Count found all this sudden approval hard to accept.

Sullyan crossed to the fire and poured herself a cup of fellan. She had been so dehydrated that she couldn't get enough. Then she sat heavily on the bed and Rienne frowned. The Major was still very weak. How would she possibly find the strength to do what she had planned?

Chapter Six

Sullyan sat watching while the men busied themselves cutting and stacking firewood, returning the hut to the condition in which they had found it. Rienne packed their food supplies and cooking gear. With Taran's help, Bull scouted the route back to Marik's mansion and reported nothing unusual. The area seemed as deserted as when they had left three days before. Sullyan felt relief.

The worst of the rain had passed by the time they were ready to leave. The Major permitted Rienne to examine her, and the healer declared herself satisfied that Sullyan could cope with the ride. The Count, who had gone outside to saddle the horses, came back looking as if he had something on his mind. He approached Sullyan where she sat on the bed and stopped before her. She gazed at him as he extended his hand, palm upward. He held a small leather pouch, closed at the neck by a thong. Embarrassed, he was unable to meet her eyes. He spoke tersely.

"I managed to save these for you. The jailor, Calder, had stolen them. He'd have been killed if Rykan found out, and anyway, I didn't want Rykan to have them."

Hardly daring to hope, Sullyan took the pouch. She loosened the tie and tipped it up. A little cascade of gold and fire opals tumbled into her waiting hand. She gasped. She hadn't expected to see them again, and it had hurt her deeply to think they were gone.

She was certain Rykan had taken them. They were a part of who she was, and she had missed them as much as she would a hand or a foot.

She sat staring at the gems through a blurred mist. Then she rose and threw her arms around the thoroughly embarrassed Count. Releasing him, she placed the ring on her middle finger and the studs in her ears. She put the necklace back into the pouch. Her neck where the spellsilver had burned her was still too sore to wear it. She handed the pouch to Robin for safekeeping.

"Ty, this is one more debt I need to repay," she said, but he waved her gratitude away.

Taran, Cal, and Marik went outside to secure the packs while Bull and Rienne swept out the hearth, folded the blankets, and checked that all was as they had found it. There was nothing they could do to replace the hay and grain their horses had consumed, so Sullyan instructed Bull to leave some coins on the table. He was about to leave when she stopped him, one hand on his arm.

"Bull, what happened to the spellsilver?"

The question puzzled him and he raised his brows. "I think Marik disposed of it. Why?"

She closed her eyes, pain and weariness swamping her. "Apart from not wanting it to cause anyone danger, there is a faint possibility that I might find a use for it. Please ask Ty what he did with it."

With a disapproving frown, Bull strode to the door and questioned Marik. The Count was alarmed by the query and stared narrowly at Sullyan. "I buried it," he said, pointing to a spot behind the barn.

"I am sorry, Ty, but I will have to ask you to undo your hard work." He scowled, but went to fetch a shovel, unearthing a dirty sacking roll. Unwilling to touch it with his hands, he used the shovel to bring the exposed silver to her.

She gazed at it. "Is there any more of that sacking?"

Bull fetched a piece from the barn, and then looked horrified as she bent to pick up the silver. "Don't touch it, Sully!"

She smiled gently. "I am intimately acquainted with the effects of this metal, Bull. It can do me no further harm."

She took up the silver and wrapped it tightly in the clean sacking. Despite her words, she couldn't quite hide the flicker of agony that touching it brought, and she knew Bull had seen. He understood that she was sparing anyone else the task of handling it, yet he still shook his head as he opened her pack so she could drop the bundle inside.

Preparations complete, they mounted up. Robin cleared the stirrup for Sullyan, and Bull helped her up to sit before him on Torka's chestnut neck. She was still too weak to ride by herself, and snuggled into Robin's arms, feeling his warm and vital body supporting her.

Rienne began the journey seated in front of Cal, and they left the safety of the drovers' hut just past noon.

✤ ✤ ✤ ✤ ✤

General Sonten strode heavily through the fear-haunted palace, for once immune to the panic waiting to strike. He grinned maliciously as he reflected on the reasons for the Duke's latest fury. He was so gleeful at this second blow to Rykan's plans that he could have laughed out loud. Only his sheer incredulity stopped him.

He was barely able to credit what had happened. Who would have thought the meek and cowardly Count had such bravery in him? Who would have guessed that such a long, melancholy face could conceal such desperate cunning? Not Sonten, that was for sure. And certainly not the Duke or he would have had the man chained, flogged, and tossed naked into the cells as soon as they had returned from Cardon. He certainly wouldn't have been left alone with that damned human witch. She couldn't have been as close to death and defeat as Rykan had thought. The two of them had clearly conspired together to cheat the Duke of his prize.

Unlikely as it seemed, the Count had managed to free her on his own, and in doing so he had done Sonten a favor, although he probably wouldn't be pleased to hear it. He had been as fearful of Sonten as he was of the Duke himself, and Sonten had done nothing to soothe those fears. This was so ironic, thought Sonten, because had he known what Marik's intentions were, he would actually have helped the man. Had he suspected for just one moment that the Count might have carried off such a risky rescue, Sonten would have joined forces with him and made the whole thing easier.

Yet Marik hadn't needed any help, and once again Sonten was in the clear. The Duke had no reason to turn his insane fury on his general. Instead, he had taken out his rage on those more expendable. Sonten had spent quite some time overseeing the clean-up of Rykan's killing spree, and the unfortunate remnants of Marik's court who had survived would be among the first thrown to the Hierarch's troops.

Emerging into the crowded compound, Sonten chuckled again. He just couldn't help it. Capricious fortune had turned his way at last and was smiling on his plans. This was not the first ironic twist of fate to befall him since accompanying the Duke to Cardon.

He stopped, glaring at the chaos, at the preparations being made. Faces turned toward him, anticipating the order to move out. He had come to deliver those orders, for his Grace could wait no longer. Unable to give chase to the traitor due to the timing of his plans, the furious Duke had been forced to rely on Sonten's patrols to intercept and apprehend the runaways.

Sonten had sent two units to Cardon in case the Count should run for his manor, although if the man was that stupid, Sonten would eat his horse. Surely no one who could snatch such a prize from under Rykan's nose would be so simple as to run straight home. No, the Count wouldn't rely on Rykan's challenge to protect him from Rykan's wrath.

Mind you, reflected Sonten with grudging respect, the Count had been surprisingly cunning there too. If his rescue had been cut any finer, Rykan would have caught him in the act. As it was, they could only have got clear with scant minutes in hand, judging by the residual warmth in the body of the jailor they had found in the cells.

Now that his formal challenge was issued, Rykan was committed to war, despite his failure to secure the witch's powers. He couldn't take the chance that the Hierarch's forces would be sent to contain him, although even that eventuality had been planned for. Fortunately, the Hierarch's generals were unaware of Rykan's increased numbers and would be totally unprepared for the strength he could field. They would simply retreat behind Caer Vellet's well-defended walls and rely upon its granite to protect them while Rykan threw his warriors at the stone.

At least, this was what Sonten had told his overlord, and he was confident he would be proved right. The Hierarch's generals would expect a siege, and that expectation would play into Rykan's hands. It would allow him to turn up his trump card—the ancient and obscure tradition that would lead to the Hierarch's downfall.

Sonten grinned widely. The Duke didn't need his despised Albian ally, the sly, self-serving Baron. He would realize that once the battle for Caer Vellet was won. This was Sonten's field of expertise. Outright warfare was much more to his taste than consorting with and pandering to humans.

Feeling satisfied, Sonten cast about for one of the Duke's commanders, the one who had replaced the late, unlamented Verris. "Reece!" he bellowed, summoning a bearded, dark-skinned fellow who scuttled to his side, fear showing in his face.

"My Lord?"

"His Grace has given the order. We ride within the hour. Muster your lieutenants and have them form their companies. Move them out by rote, and make sure you follow the marching order. His Grace is in no mood to be crossed, so keep the formations tight. Any news from the patrols?"

"Nothing, my Lord, after the initial trail went cold. The Count must have covered his tracks among ours, and in the dark—"

"I don't need your excuses, Reece. His Grace will deal with their failure if and when they have the nerve to show their faces. Just hope he calms down before he asks for your report. I can do without losing another commander. They're getting thin on the ground. Well? Why are you still here?"

Reece gave a hurried salute before turning away and yelling orders, his harsh voice betraying his fear. The general grinned yet again, thankful to be spared that heart-stopping chill. He hadn't felt it for days now, not since the morning he had returned to Marik's miserable manor with Rykan to discover that the murdering Albian Journeyman hadn't been caught in the Duke's clever trap.

What had become of him and his two male companions, Sonten didn't know. They had probably returned to their own realm, abandoning the witch to her fate. It didn't matter. The Duke's only concern was the human witch, and he hadn't noticed Sonten's air of relief. The general had even ceased to think about exacting revenge for Jaskin's death. That could wait until he was in a position to deal with it.

Then came Sonten's second stroke of luck, and he had marveled at fate's infidelity. For as soon as they returned to Kymer with the human witch at Rykan's mercy, the Duke had discovered the theft of the Staff. His rage had known no bounds. Yet instead of suspecting Sonten as the general had feared, Rykan turned to him for aid and even charged him with hunting out the culprit.

Scarcely able to believe his luck, Sonten had happily conducted a thorough search, unearthing vague and misleading clues which of course led nowhere. Rykan's apoplectic fury was directed away from Sonten, and the men he killed didn't affect their preparations for war.

Trying to keep his mirth under control, Sonten pushed his way through the mass of men in the compound. He roared for Heron. His trusted commander appeared at a run, looking alarmed. Sonten threw a heavy arm across Heron's slimmer shoulders.

"The time has come, Heron, my man!"

The Artesan commander frowned, made uneasy by his lord's familiarity and also his strange, elated mood.

Sonten turned gleaming eyes on his commander and tightened his grip on the man's shoulders. "Saddle my horse and stand the escort by the gates. His Grace is ready to ride. And don't you let me down, my valuable Artesan friend. Keep yourself well clear of the fighting and report to me every night. Keep your wits about you, and don't forget where your gold comes from. There's more at stake here than mere coinage, if my plans work out this time. Now go and join the formation and prepare our men to march. I've a good feeling about this, Heron. My fortunes are about to rise."

✢ ✢ ✢ ✢ ✢

According to Marik, it would take them just over a day to reach his mansion. In the wake of the rain, the wind was much colder. Rienne rode behind Cal, her cloak bundled tightly around her. The season was turning toward winter. The Count had predicted a frost.

The heavy folds of Rienne's cloak warmed the horse's back as well as her own. Sullyan had also drawn a cloak close about her and was sleeping in Robin's arms. Rienne marveled that she could sleep at all with the motion of the horse, but supposed that her half-healed condition and soldier's ability to snatch sleep whatever the circumstances must help.

Throughout the dark afternoon, the wind grew steadily colder and stronger. Marik led the way, Bull, Taran, and Robin taking turns to scout their surroundings. They saw nothing but wildlife and heard nothing but birds. As true twilight began to dim the countryside, Rienne suggested that Cal use the crossbow he had taken to carrying and try his hand at bringing down some game for supper. She was worried about Sullyan's lack of appetite and thought a good, warm stew might tempt her. The others agreed, and Marik took Rienne onto his horse. He told Cal to look out for a small species of woodland pig that made especially good eating.

The creatures were plentiful but shy, so Cal had to move apart from the group to stalk them. Instructed to keep in touch with Taran, he disappeared into the deepening gloom. Half an hour later Taran reported his success, and soon the Apprentice reappeared ahead of them, a small carcass slung across his stallion's withers.

Marik found a sheltered spot to make camp in a clearing in the woods through which they had been riding for the last couple of hours. Stars were shimmering in the crystal clear sky, the wind had begun to die, and the horses' breath steamed in the frosty air. Robin roused the Major, who seemed much improved as Bull helped her down from the Captain's horse. She stretched cramped muscles with only a tiny wince at the pull on her damaged ribs. Rienne guessed she had been using her vast powers to aid her healing while she slept, because the bruises on her face and arms were fading fast.

The two women skinned and dressed the meat while the men kindled a fire and saw to the horses. Marik found some herbs that would complement the pig's gamey flavor, and the resultant stew was welcome and heartening. Sullyan still didn't eat very much. Rienne commented on it, trying to encourage her. Sullyan's manner was vague and distracted, and her face was very pale. She sat in silence as the others consumed their meal, and Rienne noticed Robin watching her, concern in his dark blue eyes.

Once the food was finished and cleared away, they sat around the fire for warmth, cradling steaming cups of fellan. Bull reported the area clear of people, and Cal took his longwhistle from his pack, playing softly into the night air. Smiling, Rienne recognized one of the folk tunes she and Sullyan had giggled over during the evening they had spent together. The Major, who was sitting to her right, had also recognized the tune. Her head was turned toward Cal, and her golden eyes glittered with tears that reflected the jumping firelight.

When she noticed Rienne's regard, she smiled warmly. The healer experienced a sudden rush of companionship, friendship, and pleasure in another's esteem, such as she hadn't felt since falling for Cal's dark good looks. Then she heard Sullyan's voice in her mind.

I shall never forget your care, help, and friendship, Rienne. I could never thank you for what you have done for me.

Rienne's vision blurred and she had to turn away. Overwhelming grief welled inside her. Knowing what she would soon lose was too much to bear. She heard Sullyan give a tiny gasp and knew she felt it too.

The Major turned to Robin, her voice husky in the peaceful night. "I need you to do something for me, Robin. I need you to find out where Rykan's forces are. I dare not do it myself. Rykan is far too familiar with my psyche, and I would rather not reveal my whereabouts until I am ready. He may even think I am dead, and that sits well with me. If you look for his pattern in the substrate and read the emotions it contains, you should be able to glean some information without alerting him. Will you do this for me?"

Robin nodded. "Of course. You'll have to show me his pattern."

She did so, and they all waited patiently. Robin's eyes lost their focus as he flung his metasenses out to search for Rykan's psyche. After a few minutes, he came back to himself. His gaze found Marik's with an expression both grim and amused. The Count raised his brows in query.

Robin said, "I don't know whether this will please you or not, my friend, but it seems your reputation has gained notoriety among Rykan's forces."

The Count looked puzzled. "Oh?"

"Rykan has issued a death warrant in your name for abducting the Lady Ambassador here." Robin grinned at Marik's expression, then related what he had learned about Rykan's movements.

Sullyan nodded in satisfaction. The Duke had acted according to her expectations.

"Can he win a pitched battle by strength of arms alone?" Taran asked her.

"He has to try now he has issued a formal challenge," she replied. "The Andaryan Codes of Combat do not permit a lord to recant once such a challenge has been accepted. He must either win or concede defeat, and if he concedes then he submits to the victor's will. But Rykan has been circumspect, and he did not pin his entire strategy on forcing me to surrender my metaforce. It is my duty to make sure he cannot win by might of arms, no matter how many men he fields."

She didn't elaborate further and Taran didn't press her. Rienne thought she knew why. Taran feared that the three of them would be sent back to Albia once they reached Marik's mansion. He would be trying to deal with his feelings about that. She caught his eye and saw that he knew she was aware of his turmoil. He turned his face away.

They retired to sleep soon after that, the men agreeing on watches. None of them would wake Sullyan until morning.

Chapter Seven

It froze hard overnight, but a glorious morning met their eyes as the sun climbed a brittle, blue sky, striking sparks from the frosted trees. The ground crunched under the horses' hooves as the animals foraged beneath the boughs.

After a warming breakfast and copious amounts of fellan, Sullyan astounded Robin by asking him to fence with her. He protested, but she growled at him and he fetched his weapon with no further comment. Rienne strongly suspected that Sullyan had spent the night in healing rather than sleeping, for her face was paler and thinner than ever and she gave no sign of feeling the ribs that had only been set two days before.

She made a good showing against Robin and chastised him for going easy with her when she wanted his full commitment. After she nearly disarmed him with an unexpected move, he made no further concessions. Rienne surprised herself by watching the graceful, agile, but deadly moves with delight and some envy. She had intended to monitor Sullyan's condition, but instead found herself admiring the Major's skills. For the first time in her life, Rienne thought it might feel good to be able to handle a blade that well.

Both Robin and Sullyan were perspiring by the time the Major ended their bout. Panting, she dropped to the ground. Robin was only marginally less winded, and he leaned on his sword, regarding her with exasperation.

"Did you really have to push that hard? You'll do yourself

70

some damage if you're not careful."

She glared at him, and Rienne thought she would deliver a hard reply about it being far too late to worry about damage. Instead she said mildly, "I thought you needed the exercise, Captain. I believe you are growing a touch lazy."

This was so patently untrue that Robin snorted. He held out a hand to help her rise. Sullyan's fingers brushed his face gently as she walked past him to stow her weapon. Robin watched her, an intense expression in his eyes.

Soon they were on their way again, Marik estimating that they should reach the mansion by mid-afternoon. As before, Sullyan slept in Robin's arms, and they didn't bother with a noon meal as they were so close to their goal. Once they were within a few miles of the mansion, Sullyan roused and looked around.

"Robin, will you scout the area? If Rykan is as avid for the Count's blood as you suggest, then he will have sent men to watch his home."

Robin glanced at Bull, and the two men merged their power to search the area for patrols. As the Major had expected, they found two units of Rykan's men stationed to guard both approaches to Marik's mansion. There were no other signs of life. The servants who had been chased off had sensibly stayed away.

Sullyan paused before regarding them all. "I cannot afford for any of those men to report back to Rykan. They will have to be dealt with."

Robin and Bull were unfazed by this, but as Marik, Cal, and Taran were not under her authority, she needed their acceptance before commanding them. Taran and Cal were more than happy to follow Robin, and Marik was fatalistic about his future.

"I'm caught between Rykan and the Hierarch anyway," he muttered. "Either one is entitled to kill me on sight, so what do I have to lose?"

As Marik knew the terrain best, they took his advice on how to lure the patrols out. It was decided that Sullyan and Rienne would be left in ambush with a crossbow apiece, and the men would draw the patrols into range of their bolts. Sullyan seemed satisfied with this plan, but Rienne was far from happy. She wasn't at all sure she could aim a weapon at another living being.

"Do not try, then," said Sullyan. "Aim for the ground in front of the horses. Knowing you are shooting at them will be enough to distract the riders. Leave the killing to me."

The men rode off to alert the first patrol while the two women concealed themselves in a thicket with a good view of the land before them. The Major kept a link with Robin so she knew what was happening, and she relayed the information to Rienne.

The first patrol, ten men strong, was pathetically easy to lure out. Seeing only five men on horseback riding, as they thought, unsuspecting toward them, they wasted no time giving chase. Robin gave the order to run and the enemy closed the gap, soon coming in range of the crossbows.

Sullyan had no scruples about shooting Rykan's men, and despite telling Rienne she didn't have Robin's level of expertise with the crossbow, she brought the odds down to seven to five in the patrol's first pass across their position. Rienne's distracting shots had the effect of breaking up the group, and Robin gave the order to engage the Andaryans hand-to-hand. This made it more difficult for Sullyan to pick them off, so she stopped Rienne from shooting and had her wind each crossbow in turn. The five men maneuvered the enemy riders so their backs were to the crossbows. Soon, it was over.

Once the loose horses were rounded up, Bull tethered them out of sight. The others disposed of the bodies as best they could, so as not to warn the second patrol. Rienne took back her own horse and Marik took one of the spares. The Major also claimed one, and they rode cautiously toward the second patrol. The enemy seemed unaware that their comrades were dead, so Sullyan decided to try the same tactic as before. She guided Rienne into a nearby copse.

The second patrol also had ten men, but their leader clearly had greater experience. He refused to be drawn out and waited for the Albians to come within range. This was inconvenient for Robin, as it meant revealing he knew where the patrol was hidden. He relayed this to Sullyan, and she immediately abandoned the ambush ploy. Telling Rienne to follow her, she leaped onto her borrowed mount and galloped off to join the others.

As they pulled up alongside the men, Sullyan said, "We will have to do this the hard way. Marik, Bull, come with me. Robin, you take Taran and Cal. We will come at them from both sides at once. Let me know when you are in position. Rienne, stay close behind me."

Rienne watched uneasily as Robin took Cal and Taran off to the right flank. She kept her horse close on Sullyan's heels as she, Bull, and Marik worked round to the left. On receiving Robin's signal, Sullyan told Rienne to stay where she was, and the healer urged her horse behind a tree as the two groups charged the patrol.

Unaware that their enemy had split forces and confused by the sixth rider, the Andaryans were slow to react. Their commander rallied well, but not before four of his men were dead. Unhorsed, he suddenly found himself facing Sullyan's sword. Rienne sucked in her breath.

✣ ✣ ✣ ✣ ✣

Up to this point, Sullyan had managed to suppress her shock and fury at Rykan's abuse, using the practicalities of their situation to distract her. However, the look of stunned recognition that crossed the Andaryan commander's eyes caused Sullyan's control to crumble. He was, she realized, one of the guards who had restrained Marik the first time Rykan raped her. The suppressed boil of hatred within her abruptly burst, and a killing rage flooded her soul.

Unable to stop herself, she attacked him ferociously, raining blows he couldn't counter on his blade. Shocked, he fell back before her, his movements ever more frantic, until she disarmed him with a flick of her wrist. Her blade drove through his side and he fell, pinned to the ground while she stood over him, straddling his body and leaning on the sword embedded in his flesh.

Sick with terror, he stared up at her, seeing his death in her eyes. In the turmoil of Sullyan's mind, it was Rykan lying at her feet, exposed and helpless, just as she had lain. All the pain, horror, and madness that this sorry specimen had witnessed surged hotly into her breast. She wanted to torture and to terrify him, to use his pain to dull the anguish eating into her heart.

He made a small whimpering sound, and it inflamed her further. For all the agony and desperation she had felt at Rykan's hands, she had only allowed herself to scream at the most extreme pain. As soon as she recovered from the drug he had given her, she made up her mind not to betray a single sign of pain or terror, no matter what he did. Mostly, she had succeeded. She wasn't shamed by the times she had begged, pleaded, and cried, for eventually her choices ran out. By that time, her hopes of rescue had vanished and it no longer mattered.

Now, seeing this reminder of what she had endured lying so craven before her, the crushing despair came back. The man's palpable fear and whimpering pleas disgusted her, and a ferocious need for revenge overwhelmed her. If she could not yet have Rykan, then one of his men was almost as good. An enveloping surge of fury rose within her and she grasped the hilt of her sword, intending to twist it in the wound.

A restraining hand clamped onto her arm and she spun round, staring into Robin's dark eyes. He recoiled from the savagery in her face. She tried to shake him off, enraged at being held back from her prey. The others were staring, not sure what was happening. Robin stood his ground, radiating unease. He almost didn't recognize her.

A flash of movement caught her attention. She swung round just in time to see Marik bend and slit her prisoner's throat. The Andaryan died in a gurgle of blood, and the Count stood up to face her.

"How dare you?" she hissed.

Marik shrugged and stared back at the dead man. "I was owed that. Besides, you'd already killed him."

He walked away. Wordlessly, she stared after him. His undeniable right to vengeance—as urgent and valid as hers—drained her anger and resentment, leaving her lost and empty. She gazed down at the dead man, scarcely seeing him. Abruptly, she pulled out her sword and thrust it at Robin. When he took it, she stalked away.

✤ ✤ ✤ ✤ ✤

Rienne's heart was in her mouth as Robin moved over to the horses. He shrugged off her questioning look, cleaned the sword blade, and returned it to Sullyan's pack. Then he sent Cal to collect the other horses while he, Bull, and Taran unsaddled the remaining Andaryan mounts. When Cal returned, all the riderless horses were set free with a slap on the rump.

Finally, Robin approached Rienne. "Would you go talk with the Major?" he said. "I've never seen her like this before. It was as if a kind of madness went through her. I hardly recognized the look on her face. She isn't armed at the moment, so she'll do you no harm."

"Surely she wouldn't…?" Rienne stopped when she saw the tears in Robin's eyes. "Very well," she said, "I'll see what I can do." Moved by his distress, she added, "Try not to worry, Robin.

Remember what she's been through and what she carries inside her. She isn't the person she was before Rykan raped her."

Robin hung his head. Rienne moved over to where Sullyan was sitting on a fallen log some distance away, staring out into the woods. She made sure the Major heard her coming and tried to project feelings of friendship and understanding as she approached. She stopped a few feet away, unsure of her reception.

"Oh, Rienne, you are quite safe. I would never hurt you." Sullyan's husky voice radiated grief.

Rienne sat down. The Major turned to face her.

"It is beginning to erode my control, Rienne."

The healer was under no misapprehension as to her meaning. In the pallor of the Major's skin, her golden eyes seemed feverishly bright.

"If I am to succeed in thwarting Rykan's plans, then I shall need all the control I can muster. I cannot give in to it yet, it is far too soon."

Rienne knew she had to quell the rising panic in Sullyan. Taking her hand, she spoke calmly.

"We're nearly at the mansion now. Once we're there, perhaps Marik and I can do more to help you seal it away. The others will help too, you know that. We'll do everything we can. And you're still exhausted. You're nowhere near full strength. Perhaps that's affecting your resistance too."

Sullyan returned the pressure of Rienne's hand, tears sliding down her face. "What have I done to deserve such good friends?" she whispered.

Rienne smiled. "Given as much, if not more, than you've ever received."

Sullyan released Rienne's hand and rose to her feet. "I am going to miss you all so badly. But I know that all the healing in the world will not avail me now. I shall have to find the strength to deal with this myself."

✢ ✢ ✢ ✢ ✢

The incident with the Andaryan commander had shaken them all. Taran was as silent as the others as he rode alongside Cal for the rest of the way to the mansion. When the gates came into sight, he saw Marik regarding his home with tight lips, doubtless wondering if he would ever be its rightful lord again.

The Count led everyone round to the servants' entrance by the kitchens and showed them the stables. Although the servants had been driven off and all Marik's people taken by Rykan, the building itself had not been looted. There was grain and hay for the horses, and Taran did his share of work as they were fed, rubbed down, and bedded on fresh straw. Then he followed the others inside the smallest of the mansion's three kitchens and helped Bull attend to the great hearth. Soon a roaring blaze cheered the room and the familiar aroma of fellan filled the air. Sullyan's earlier fey mood seemed to have lifted and she was almost restored to her old self. Following Bull and Robin's lead, Taran allowed himself to relax.

While the light outside faded, they all sat round the large kitchen table partaking of what unspoiled food they could find. As the meal ended, Taran realized that the Major had grown increasingly withdrawn and was studying their faces, as if committing them to memory. Rienne had seen it too, for she put her hand on Sullyan's arm.

"Are you alright?"

It was a trite question, but Taran knew she was offering what comfort she could. The warmth in Sullyan's eyes and her smile were answer enough, although Taran could still see the underlying grief and sorrow.

Looking past Rienne to Cal, Sullyan said, "Do you have your whistle about you, Cal? I am in the mood for some music."

Cal, who never needed persuading to play, grinned and produced his beloved silver longwhistle from his pack.

"Marik," said Sullyan, startling the Count from a morose reverie. "I know you kept musicians. Would their instruments still be here?"

The Count shrugged and rose to his feet, returning with two guitars and a lap harp. Bull passed the fellan round before producing the bottle of firewater. Sullyan covered her cup as he uncorked it, but everyone else—including Taran—accepted the liquor.

The Major took the harp and indicated that Marik give one of the guitars to Rienne. Taran was mildly surprised when the Count kept the other for himself. Sullyan tested the harp strings and Taran thought it sounded inferior to her own instrument back at the Manor. Yet it sounded pleasant enough, and she gazed round at her friends.

"This may well be the last night we spend together."

Taran felt his heart lurch, and Robin took a sharp breath as if he would speak. He remained silent, though, and the others just stared at her or at their hands, too full of emotion to say anything.

"Tomorrow," she said, "you will return to Albia while the Count and I make our way to Caer Vellet. Bull, I want you to run a few errands for me. There are some things I will need. But we will speak of that later. Tonight, let us make the most of this evening and try to enjoy ourselves."

Robin made a small sound of protest, but no one else spoke. Taran saw Bull's eyes fill with tears and Rienne's were red-rimmed. He dropped his gaze to his hands and left Cal to lighten the mood. Raising his whistle to his lips, Cal played exactly the right sort of melody, a saucy little folk tune that banished morbid thoughts. He ran through it once, and as he began it again, Sullyan started to sing, playing a soft accompaniment on the harp. Rienne picked up the chords on the guitar, and then, surprising them all, Marik added his voice to Sullyan's. They sang the folk song through.

By tacit agreement, no one played any laments that night. The only poignant note came from Marik, who had a light and pleasant voice belying his melancholy nature. His offering was a song about a handsome young man who fell in love with a fairy girl, only to see her turn into a butterfly and fly away. The way his eyes kept straying to Sullyan left Taran in no doubt of his meaning.

Bull and Robin sang some marching songs, the Captain's light tenor blending nicely with Bull's rich bass rumble. Then Rienne and Cal sang a couple of lover's songs, and had everyone laughing as they lampooned two love-struck youngsters. Rienne and Sullyan even sang a couple of the songs they had shared during their evening together at the Manor—with the proper words this time—and the warmth and friendship flowing between them was plain for all to see.

Eventually, the hour grew late and the fire died down in the hearth. Bull's supply of liquor was exhausted, and their fingers and voices were sore from use. They lay the instruments aside, and Taran suddenly noticed that both Bull and Robin had blank looks on their faces. Turning to Sullyan, he saw the dilation of her eyes, a sure sign she was communing with the two men. He wondered why they were being so secretive, but before he could speculate further, the contact was broken.

Sullyan smiled and nodded at Robin, who stood, drawing their attention. Bull remained relaxed, a small smile on his face. Taran waited to see what was coming and was surprised when Robin turned to him, inclining his head.

"Journeyman, are you feeling strong tonight?"

Taran was startled. He hadn't thought of himself as a Journeyman since opening the tunnel through the Veils, since

Robin told him he had passed the test of Water. Then he remembered Robin saying that Sullyan would confirm him when she could. Something his father once said suddenly slipped into his mind, and he could hear Amanus's pedantic tones as if he were present in the room.

You owe allegiance and duty to anyone of higher rank than yours. But above all, you owe duty to the Masters. Anyone of higher status can confirm you in the next level, but Masters hold the right of confirmation over all. To be acclaimed by a Master Artesan is the ultimate accolade.

At that time, of course, Amanus had never believed his son would ever be so acclaimed, let alone by an Artesan as exalted as Sullyan. Taran felt a shiver of apprehension down his spine. Thoughts of his father always sapped his confidence. Yet the smile on Robin's face and the warmth in Sullyan's eyes reminded him that he had already passed the test and had nothing to fear from his friends. Taking a steadying breath, he rose.

"Yes, Adept-elite. I am feeling strong tonight."

Robin's grin told Taran that he had answered correctly, entering into the spirit of the occasion. Sullyan then rose, as did Bull, who indicated that Cal and Rienne do likewise. Rienne looked puzzled, but did as he asked with no question.

Marik moved off into a corner and sat watching while Robin and Bull moved the large wooden table, clearing an open space before the fire. Bull found a silver basin and filled it with water, placing it in the center of the floor. Sullyan moved to stand with her back to the fire. Robin joined her, standing on her left side. Bull took her right, and directed Cal and Rienne to complete what became a large circle with the silver bowl in the center. Taran remained on the outside.

He stood alert, not knowing what to expect. During their time fighting the invasion with the Major's company, he and Cal had listened to Robin's tales of life at the Manor. The Captain described some of the promotion ceremonies he had seen, both military and metaphysical. They fascinated Taran, but he had never expected to witness such a ceremony himself. Now he was the focus of one.

He realized he was trembling. Whether it was from nerves or anticipation he couldn't tell, so he kept his attention on Sullyan. Her eyes were huge and black, and he could sense her calling on her metaforce. He watched as she stretched her cupped hands out, palms upward. To his amazement, an amber glow blossomed in the bowl of her palms. Golden radiance lit her face, lending luminosity to the room.

She separated her hands, each still glowing, and held out the left one to Robin. The amber light extended toward him, becoming a thin line, and as the Captain reached out his right hand, the power touched his fingers, flowing up his arm and into his body. When it reached down his left arm, he held out his left hand to Rienne. Confused, she looked to Sullyan for reassurance.

"Do not fear, Rienne, my power will do you no harm. Just accept it in your hand as Robin did and pass it on to Cal."

Rienne did so, and Taran could feel her awe the moment Sullyan's power filled her body. She smiled, as if at a joyful memory. Cal accepted it from her, his expression turning to amazement, and Rienne had to remind him to pass it on to Bull. The circle was closed by Bull passing the power back to Sullyan, and she gathered it once more into her two cupped hands. The members of the circle stood joined in friendship and in power.

The Major stood wreathed in her own amber metaforce, her tawny hair shimmering in its glow. A warm breath of air moved gently in the room, stirring her hair and bringing the fire back to life. Taran was stunned—she had manipulated Air! He saw Robin frown, and even Bull, who must have known Sullyan's strength better than anyone, was startled by her skill. Awe flooded Taran. Control over the four elements was an Artesan's final test of Mastery.

Sullyan took no heed of their surprise. She merely gazed across at Taran, saying quietly, "Artesan Elijah, what rank do you hold?"

Despite his awe and mounting excitement, he managed to answer her calmly.

"I hold the rank of Journeyman, confirmed by the late Amanus Elijah, Adept-elite."

Approving this with a smile, she said, "Artesan Elijah, what is your wish?"

Her psyche radiated tranquility and reassurance as he gazed at her from behind Cal's right shoulder. "It is my wish to be confirmed in the rank of Adept if the level of my skill permits."

She inclined her head. "Very well."

She raised her cupped hands, still cradling the aura of her extended power. When her hands reached the level of her eyes, the water in the silver bowl stirred and rippled. A fine mist rose from it, catching in her web of power like tiny, glittering spiders. The rope of metaforce changed from amber to an opalescent shimmer. The color change flashed through everyone in the circle, returning once more to its maker.

The only illumination in the room came from the fire and Sullyan's shimmering rope of power. Once more she turned her eyes to Taran.

"This barrier of metaforce is now alloyed with the element of Water. Artesan Elijah, I bid you enter the circle."

Chapter Eight

Taran frowned. This was not what he had expected. He could feel the barrier's force from where he stood. If he tried to cross it unprepared it would burn him. This was another test, and one that could not be beyond his capabilities or Robin would never have been permitted to tell him he had reached the level of Adept.

Taran glanced at the Major, but there was no clue in her eyes, only watchfulness. He trusted that if he made a wrong move, she would not allow her power to harm him. He wouldn't choose wrongly, though. This time he would fail neither himself nor his father's years of impatient teaching. He had struggled too long and too hard to allow that to happen.

As he searched his memories, he heard his father's voice again.

Look for the place of least resistance. Look for the power which most closely matches your own. Merge like with like and you will pass through unscathed.

These instructions had been intended as a guide for the best place to build a portway, a place where the Earth energies could be matched to an Artesan's psyche. Taran wondered whether the same principle might also apply here.

He inspected the shining snake of power, perceiving how it subtly changed after passing through each person. On leaving Sullyan, its maker, it was pure silver, warm and alive. Passing through Robin, it gained a core like grey steel, solid, dependable, strong. From Rienne it emerged muted, as if wrapped in satin, less inclined to ripple. Cal added a mysterious, dark quality to it that carried an edge of unpredictability. From Bull it snaked away calm, smooth, honed and deadly, until finally uniting tail with head in the crucible of Sullyan's hands.

Taran smiled. He knew where his gateway lay.

Positioning himself at Cal's left shoulder, he concentrated on the flaring, twisting rope with its dark core of uncertainty. He suffered a guilty flash of understanding as he accepted that this flaw in Cal was of his making, an unwanted legacy from his father that he would have to correct for both their sakes. Yet its familiarity was his pathway, his route to becoming what he had long thought out of reach; the rank of Adept.

Taran stretched out his right hand and caught the shining rope. Instantly, metaforce flooded his soul. He sensed and acknowledged the separate components added by the five people in the ring and knew the power could never hurt him while those people were his friends. Glancing into Sullyan's proud and approving gaze, he passed through the shimmering line and entered the circle unscathed.

He stood before her, triumph washing through him. Despite his overwhelming joy, he gave a start of amazement as Sullyan, with a deft movement of her hands that he didn't quite see, detached herself from her own power and left it hanging in the air. She moved forward to face him, and Taran shook his head. Never would he achieve such casual competence.

Discerning his thoughts, she smiled. She reached out, took his right hand, and placed her left on his shoulder, gently requesting him to kneel. Then she gently touched the first two fingers of her left hand to her brow before pressing them to his.

"Artesan Elijah. By the Mastery of my calling, I confirm you in the rank of Adept."

Her fingers went to her lips before she gently touched his.

"By the love in my heart, I confirm you in the rank of Adept."

Finally, she laid her hand on her heart before pressing it to his chest.

"By the power of the craft we share, I confirm you in the rank of Adept."

He had only ever used it once—to his father—and it took Taran a moment to recognize the traditional salute due to Artesans of superior rank. It signified allegiance of duty, love, and power. Suddenly, he felt overawed.

Sullyan raised her eyes, gazing round at the others. "I bid you hear me well. By the power I wield as Master-elite, I, Major Sullyan, do confirm Taran Elijah as Artesan Adept. I call you all to Witness. Taran, use your power well and wisely. Learn to control and discipline the forces within you, and do so with humility. Taran Elijah, Artesan Adept, I bid you rise."

Taran raised his face to hers. Tears of pride glistening in his eyes, he performed the ancient salute, signifying his acceptance of her Mastery and confirming his allegiance and duty. The answering gleam of moisture in Sullyan's eyes gave him a sharp pang. If he ever gained enough knowledge to progress to an even higher rank, she wouldn't be there to confirm it.

Before he could think better of it, he rose and caught her fast in his arms, trying to convey the gratitude, love, friendship, sorrow, and sympathy he felt. She was taken off guard and let out one uncontrolled sob before using her power to calm herself. Bravely, she returned his embrace.

He realized his error and released her, but she smiled and forgave his lapse before carefully dampening her rope of power, freeing the others to move again. In the mêlée of backslapping, congratulatory hugs, and remarks from the others, only Taran caught sight of the slim woman slipping outside into the chill night air. He didn't dream of following her.

Worn out by the strength of their emotions, they all sought beds in the servants' rooms. Although basic, the quarters were well kept and clean, and all the little cots had good quality linen. Despite his obvious lack of wealth, Count Marik had been a good lord to his people.

Marik had gone off to his own rooms earlier to gather what he needed for the coming journey and to bolster his fast-fading courage. He might trust Sullyan to try her best with the Hierarch on his behalf, thought Taran, but he clearly doubted whether the ruler of Andaryon had need of a cowardly and minor noble such as himself. Especially as his allegiance had always been given—however unwillingly—to the Hierarch's rival.

Before retiring, Robin and Bull took the opportunity to sound each other out on the plans each had made concerning the future. They spoke in low tones, and Taran wouldn't stoop to eavesdrop, but he did catch them stating that they could not—and would not—disobey a direct order from the Major. However, it was plain to Taran that each had his own idea on how to interpret such an order. Bull then ushered everyone off to bed, leaving Robin to await Sullyan's return.

✤ ✤ ✤ ✤ ✤

She didn't make him wait long. The warmth and homeliness of the small servants' kitchen, with its smells of herbs, meat, and fellan, called to her. The ceremony she had performed for Taran served to remind her of what she was going to lose, and she had needed some time alone to regain her composure. It was fragile, though, and she was relieved to find only her Captain seated by the dying fire when she returned, as she didn't need to pretend with him. After the incident over the duel with Parren and the terrible rift it had caused between them, she felt closer to him than ever. The thought of not being able to spend the rest of a long life with him now that they had openly declared their love cut into her heart like a knife.

She stood silently in the doorway, watching the firelight flicker on the planes of his handsome face, seeing the reflected warmth in his deep blue eyes and the glints of gold in his soft, brown hair. Strong, well-shaped hands lay at peace on his knees, and his slim, muscular body sat easy in the plain wooden chair.

He sensed her regard and turned his head, his eyes dilated and dark. She knew he had something on his mind and put her own thoughts aside as she closed the door on the frost-laden air. She came toward him and he stirred, smiling up at her.

"That was some show you put on for our new Adept. Since when have you been able to manipulate Air so well?"

She knew this wasn't what he really wanted to say, but she accepted the topic.

"Do you think I do not practice my own teaching, Robin? I trust you are still working on the test I set you as confirmation of your Mastery."

This reminder of a happier day was almost too much for Robin. He came to his feet and stood close to her, taking both her hands as if clutching at his courage.

"Sullyan, I'm begging you. Please don't send me away with the others tomorrow."

His soul shone naked in his indigo eyes, and she had to look away. She drew a deep breath, sensing the fear sparking in his breast at what she might say.

"Oh, Robin. If it were only up to me, I truly would never be parted from you ever again. In all honesty, I fear I might not be able to complete my task without you."

She looked up, seeing hope, despair and love playing in his eyes. "But," she added, "the decision is not mine to make."

He was astounded and opened his mouth to reply, but she

firmly forestalled him. "Neither is it yours."

"Sullyan!"

She placed the fingers of her left hand across his lips. "No, Robin. I cannot let you throw away a brilliant career and potential for Mastery for nothing."

Again he opened his mouth, no doubt to protest her use of the word 'nothing', but she cut him off.

"My love, it will help me more than I can say to know that whatever befalls me, you are still there, using your training, being what you are, and becoming what you will be. There is much of me in you, both in your control over your powers and in your command of the men of my company. Would you give that up as if it were of no account? You must not. It is part of who you are, and what you would gain in return would soon be just ashes and memories. That is no trade, Robin, believe me. However, for the sake of our love, I will make you a concession."

He gazed at her through tear-filled eyes, but there was not much hope within them. She tried to smile for him but failed.

"You may wait with me while Bull returns with the others to the Manor. He must speak to the General for me, tell him the situation, and explain why I cannot return. There are also some things I will need. We will have one day to ourselves, but once Bull returns, you must go back with him to continue your career.

"You will always have my love, Robin, you know that. But I will not, I cannot, go through this knowing I have let you destroy the life you love. Can you understand that? Can you … forgive me?"

He dropped her hands and stepped away, tears falling unchecked. He couldn't speak, his throat too constricted by grief. Silently, she watched him, wanting to comfort him, yet knowing he had to come to his own acceptance of what must be.

He moved to the table and leaned both hands on it, bowing his head. She saw his shoulders shake as sorrow overwhelmed him. Unable to bear it, she came to his side. Without touching him, she extended her senses until she felt the essence of him within her mind. Carefully, she let him see how deeply she loved him and let her own warm, amber essence mingle with his.

After a few moments, the tremble of his body eased and she felt his spirit respond. He raised his head, turning slowly to look at her. Those deep indigo eyes, shimmering with tears, pierced her heart as they always did with the reflected clarity of his soul. Fractionally, they widened as he caught an echo of her thoughts. Now they held a question.

She brushed her fingers tenderly along the side of his face, feeling the smoothness of his skin. Hesitantly, she smiled. "Robin," she said, a husky note creeping back into her lilting voice, "I would rather not sleep alone tonight."

He gave a sharp gasp, half of hope, half of fear. Her heart nearly broke to think he might suspect her of falseness. She met his uncertain gaze with honesty, letting him see her intentions.

He whispered, "Are you sure …?"

She moved closer, smelling the sweetness of his breath and his other, subtler, masculine odors that she had always found most compelling. Her face came close to his, their lips almost touching. An electric tingle shot through her skin.

"My only love, I have never been surer. Rienne told me once that I should not cast away my one chance of happiness because of duty. She was right. I should not have waited so long, not when I knew how you felt. I was afraid it might … complicate matters between us. I was wrong. I should have trusted you. I have given us both needless pain, and I am sorry."

He drew back so he could look in her eyes. He cupped her face in both hands, trembling.

"You did what you thought was right, and I … well, I have

tried to do what you wanted. I will do the same now, but you must be very certain that this is what you want. I couldn't bear to hurt you—not after what you've suffered. But I tell you now, if we go much further than this, I may not be able to help myself."

"I appreciate your candor, Robin, but I intend to go much, much further than this." Leaning forward, she kissed him on the lips.

Their minds were still linked, so each felt what the other did. Neither thought they could contain it. After a long moment they broke apart, both breathing heavily. Robin's eyes were as dilated as Sullyan's when she expended power. Hers were amber and glowing.

Taking his hand, she led him to the room she had chosen for the night. It was dark within, but the low fire laid earlier lent a pearly quality to the shadows climbing the walls. Robin closed the door behind them and leaned his back to it, his heart thumping in his breast.

Sullyan crossed to the bed and raised her arms to unbraid her wealth of hair. Its silken softness cascaded down her shoulders and back, rippling like liquid fire in the glow of reflected flames. He came silently up behind her and buried his face in the fragrant waves at her neck. She took a deep and trembling breath as she felt his hands upon her. He could feel her tremor as she turned to face him.

"I need you, Robin," she whispered. "I need you to take away the fear and the pain. I think you are the only one who can."

Taking their time, they undressed before the fire. Although they had seen each other naked many times during their two years together, that had been a necessary part of their military life and didn't mean anything. This time, each felt they were learning about a stranger. Reveling in smooth skin, firm muscles, and strong arms, they finally twined themselves together on the bed. Despite his mounting ardor and overwhelming arousal, Robin had the presence of mind, before it was too late, to raise himself from her lips and ask, "Are you still sure?"

His only reply was a pair of slim and urgent arms linking behind his neck and smooth legs locking around his hips. And then it was far, far too late.

Chapter Nine

No one rose early the next morning. Nevertheless, by the time Rienne wandered into the kitchen in the frosty light of the new day, Sullyan and Robin were already seated at the large wooden table, mugs of fellan before them.

Sullyan was oiling her sword blade while talking quietly to the tall, handsome Captain by her side. Rienne glanced at them, and her morning greeting remained unsaid as she took in the relaxed attitude of their bodies so close together, the slight pink flush on the Major's cheek, and the way their eyes shone when they met.

Sullyan looked up to greet her and Rienne watched her eyes narrow in suspicion as she registered the broad, knowing grin that Rienne failed to hide.

With the merest hint of suggestion, Rienne said, "I trust you both, um, slept well?"

As she picked up two mugs of fellan, eager to tell Cal the news, she saw Sullyan trade a glance with Robin. To her amazement, a shy grin appeared on the Captain's face.

Bull came in then and walked straight up to the pair at the table. He slapped Robin roundly on the back and gave the startled Major an enormous bear hug. Rienne could see unshed tears standing in his eyes and presumed that his close bond with Sullyan had allowed him to sense what had happened.

Sullyan scowled at him. "Does everyone know our private business?"

Her voice was hard, but Rienne noted the slight curve to her lips.

Bull casually helped himself to fellan. "Only those of us who care about you."

Snorting in disgust, Sullyan took her gleaming sword back into her room.

Once breakfast was out of the way, there was no avoiding the inevitable painful farewells. Packs were gathered and horses saddled. They moved out into the brittle morning that at any other time would have dazzled with its beauty. A thick frost lay over everything and myriad crystals sparkled in the winter sun. The horses' breath plumed in the frozen air.

Marik had made only the briefest of farewells. Wisely deciding his presence would not be required, he had taken himself off to visit old Harva. Robin and Sullyan walked beside Rienne and her friends as they led their horses out into the sunshine. They fussed around, securing packs and adjusting girth straps, until the atmosphere became strained.

Suddenly, Sullyan could stand it no longer.

"It is time," she announced. "Bull must report to the General as soon as possible."

Turning to Cal, who stood nearest, she took up one of his hands. "I thank you for your friendship and help over these past weeks. Be sure to take extra care of your lady, there. Rienne is a very special person and has become very dear to me."

"Of course I will," mumbled Cal.

Sullyan embraced him, surprising him with a kiss on the cheek. She turned to Taran, who was standing behind his Apprentice. He came forward and placed both hands on Sullyan's shoulders before she could speak.

"I have to thank you for last night," he said, a catch in his voice. "If not for you, I'd still be floundering around in my own self-pity. You've given me direction and more knowledge than I ever thought I'd have. If there's ever anything I can do for you, you only have to ask." Going down on one knee before her, he once more made the brow-lips-heart salute due to a Master-elite.

Her eyes were damp as she raised him. "What you can do for me now, Taran, is continue to fulfill your potential. You have the capacity to become Master at least if you are willing to strive for it. Your father would be very proud of what you have achieved. Whatever you decide about your future, know that Robin and Bull will always be ready to help and guide you. Keep in touch with them and share your strengths. You need never be so alone again."

She embraced him too and kissed him, and then turned quickly away so he wouldn't see the moisture in her eyes.

Rienne was next, and the two women stood for long moments just looking at each other, tears making tracks down their faces. Then they fell into each other's arms.

"I owe you far too much for thanks, Rienne," murmured Sullyan. "But you were right about not letting happiness go by, and for that alone I'll always remember you. Will you do me one last favor?"

Rienne nodded, too choked for speech.

"Will you look after my harp and guitar for me? I would hate to think they might never be played again, but with you they will always have an echo of that evening we shared. I wish ...." She couldn't finish and had to push herself away from the heartbroken healer, leaving Cal to try and comfort Rienne.

Coming over to Bull, she managed to regain some composure. She took a deep breath and looked up into his brown eyes as he towered over her.

"You already know what I need you to do to tidy up my affairs," she said, "but there are two other favors I would ask of you." Bull raised his brows. They had already spoken of what he was to do back at the Manor. "The first," she said, "is to ask the

General to lend me Drum. I will need his battle skills to help me accomplish what I intend. I will have him returned when my need is over."

Bull nodded, and Rienne knew that if he had his way, the General would never learn of this request.

"And the second is this."

Reaching to the double thunderflash rank insignia gleaming above her left breast, Sullyan unclasped it and held it in her hand a moment. Then she thrust it toward Bull. Rienne heard Robin gasp, but the big man made no move to take it. Muscles along Sullyan's jaw jumped with strain as she grasped Bull's right hand. She placed the badge in his palm and firmly closed his fingers over it. His eyes were wide with shock and he shook his head in denial.

Sullyan's voice was hoarse as she said, "Give this to General Blaine and explain for me, Bull. I would go myself, but you know I cannot. He will understand."

Finding his voice, Bull said, "Sully, no!" but she stepped away and refused to meet his gaze.

"Go now," she said, a catch in her voice. "Go quickly, Bull."

There was nothing more to be said. They mounted up in the brittle sunlight, the icy cold catching their throats and stinging their eyes. As she turned the corner of the mansion, Rienne risked one final backward glance. Her last sight was of the two of them standing together, Robin's strong arm around Sullyan's shoulders, the sun tinting her glorious hair with russet sparks. Her hand was raised in farewell.

It was a long time before anyone spoke. They each rode absorbed in their own thoughts, some with tears still wet on their cheeks. Bull's hand was clasped tightly about the gold badge in his palm, as if desperately holding on to the warmth from Sullyan's body. Abruptly, he spurred his horse into a wild gallop, trying to outrun his grief and fear. Rienne and the others followed, but in the end it didn't help.

✤ ✤ ✤ ✤ ✤

Sullyan watched them go, holding tightly to Robin for comfort. It was also for support, although she was valiantly trying to hide from her lover what she had managed to hide from Rienne. The pain of the poison inside her was growing worse.

The distress of watching her friends depart had weakened her and she couldn't conceal a sudden, agonizing pang. Robin had to help her back into the warmth of the kitchen. Once more, she turned her powers over to him. With her direction, he managed to repair the breach that had allowed the poison to surface. In the process, Robin felt her growing desperation that she wouldn't be granted the time she needed to implement her plan against Rykan. He tried, but there was nothing he could say to reassure her.

They spent the morning resting and loving, not speaking much, just taking comfort from each other's presence. Sullyan knew Robin was painfully aware that this was their last full day together. Bull would return sometime late the next day, and it was inevitable that Blaine would order Robin back to the Manor. Sullyan had deliberately made it impossible for him to follow his instincts and disobey the General, and she knew he couldn't bear the thought of leaving her again.

For her part, Sullyan's heart was heavy. The knowledge that she would lose Robin just when they had discovered the depths of their love was a tragedy too painful to dwell on. So, after a light noon meal which improved her strength, she again asked her Captain to fence with her, taking refuge as she often did in the physical skills of her profession.

Robin recognized her need and raised no objections. He was happy to indulge in any activity that reaffirmed their awareness of each other, although he was obviously concerned for her lack of strength. Yet her skill with a sword was so great that it was Robin who had to call on his greater physical strength in order to avoid her swift and agile attacks. What she lacked in muscle and stature, she more than made up for in speed and cunning. She had been well taught from the beginning by Master Ardoch, the King's legendary swordmaster, and her supple musician's fingers gave her great control over the handling of her sword. Both of them were soon thoroughly enjoying their practice bout, and the afternoon slipped away.

They were still at it when the Count returned. Seeing him, Sullyan ended her bout with Robin by putting her sword to the salute. She couldn't suppress a measure of surprise that Marik had decided to throw in his lot with her after all. His going off alone hadn't concerned her—he didn't want to end up Rykan's captive again any more than she did—but she had wondered whether he might prefer to disappear, to take his chances somewhere else.

She smiled as he approached, and he gave her a challenging stare. "So, you did think I might not return."

She stared him down and he flushed. "It crossed my mind, Ty. I confess I am glad to see you safely back."

"Where else would I go? I might just as well go along with your plans, although how you're going to convince the Hierarch to accept me, I can't think."

Shaking her head at his gloomy tone, Sullyan took his arm and drew him into the kitchen. "How was Harva?"

He accepted the change of subject gladly and launched into all the things he had promised the old woman to tell her.

The evening passed quietly. Once they had eaten and exhausted what little conversation they felt like making, they lapsed into silence. Marik went out to tend the horses and came back shaking a dusting of snow from his shoulders. Sullyan hoped it wouldn't snow too much, as a heavy fall might delay them on the four-day journey to Caer Vellet.

The Count retired early again, diplomatically leaving the two lovers to spend as much time alone as they could. Sullyan appreciated his thoughtfulness, although it pained her to remember why it was necessary.

Once more, Robin tried to coax her into allowing him to stay with her, but she was adamant he must obey the General's orders, whatever they were. Reluctant to vex her on this last evening together, he desisted, and they retired to the simple little room that had become the focus of their love.

Their union that night was sweeter and more poignant than ever, minds linked as closely as bodies. Robin had a couple of brief affairs before meeting Sullyan two years ago, but apart from her brutal initiation by Rykan, Sullyan had never known a man's touch. Robin found her a quick and imaginative learner, as she was in all things, but the one new thing she brought him was the depth and strength of her power.

He had never made love to anyone gifted and had no idea how the power could intensify the pleasure they experienced in each other. It also prolonged their physical endurance, but as they lay entwined together afterward, breathless and utterly spent, he wryly reflected that all power must be paid for. Their sleep that night was deep and profound.

She tried so hard not to disturb him, but in the end, the pain was too much. Her cry in the cold pre-dawn startled him awake. She was kneeling on the floor by the bed, arms wrapped tightly round her belly, a small patch of bloody vomit on the floor. Instantly he was beside her, holding her while the spasm of trembling passed. Then he fetched a damp cloth from the kitchen and wiped the bloody froth from her lips. She allowed him to help her back into bed and then lay there panting, watching the fear in his eyes.

He took her cold hand, his face pale with concern. "Maybe

you shouldn't have sent Rienne away."

"There was nothing Rienne could do, Robin. There is nothing anyone can do, except maybe Pharikian."

He frowned. "Who?"

She could hear a hint of jealousy in his voice and tried a smile. It failed. "Timar Pharikian, the Hierarch of Andaryon."

The frown deepened, and she realized he had never heard the Hierarch's name before. Then he raised his brows. "Are you telling me you actually know the Hierarch?"

This time, the smile succeeded. "I have not been presented at Court, if that is what you mean. But I have seen him once or twice, and I know of him by reputation. He is the only Senior Master in existence, as far as I know, either in Andaryon or in Albia. It is possible that his greater power might be able to mitigate the poison's effects for a while, before it grows too strong. Long enough, perhaps, for me to accomplish my task."

"Well, I hope so, love." Robin's tone was bleak. "Because if it leaves you like this now, what's it going to be like when it's really bad?"

"Far worse." She smiled again, unable to give him any real comfort, then reached up and drew his cooling body under the covers. "But we will not think about that now."

✤ ✤ ✤ ✤ ✤

They woke in the early dawn, the sky smudgy-grey through the thick-paned window. They lay twined together, Sullyan's head cradled on Robin's chest, one of her legs thrown over his and her wealth of tawny hair spread out like a glowing cloud. Neither one wanted to speak. Both were aware that the other was awake, both were aware of tear tracks on the other's face. Neither wanted to stir and further the day.

Eventually, the increasing daylight made speech inevitable, and Sullyan finally found the courage to move. She raised herself on one elbow, her small breasts brushing the smooth skin of Robin's chest. Her lover's deep blue eyes met her gaze. They were damp with grief, and she ran her free hand through the soft curls of his short, brown hair. Gently, she brushed away the moisture from his face and kissed a smile to his lips. He returned it hesitantly, not knowing how he would bear the day's events.

His profound unhappiness made Sullyan twist at the fire opal ring on her right hand. She drew it off and held it out on her palm. "My love, would you keep this for me?"

He struggled upright. "No, Sullyan, I can't take that from you. I know how highly you value it."

"I do value it, but not as highly as I value your love. Please, Robin?"

He couldn't refuse the look in her eyes.

"Will you exchange rings with me, then?"

It was tentatively spoken, for an exchange of rings was normally part of a betrothal contract.

Her smile grew warmer and her gaze blurred as she watched him pull off the tiny gold ring he wore on the little finger of his right hand.

"But that is Jessy's ring, Robin. Are you sure?"

Jessy, Robin's beloved younger sister, had died of a wasting illness just over two years ago. Sullyan had tried her best to heal, and then soothe, the young girl and grew to love her in the short months she had known her as much as she did her tall and handsome brother.

Robin's gaze dropped to the tiny ring of gold.

"Jessy would have been overjoyed to see us betrothed. She would have been so proud to see you wearing a ring that was once hers."

"Then I accept it gladly."

Sullyan reached out and placed her fire opal on the little finger of Robin's left hand. She saw his eyes widen fractionally when he realized she had chosen the marriage hand. Then she held out her own left hand and smiled when he slipped Jessy's ring onto her middle finger.

Chapter Ten

A couple of hours later, they finally emerged into the kitchen. Such an open admission of commitment and love had put all thoughts of the day from their minds. Marik had set out a light breakfast for them and water was heating over the fire. Robin made some fellan and the two lovers sat drinking it together in silence.

The skin around Sullyan's neck where the spellsilver had burned her was finally healed, so she was now wearing her fire opal necklace. She would probably carry the marks of those wounds forever, she thought, and then remembered with a lurch that she wouldn't likely have the time to heal further.

Sunlight glared into her eyes as Marik opened the door and entered. He stamped a light dusting of snow from his boots. She saw his eyes swivel toward the full packs lying on the table. He raised his gaze to her face and she regarded him calmly, knowing he could see the pallor of her skin and the hint of dark bruises under her eyes. The obvious marks of Rykan's abuse had almost disappeared, but she knew he was wondering if she could survive the four days of hard riding it would take them to reach Caer Vellet. Although she would never admit it, the same thought had crossed her own mind.

To distract them both, she smiled. "I trust you have everything you need, Ty? Bull should return sometime late this afternoon, and we must be away soon after."

From the corner of her eye she caught the paling of Robin's

face and the expression of pain which flitted across his features. So, she thought, his outward calm did not extend very deep.

Marik crossed to the fire and helped himself to fellan. "I'm as ready as I'll ever be. It's perishing out there. Do you have enough warm clothes?"

"Bull will bring what I need." Sullyan squeezed Robin's hand as she sensed the clenching of his heart. There was nothing more she could do or say to ease him. He would have to find his own strength now.

She turned back to the Count. "What is the state of your armory, Ty?" Marik's head came up at the unexpected question. "Did Rykan's men loot it when they took us away?"

The Count shrugged and she realized he hadn't bothered to check the arms store. "I'll go and see if you like," he offered. "Why?"

"I need an Andaryan longsword, if you have a spare. The Hierarch's forces use heavier blades than my Albian steel."

Marik cocked his head. "Can you wield a longsword?" He sounded dubious, as if he couldn't imagine her even holding such a heavy blade, let alone using one effectively.

Robin snorted and Sullyan smiled. "Perhaps you could give me some pointers, Ty."

He fell for it. "Well, I will if you like, but I warn you, it'll be very different to what you're used to."

He left the room. When he returned, he carried his own blade, plus two more. They all went out into the bitter sunlight of the early winter day. The mansion's training ground was more sheltered than the kitchen yard, and no snow had settled there. Marik offered Sullyan the two blades to test and she weighed each in her hand for balance. Satisfied with her chosen blade, she took it in her right hand and faced Marik, ready to fence.

His face showed concern. "Just let me know if you get too

tired," he advised. "Use a double-handed grip if it's easier."

She smiled sweetly at him, a look that would have put Robin instantly on his guard. He moved to one of the benches surrounding the training ground to watch.

Marik began the bout gently and didn't press her too hard. She responded in kind, testing her agility and stamina against the unfamiliar feel of this heavier weapon. After a few minutes of what she regarded as a gentle warm up, she was comfortable enough with the balance of the weapon and her own reactions to practice some advanced moves. Marik suddenly found himself harder pressed. Sullyan saw his eyes narrow.

She had already noted that his attention often wavered. Unlike most well-trained swordsmen whose eyes never left their opponent's upper body, Marik didn't seem capable of making up his mind which part of her to watch. His focus often flickered from her eyes to her upper body, even to her sword arm. This was a grave mistake, for by the time the sword arm moved, it was far too late to take evasive action. Watching anything but the body—and especially the eyes—was a complete waste of time, and in fencing, as in most things, Sullyan never wasted time.

A sharp twisting movement of her longsword sent Marik's blade skittering across the ground. He stood dumbfounded, staring at her.

"You evil witch! You've bloody done it to me again, haven't you?"

Hearing Robin's dry chuckle, she smiled, remembering her first meeting with Marik and the duel that had resulted in a humiliating defeat for the Count. Retrieving his weapon, she handed it prettily back to him, giving him a small bow. He shook his head and grimaced as he accepted it.

She switched the sword to her left hand. "So, shall we do it properly now?"

Marik looked both annoyed and alarmed. "I think I'm the one who needs lessons!"

A lesson is exactly what she gave him for the next hour or so, leading him with painstaking precision through the various moves and improving his technique. Robin shouted helpful comments about his footwork from the bench, comments which were not always gracefully received. The three of them were so engrossed in what they were doing that Sullyan only belatedly realized she could feel a familiar prickle in her mind. Someone was opening a substrate tunnel nearby.

Robin felt the prickle too. She could see him looking around. Surely, she thought, it was far too early for Bull to return? Although, judging by the angle of the winter sun, it was mid-afternoon. How could the hours have passed so quickly? Tears stung her eyes. Her time with Robin was nearly over. Suddenly, she resented the time she had spent coaching Marik, although it made sense if the Count was going to be guarding her back from now on.

She broke off their bout by sweeping her blade to the salute. Marik was panting and sweating heavily, but Sullyan felt healthier than she had since emerging from Rykan's cell. Robin hissed her name and she went to his side.

By the mansion gates, about a hundred yards from the training ground, the familiar flowerlike end of a trans-Veil structure blossomed. Bull rode his stallion through, leading another horse by the reins. It was a huge, coal-black beast with no white markings whatsoever. Even to someone who knew nothing about horses, its relationship to the Manor's lead stallion, Mandias, was unmistakable. It had the same fine head and small ears, the same strong-boned legs with profuse feathering, the same silken wealth of ebony mane and tail. If anything, it was even larger than Mandias by about a hand's height. It bore a small, light saddle and a plaited leather bridle with no bit. It tossed its magnificent head against Bull's hold, snorting and dancing surprisingly lightly for such a huge animal.

It wasn't the horse, though, that drew Sullyan's eyes and provoked an indrawn breath. Following Bull through the tunnel on a dark bay stallion was the imposing figure of General Blaine.

Sullyan's hand went to her mouth. "Mathias?"

She could hardly remember the last time Blaine had used his Master level powers, let alone travelled the Veils. Frozen, she watched as he and Bull rode nearer, the General looking round with interest.

A sudden squeal rent the air, breaking Sullyan's shock. The coal-black stallion wrenched the reins from Bull's hand and reared, then came thundering toward her. The ground shook under his massive hooves, and Marik dived for safety behind the benches. As the horse charged nearer, Sullyan gave a soft, trilling whistle. The big beast flung up his head, and with a snort, skidded to a dust-showering stop in front of her. Gently, he lowered his nose to her hair, blowing and snuffling. Then he buffeted her shoulder.

She stroked the side of his face, murmuring, "Oh, Drum, you big show-off."

Bull and the General dismounted, and Bull lowered a full pack to the ground. Blaine passed his reins to the big man and approached Sullyan, who watched him around the stallion's sleek neck. She saw Robin glance at Bull and the big man's cryptic answering look. The General's expression was impassive as he approached, and although Robin snapped him a salute, Blaine ignored it. Sullyan could feel the waves of Robin's despair.

Turning to the stallion, she pushed at his neck, sending him ambling away. Calmly, she faced the General, came to attention, and saluted. He stopped in front of her and flipped a casual hand back. He studied her for a long moment in silence while Robin fretted on the verge of tears and Bull stood alone, holding the reins of the two horses.

At length, the General spoke. His voice was low, carrying a tone she had never heard before.

"Major Sullyan. So it's true, then?"

Moisture started in her eyes, but she managed not to flinch. "I fear so, General."

He briefly looked away. She saw lines of pain on his stern face and was amazed. Turning back, he said, "Can nothing be done?"

She took a deep breath. "Not that I am aware of, sir. The Hierarch may be able to help, but it would only be temporary."

Blaine stood in silence a moment more, digesting the news. Then he squared his shoulders and became once more the familiar, impersonal commander. He held out his left hand and Sullyan saw the gleam of gold. This time she couldn't hide her start of astonishment.

He spoke formally, his voice rough and stern. "Major Sullyan, I am charged to tell you that your resignation has not been accepted. The King will not release you."

Her eyes widened. "The King? But, General—"

"Major!"

She fell silent.

Blaine removed a parchment from within his jacket and passed it to her. "I am instructed to pass these orders on to you. You were already the temporary Albian Envoy to Count Marik, and now King Elias has decided to make the appointment permanent."

Stunned, her hand shaking, Sullyan accepted the orders. She opened them and read them swiftly. When she looked back up at the towering General, her gaze was blurred by tears.

"I am to be King Elias' Envoy to the Hierarch?"

She saw Robin's start. The post of permanent Envoy was a prestigious one, very seldom bestowed.

Stepping close to her, the General pinned the double thunderflash insignia of her rank above her left breast, where it belonged. Then he added another badge; the King's Envoy shooting star.

She shook her head, unable to speak. Robin's mouth was hanging open and Bull was grinning widely, his eyes full of tears. She thought she saw a gleam of moisture in the General's eye, but she must have been mistaken, for when he turned toward Robin his expression was as hard as ever. Robin's fists clenched and she knew that her own face was as pale as his.

As the General turned to him, Robin came to attention, trying vainly not to look in his superior's hard blue eyes.

"Captain Tamsen, I trust I'm not going to have any trouble from you?"

Robin turned despairingly to Sullyan, but she could offer him no comfort. He had given her his promise to obey the General, but now that the moment had arrived, she wasn't sure he could do it. She sensed him gathering his courage and hardening his resolve, and she silently begged him not to rebel.

His voice came out as a croak. "No, General."

"Well, that'll make a change." Blaine studied Robin's pinched face before continuing. "Your orders, Captain—and I trust you'll obey them to the letter?" He paused, forcing Robin to nod his unhappy acceptance. "You are to remain here with the Major, to stand for her, aid her in her new duties, and guard her back until such time as she … no longer needs you."

Robin stared, taking a few moments to assimilate what the General had said. He had been so sure of a recall. His face flushed and then paled again as he struggled to control himself. Bull was openly weeping, and Sullyan lowered her face to her hands.

Trembling with reaction, Robin managed to stammer, "Th-thank you, General. You can rely on me to follow your orders implicitly, sir."

Blaine frowned. "Yes, I expect I can. But, Captain?" He captured Robin's gaze again. "I want you back the moment your duties here are completed, do you understand? Sergeant Dexter has temporary command of the Major's company, but you will be required to take over when you return." His voice lost some of its gruffness. "Despite my reservations, I find that you are too good an officer to lose, even allowing for your past ... indiscretions."

Robin gave a feeble grin and Blaine's face twisted wryly. "Major," he said over his shoulder, "see if you can instill a bit more discipline into this young man, will you? He could certainly do with it."

"I will do my best, General, but I fear it will not be easy."

On hearing her voice, Blaine's expression changed. Now, as he came toward her and took her hands, Sullyan could clearly see the unshed tears in his eyes. She followed as he guided her out of earshot of the others. She was still wrestling with the unexpected turn of events and was grateful for the respite. He stopped and she looked up at him.

"I hardly know what to say, Mathias, except to thank you. I was trying not to think how I would cope without Robin. And as for the orders from the King ...." She shook her head, unable to finish.

Blaine took her shoulders, turned her to face him, and looked down into her eyes. "You've never realized how highly Elias and I value you, have you? The King has followed your career with great interest. Yes, I admit, I had to be persuaded at first, and I know our relationship hasn't always been easy for you. I can be stern and uncompromising, I know, but you always went out of your way to observe the proprieties, and for that, I thank you."

"You have no need to thank me, Mathias. If not for you, I would never have found my place in life, would never have come to know the profession I love or fulfill my reason for being. You have been my commanding officer, but also, as much as your duties allowed, my friend. I hope you know that I love you."

He ducked his head and she could feel him struggling for composure. When he was able to look at her again, he said, "Bull tells me that you and that hot-headed Captain of yours have finally decided to acknowledge what the rest of us have known for months."

"Oh, has he?" She glanced archly at Bull, who grinned and shrugged. "Well, he had no business to."

The General snorted. "He couldn't have kept it to himself if he'd tried, not with your other friends so full of it." He suddenly sobered. "Your dark-haired healer is very distressed, you know."

She looked away. "As am I, Mathias. Will you tell her you found me well?"

"Lie to her, you mean? She'll not believe me."

After an awkward pause, she said, "I must ask you two small favors, General."

Warily, he said, "What favors?"

"The first is that you will do what you can for Taran. He has had a difficult life so far. He has much talent, but all this will have confused him. He will be concerned for his future."

Blaine regarded her with raised brows and hard eyes, but she said no more. "And the second?"

"I want you to see that Robin gains his Mastery." She glanced over to where Robin stood talking quietly with Bull. "I may not be capable of it myself and he is very nearly ready. He may not think so, at least, not when he first returns, but given a little time I believe he will want it again. He is very strong, Mathias. Do not waste that strength."

The General considered this, looking off into the distance. Then he said, "Do you think he'd accept it from me?"

She smiled. "Persuade him. You can be very persuasive when you want to be."

He grinned. "Very well, Sullyan. I'll do what I can." To her eternal amazement, he suddenly gathered her into an emotional embrace which, after a stunned moment, she returned. "Take care of yourself," he murmured, "as much as you can."

He released her quickly and stepped away, but not before she had seen the tear on his cheek. He marched back to his horse and all but snatched the reins from Bull.

The big man dropped his own reins and came hesitantly toward Sullyan. She was trembling, dreading the moment. She simply couldn't believe she would never see him again.

He stopped a few paces off and she realized he was trembling as hard as she was. Awkwardly, he said, "I have a message for you from Solet. He said to tell you that Mandias will be alright. He won't recover completely and he'll never work again, but he'll still be able to cover the mares and live out his life with the breeding herd."

She swallowed painfully. "Thank him for me, Bull."

They stepped into each other's arms, allowing the grief to flow freely, neither hiding anything from the other.

"Oh, Sully, Sully," Bull gasped when he could finally speak again. They reluctantly moved apart, still holding fast to each other's hands. Bull's big fingers softly stroked the unfamiliar ring on Sullyan's left hand, and he smiled through his sorrow. "I'm so glad for you both."

Robin spoke from behind him. "I don't know how you managed to persuade the General to let me stay, Bull, but I'm very grateful."

The big man shook his head. "It was nothing to do with me, lad. It was his idea." Giving the stunned Captain a hug, he said, "Look after her." Robin could only nod.

"He will, Hal," breathed Sullyan. "You know that. And now I stand a chance of accomplishing my task before—" She broke off. Taking a steadying breath, she hurried on. "Look after Rienne and the others for me. We never did get to the bottom of that business with the Andaryan artifact, so they will need your help with that. Robin will keep in touch with you, let you know how things progress. And I … I will be thinking of you and missing you and wishing we were all together again. Oh, Hal!"

She let the floodgates open again as he wrapped her desperately in his arms.

A few minutes later she stood with Robin, watching as the two men rode back into the trans-Veil tunnel. The General kept his eyes resolutely turned to the fore, but Bull strained back to catch the last possible glimpse of them before the structure collapsed. Then they were alone.

Marik had already left to go ready his gear. Robin picked up the extra pack of Sullyan's things that Bull had brought and put his arm around her trembling shoulders.

"Well then, Major Sullyan, Lady Ambassador, King's Envoy to the Hierarch of Andaryon. Shall we go?"

His forced cheerfulness bolstered her flagging strength and she smiled at him. They walked back to the mansion, Drum trailing at their heels like some huge, black dog.

Chapter Eleven

The journey to Caer Vellet, four long days' ride to the north of Marik's lands, was not one on which any of them later looked back with pleasure. Count Marik, fearing for his life, withdrew further into himself the nearer they came to the Hierarch's stronghold. Sullyan rode lost in her own thoughts. Never one for moodiness, this was completely out of character, but she hoped Robin would understand. She had never been in a situation quite like this before.

Although the two of them shared their blankets during the bitterly cold nights, out of deference to the Count they did no more than hold each other. The closeness and passion they had experienced in the acknowledgement of their love had been walled away, too intense, too consuming, to speak of at this time.

Sullyan knew that Robin thought she was merely going through the motions of living. She cared for Drum as assiduously as ever, took her share of camp duties and resumed her preferred pre-dawn watch as normal. Yet she was aware he thought the reasons for doing these things had deserted her. She replied if spoken to, but rarely initiated speech, and Robin soon took over responsibility for scouting their route. He had formed the impression that she didn't much care whether they were discovered or not, and she didn't put him right.

His assumption, however, was completely wrong. Most of her attention during that time was spread out through the countryside, searching for signs of raiding bands or scouts from either Rykan's or the Hierarch's forces. It did not suit her plans for anyone to discover them before they reached Caer Vellet, and the last thing she wanted was for Rykan to learn what had become of her.

They circled westwards in their journey, and as any serious fighting was likely to be concentrated in the forests to the east, she felt they were safe from Rykan's forces. Even so, she pushed on hard, rarely stopping for longer than to breathe the horses. She was desperate to reach the Caer and deliver her information before the two sides fully engaged, and with every passing day she could feel the poison of Rykan's seed creeping closer to her heart.

In the evenings, when they sat to eat their rations before a small, screened fire, she often caught Robin gazing at her as she sat brooding over her fellan. Did he know she was thinking of Bull in those dark and lonely moments? Maybe, for he sat as close as he could to her, sometimes with an arm across her shoulders. Although she never let herself melt against him, she was glad of his uncomplicated support.

The weather worsened as winter drew on. Finally, they crested a small knoll within a circling wood of bare trees. Looking away to the north, three miles or so across frozen, snow-softened plains, they saw a tall hill.

The hazy sky and diffused, watery sunlight made the details unclear, but still the fortress rearing from the top of the hill was impressive. It commanded views of the plains all around. Dark, encircling walls, buttressed and crenellated, surrounded the lower town. From the top of those walls came occasional flashes of sun glancing off weapons as swordsmen patrolled the walkways. Huge wooden gates in the south wall were shut fast, but there was movement by their feet. Doubtless a detachment of guardsmen patrolled there.

The massive, grey towers of the Citadel's palace stretched smoothly upward among the buildings of the upper town, standing like vast fangs against the steely sky. Pennons flew from their tips, gaudy patches of purple slashed with gold. The colors of the Hierarch, Sullyan thought, the House of Pharikian. In peacetime, the gates to the Citadel would stand open, and even in winter a steady stream of petitioners, craftsmen, peddlers, and market men would pass between them. Now, all they could see were companies of soldiers drilling among a huddle of tents, the daytime enclave of the craftsmen who supported and equipped the Hierarch's fighting forces.

Sullyan leaned on Drum's ebony neck and regarded the Citadel. Her eyes ranged further east toward the forests where she thought skirmishes against outriders from Rykan's army must surely have already taken place. Yet no columns of smoke stained the horizon, no circling carrion birds indicating major confrontations. She was surprised but relieved, guessing that the loss of Rykan's trump card—her powers—had caused the Duke to rethink his strategy. Smiling grimly—the first expression she had ventured since leaving Marik's lands—she turned to the two men beside her.

"Gentlemen, behold Caer Vellet, Citadel and stronghold of Timar Pharikian, Hierarch of Andaryon. Let us pay him a visit."

She touched her heels to Drum's sides and sent him plunging down the knoll, through the barren wood, and toward the plains. Marik's horse came after her, followed by Robin, guarding their backs.

On that particular frosty afternoon, Taran and Cal returned to their quarters to find Rienne sitting alone and miserable by the fire. Taran glanced worriedly at his Apprentice. The healer hadn't heard them come in over her uncontrollable sobs.

"Oh, Rienne." Cal went over to her and folded her tightly in his arms. She turned her face to his chest, sobbing as if her heart would break. She was obviously beyond words, and neither man wasted breath asking what was wrong. Even though the intensity of Rienne's emotion was unusual, they both knew its cause. It troubled their hearts too. Cal merely sat and held her while the shuddering eased, and Taran silently fetched glasses, pouring each of them a shot of firewater. Ruefully, he reflected that they were becoming a little too addicted to Bull's favorite drink.

He passed a glass to Cal, who offered it to Rienne. Trying desperately to calm herself, Rienne accepted it, drinking it straight off in one swallow. She coughed as it burned her throat, and wiped her eyes with the back of one hand. Cal handed her a cloth with which she did a thorough job. Then she noisily blew her nose.

Cal's dark eyes scanned her face. "Better, love?"

Rienne drew a shaky breath, looking from Cal to Taran, profound unhappiness clear in her soft, grey eyes. She shook her head. "I can't stand this, it's not right. How can we walk away from here and pretend everything's normal? Our lives are never going to be the same again. I can't just forget all this ever happened. How can I go back to my patients with their ordinary problems knowing I might have helped her, might have saved her?" Her voice broke. "Why did we leave her like that?"

Her intensity alarmed Taran. Rienne was usually more level-headed. Cal gathered her close, tried to soothe her. A questioning look passed between him and Taran. When they hadn't been practicing their skills over the last few days, they had asked themselves the same thing.

"I think Bull feels the same way you do, love," said Cal. "In fact, we're a bit surprised he hasn't gone back to be with them. He's been very unhappy since returning with the General."

Hope immediately bloomed in Rienne's tear-filled eyes. "Is he considering going back, then? If he is, I want to know. We can't let him go without us."

Cal frowned. "I know how you feel, love, but just think about what's happening there. Do we really want to walk straight into a war? Because that's what we're talking about. Full-scale civil war. It would be very dangerous, and they wouldn't want us interfering or getting in the way."

Unimpressed, Rienne sniffed. "But we wouldn't be in the way. We'd keep to the sidelines and just be there if she needs us." Seeing Cal's expression she said, "At least go talk to Bull and see what he thinks. If he's dead against it, we won't go, but I for one need to know what's happening. I can't sit around here day after day waiting for bad news. It's driving me mad."

When Taran asked Bull into the apartment a little later to broach the subject, he had the distinct impression that the big man had been thinking along very similar lines. He was unwilling to commit himself, though. "I don't know, Taran. I'm in two minds. I'm not at all sure we'd be welcome."

"What do you mean?" said Rienne. "Why on earth wouldn't we be welcome?"

Bull sighed. "For a start, she as good as ordered me not to follow her. And she's already made her farewells. Knowing her as I do, I don't think she'd want to go through all that again. She's a very private person, sometimes. I don't think she'd appreciate us coming to watch her die."

Rienne sounded strained. "That's not why we want to go! We want to help."

"I know, dear heart, I know. Let me think about it a little longer. I've not heard from Robin yet, although I can feel he's alright. Let's wait and see what the situation is before we go rushing into anything. It'll be a tricky time for them, entering the Citadel. They don't know what the Hierarch's reaction will be, whether he'll even see her. We have to wait for them to contact us, and then perhaps we can make a decision."

Rienne saw the sense of Bull's words, even though they didn't pacify her. Taran understood how she felt. It was hard not knowing what was happening.

✤ ✤ ✤ ✤ ✤

Sullyan cantered Drum across the plains for the first mile or so, weaving through the trees, Robin and Marik at her back. Then she slowed the stallion to a brisk walk, allowing the other two to catch up. She made for the high road leading directly to the fortress gates, seeing with satisfaction that they were the only people on the road. Warning Marik and Robin to keep their hands well away from their sword hilts, she rode confidently forward, eyes narrowed against the snow glare.

The Count nudged his horse up on her left side, a gloomy expression on his face. "I expect the sentries and outriders will see us soon."

She gave a snort. "My dear Count, there have been loaded crossbows aimed at our hearts for the past half hour."

Marik started and looked wildly about, but there was no one in sight.

Sullyan continued in silence, highly visible on the coal-black Drum. Her borrowed longsword reared in its harness over her shoulder.

They were about a mile and a half from the gates when the sentries rode out of cover and confronted them. Sullyan immediately halted in the middle of the road, waiting for the twenty-strong patrol to approach. Marik and Robin flanked her. She studied the Hierarch's men with professional interest. The purple and gold of his livery was evident on their combat leathers, and their leader bore a Lieutenant's rank insignia, the equivalent of an Albian Captain. A medium height man in his middle thirties, he halted his men a few paces from Sullyan and rode forward alone. He sat his dark bay stallion easily and his hand never left the hilt of his sword, despite the ready crossbows behind him.

He ignored Robin, swept Marik a contemptuous glance, and then turned his attention to Sullyan. He regarded her for a few moments, his pale brown eyes taking in her gold insignia, her battle honors, and King's Envoy shooting star. When he addressed her, his tone was barely respectful, the attitude of a confident man unused to dealing with armed women.

"Major." He gave her a slight nod, the only sign of respect she would get.

"Lieutenant." She accorded him the same bare courtesy, giving her voice an identical inflexion.

His eyes narrowed as he reassessed her, taking in her relaxed but alert attitude and the casual way she sat the huge black stallion with its light saddle and bitless bridle. His own mount bore the usual heavy cavalry saddle that could keep a dying man upright, and foam was dripping from the iron bit in its mouth.

He motioned for his men to put up their weapons. They obeyed instantly, a fact not lost on Sullyan. She approved of discipline, and this smooth obedience spoke of an able officer and good leadership. She didn't take her eyes from the Lieutenant while she assessed his men, and she could see he didn't like her forthright gaze. It made him nervous, and she guessed he was unused to being made nervous, especially by an armed woman.

There was tension in his voice when he addressed her again. "What is your business here?"

"My name is Major Sullyan, and I am an Ambassador of Elias Rovannon, High King of Albia. I am here to request an audience with the Hierarch at his earliest convenience."

The Lieutenant gave a bark of laughter. "Have you not heard we're on the brink of war, Major? His Majesty will see no one at this time, and certainly not a human Ambassador. What on earth makes you think he would grant you an audience?" He shot a glare at Marik, who flinched. "Especially when you come in the company of traitors."

She stood her ground. "My business is with his Majesty, Lieutenant, although it is precisely because you find yourselves at war that I have come. As for Count Marik, he is under my protection and is no traitor to the Hierarch's rule. I think you will find that the Hierarch *will* see me, if you will be good enough to escort us."

She urged Drum forward, pushing past the Lieutenant's horse. Robin and Marik hastened to follow, the Captain keeping a nervous eye on the men of the patrol. In the absence of orders from their officer, though, they allowed the three strangers to ride through. Robin might have laughed at their confusion had he not been so wary.

The Lieutenant recovered quickly and barked orders at his men. As they closed smoothly around the three, he pushed his mount close beside Drum. The big black laid back his ears at the unfamiliar stallion and sidestepped menacingly. Sullyan calmed him with a word and rode serenely on, ignoring the seething officer.

As they neared the gates of the fortress, the Lieutenant once more nudged his horse across Drum's path. Sullyan halted. The patrol ranged around her, whether protectively or defensively wasn't clear. The sentries on the walls all had crossbows aimed at the party, and the guards stationed at the foot of the gates were likewise alert. With a hard stare of unmistakable meaning, the Lieutenant turned his back on Sullyan, rode forward, and called out to someone behind the gates. A small postern opened and he conferred with whoever was behind it. Sullyan heard her name mentioned and guessed he was sending for someone of higher rank to deal with the unwelcome visitors.

All around the battlemented walls were the signs of

preparations for war. Sentries patrolled every section and guard tower, and the crust of frozen snow on the ground outside was churned with the hoof marks and boot prints of many troop movements. Cart ruts also ran through the gates, and Sullyan guessed they were laying up provisions in the event of a siege. It made her heart clench. She stared impatiently at the Lieutenant, who was fretting before the gates.

At length, the postern reopened and a single man emerged. He was tall, strongly built, and had pale grey eyes. His hair was black, lightly peppered with grey, and over his uniform he wore a heavy purple cloak edged with gold. A longsword rode at his left hip, and he walked with the confident air of command. On seeing him, the leader of the patrol immediately relaxed.

As the newcomer approached Sullyan, she swung elegantly down from Drum, her heavy riding cloak swirling around her. She gestured for Robin and Marik to do likewise. The tall Andaryan halted before her and she accorded him a formal salute, giving him the level of courtesy she would have shown Mathias Blaine.

"General."

He returned the homage while appraising her, although his salute wasn't as respectful as hers. When he spoke, his tone conveyed wary interest.

"Major Sullyan. I have heard of you."

She inclined her head, hearing Robin's surprised intake of breath before the tall Andaryan went on.

"I am General Ephan, overall commander of the Velletian Guard and responsible for the Hierarch's security. We are currently under threat of war, as I'm sure you're aware. The Citadel is closed to outsiders. However, in deference to King Elias of Albia, I will permit you and your Captain to enter and seek an audience with the Hierarch. But I warn you, he is a busy man and these are troubled times. He may not be inclined to see you."

"We will take that chance, General Ephan. I thank you for your courtesy."

The General's pale eyes hardened and his voice became harsh. "I will not, however, admit traitors, no matter who speaks for them. The renegade Marik will be taken under arrest and held in confinement until such time as his Majesty decides his fate."

Marik gasped and stepped back, but he was too late. The patrol tightened around him, crossbows raised. He looked desperately at Sullyan, his eyes a little wild. She made a calming gesture and turned back to the General.

"Count Marik is under my personal protection, General Ephan, and only accompanied me here at my insistence. I pledge you my word he is no traitor."

Ephan brushed her protest aside. "That is not for you to say. While his overlord threatens the Citadel, I cannot permit this man to go free in the Hierarch's domain." He nodded to the guards. "Take him."

Two of them grasped Marik's arms. He struggled at first, but then thought better of it and subsided, his expression gloomy.

Sullyan gave him a reassuring smile. "I am sorry for this, Ty. Rest assured, I will do my best to resolve the situation. The Hierarch will understand once I explain why you are here."

The General gave a grunt, and Marik hung his head as he was hustled away. Sullyan turned stiffly back to Ephan. "That was not well done, General. I do not extend my protection to traitors. The Count has much to offer his Majesty and has suffered greatly at Lord Rykan's hands. He was coerced into supporting the Duke, as I suspect you already know. Be sure he is well treated while under your care."

Ephan chose not to respond. Instead, he turned to the leader of the patrol, who was awaiting release. "Get back to your duties, Lieutenant Barrin."

The man turned his horse and rode back through his men, leading them south along the road. Ephan strode to the postern gate and barked orders to the guardsmen behind. Grooms arrived to take the visitors' horses, and Ephan indicated that Sullyan and Robin should follow him into the Citadel.

Once through the postern, Sullyan looked round with interest. The walls on the inside were lined with guard posts and towers, and scaled by laddered platforms leading up to the battlements. The interior road running round the perimeter was teeming with swordsmen, all of whom bore the purple and gold livery of the Hierarch's elite corps, the Velletian Guard. Buildings nearby were obviously barracks, supply depots, and armories. There was one clear road running up from the gates, between these buildings, and on into the center of the Citadel.

Ephan spotted a servant wearing the livery of the Hierarch's personal service and hailed him. "You, man. Take Major Sullyan here and Captain ...?" He raised a brow and Sullyan supplied Robin's name. "Captain Tamsen to Baron Gaslek. Tell Gaslek the Major is an Ambassador from King Elias of Albia, and that she desires an audience with his Majesty." The servant's eyes widened, but he didn't speak. "Have him assign them quarters while they wait."

Ephan turned back to Sullyan. "Major, you will excuse my not escorting you, but as you see, we are preparing for war. The Baron is his Majesty's secretary. He will present your petition and see to your comforts. I wish you good fortune. If his Majesty is gracious and grants your request, maybe we will meet again."

He swept away. Sullyan watched him go, a small smile on her lips. Then she turned to the servant, who was hovering anxiously at her elbow. "Please, Lady," he said, as he turned to lead them through the town.

The servant guided Sullyan and Robin up the straight road

leading through the center of the Citadel. They passed shops and houses, the dwellings and business places of the lower town. The Caer was thronging with people, all going about their daily lives despite the insecurity of their future.

Sullyan studied the faces of the people they passed, most of whom didn't pay the party any attention at all. A few of the men, mainly swordsmen, glanced their way. Without exception, they regarded Robin with professional interest and were openly startled when they realized Sullyan was armed. They stared at her with varying expressions. Chief among these was plain disbelief, but some were blatantly hostile.

Occasionally, they passed groups of women, all escorted by either household servants or guards wearing the Hierarch's colors. The servants' liveries were trimmed in whatever color their noble had adopted, and the resulting clash of color made Sullyan feel sick.

The highborn women, gaudily dressed in court finery and with lavishly made up faces, were open in their condemnation and scorn for Sullyan's attire. Their snide comments, outraged gasps, and sniggers behind fluttering fans made Sullyan's hands itch to slap. Yet she moved serenely through them, never giving a sign that she heard their wounding remarks. Much as she could appear refined when she chose, as at Marik's feast, she always felt more comfortable in her leathers. Such sentiments, she knew, would scandalize these chattering, painted parrots.

The silent servant led them through the town toward a steeper rise in the land. They emerged onto the Processional Way, the state road leading to the ornately wrought gates of the Imperial Palace. Ornamental trees, bare of leaves yet still graceful, lined the avenue, and the gleaming white river cobbles underfoot had been swept clear of snow. The crowds were absent now. No one approached the Palace save servants and military officers.

Their guide didn't lead them through the huge main gates, but turned left before reaching them. Guards patrolling behind the gates watched the two Albians with cold and wary eyes. Following the pale stone wall surrounding the Palace gardens, the servant took them through a much smaller gate. The two sentries stationed there stared with unfriendly curiosity and whispered to each other as Sullyan passed. If the gaudy gossips in the town had not already spread it, she thought, news of their arrival would soon be common knowledge.

The servant now took them through a pleasant but winter-bare rose garden, toward a wing of the vast and sprawling Palace. Opening a pair of fancy, carved wooden doors set with glass, he ushered them inside. A young maid standing close by scurried forward to take their heavy cloaks. Her pale yellow eyes nearly started from her head when she saw Sullyan's combat leathers. The Major smiled at her, but she didn't respond.

"Please, Lady," said their guide, beckoning them on. They followed him through a succession of large, empty reception rooms, their ceilings heavy with gilded bosses, the door lintels ornately carved. The furniture was solid and impressive, yet none of it looked comfortable. Expensive woven carpets covered the floors and scented bowls of flowers stood in every room. Robin frowned as he smelled their heady perfume, and Sullyan guessed he was wondering where the Palace got such flowers in winter. He was still frowning as they arrived at a green baize door. The servant stopped and rapped sharply on the wood surround. At the response from within, he opened it and ushered them through.

Chapter Twelve

The room they entered was plainer than any they had yet seen. Clearly an office, it held only a fruitwood table with a matching chair, and several other chairs ranged around the walls. A large window overlooked an inner courtyard where a fountain of marble nymphs played over an icy pool. There was an overriding smell of beeswax, as if someone had recently polished the furniture.

The man seated behind the desk rose to greet them. He was small, stout, and fussily dressed, and he sported a pair of thick spectacles which perched precariously on the end of his small nose. Peering shortsightedly at them, he came around the table to get a better view. He wore the purple and gold of the Hierarch's personal staff, and his short, thick fingers were covered in rings. His robes had the appearance of hampering his movements, and his hands constantly twitched at his clothing.

The servant bowed. "My Lord Baron, may I present Major Sullyan, Lady Ambassador and Envoy of King Elias of Albia. Also, her escort, Captain Tamsen. They seek an audience with his Majesty. General Ephan asks that you see to their comfort." He turned abruptly and left the room as if well pleased to be rid of his duty.

Sullyan stood at ease and studied the Baron. She immediately noticed his pale grey eyes flicking nervously from her face to the sword at her back and guessed he had never seen a woman go armed before.

The little man cleared his throat before speaking. "I am Baron Gaslek, his Majesty's secretary. I bid you welcome, Major Sullyan. To what do we owe this honor?"

His voice was light and ineffectual, yet she had to give him his due. Despite this unprecedented situation, he was faultlessly polite.

She smiled. "I seek an audience with his Majesty on urgent matters of state, and we would appreciate the chance to rest and refresh ourselves as we have travelled a long and weary way. But first, my Lord Baron, I must make a request." She saw the little man's eyes narrow in suspicion. "I wish to see Count Marik, who was summarily imprisoned by General Ephan. I must be convinced of his comfort and welfare before I can consider my own."

He made a disparaging gesture. "I'm afraid that will not be possible, Lady. The Count is under the General's authority. He commands the garrison here."

Sullyan's eyes hardened. She was weary and in pain, in no mood to be thwarted. She took a step toward the Baron, and although her hand never reached for her sword hilt, the little man glanced at the weapon. With the faint smile still on her lips, she murmured, "My Lord Baron, it is my intention to see the Count with or without your help. Notwithstanding General Ephan's authority, the Count is still under my personal protection. Now, may I suggest that you arrange for us to be taken to where he is being held? If not, I will find my own way. And I think you would not want us wandering the Palace unescorted. That would not reflect well on the Hierarch's hospitality."

The thought of the two of them walking through the Palace, alone and armed, clearly unsettled the Baron. He decided to humor her, although his displeasure showed in his tone. "Very well, Lady. I will arrange for you to be escorted to the cells. But authority for you to see the Count will have to be gained from General Ephan."

Sullyan smiled coldly. "I thank you, Baron."

Swallowing nervously, he picked up a small gold bell and rang it with a practiced flick. Sullyan's eyes never left his, and she saw a glint of moisture on the man's upper lip. Robin was regarding him too, and she felt her Captain's amusement at the Baron's discomfiture.

A liveried servant arrived promptly and was given instructions to convey the two of them to the cells. Afterwards he was to take them to a suite of rooms where they could be comfortable. "I trust you will find the accommodation satisfactory, Lady," said the Baron as they made to leave.

Sullyan turned a smile on him, prepared to be gracious now that she had what she wanted. "I have no doubt of it, my Lord. You have been most helpful. I am sure we will meet again." Briefly, she gave him her fingers before sweeping from the room.

As the door closed, she was sure she heard the Baron sigh with relief.

This new servant took them through the Palace once again, a different route this time, and they came out under a colonnaded walkway leading to a low, functional building attached to the rear of the Palace. There were sentries patrolling here, all of whom stared narrowly at the two armed Albians as they were led to a pair of solid wooden doors. Guards stationed there stepped toward them, barring their entry.

The servant turned to Sullyan. "I'm sorry, Lady, but without General Ephan's express command, you can't enter here."

She planted her feet, making it obvious she wasn't going to leave. "Then I suggest his express command is obtained immediately." The servant shrugged and turned to one of the guards who, noting the Major's stern expression and alert attitude, decided to duck the arrow.

"Wait here," he said, and strode off.

They stood in the frosty air for some minutes, the remaining guard watching Sullyan as closely as she watched him. The other man returned, bringing with him a senior officer in the now familiar uniform of the Hierarch's personal guard.

Instantly, Sullyan shifted the focus of her attention to the newcomer. He was lithe and loose-limbed and walked with one hand resting on the hilt of his sword. Tall and spare, he moved with purpose. Yet it wasn't his body which arrested her gaze, but his eyes. Dead white with slit pupils, they gave nothing away. They were a killer's eyes, emotionless eyes, the eyes of an implacable warrior.

He came to a fluid halt before her and swept her casually with a flat gaze. She knew he had dismissed her as a woman and therefore powerless. *Your first mistake,* she thought grimly.

"I am Commander Vanyr of the Velletian Guard," he announced. "What is your business here?" His insulting omission of her title, plus his curt tone and clipped speech, conveyed his annoyance.

She refused to be cowed by his menacing stance and answered in the same terse manner. "A simple enough request, Commander. I wish to satisfy myself as to the wellbeing of one who is under my personal protection."

Unaccustomed to such boldness from a woman, the Commander allowed irritation to flash in his eyes. Yet she was an Ambassador, the Albian High King's Envoy, and he grudgingly gave way.

"Very well ... Lady." He gave the title a slight, disparaging emphasis. "But you will not enter the security building armed."

He held out an imperious hand for their weapons, and it was with only the slightest hesitation that Sullyan unhooked the sword from her shoulder harness and passed it to him. Robin did likewise. The man seemed surprised to feel the weight of Sullyan's weapon, almost as if he hadn't expected it to be real. He handed their blades to one of the guards and turned on his heel to lead them into the building.

Bare and functional, this place would offer no distractions to those carrying out whatever security measures might be necessary, thought Sullyan. The taciturn Commander stalked past various rooms and offices, leading them deeper into the building. He finally halted outside a door with a single guard and motioned the man aside.

The door, which wasn't locked, opened onto a small but pleasant room. It was warmed by a fire and lit by two tiny, barred windows set high into the walls. There was a table and chair, and a small settle drawn close to the fire. Another door led off into a sleeping room. The suite's occupant, who had been lying listlessly on the settle, started to his feet as they entered. He looked a little strained around the eyes, but brightened when he saw who his visitor was.

Sullyan crossed the room and took his hands. "Are you well, Count? Have they treated you fairly?"

He glanced over her shoulder toward Vanyr, who stood brooding in the doorway. "I'm fine, Sullyan. I could do with something to eat and drink, though."

She turned to the Commander and raised her brows. He stared back before saying, "It will be arranged."

"I thank you, Commander." She turned back to Marik. "I am truly sorry about this, Ty. It will be resolved once I have spoken with the Hierarch. Can you be patient until then?"

"Oh, don't worry about me," he muttered. "It's only what I expected, and better than I deserve. I'll be alright."

He gave her a wan smile. She pursed her lips and squeezed his hand.

They collected their weapons from the guard by the outer door and walked away under Vanyr's hard stare. The waiting servant led them to a sumptuous suite of rooms on the ground floor of the Palace. He bowed them into the suite, only leaving once he had seen that their packs had been brought up from the stables and their heavy riding cloaks had been brushed and hung to air.

With a sigh of relief, Sullyan removed her sword and placed it on the rack provided. She looked round with appreciative eyes. On a low table in the lavishly furnished living area sat a tray of various meats, bread, wine, and sweet rolls. There was a roaring fire in the hearth, and the heavy drapes at the two floor-to-ceiling windows had been closed against the early evening cold. Trimmed lamps flickered brightly along the walls.

She crossed to one of the doors that opened off the living area and discovered a sleeping room, a vast bed occupying most of the floor space. Robin glanced in over her shoulder. "Looks comfortable," he murmured. "Want to try it out?"

She grinned. "Later." She crossed to the other door. "First I want to see … ah, Robin, look at this!"

The second door opened to reveal the largest bathing room they had ever seen. The walls were completely covered in ceramic tiles of yellow and green, while the vast pool in the middle of the floor was lined with deep blue tiles that made the steaming water look especially appealing.

Robin whistled in amazement as he trailed his fingers in the water. "How do they keep it so hot?"

Sullyan was already removing her jacket. "I have heard of these, but never had the chance to try one. It is said that a thermal spring rises under the Palace, and I believe that the ancient Andaryan word 'Vellet' translates as 'volcanic'. The hot water from the spring will be channeled into these pools through a system of baked clay pipes. This is why the majority of the Palace is built on one level."

She let down the masses of her hair and Robin came over to

help remove the rest of her clothing. He watched as she carefully slid her slender body into the water, the scars of Rykan's abuse still visible on her creamy skin. It felt so good. She lay back, luxuriating in the sensual warmth. She could float full length in the enormous pool. Seeing the look on Robin's face, she moved to the edge, languidly flicking water at him.

"Why not join me, Robin? Have you ever made love underwater?"

He needed no second invitation.

Eventually, warm, clean, and spent, they wrapped themselves in the heavy house robes provided and relaxed by the fire, now and again sampling the meats and bread left earlier. Sullyan would have given much for a cup of Bull's strong fellan, and thoughts of her big, loyal friend dispelled the delicious languor brought on by the bath and Robin's attentions.

It was fully dark outside and most of the food was gone by the time she heard the discreet tap on the door. Robin got up to answer it, revealing the stocky form of Baron Gaslek. Sullyan beckoned to him and the Baron entered nervously, his constantly moving eyes settling anywhere but on her. She was lounging casually on the settle, her damp hair spread to dry over her shoulders. Lazily, she watched the Baron, enjoying his discomfiture.

"Will you not sit, Baron?" She patted the settle beside her. Robin had to choke back laughter as the Baron struggled to politely refuse.

He had to look at her to deliver his message. As he drew himself up, gathering his dignity around him like an ill-fitting cloak, his ringed fingers fluttered at his sides like crippled butterflies. "My Lady," he said, before clearing his throat. "My Lady Ambassador, I am charged to inform you that his Majesty sends his profoundest apologies. As I warned you, he is much too busy with matters pertaining to the war to see you. However, you are welcome to ...."

Sullyan rose with threatening grace and the Baron's words trailed off. Her eyes were hard and she fixed them on him as she moved closer. He took an involuntary step back before managing to stop himself.

Sullyan knew how to exude menace, and the Baron certainly felt it. She could see the tremble of his body in the reflected light from his spectacles. When she spoke, her voice was deliberately low.

"I think, my Lord, that you cannot properly have conveyed my message to his Majesty."

The Baron wrung his hands. "Yes, I ... yes I did, Lady. I told him you were here, but he is too busy. You must understand—"

"No, my Lord Baron, *you* must understand. You are to return to his Majesty with this message. Tell him that Major Sullyan, Ambassador and Artesan Master-elite, wishes an audience with him. Can you remember that?"

Her eyes bored into his. Faintly, he repeated, "Master-elite?"

She nodded, smiled, and stepped back, breaking the tension between them. He shook himself, fluttering his hands in confusion. "Yes, Lady, of course. I'll go at once." Bowing hastily, he left the room.

Robin closed the door and leaned on it. He was shaking with laughter, and Sullyan regarded him narrowly. She was expending power to hold at bay the nagging ache in her belly and could do without these obstacles to her plans.

"Men!" she snapped.

Within half an hour, the Baron was back. His manner was completely different. Gone was the fussy nervousness. He was deferential and polite. After conveying the Hierarch's concern for their comfort and invitation to remain as long as they chose, he informed Sullyan that his Majesty would see her later that evening, once he had closed his business with his generals. The Baron then enquired after their needs, offering Sullyan the services of a maid, which she graciously refused. Her manner had also changed. She was every inch the lady with no sign of her earlier irritation. As the little man turned to go, however, the Major called him back.

"There is one small favor you could do for me, my Lord."

He turned fawning eyes on her and bowed, eager to please someone whose rank commanded his sovereign's respect. "Whatever you wish, Lady."

"Will you personally see to Count Marik's comfort? I am sure it would distress his Majesty to learn that one of my friends was being treated with less than due respect."

She looked down at her hands as she spoke, yet still caught the Baron's irritated expression. His voice was tight as he replied, "Of course, Lady. I'll ask the General to move him to a more suitable suite."

"I thank you, my Lord. I would deeply appreciate it."

It was left to Robin to show the defeated man out. The Captain shook his head once the Baron had gone, and grinned at the Major. "You're incorrigible."

She didn't reply.

✣ ✣ ✣ ✣ ✣

A few hours passed before a page arrived to convey them into the Hierarch's presence. Sullyan had dressed carefully in a plain and simple dove grey gown. She left most of her hair loose, only braiding part of it to keep it out of her face. The rest fanned out around her shoulders, tumbling down her back like a tawny cloak.

Robin had put on his dress uniform, and Sullyan coached him in the protocol of the meeting.

"We must remain kneeling in his presence until given permission to rise. Do not speak unless you are addressed, and be unfailingly polite whatever is said. Always remember, Robin, that not only is Timar Pharikian the supreme ruler of this realm, but he is also a Senior Master, and therefore doubly deserving of our respect."

They followed the young page along the corridors, passing various members of Pharikian's Court, a few of whom gave them cursory glances. Sullyan was amused to observe that she wasn't attracting half as much negative attention dressed in women's clothing as she had in her combat leathers. The absence of the sword, she thought, probably had much to do with that. There were a few groups of women, however, who gave her much more than a cursory glance, no doubt comparing her simple, elegant gown with their gaudy, ruffled plumage. Robin also drew a fair share of the ladies' attention, due to his handsome face and slim, muscular body.

At the end of a long, ornate corridor, they finally came to a pair of massive gilded doors. Carved with fantastical designs of mythical beasts, the doors were guarded by two swordsmen of the Velletian Guard, both of whom held lances crossed before them. The young page stopped at the doors and announced, "Master-elite Lady Ambassador Major Sullyan, and Adept-elite Captain Robin Tamsen, invited to an audience with his Majesty."

The guards stepped apart, opening the doors wide as they did so, revealing a cavernous, lavishly appointed formal audience chamber. Gilded bosses and painted timbers adorned the high vaulted ceiling, while two lines of intricately carved columns formed an aisle down the room's center. On either side of the aisle, chairs sat against the white plaster walls, beneath the multi-colored banners and crests of the Hierarch and his underlords. The floor was pink marble shot with gold, and a raised dais at the far end of the aisle bore an ornately carved and gilded throne, currently unoccupied.

The page ushered Sullyan and Robin toward the end of the

hall. When they reached the platform leading up to the dais, he instructed them to kneel upon a cushioned carpet and await the Hierarch's arrival. Robin looked round the room with interest, but Sullyan kept her eyes downcast. She was struggling to maintain her composure, for the pain of Rykan's poison was increasing once more. She used metaforce to try to bolster her flagging strength, but the pain refused to abate.

A blare of trumpets from outside the room caught her attention, and Baron Gaslek entered through double doors in the far wall to the right of the dais. As he came forward to stand beside the throne, he glanced down at Sullyan but didn't speak. Behind him came four men, all attired in military uniform. They marched to the throne and ranged themselves around it. Their leader was Commander Vanyr, and he stared at the two Albians with undisguised dislike. Sullyan guessed he had heard of her request regarding Marik and was infuriated by her interference.

As soon as Gaslek and the honor guards were in place, the fanfare sounded again, longer and louder than before. Another man entered the room, preceded by two pages and followed by two more. Sullyan had seen him before and knew what to expect, but Robin gave a start of surprise when he saw that the Hierarch was old. Over seventy years of age, thought Sullyan, but he still moved with the fluid grace of a trained swordsman. His body was tall and spare, his brown skin weathered and lined with age. He had a lean, patrician face with a long, straight nose and generous mouth. His eyes were golden yellow and not as pale as most Andaryans', and his shoulder-length hair was nearly white.

A long purple cloak of rich silk flowed around his legs as he walked. Under it, his belted robe was soft gold velvet. A thick chain of gold lay about his neck, and a large carved amethyst bearing the tangwyr crest of the House of Pharikian adorned a heavy gold ring on the third finger of his right hand. He strode to the throne and sat, the pages taking stations around him. When he was settled, the four guards stood at ease.

Baron Gaslek turned to him and bowed low. Descending the dais, he came to stand beside Sullyan. She neither reacted nor raised her eyes, but kept them modestly downcast. The little man spoke up.

"Most Noble and Exalted Majesty, may I present Master-elite Lady Ambassador Major Sullyan, Envoy from High King Elias Rovannon of Albia."

She heard Commander Vanyr stir as her full titles were revealed. The Hierarch leaned forward in his chair, eagerly studying her as she afforded him the reverent brow-lips-heart salute due to her superior in the Artesan craft. Robin, who had never seen her make this obeisance before, was gaping at her, and she had to remind him to follow her lead.

When they were done, the Hierarch rose and stepped forward. Holding out his right hand, he spoke in a deep, smooth voice that belied his age. "Ah, Lady Brynne Sullyan! You are very welcome here, my dear. I have long wondered when I would have the pleasure of beholding you once again."

Caught in the act of kissing the dynastic ring, Sullyan gave a start. She glanced up for the first time into the Hierarch's golden yellow eyes.

"Why do you name me so, Majesty? And we have never met, to my knowledge."

He frowned and withdrew his hand. "But are you not Brynne Sullyan, daughter of Morgan and Bethyn Sullyan?"

She felt the blood drain from her face and saw Robin's look of concern. Her voice wavered as she replied, "I ... do not know, Majesty. I never knew my parents."

The Hierarch's frown deepened and his eyes narrowed. "No, but ...." He hesitated, and then beckoned to her. "Come here, child."

She rose and approached him as he seated himself once more on his throne. Holding out a veined hand, he asked, "Will you permit?"

She realized he was asking to read her, to look inside to where her private power rested. This was a very intimate thing for an Artesan, a request never pressed on anyone unwilling. Yet something urged her to comply, and bowing her head, she gave him her left hand. He took it gently and she watched in silence as the Hierarch's yellow eyes focused on her face. She felt him attune to and mesh with her psyche, and her own eyes dilated widely as she allowed his scrutiny.

After a few moments, he smiled and let fall her hand.

"I was right, child. You are indeed Brynne Sullyan, daughter to my very good friends Morgan and Bethyn. You are so like your mother that I could hardly fail to know you. You even wear her jewels, although there was also a ring?" He looked questioningly at her hands.

Sullyan was silent, although her heart was pulsing so violently she felt sure they all must hear it. She was unable to take this in. After twenty-three years of not knowing her origins, she had just learned more of her life history than she had ever thought to hear. Her head spun with it and she began to tremble.

"Yes, Majesty," she managed, "I still have it."

The Hierarch's eyes took on a far-away look. "The last time I saw you, my dear, you were a tiny babe in your father's arms. Oh, you are so like your mother! She was extremely beautiful too."

Suddenly, it was all too much. The control Sullyan was exerting over the pain in her belly—pain she had managed to conceal from the Hierarch's scrutiny—slipped as she desperately tried to assimilate what she had heard. She could feel herself fading and fought for composure. Yet the shock of the Hierarch's revelation, coupled with the effects of Rykan's poison, was just too strong.

"Dammit, not now!" she gasped, mortified as pain ripped through her, sapping her strength and shearing her control. Helpless, she sank to her knees, clutching her belly.

The Hierarch looked startled. "Are you unwell, child?"

Robin, forgetting protocol, leaped to his feet, only just managing to catch her as she lost control over her body. She slumped into his arms, her vision blurred, her hearing muffled. Strange sounds roared in her mind and she barely heard the Hierarch rapping out an order for Vanyr to fetch a physician. As the sullen Commander left the room, his footsteps resounded through her head. She felt Robin stir as he looked up at the Hierarch from where he sat cradling her. Even through the suffocating fog in her mind, she could hear the fear harsh in his tone.

"I doubt your physician will be able to help, Majesty, unless he is also an Artesan."

No, Robin, she thought, desperate to stop him uttering her secret. *Please, no!*

"How so?" demanded the Hierarch, his voice sounding distorted, strange.

"This is demon induced poison, Majesty, and it's killing her."

She sagged as Robin sealed her fate, pain and nausea roiling through her gut. The guards crowded forward, concerned despite themselves, and Baron Gaslek wrung his hands.

The Hierarch came down from the dais to crouch beside Robin. He took one of her hands, his skin warm against the ice in her veins. "What do you mean?"

Robin lowered his voice, and Sullyan retained just enough sense to be grateful. "It's Lord Rykan's doing, Majesty."

The ruler glared at him. "Rykan? How has he done this?"

Through the terrifying pain and sickness that swamped her, Sullyan could feel the power of his anger. She knew that Robin could never have resisted it, even had she been able to command him to silence. The information she so desperately wanted to hide was about to be revealed. Robin was compelled to answer, and there was nothing she could do. The pain finally overwhelmed her as Robin harshly ground out the words.

"He took her captive, Majesty, and he ... he raped her."

Chapter Thirteen

obin could hardly contain his anguish as he felt Sullyan's spirit once more slipping away. He knew she didn't want him to do what he had just done, but what other choice did he have? He couldn't sit back and let her die, not if there was the slightest chance this Andaryan ruler could help. So he stayed silent, helplessly hugging Sullyan's unconscious form to his chest, while the Hierarch took charge of the situation.

Calling to his guards, Pharikian rapped out orders. One of them came forward to take Sullyan, but Robin waved him away. "I can manage." He stood and lifted her, then followed the Hierarch through the doors behind the dais. The Hierarch led him to a lavishly appointed suite and told him to lay Sullyan on the huge canopied bed. The pages who had accompanied them bustled around, doing the Hierarch's bidding. Robin ignored them. He sat on the bed beside Sullyan, holding her hand and smoothing the perspiration from her face.

One of the pages brought a cloth and a basin of cool water smelling of fresh herbs, which Robin used to soothe Sullyan's overheated skin. Her face was white and bloodless, but she was burning underneath, and Robin was thankful when the sound of hurrying feet heralded the arrival of Pharikian's physician. He was a short, extremely thin man with a hooked nose and a long face. His name was Deshan, and he was a Master Artesan as well as a

Master Healer.

Deshan moved to examine Sullyan and Robin stood back to give him room. He was relieved that the Hierarch's pages had closed the door after Deshan's arrival. He had caught sight of Vanyr's disapproving face out in the passageway and knew Sullyan would hate being stared at. He soon forgot the sullen commander, for the Hierarch demanded to know everything Robin could tell him concerning Rykan's abuse. The Captain related what Marik had said in the drovers' hut, and both Andaryans wore thunderous expressions by the time he was done.

Sullyan showed no sign of regaining consciousness. Deshan sat with his hand on her brow, his eyes narrowed in concentration. Finally, he shook his head and rose.

"I am sorry, Timar, but I don't think there's much I can do. The poison has been there too long. It has eaten into her soul and there's much damage."

Robin leaped to his feet and pushed between them. "But there must be! She said you would be able to help her, Majesty, she said you were the only one who could! Marik was able to help her and he hardly has any power, so why can't you?"

The Hierarch put his hands on Robin's shoulders, choosing to ignore rudeness born out of desperation and love. "What was it that Count Marik was able to do?"

Robin shook his head in frustration. "I don't know, sir, I wasn't involved. He sang to her or something. I didn't understand it. I only know that he was able to seal the poison off because he was Andaryan. Why don't you ask him?"

Pharikian snapped an order and one of his pages ran for the door. "We'll do just that." He moved around Robin and sat on the bed beside Sullyan. Taking one of her pale hands, he clasped it in both of his. "This would be a tragedy indeed," he murmured, "to lose you before I have gotten to know you properly. You look so like your mother, yet in your strength and power you are much more like your sire. They would both be so proud of you, to see what you have achieved and how beautiful you have become."

Sullyan lay still and silent.

Robin dared to ask, "Majesty? Where are her parents?"

Pharikian looked up, his eyes full of sadness. "It grieves me to hear she's lived all these years never knowing who they were. I can't imagine what went wrong. Morgan was going to leave her with relatives to be brought up. That's what he told me he'd done."

For some reason, Robin felt defensive. "She was found abandoned as a baby by some villagers, brought up an unwanted orphan."

He was startled when moisture suddenly appeared in Pharikian's eyes.

"Unwanted? Ah, no." He turned his gaze on Sullyan's pallid face. "She was never unwanted. Her parents tried for years to conceive and carry a child to term. She was her mother's dearest wish."

He looked up again and Robin saw memories filling his eyes. "Brynne was conceived here, and later born here, in this very room. In this very bed, in fact."

"Here?" Robin stared at the old man. There was such care in Pharikian's tone, such sadness. He swallowed. "And are they ... are they still alive, sir?"

The Hierarch's voice was so low that Robin strained to hear it. "Alas, no. I can't tell you how much I wish they were. Poor Bethyn died bringing her baby into the world, and Morgan couldn't live with the loss. So the one thing they both wanted above everything else finally killed them."

Robin thought he was going to say more, but at that moment the page returned, ushering a bewildered Marik into the room. When the Count saw who Robin was talking to he fell to his knees, bowing his head to the floor.

With a heavy sigh, the Hierarch rose, crossed the room, and raised Marik by the arm. "Get up, man, there'll be time for all that later. Right now we need you. We have a crisis here, and this young man thinks you might be able to help."

Marik allowed himself to be drawn to the bed. When he saw the color of Sullyan's face, he gasped in dismay. Robin gripped his arm. "Tell his Majesty what you did to help Sullyan seal off the poison."

Marik glanced at him and nodded, but his nervousness caused him to stammer when he tried to describe what he had done.

"Show us," commanded Deshan and the three Andaryans crowded round the bed. Robin could sense them concentrating the power of their minds on suppressing and walling off the creeping poison of Rykan's seed. Redundant and fearful, he retreated to the side of the room.

✤ ✤ ✤ ✤ ✤

It was daylight when Sullyan woke. She lay still, unwilling to move. Her body seemed so heavy she felt like never moving again. Slowly, she opened her eyes. There was a canopy over the bed, and what she could see of the ceiling was white, completely unlike the suite she and Robin had been assigned. She frowned, knowing without turning her head that she was alone in the huge bed. She couldn't hear any sounds and wondered where Robin was.

Coming fully awake, she suddenly realized that the heavy ache in her bones was the only pain she could feel. For the last few days she had lived with the constant, nagging cramp in her belly caused by Rykan's poison. Now that pain was gone. She considered this, unwilling to use her metasenses to probe for the reason. She left it alone, grateful for the respite no matter its cause. Briefly, she entertained the thought that the lack of pain was a sign the end was near, but apart from aching as if she had fought an entire army single-handed, she felt remarkably healthy. In fact, she felt better than she had since her capture.

She even felt hungry and very thirsty. Where was Bull with his fellan when she needed it?

Thoughts of Bull brought a tiny, sobbing breath to her throat. Now she heard a sound. Someone was moving toward her. Too weak to turn her head, she stretched out her senses and touched a familiar presence.

"Marik? What are you doing here? Or have I been arrested too?"

She heard a noise which could have been either laughter or a sob. Then Marik leaned over the bed, and she saw care and strain etched into his melancholy features. Sudden fear clenched her heart. "What is it, Ty? Is it Robin? Is he hurt? Where is he?"

"Don't worry, I'll fetch him. Don't move!"

He disappeared. She heard him open a door and caught the break in his voice as he called Robin's name. There was a flurry of movement, and then the warm and comforting presence of her lover was beside her on the bed. He covered her face with kisses and looked down into her eyes through a blur of tears. He was saying her name repeatedly. She moved one hand, surprised when she could actually raise it to his face and brush her fingers over his lips. He moaned and buried his face in her hair, and she couldn't imagine what was causing his grief. Very worried now, convinced some tragedy had befallen one of their friends, she reached out to his mind. It was so clouded by conflicting emotions that she couldn't touch him. She began to panic.

"Calm down, Robin," urged Marik. "You're frightening her."

The Captain drew back, taking a deep breath to bring himself under control. He smiled down at her, letting her into his mind, showing her that it was only his love and fear that had upset him so. She relaxed and tried to smile back, amazed when she found that she could.

Robin sat straighter on the bed and his breathing slowed. "How are you feeling, love?"

She thought about it. "Good. Robin, I feel good."

His emotion overflowed again and she frowned. Marik approached and sat on the other side of the bed. He was grinning.

"Oh, stop it, you great turkey! Can't you see you're confusing her? She's been asleep for nearly twenty hours. She hasn't got a clue what's been going on."

Sullyan struggled to sit up. "Twenty hours? What do you mean?"

Robin put a hand on her shoulder to prevent her rising. "It's alright, love, just lie still. You gave us a bit of a scare, that's all." She stilled, hearing the raw emotion in his tone. "We nearly lost you, you know. It took the combined strength of the Hierarch and his physician to save you, but if it hadn't been for Ty here telling them what to do, they'd never have done it."

The realization that Robin and Marik were now on first name terms made her smile. Then she turned her attention to what Robin had said.

"I remember feeling very ill. I remember being so angry that it happened when it did. But I remember nothing after that. Robin, where is this place?"

He snorted. "Only the Hierarch's private apartments! He wouldn't have us put you anywhere else."

He regarded her narrowly, trying, she realized, to gauge her mental state. She stared back, wondering what was on his mind. Before he could speak, however, Marik stood up. "We'd better let his Majesty know she's awake." He winked at Sullyan. "He was very insistent about that, you know. He's been sitting here beside you most of the time you were asleep. And Robin's only had a couple of hours sleep himself. You've worn us all out."

She hung her head. "I am very sorry."

Marik just grinned. He crossed to the door, opened it, and spoke to someone in the hallway. Then he returned and sank into a chair by the fire. Robin settled himself against the pillows beside her and helped Sullyan to sit, cradling her body against him. She was grateful, for she knew she couldn't have managed it by herself. She had just gotten comfortable when the door was pushed open and Pharikian entered the room.

He was wearing a more functional robe this time, plain dark blue trimmed with gold, and belted with a purple sash. His aging face looked strained and his yellow eyes were full of concern. He walked to the bed, took Sullyan's hand, and studied her face. Then he smiled and breathed a sigh of relief. She responded shyly, not at all sure how to react. It was outside of her experience to conduct an audience with such a powerful man from the bed in one of his own chambers. His relaxed and casual manner, however, soon put her at ease.

"Well, my Lady, I am very pleased to see you so much improved. You gave my physician a very difficult time."

She ducked her head. "I thank you, Majesty."

"Your Captain has told me the circumstances of your … malady." His voice grew harsh. "You did well to come to me. Rykan shall pay for what he did to you."

"Majesty, I did not come here to present a complaint of the Duke's maltreatment. I came because I carry important knowledge of his battle strategies and other … plans. My illness has wasted yet another day, so it is imperative that I speak with you concerning his challenge."

Pharikian held up a hand. "All in good time, child, there is no immediate threat. My generals are well aware of the position of Rykan's forces, and for the past few days he has not advanced. We are fully prepared. My senior commander, Lord General Anjer, has all the information he needs to direct the Caer's defenses. You can rest easy."

Sullyan shook her head. "He does not have the information I carry, Majesty! Rykan would never have revealed it had he suspected for one moment I might survive his brutality. His own vicious nature will be his undoing, for I will not see him overthrow your reign if I can prevent it. That is why I am here, Majesty, to play as large a role in his defeat as I can. I owe him that much for the premature ending of my life."

Pharikian raised his brows. "He hasn't ended it yet, child, and if we overturn his challenge you may yet cheat him of your death."

Robin hissed in shock and Sullyan froze. She felt the blood drain from her face. "How so, Majesty?"

He cocked his head. "Surely you are aware that Rykan can cleanse you of his poison?"

Her flare of hope died instantly and her reply was bitter. "Oh yes, Majesty, if he wills it! Can you see Rykan, once defeated in his challenge, agreeing to spare my life?" She snorted. "How he would enjoy that! By then he would have lost everything. What could possibly persuade him to be merciful to me?"

Pharikian began to speak but she stopped him. "I will not beg him, Majesty, not again. This I have sworn. I will never lie helpless before him or put myself in his power again. Not even to save my own life."

The Hierarch chose not to argue with her, seeing how even this small discussion had tired her. "Very well, child, do not distress yourself. We will discuss this later."

She began to protest, but he held up a hand. "No, my dear, no more. If it will calm you, I promise to keep you informed of any change in the Duke's position. Otherwise, you are to forget him for now." He rose to leave and turned his stern gaze on Robin. "Young man, you are to keep her in bed for the rest of the day. Deshan will come by later to check on her, and I will send for some food for you both. Which do you prefer, spice-tea or fellan?"

Sullyan replied for them both. "Fellan, please, Majesty, as strong as possible."

He stared at her, a slow smile coming to his lips. "Fellan, as strong as possible? Yes, of course."

His evident amusement puzzled her, but he continued before she could ask.

"I am also having your things brought here from the other suite. I want you close to me, here in my private apartments."

Sullyan was touched and thanked him earnestly, but he caught the wistful tone of her voice. "What is it, Lady?"

She lowered her eyes. "Majesty, does this suite have a bathing pool?"

He laughed, a sound of genuine pleasure. "Ah, you enjoyed that, did you? Yes, child, all the Palace suites have pools. We're very civilized here! And the private apartments have the largest pools." His eyes took on a distant look. "Your mother loved bathing too."

Shortly after his departure, a servant brought fresh food and fellan. The brew was easily as strong as Bull's, and tears came to Sullyan's eyes as she drank it, remembering his big, comforting presence. She glanced over at Robin, who sat in one of the chairs by the bed. Marik was still there too. As the Hierarch passed him on his way out, he told the Count he was released to Sullyan's custody. He cautioned Marik to remember it. The Count was more than happy to obey. Now he sat across the room from them, quietly drinking fellan and thinking his own thoughts.

"What would Bull make of all this, Robin?"

The Captain chuckled and looked around the lavish room. "He'd never believe it. Mind you, I can hardly believe it myself." He smiled shyly. "Do you remember that you have a name now?

Does it feel like it fits?"

She hadn't really thought about what she had heard in the Hierarch's audience chamber. Her memory of that time was mingled with the pain of her illness, and she wasn't entirely sure she had heard correctly. Robin told her what Pharikian had said about her birth and her mother's death—here in this very room— and her soul was in turmoil, desperate to know more.

She glanced down at her hands and tried the name on her tongue. "Brynne ... I hardly know, Robin. I have had only one name all my life, so to suddenly have another seems somehow ... superfluous."

The Captain laughed aloud and Marik grinned. Robin took her in his arms.

"Oh, my love, only you could think that having such a lovely name was superfluous!"

Later that evening, after a page had shown Marik to his rooms across the hall, and Deshan had come by to check Sullyan once more, Pharikian returned. Despite his orders and Robin's protests, Sullyan was not in bed. She had risen shortly after eating, yet she only went as far as the bathing pool. The warm water did wonders to ease the deep ache in her bones, and she reveled in the clean, buoyant feel of it, her tawny hair floating out around her.

Worried she might overtax herself, Robin sat by the pool and watched her closely. She emerged feeling much improved. Now, wrapped in a soft, voluminous house robe, she lounged on a settle by the fire, spreading her damp hair to dry.

A discreet knock sounded at the door and Robin went to open it. Three servants entered, bearing trays laden with food, wine and fellan. A page came behind them, and then to Sullyan's amazement, the Hierarch appeared. He looked strained and tired, but his tension eased when he saw her. He did, however, point a stern finger at Robin.

"Young man, I thought I told you to keep her in bed."

Robin was about to explain but Sullyan got there first. "Do not blame the Captain, Majesty. I could not resist the bathing pool. Once I have eaten a little and drunk more fellan, I will be more than happy to return to my rest."

The servants laid their trays on the low table near Sullyan and departed. Pharikian's page, a young lad of about twelve who reminded Sullyan strongly of the Manor kitchen boy, Tad, closed the door behind them. His master approached Sullyan and indicated the space beside her. "May I?"

She blushed. "Majesty, you need ask no leave of me!"

He sighed and wearily lowered himself to the settle. "Child, I have had people bowing and scraping and generally fawning over me all day long. Would you do me a very great favor?"

Her eyes widened. "Anything, Majesty."

"Then, when we are alone, will you do me the courtesy of using my name and forgetting that I am Andaryon's sovereign lord? That is how it was with your parents, and I found it very refreshing. Your father was one of my closest friends, Brynne. It would give me inestimable pleasure to think of you in the same way."

She stared into his yellow eyes, and as she offered metaphysical contact, her pupils dilated wide. "It would give me great pleasure also, Timar."

He accepted her offer with a pleased grin that took years off his face. She smiled shyly. "Dare I ask you a favor in return? Not that I do not already owe you everything for saving my life."

His eyes flashed. "That was just due recompense for what you suffered at the hands of one of my so-called subjects. An accounting will be sought, of that you can be sure."

Her smile vanished. "May we talk of that later?" He gave a terse nod and she broached the subject that had been filling her heart and mind since his astonishing revelation in the throne room. "Timar, will you tell me about my parents? Robin has told me what you said concerning my birth and how my mother ... died, but I would love to hear more. I always hoped someday to find someone who could tell me about them."

Pharikian reached for a plate of meat and offered it to Sullyan. She took some and he helped himself before passing the plate to Robin.

"I will tell you while we eat, but I don't want to tire you. Deshan thinks you will feel much better tomorrow, and we will discuss then what can be done about my rival. I should warn you, though, that your arrival and the news that you carry information concerning Rykan's plans have already spread throughout the Caer. It has stirred up my generals, Brynne, which may be no bad thing!"

Her heart gave a lurch as she heard her given name. It would take some getting used to.

"Please, Timar, I would rather that the details of my ... circumstances do not become public knowledge. I want no pity, only the chance to play my part in thwarting Rykan's challenge."

"I know, child, rest easy. No one else knows but Deshan, and he is very discreet. Have no fears on that score."

Companionably, they sat together and consumed the fine food provided by the Palace kitchens. As they did so, Pharikian told Sullyan about his friendship with her parents.

Chapter Fourteen

"I first met Morgan Sullyan around forty years ago. He was a well-respected bard and a gifted storyteller. His fame reached us even here. For this he was made welcome by my father, the previous Hierarch. Morgan became a regular visitor at Court. At that time, I had an elder brother, Selmar, who was my father's Heir. Many of the higher ranking nobles had sworn allegiance to my brother and were pledged to support his succession. But Selmar died unexpectedly in a dueling accident, and I became the Heir. The nobles, judging their oaths annulled by Selmar's death, rebelled, for they felt no loyalty to me.

"You may be aware that in Andaryon, an Heir's right to the throne is only as strong as his power, and much of that power depends on the support he has gathered around him. Such support in turn depends as much on his physical strength as his metaphysical prowess, for the death of a Hierarch almost always results in a bloody scramble for position, and no one will support an unprepared or physically weak candidate. Many an Heir has been ousted by a noble with greater power, and I had been thrust into the position with no time to prepare.

"My father was still alive, of course, but he was weakening, and he could see the nobles circling like tangwyrs above a corpse. Their rebellion infuriated him, and his efforts to whip them back in line put a strain on his aging heart. He died with the situation still unresolved, leaving me facing a serious challenge to my succession.

"Partly out of respect for my father, and partly because the strongest of the nobles was a man known to be hostile toward Albia, Morgan, who was then about twenty-five, offered me his aid in suppressing the insurgents. I was happy to accept. In addition to his bardic skills, he was a powerful Artesan, a talented swordsman, and a gifted tactician. Such qualities persuaded the nobles still loyal to my House to respect him, and his counsel proved invaluable. Together, we defeated the rebels and secured my right to the throne. Morgan's selfless endeavors on my behalf earned him my deepest gratitude and undying friendship.

"Three years after my coronation, I married the Lady Idriana, daughter to the Lord of Selkiar, one of our southern provinces. Morgan was my guest of honor and groom's man. He played for us that day, music he composed especially for the occasion. I remember it still so clearly. The melodies come readily to my mind although I have not heard them for many years now …."

"What instrument did my father play?" Sullyan was reluctant to interrupt, yet desperate for any knowledge that would bring her closer to her sire.

Pharikian's gaze sharpened and he smiled at her. "He was accomplished on many instruments, child, but mostly he favored the harp."

She flushed with pleasure. "I have some skill with the harp myself."

Pharikian was delighted. "I shall have Gaslek unearth his scores, child, and you shall have them. But only on the condition that you play them for me."

Her heart too full for speech, Sullyan nodded. She closed her eyes as Pharikian went on.

"Two years after our wedding, I learned that Morgan had married his long-cherished sweetheart, Bethyn. He had spoken of her many times, but I had never met her. Once they were wed, I insisted he bring her to Court. I had to see her for myself, as I could scarcely believe his descriptions of her beauty. But when she came, when I saw her walking beside him with the light in her tawny hair and the love shining bright from her eyes, well, I could see he had spoken the truth. She was a gentle beauty indeed and well suited to Morgan's generous heart. I gave her a wedding gift of four rare fire opals set in gold. It gives me immense pleasure to see you wearing them, Brynne. They sparkle as brightly on you as they did on her."

Sullyan still could not speak. Her throat was too tight. Pharikian squeezed her hand, his own voice unsteady.

"My lady Idriana took Bethyn to her heart, and we found much pleasure in each other's company. After that first meeting, Bethyn often accompanied her husband when he came to Court. The following year, Idriana gave birth to twin daughters. One of them died within hours. Morgan and Bethyn grieved with us, for Bethyn had recently suffered a miscarriage, and she and my lady comforted each other.

"Two years after that, my son Aeyron was born, but Bethyn had miscarried twice more in that time. She was very brave about it, but we all knew how sad she was. A child was her heart's wish, and she felt incomplete without one. But that sorrow aside, they were happy. Over the next six years, our friendship deepened and I was pleased to be able to help Morgan achieve his potential as an Artesan. We held a lavish celebration here when I acknowledged him as Senior Master."

Sullyan finally found her voice. "Was my mother gifted too?"

Something flashed in the Hierarch's eyes, but his voice remained level. "Bethyn was an empath, child, as my dear late wife had cause to know. It was your mother's deep understanding of Idriana's sorrow over the death of our child that helped her overcome her depression and enabled her to conceive our Heir. We were all distressed when Idriana didn't live long enough to see Bethyn carry a child to term."

There was a brief silence. Then Pharikian sighed and took up the tale once more.

"One day, one of my physicians—a talented and precocious youngster named Deshan—came to me, saying he thought he had found the reason for Bethyn's trouble. After her third miscarriage, she had not quickened again in six years and had given up all hope of ever bearing a child. Deshan's news encouraged us all, and Morgan brought his lady to stay at the Caer for treatment. They lived here, in this very suite, as they always did when visiting us. To our delight, the treatment was successful. Bethyn conceived and managed to keep the child past three months. However, once that dangerous time was over, Deshan advised her to return to Albia, as remaining here in an alien realm might prove damaging to the baby.

"I was sad to see them go, but Bethyn decided she would give birth here at the Caer, in order to take advantage of my experienced physicians. And I think she wanted me to be the first to see the child. She felt it would in some way repay me for what I had been able to give her."

Sullyan leaned forward. "Where did they go? Where was their home?"

He shook his head. "I'm sorry, child, I don't know. I travelled the Veils only rarely in my youth, and never after I became Hierarch, so I never visited them there. Morgan rarely spoke of Albia when we were together, and he never mentioned his home. I'm sorry."

"No matter."

Her tone was light, but it still made Pharikian frown. Changing the subject, he reached for the plate of sliced meat and offered it to her again. "You don't eat enough, Brynne."

She smiled, accepting his tactic along with another slice of the delicious meat. "So Rienne has told me."

"Rienne?"

Her smile faded. "A very dear friend. She is a gifted healer who is also an empath. She helped save my life when I was brought half dead out of Rykan's captivity."

At the mention of his rival's name, the Hierarch's expression darkened. "Then I would welcome the chance to thank her." He took a sip of wine before continuing his tale, his tone warning her that this part wouldn't be easy to hear.

"When Bethyn was close to her time, Morgan brought her back. All was well, Bethyn was happy and healthy, although sad that my lovely Idriana had died of a fever during the winter and wouldn't see her child."

Sullyan closed her eyes, but not before a tear managed to squeeze under the lids. Pharikian touched her hand, lending her some strength. She pressed his fingers gratefully.

"Bethyn's labor began normally," continued the Hierarch, striving to keep the emotion from his voice. "All seemed to be going well until Deshan realized that the baby wasn't moving along the birth canal. Hours went by, the contractions got weaker, and there was still no sign of the baby coming. Deshan and his team did all they could. Both Morgan and I tried to lend Bethyn the strength to carry on pushing, yet nothing we did seemed to help. For some reason, we couldn't reach her. Even our combined metaforce couldn't break through the barrier that blocked us.

"And then Bethyn began to hemorrhage, and Deshan reluctantly decided that our only option was to remove the baby. It was not an easy decision, as it meant almost certain death for either mother or child, maybe both. But as both would certainly die if we did nothing, we had no choice. Bethyn, weak and fevered though she was, begged us to save the baby, so Deshan opened her stomach and delivered it. It was a beautiful, healthy baby girl. It was you, Brynne."

Sullyan was weeping openly now, neither hiding nor denying her grief. Robin came to her side and held her hand as Pharikian, his voice betraying his emotion, continued the tale.

"Bethyn had lost so much blood and was so weak. Despite Deshan's best efforts, there was no saving her. She was able to hold her baby briefly and speak her name, the name she and Morgan had decided on only a few weeks earlier. She died with you in her arms. Morgan was devastated by her loss, and we had to lend him strength to get him through that terrible day."

Sullyan was overcome by guilt and sorrow. "Did he blame me for the death of my mother? Is that why he abandoned me?"

The Hierarch gripped her shoulders. "Oh no, child, no! Your father was full of love for you. It was only that he had poured everything he had into willing Beth to survive. He simply had nothing left for himself and was dismayed by his failure to save her. He blamed himself for not being strong enough, but the truth was no one could have been. We were simply unable to reach her. Morgan couldn't accept that. He was so distraught that he became suicidal. We nearly lost him too that day."

Pharikian fell silent, his eyes seeing that long ago day, a fateful day that should have been so joyous. Sullyan sat fingering the fire opal at her throat, the jewel worn by her mother as she died giving birth to her child.

Her gaze briefly met the Hierarch's, and she knew he was trying to gauge how she was taking such grief-laden family history. He had been gentle in the telling, yet his words would inevitably take their toll on her weakened vitality. She knew there was more, and knew also that if she didn't hear the whole tale now, she wouldn't rest. And she badly needed to rest. She would have to be at full strength on the morrow if she was to break through his generals' prejudice and convince them to listen.

Pharikian waited quietly until she was ready to continue. She took a deep breath, met his gaze, and nodded. He smiled slightly and she cocked her head, puzzled by his wry expression. "What is it, Timar?"

"Nothing, Brynne. Only that I've seen that determined look before on your father's face."

Tears threatened again, but she fought them down. "Tell me, please, Timar, what became of him?"

Pharikian sighed and glanced down at his hands.

"In the years following my succession, there was much civil unrest in Andaryon. The faction that opposed me had been repressed but not destroyed, and they continued to gather supporters from many provinces. I was forced to fight several battles over those years, and the constant strife was damaging the realm. In practical terms, Andaryon was split in two and the economy was on the verge of collapse. By the year of your birth we had reached an impasse, neither side being strong enough to conclusively defeat the other.

"Eventually, it was agreed that the most powerful nobles of each faction, together with their military leaders—many of whom were also Artesans—should call a temporary truce and convene a Grand Council in order to reconcile our differences before we completely destroyed the realm. This Council was scheduled for the week after your birth."

Sullyan leaned forward. "My father attended the Council with you."

The Hierarch shot her a look of surprise. She waited for him to continue, a tremor starting deep in her body.

"Yes, he did. Although he was Albian, Morgan was one of my most trusted advisors, and despite his despair, he wouldn't stay away. But you had only just been born, and Bethyn wasn't there to care for you. He had to make hurried arrangements for your safety before he could attend the Council. The original plan was for you and your mother to return to Albia and for Morgan to follow once the Council was over. With Bethyn gone, he was forced to take you himself. When he came back, he told me he had left you with relatives who would care for you until he could return."

Sullyan's eyes closed in pain. She was unlikely ever to know why her father's family had rejected her. "But he did not return for me," she murmured. "Let me guess what happened at the Council meeting."

Pharikian raised his brows, inviting her to continue.

"The two sides could not reach an agreement. The balance of power was equally distributed, and no one was willing to back down or give ground. Only one course of action remained, only one way to avoid the carnage that outright war would inflict upon the realm." She stopped and Pharikian bowed his head. He stared at his hands as she added, "And that was the Primal Sacrament."

Robin's hand tightened on hers. "Primal Sacrament? What's that?"

"It is an ancient Andaryan tradition, one that goes back to the times when a much higher percentage of the nobility possessed great powers which could be used equally for good or for ill. Many held the rank of Master-elite, Senior Master, and even, I believe, Supreme Master."

Robin frowned, he hadn't heard of that particular rank.

Pharikian nodded. "That is true. You seem to know much of our history, Brynne. But there hasn't been a Supreme Master for time out of mind, and it's my belief that we're slowly losing the abilities our forebears once had. It's a great tragedy, I think, but all things change. Please carry on."

She gave a tight smile. "Terrible wars had been fought by those possessing such tremendous forces, and they caused great devastation. If the realm was not to be literally torn apart by such strife, then a new way of settling conflict had to be found. The formalized Codes of Combat came into being at that time, but they were aimed primarily at individuals, not those commanding vast numbers of troops. For warfare on this scale, a new treaty was needed, a powerfully binding and unbreakable contract. The kind of contract which would actively discourage the disputes it was designed to resolve.

"And so the ritual known as the Primal Sacrament was devised. Should two or more powerful factions find themselves in stalemate, they were obliged under law to either undergo the ritual or forfeit their claims. Whichever side produced an Artesan willing to make the Sacrament—and he had to be willing, he could not be coerced—that side would be judged the victor. Each Artesan involved in the dispute would then surrender a tiny portion of his psyche to the willing one, signifying the end of all grievances. They were bound by this not to resurrect those grievances while they or their Heirs survived."

She captured Pharikian's gaze. "It was by this ancient ritual that the Council decided to resolve the strife that followed your succession."

His expression was rueful. "I'm impressed by your knowledge, Brynne, and you're quite right. The nobles all agreed to be bound by the Sacrament and even accepted my stipulation that wholesale raiding into other realms should also cease."

Her reply was barely a whisper. "They accepted it because they never expected to find someone willing to make the sacrifice."

"Hang on," said Robin. "Sacrifice?"

She glanced at him. "You know of the Sacrament, Robin. In Albia, we call it the Pact."

Understanding flooded his face. He knew that a Senior Master

Artesan had died to broker the Pact, but no one knew who he was or why he had lost his life. "Are you saying …?"

Sullyan couldn't answer him. Confirmation was left to the Hierarch, who gently gathered her trembling form into his arms.

"The Senior Master who gave up his life to the Sacrament that saved my rule and my realm, and also ended the tradition of raiding into Albia, was my dear friend, Morgan Sullyan."

A few moments of silence passed. When she was calm again, Sullyan said, "What drove him to it, Timar? Did he so wish to die?"

Pharikian paused before replying. "I cannot truthfully say, child. I would never have taken him with me had I thought he might offer himself. I think the simple truth is that he was totally devastated by your mother's death. He knew that without the Sacrament I would have to abdicate, and that would lead to yet more years of civil war being unleashed upon the realm. He also knew how much this land meant to me, so maybe in some way he thought he was repaying me for our friendship. And as I said before, he believed he had made suitable arrangements for you."

His eyes strayed to the fire opal glinting at her throat. "You know, I never realized he had taken Beth's jewels and left them with you."

She put a hand to the stone. "They are the reason I knew my family name. They were in a small leather pouch around my neck when I was found, and although it was badly worn, the name 'Sullyan' could just be read upon it. The stones and that name were the only things I had in the world."

He shook his head. "Oh, my dear child, I'm so sorry you spent all those years not knowing who you were. It shames me, and it would have distressed your parents greatly. I am grieved that I can tell you nothing more about your father's family, but I can perhaps offer you a small grain of comfort once I finish Morgan's story."

Sullyan shrugged, doubting that any comfort would make a difference now. She had grown up knowing she was abandoned, but somewhere in the deepest part of her soul she had nurtured a tiny hope that her parents might still be alive. Now she knew they were not. Nothing else mattered. There was no comfort to be had.

Pharikian returned to the subject of Morgan's sacrifice.

"After Bethyn's death and before the Council meeting, Morgan merely went through the motions of life. I could see he was becoming increasingly withdrawn, but nothing I said made a difference. He had been with Beth so long—they were childhood sweethearts—that he simply didn't know how to live without her.

"Morgan rarely drank liquor, even wine. He was addicted to fellan, the stronger the better, but he began to find solace in drink. Never enough to incapacitate him, but enough to impair his control. Given time, perhaps we could have helped him overcome his depression, but the Council meeting came too soon."

His gaze turned inward, his expression sad. "The session was long and stormy. No one was in the mood to give ground. Accusations were flung, offences given and taken on both sides. There were angry words and drawn swords and the whole thing was about to degenerate into a brawl when my father's chamberlain, Baron Arlow, mentioned the ritual of Sacrament. It stopped us in our tracks, and the nobles, many of whom had never heard it mentioned before, demanded to see evidence of this ancient law. Arlow had brought the parchment with him, and there was no disputing its authenticity. To be brief, each noble, including myself, eventually agreed to be bound by the law. I am sure you are right, child. Most never dreamt that anyone would be willing to take such a burden.

"They reckoned without Morgan. As soon as he understood the implications of the Sacrament and what was bound to happen should we refuse it, his clear voice rang out over our heads. 'I am willing' was all he said."

Sullyan nodded slowly. "He had rediscovered a purpose to his life. Having lost everything, he suddenly saw hope. Something only he could do, something that would rectify an impossible situation."

The two men stared at her in silence, and Robin's expression told her he was afraid she had found a parallel to her own situation in her father's story. He feared she foresaw a similar end for herself.

Pharikian nodded. "Yes. Once his mind was made up, there was no dissuading him, no matter what I said. Skeptical about his ability to carry it through, and half suspecting that he would renege at the last moment, the nobles signed the Sacrament. We all surrendered a tiny portion of our psyche to Morgan. I kept trying to talk him out of it, but he knew what would happen if the Sacrament was refused. My rule—indeed, the very stability of our realm—depended on him.

"And then it was too late. The Sacrament was signed and it had to be fulfilled. I had to stand strong and allow him his wish. I had to bid farewell to my dearest friend. It was one of the hardest things I've ever done. Before he left us, in the name of our friendship he asked me to look out for you, Brynne, to extend the same friendship if ever we met. I was more than happy to agree. I would have done so without his asking."

Robin glanced sideways at Sullyan, hoping his question wouldn't give her too much pain. "But how did it happen? How did he fulfill this ... Sacrament?"

Pharikian was silent, watching Sullyan's face. She felt numb, as if all her senses were in stasis. Raising her eyes to Robin's, she sent him a flash of memory. He saw again the little drovers' hut the day after her rescue and felt again her anguished spirit brushing past him on its wild dash for oblivion. His face drained of color as understanding dawned. "Oh!"

Such power came with the increase in strength required to become a Master Artesan. Anyone who reached that rank had the power to relinquish their hold on life and choose to pass on to the next existence, whatever that might be.

Sullyan included Pharikian in the exchange and felt his horror on learning that she had so nearly done what her father had chosen to do, and in such extremity. His yellow eyes filled with pain and he leaned forward, his voice rough and urgent.

"I swear to you, I will have an accounting of Rykan for his brutal treatment."

She shook her head firmly. "Majesty, I claim that right. His life is mine."

There was naked venom in her tone and Pharikian recoiled. "As you wish, child. I acknowledge your right. I grant you his life."

She reached out, took his hand, and pressed it in apology and gratitude. His expression softened. "Brynne, would you like to see your parents?"

She startled before she realized what he meant. He could show her their faces from his own memory. Finally, after years of futile wonder, she would know what they looked like. Her heart gave a lurch. "That would please me very much."

Her eyes dilated as she accepted the Hierarch's contact. Reaching for Robin's hand, she prepared to share the experience with him. When Pharikian's mind opened in hers, she saw the image of a medium height, slightly built man with short, dark auburn hair. His eyes were a warm brown, his pleasant face serene, his lips relaxed in a gentle smile. Catching her breath, Sullyan drank in the face of her sire.

Then a second figure came into focus alongside Morgan, and it was Robin's turn to gasp. Standing at her husband's side was a woman who, but for the deep brown of her eyes, could have been Sullyan herself. The wealth of tawny hair was the same, although Bethyn wore hers shorter than her daughter did. Her build and height were the same, as were her small, finely featured face and creamy skin. As she turned to look lovingly at her husband, the opals at her throat and ears glinted in the light of some long ago summer's day.

A sob escaped Sullyan's throat and Pharikian let the images fade. Once again, he gathered her into his arms and rocked her like a child.

It was growing late and what remained of the food had long since gone cold. Taking the fellan pot from the fire, Robin poured some into a cup and touched Sullyan on the arm. "Brynne?"

The name sounded unfamiliar on his tongue. She pushed away from Pharikian, responding to the care in Robin's voice. As she accepted the cup, she allowed her fingers to caress his. Once she had taken a few sips, she was able to speak again. "Timar, I have one final question, and then I think we both need to rest."

She did indeed feel very tired, and knew she looked strained around the eyes. Pharikian looked no better.

"Anything, child."

"You said earlier that my mother wanted you to be the first to see her child, to repay you for what you had given her." He nodded, his gaze sharp on her face. "Both my parents were dark-eyed, and no one in Albia has eyes like mine." She stared back at him. "Timar, where do I get my coloring from?"

His smile broadened. "Well done, child, you are very quick. I wondered if you'd guess this final twist to the story. Deshan had discovered that Bethyn's miscarriages were due to her spending too much time in our realm. He found that her body had suffered slight damage and so was unable to carry a child for more than a few weeks. As he looked through our archives for a way to help her, he unearthed a parchment which led him to believe that if she was treated with small infusions of Andaryan blood her body would become acclimatized to our alien atmosphere."

Robin frowned. "Are you saying that someone gave blood to Sullyan's mother, and that this blood somehow affected the color of her eyes?"

"Indeed I am, son. None of us foresaw that outcome—not even Deshan—and no one has ever been able to explain it. Nevertheless, that is what happened." He turned back to Sullyan. "So you see, child, you are not entirely alone in the world. Should you wish to acknowledge the connection, you can claim that we are related. You get your golden eyes from me, Brynne. The blood Bethyn received that allowed you to be born was mine."

Chapter Fifteen

Exhausted by the Hierarch's startling revelations, Sullyan and Robin slept deeply. A gentle tap on the outer door woke them just after dawn. Robin threw a robe about his slim body as he padded through the living area to answer it. A servant brought in breakfast, followed by another bearing their clothes, which had been cleaned and pressed. The Hierarch had arranged that courtesy the day before and Sullyan was grateful. She wanted to appear at her professional best today, and travel-stained clothing would do her no favors.

Lying still in the bed, she was unwilling to surrender the peace and wellbeing she felt. She hadn't realized how debilitating the cramp in her belly had been, but now that she wasn't expending power to keep it at bay, she felt fit and strong. Raising herself on one elbow, she watched Robin as he returned from seeing the servants out. His robe had fallen open and she saw, with loving admiration, that he was also feeling fit and strong.

They finally found time to attend to the food on the tray before putting the final touches to their attire. Sullyan had decided to wear her dress uniform rather than her combat leathers, and was startled and pleased when she discovered a gold Andaryan rank badge—a crown surmounted by a single star, equivalent to her own double thunderflash—lying on a dress jacket which was subtly trimmed with purple. She attached the badge to the jacket before putting it on.

Robin whistled. "He doesn't want anyone to be in doubt of his support, does he?"

Smiling, Sullyan held up a second jacket bearing a lieutenant's insignia, obviously intended for Robin. The Captain raised his brows in appreciation and shrugged into it.

Sullyan braided her hair with care. She wanted to divert attention from her gender today, if that was at all possible in this male-dominated society. The meeting would be difficult enough without inviting their prejudice.

Soon, one of Pharikian's pages arrived to escort her to the royal presence. This was a private meeting between Sullyan and the Hierarch, but Robin knew he would be accompanying her to the main briefing session later.

Sullyan returned from her private meeting with Pharikian looking calm. The page who bowed her back into the suite grinned cheekily at her, reminding her even more strongly of young Tad. Sullyan smiled and ruffled his blond hair before sending him scampering off.

Robin looked up from his place on the settle. "I finally managed to contact Bull while you were gone. How did it go with the Hierarch?"

She relaxed beside him. "Much as I expected. Timar is now fully aware of Rykan's intentions as well as his hidden strength, and he agrees with my assessment of the Caer's defense. However, Timar does not personally command his troops, neither is he skilled in military tactics. He leaves both to his generals. I have his permission to address the Lord General and put my proposals before him. Further than that, I did not expect him to go. Despite his support and offers of friendship, not even the Hierarch can order his warlords to trust me. That is something I must secure for myself. But at least we have time. As of yesterday, Rykan has still not begun his advance.

"My love, I have a feeling that this meeting will be awkward and uncomfortable. Maybe even hostile. I must ask you to listen and observe closely, but remain silent. I may have to play these men very carefully indeed."

A couple of hours later, Sullyan and Robin were ushered into a much smaller but no less grand audience chamber than the one where they had first met the Hierarch. It was functional rather than formal. The throne sat at the head of a large oval table with chairs arranged around it to accommodate the other participants. The room was empty when Sullyan and Robin entered, and the page directed them to chairs at the side of the room where they could await the Hierarch and his generals.

Sullyan sat quite still, trying to appear calm and composed. She saw Robin watching her and knew he was nervous, never having attended such a high level meeting before. The fire opal pulsing at the open neck of her shirt betrayed the rapid beat of her own heart, and she knew Robin could see it. She sat in silence, hands folded in her lap, rehearsing what she would say. Much depended on the reactions of the generals, both to her news and her presence.

She didn't have long to wait. Two guards opened the doors at the far end of the chamber and four men entered the room. At their head strode a truly massive and muscular man around forty-five years of age. He was black-haired and black-eyed, which was highly unusual for an Andaryan, and he wore full military uniform. His mouth was hidden by a dark mustache, and a rank badge showing a gold crown surmounted by three stars glittered on his chest.

Sullyan murmured, "Lord General Anjer."

General Ephan followed Anjer, talking quietly to a shorter, stocky, pale-eyed man. Both bore double starred crown insignia. The last man was Commander Vanyr. He glanced sourly in Sullyan's direction as he took his place behind one of the purple upholstered chairs. He stood there frowning, his white eyes cold and hostile. Sullyan ignored him.

Next to arrive was Baron Gaslek, and he nodded politely to Sullyan as he positioned himself to the right of the Hierarch's throne, parchment and quills in hand. His expression bore a trace of speculative respect, and the Major inclined her head to acknowledge him.

Lastly, the Hierarch himself entered, flanked by two of his personal Guard. They escorted him to the throne before retiring to the door. At his entrance, everyone accorded him the Andaryan military salute; a closed fist held above the heart. Sullyan and Robin did likewise, adding the homage due to a Senior Master Artesan.

As the warlords took their chairs, Sullyan noticed Ephan regarding her curiously, no doubt weighing the implications of the Hierarch's colors on her jacket. She didn't allow herself to react, but kept her eyes on Pharikian. When they were all settled, he greeted them, his blue veined hands resting lightly on the table. He swept them with his yellow gaze, as if judging their mood. Sullyan thought he looked tired.

When he spoke, however, his voice was deep and strong. "Gentlemen, I believe there have been some developments in the deployment of Rykan's forces. Your thoughts and reports, please."

He sat. There was a slight pause as Ephan glanced at the two Albians and gave a disapproving frown. The Hierarch didn't comment, and so Ephan gestured for Vanyr to give his report. In a light, clipped voice, the Commander obeyed.

"Majesty, at first light this morning my patrols returned to report that Lord Rykan's forces have finally begun an advance on the Citadel. They are moving slowly and keeping to their marching formation. It is my opinion that if they continue to advance at this rate and remain unopposed, they will be able to adopt siege positions in around four days' time."

Sullyan stiffened and stared hard at the Hierarch, but he was considering what Vanyr had said.

"Based on this information, Ephan, what is your recommendation?"

The General turned his head, his pale eyes regarding his ruler. "My recommendation remains unchanged, Majesty. We should sit tight. Rykan doesn't field enough men to mount an effective siege, and the Caer is well provisioned. His lack of action since issuing the formal challenge has allowed us ample time to lay in extra stores. So let him surround us. Let him break his forces against our walls. We can pick off his men at leisure, and he'll soon grow tired of his losses. And if he doesn't, then our reserve troops can be summoned and they will dissuade him from continuing the siege."

Ephan's casual reaction to the possibility of Rykan besieging the Caer made Sullyan gasp aloud. The other general, whose name she had yet to hear, turned to stare at her in undisguised annoyance. When Ephan had finished, this man eyed the Hierarch, pointedly clearing his throat.

"Yes, Kryp. Do you wish to say something?"

Gesturing with a heavy arm, General Kryp indicated Sullyan and Robin. He spoke deferentially, but his stiff tone suggested censure. His wheezy voice grated on Sullyan's nerves. "Majesty, might I enquire as to why there are two Albians present at an Andaryan war council?"

The Hierarch smiled coldly. "You may, Kryp." He beckoned, inviting Sullyan to approach the table. She stood, placing a restraining hand on Robin's shoulder when he would have risen also. Alone, she moved to the opposite end of the oval table and stood facing Pharikian. All four war leaders turned to stare at her. Lord General Anjer showed open but impassive curiosity. Ephan looked resigned. Both Kryp and Vanyr wore expressions of unveiled hostility. Sullyan ignored them all.

"Gentlemen," announced the Hierarch, "may I present Major Brynne Sullyan, Master-elite, Ambassador and King's Envoy to Elias Rovannon, High King of Albia."

Kryp's eyes narrowed and Sullyan would have given much to know which of her titles concerned him the most. Ephan, who already knew something of her reputation, looked speculative. Vanyr's hostility hadn't changed. Anjer's expression was wary and he leaned forward, cocking his head at Pharikian. "Did you say 'Sullyan', Majesty?"

The elderly ruler met his General's gaze. "That's right, Anjer."

"I see." Anjer turned to face Sullyan and inclined his head. "Major Sullyan."

She had to give him credit. There was only the mildest hint of condescension in his tone. She responded by according him a very respectful Andaryan-style salute, and he raised his brows. After the briefest of hesitations, he returned it.

"Might I ask why you are here, Major?"

She answered calmly and clearly. "Because, my Lord General, I carry vital information concerning the Duke of Kymer's forces and battle plans."

She stood easily, her hands clasped behind her back as if she was facing General Blaine, not four hostile and powerful alien lords. She hoped they would at least respect her courage.

Anjer's smile was disdainful, and his black brows rose higher. "And how, pray, did you come by this 'vital' information?"

Sullyan kept her tone neutral. "I had it from the Duke's own lips, my Lord."

There was an angry stir and mutters of disbelief. Anjer's smile and tone turned patronizing. "Are we supposed to accept that the Duke of Kymer took you into his confidence before sending you here to conveniently tell us of his plans?" He snorted and turned to Pharikian. "Come now, Majesty. I can understand your desire to accept her given your old friendship with Morgan, but really! What is this?"

The Hierarch faced him down. "I think it would behoove us to listen to what the Major has to say, Anjer."

He put a slight emphasis on her rank, and this provoked a loud and irritated snort from Kryp, who gestured in her direction. "Major? Don't make me laugh! Look at her, Majesty. She's no more than a child. Don't they have enough men in Albia that they have to let women run around playing soldier? Have they all been emasculated?" He stared at Sullyan, his pale eyes roving insultingly over her slender body. His voice dripped contempt. "What can you possibly know of military matters, girl?"

Slowly and deliberately, Sullyan turned her gaze on him. Her eyes were hard and clear, showing no fear.

"You may consider me no more than a girl, General Kryp, but let me tell you that I have spent thirteen years in the active service of my King—most of it in the field. I went through the same rigorous training process as any other cadet, only being accepted by the King once I had passed the tests and proved my abilities. I won my own command at the age of eighteen and have held it ever since, spending five years as a Captain and three as a Major. The men of my command are disciplined, ordered, and successful, as these battle honors above my heart bear witness. They were presented personally by the High King, and I wear them proudly. Ask Elias Rovannon whether I merit my rank! Any one of you is welcome to check my credentials. I carry a copy of my orders signed by his hand, as well as my appointment to the post of King's Envoy.

"I am an Artesan of Master-elite rank, and these skills have also been proven in King Elias' service. I hereby lay them at his

Majesty's disposal. Test them if you will. If that is not sufficient, gentlemen, and you require more of me, then I am more than willing to prove my skills with a sword against any you care to name. Even you, General Kryp. I wonder—when was the last time you used your sword in the field?"

This last acerbic comment brought the General surging to his feet. He spluttered with outrage, his face flushing. The Hierarch removed the hand he had been using to cover a small smile and rapped it sharply on the table to get Kryp's attention. Sullyan neither moved nor dropped her eyes, showing not the slightest sign of backing down in the face of Kryp's anger.

"General!" snapped Pharikian. Kryp struggled to bring himself under control. Vanyr's face was thunderous and Ephan rolled his eyes, but Lord General Anjer leaned back in his seat with his arms crossed over his massive chest. He regarded Sullyan with what might have been respect awakening behind his jet black eyes.

Once Kryp, still muttering, had resumed his seat, the Hierarch glanced at Sullyan. "Major, I am sure General Kryp meant no offence. I believe you owe him an apology."

She meekly bowed her head. "General Kryp, if you perceived my comment as a slur on your abilities, then I apologize unreservedly. It was not intended as such. I am sure you set the men of your command a splendid example."

The Hierarch again used his hand to cover a smile, and Sullyan thought she saw Anjer's mouth twitch under his black mustache. The furious Kryp wasn't pacified by her barbed apology, but had no opportunity to respond.

The Hierarch continued. "It may interest you to know, gentlemen, that I have already done as the Major suggested. Not only have I seen the documents she spoke of, but I have also conferred by messenger with her King. As you know, I have always had the greatest respect for Elias of Albia, and he has confirmed everything the Major told us. Major Sullyan, you should know that I also contacted your General Blaine. He spoke glowingly of your capabilities and bade me make full use of your unique talents."

"I thank you, Majesty." A faint flush stained her cheeks. This was unaccustomed praise from General Blaine.

Ephan stirred in his seat, adding, almost reluctantly, "I too have heard reports of the Major's prowess, Kryp. Unlikely though it sounds, I believe she has told us no less than the truth."

Sullyan was amazed that Ephan should support her and turned an evaluating look on him. Kryp remained unconvinced and brushed their comments aside.

"That's all very well, Majesty. She may have some standing among the Albians. We all know how weak their warriors are. But it doesn't answer the question of how she has come by information concerning so powerful and ambitious a man as Rykan of Kymer. Why would he tell her his battle plans and then allow her to inform you of them?" His eyes narrowed and he shot her a venomous glance. "Unless it's a trap, of course."

Robin's angry gasp was clearly audible, as was the harsh scrape of his chair as he rose. "A trap? You think she'd work for Rykan? After all she's been through? After all his—"

"Robin!"

Sullyan's reprimand came out sharper than she intended but she had to stop Robin revealing too much. The anguished glance he shot her and the sudden pallor of his face showed he realized how near he had come. Slowly, he resumed his seat, color flooding back to his cheeks.

The Hierarch ignored Robin's outburst as if it hadn't happened. "There's no need for accusations, Kryp. I'm sure the Major can satisfy your doubts."

He gave her a look of regret for his inability to help her

further. Sullyan accepted his tacit apology and turned to face Kryp.

"It is no trap, General Kryp. My information is correct, and imparting it to you will seriously damage the Duke. I learned it in the cells of his palace, where he held me confined. It was not his intention that I should survive."

Ephan sucked his teeth and Anjer's brows shot down over his eyes. Vanyr didn't react, although his arch expression suggested disbelief. It was left to Kryp to ask, "And why was he holding you captive, Major?"

Judging by the way they watched her, both Robin and Pharikian wondered what she would tell them. She took a deep breath. "General, he intended me to be an integral part of his plan to topple Andaryon's ruling House."

"I don't understand."

"He tried to force me to yield my powers, General, in order to augment his own. If he had succeeded, he would have been strong enough to overpower his Majesty, leaving him no choice but to abdicate. Fortunately for me—and for you—I was rescued before it could happen. But not before his arrogance and confidence, and my weakened state, led him to boast of his plans in my hearing. This, gentlemen, is the reason why he has waited so long before bringing his troops to bear. He was cheated of his primary weapon—my powers—and was forced to rethink his strategy."

This caused a buzz of concerned conversation. Wondering if she would get away with her gloss over the whole truth, Sullyan was waiting for someone to ask the obvious; namely, how had Rykan tried to force her to yield. Instead, Vanyr spoke up.

"Would the ... Major ... then care to explain why she has brought this news to us? As the Duke didn't succeed in taking her powers, he can't challenge the Hierarch's Artesan skills. And as General Ephan has already pointed out, neither can he field sufficient trained numbers to trouble the Caer. The forces he can raise from Kymer are not nearly enough to defeat us. So why bother his Majesty with such trivial matters? Have you come to complain of the Duke's behavior, girl? To demand redress? If so, you'll be disappointed. Why should we care if Rykan takes Albian captives? It's hardly a crime, and it wouldn't be the first time."

Vanyr's discourtesy and vicious tone caused the Hierarch to frown in displeasure. Sullyan had been expecting something of the sort from either Vanyr or Kryp, and the Commander's scornful comments at least diverted attention from what she would rather keep hidden.

"Commander, I have 'bothered' his Majesty because if Rykan does succeed in his challenge, either now or sometime in the future, he intends to rescind the Pact and resume full-scale raiding into Albia. That is very much my concern, as I think you would all agree."

Anjer nodded once. Ephan then raised his voice, having gained Pharikian's attention.

"Majesty, interesting as this is, I don't see how it affects our traditional response to a force the size of Rykan's. Commander Vanyr is correct. The Duke cannot match our numbers, and sitting tight is still our best option. Let him spend his men on the Citadel walls. His best force of five or six thousand would never break us in siege."

Planting her hands very deliberately on the table, Sullyan leaned forward. Her menacing stance surprised Ephan and made him turn his head.

"Maybe not, General. But a force of fifteen thousand might."

There was a slight pause before the room erupted. Ephan, Kryp, and Vanyr all rose their feet, shouting. Kryp's face was an angry shade of red, Vanyr's pale with fury. His voice was sharp with disdain. Anjer sat in silence, arms still folded on his massive chest, eyes flicking alternately from Sullyan's calm expression to the Hierarch's. He clearly deserved his post at the head of his ruler's forces, thought Sullyan, a shrewd man who considered his options, not scorning any information which might help him protect the Caer.

The Hierarch raised his hand for silence, but it was a few moments before they noticed. Subsiding angrily, they resumed their seats. Pharikian turned to Sullyan.

"Major, are you certain of your facts?"

"Completely, Majesty."

Before she could continue, Kryp interrupted. "It's ridiculous, there's no possible way Rykan could field so many men! This must be some kind of trick. And if it's not, if she's right, where have the extra numbers come from?"

Once again, the Hierarch deferred to Sullyan, and she saw Anjer take note.

"From the boasts he made, it would seem that the Duke has been covertly annexing land for the past few years. Two minor nobles were relieved of their holdings on the pretext of bad management. I do not know their names, but they are almost certainly dead. Three other lords lost their provinces. Two were infirm and unable to defend against the Duke. They have either been bribed or coerced to join his cause. The third he murdered. My estimation of his strength is probably conservative. In all, he may be able to field more than fifteen thousand." She glanced at Anjer. "My Lord General, what is the sum of the forces loyal to his Majesty?"

Anjer considered this and glanced briefly at Pharikian before replying.

"The Caer retains eight thousand fighting men, Major. If we were to call in all our available reserves, we could match your estimation of Rykan's numbers."

She held his gaze. "Then given your previous expectation of

Rykan's strength, my Lord, how quickly could those reserve troops arrive? How many lords keep such numbers ready to march?"

Anjer's eyes narrowed and she didn't press him. Instead, she swept her eyes around the table.

"So, gentlemen, the last thing you want is to allow a superior force to pin you inside the Caer. That would give Rykan control, and that would spell your defeat. He will not risk coming under attack from your reserves, and neither does he intend to starve you out under a protracted siege."

She paused, capturing their attention. The Hierarch knew what was coming but was caught up in her compelling gaze. Even Robin, who had seen her dominate a room like this before, sat in awe.

She stepped back from the table, drawing their eyes.

"Instead, he will challenge his Majesty to single combat."

Chapter Sixteen

This time they all rose to their feet with angry shouts. Anjer's black eyes were blazing. Sullyan remained still while the wave of their ire washed over her.

Unable to gain silence by raising his voice, the Hierarch gestured at Gaslek. The fussy little man seemed stunned by the noise and Pharikian had to dig him in the ribs to gain his attention. Startled back to awareness, the Baron slapped the table with his hand. Silence fell, and they all sat slowly, the atmosphere charged with indignation. Four pairs of eyes glowered at Sullyan.

Eventually mastering his temper, Lord General Anjer spoke, his tone once more patronizing.

"Major Sullyan, what you've suggested is impossible and shows your ignorance of our customs. The Codes preclude anyone from challenging the Supreme Ruler to single combat. Rykan knows this, so the whole idea is ludicrous."

She regarded him steadily. "You are correct, of course, Lord General. His Majesty is not personally bound to accept a challenge of single combat. But if you consult your ancient records and Codes, I believe you will find that if a formal challenger gains a controlling position and challenges the Supreme Ruler upon a field of combat, then the Crown is obliged to appoint a Champion to fight on its behalf."

Anjer stilled. He stared at her and then the Hierarch, who sat contemplating the table over steepled fingers.

"Is this correct, Majesty?"

The Hierarch glanced up as if only now registering the debate.

"Oh yes, Anjer. The Major mentioned it to me earlier and I had Gaslek check it. It goes right back to our oldest records. I was aware of it before, but it has never been used to my knowledge, so it had slipped my mind."

Kryp's face was purple with anger. "Then how does she come to know of it?"

Sullyan regarded him with hooded eyes. "It pleased Rykan to taunt me with it, General. I thought it worthy of verification."

Kryp subsided, still muttering. While he had been venting spleen, however, Anjer had been thinking. "If such a thing were to happen, Majesty, who would you appoint as your Champion?"

The Hierarch turned his yellow gaze on Anjer. Massive and muscular though he was, the man was in his mid-forties and past the flush of his prime. As the Hierarch's deputy on the field and overall commander of his forces, Anjer was the obvious choice. Before he could speak to accept or refuse, Sullyan raised her voice.

"Majesty, gentlemen, a word of caution, if I may. Be aware that whoever is chosen must be a match for Lord Rykan on more than a physical level."

Anjer swung round on her. "What do you mean?"

"I mean, Lord General, that if the Duke of Kymer gains a controlling position, then the method of combat is his choice by right. But the choice is not made until the Champion is declared, and it is by no means guaranteed that Rykan would choose the sword. Even if he did, his ambition is so great that I would not place any faith in him standing by that choice, Witnessed or not. None of his faction would dare protest if he broke the Codes, and if he emerged victorious, then no one on his Majesty's side would live to tell the tale.

"So, my Lords, the question should be who among you is a match for his metaphysical prowess?"

That silenced them. From her earlier interview with the Hierarch, Sullyan was aware that Anjer, the most powerful of Pharikian's generals, was a Master Artesan. The other two were a rank lower at Adept-elite, and Vanyr was only a Journeyman. She watched the play of emotion across their faces as they considered her words. She was sure of Anjer and Ephan now. However reluctantly, both recognized and accepted her rank and experience. Kryp was entirely prejudiced but would ultimately follow the Lord General's orders. Vanyr was the only one who might obstruct her if he felt he could do so without incurring his superiors' wrath. He would bear watching.

She waited them out, as did Pharikian. They had discussed some of this prior to the meeting, and he had given her some idea as to how each was likely to react. Still, she wondered how they would take the next phase of the plan. Not even Pharikian would bet against Rykan somehow utilizing his superior metaphysical powers to win a sword fight. The Champion had to be someone who could match Rykan's powerful Artesan skills.

As Pharikian had predicted, Anjer reacted first.

"So, Major, what would you suggest?" His voice lacked any trace of its former condescension.

"As you do not have the numbers to defeat Lord Rykan outright, you must employ some subtlety, my Lord. He has no idea of my whereabouts and is unaware that I survived his brutality. Indeed, I was fortunate to do so. He will be expecting what you first proposed, that you will be confident of your security and will retreat into the Citadel. You must allow him to believe that this is the case while preventing him from consolidating his position and besieging the Caer. You should not, under any circumstances, reveal your knowledge of his true strength.

"He will wish to conceal his numbers until he is ready to surround you, so he has no option but to approach through the forests. You can use this to your advantage. Send out small mounted units to harry and scatter his forces. Isolate pockets of his men. Many of his troops are recent acquisitions. Given the chance, their leaders might even slip back to their own lands, hoping Rykan will suffer defeat. Considering the size of his forces and the absence of his Majesty's reserves, it is highly unlikely that you can beat the Duke in open battle. Not without severely depleting the Hierarch's resources, which would leave him vulnerable to anyone with similar aspirations. So, if you are to avoid such a bloodbath and adhere to the Codes, yet still remove the Duke's threat to both Andaryon and Albia alike, you must hold Rykan to a stalemate, force him to retract. This will put his Majesty in the controlling position. He can then issue his own challenge to single combat."

This statement brought another flurry of angry objections. Content to go along with the first part of her plan, Anjer now grew irate.

"You're not making any sense, Major! You know very well that his Majesty cannot involve himself in single combat. You said as much yourself. And in order to make a challenge of his own, he must still appoint a Champion who can stand against the Duke. As you also pointed out, we have no one suitable. You're talking in circles, girl!"

He turned his face away and the others added their agreement, Kryp being loudest in support.

Softly, Sullyan said, "Lord General?"

He turned back, a retort on his lips. When he saw her slight smile, he frowned.

"With the greatest respect, my Lord, you have missed the point. If Rykan makes the challenge, he has the right not only to choose the method of combat, but he also has a measure of veto over his opponent. Yet if his Majesty holds the controlling position, then the Duke would be forced to accept the Crown's choice."

"So?" Anjer threw his hands in the air. "What use is that if there's no one qualified to face him?"

"Ah, but there is."

His black eyes narrowed, then suddenly widened. Sullyan swept the assembled men with her gaze.

"My Lords, my skill with the sword is sufficient to match Lord Rykan in a duel, as are my metaphysical powers. I will be his Majesty's Champion."

The stunned silence was profound. They stared at her while she stood at ease, her hands clasped behind her back. She could sense Robin's amazement and realized that even he hadn't seen this coming. To cover his lack of intuition, he was studying the generals' faces. In order to gauge their reactions, she did the same.

Despite his obvious opposition to the very thought of it, Anjer was going over the plan for flaws. He leaned back in his chair, arms on the table, one hand tapping absently on the wood. There was more speculation and respect in his eyes than anyone else's.

General Ephan was also chewing over what he had heard, no doubt recalling what he knew of her reputation. His eyes remained unfocused, but his expression held no censure. He sat forward in his chair, elbows on the arms, hands clasped beneath his chin.

Opposite Ephan, General Kryp stared at Sullyan with open hostility. His paunch heaved with every indignant breath and she waited for his outburst. Commander Vanyr's face was stony and sullen, but it seemed he was willing to let Kryp do his objecting for him.

After a few more moments of silence, the Hierarch stirred, collecting their attention.

"Anjer?"

The Lord General straightened. "Majesty, I will not ask if the Major's offer is acceptable to you. The fact that she bears your colors answers that. And she is right, we have no one qualified to face the Duke in combat. Only one of us here has first-hand experience of his skill, and I doubt that man would want to repeat it."

He paused, and the Hierarch inclined his head. Sullyan would have given much to know who Anjer was referring to. None of them gave it away, though, and despite his impersonal phrasing, she strongly suspected it was Anjer himself, or maybe the Hierarch.

"All I ask is this. Do you have any proof—beside the word of her King and General, who might be biased—that her combat skills are as great as she claims? Leaving aside what Ephan has heard, she is still a woman, and Rykan is reputedly the best swordsman in our realm."

"Well said, Anjer," snapped Kryp. "The very idea's preposterous."

Anjer's eyes betrayed annoyance at Kryp's derisory tone. He ignored the man and turned to Sullyan.

"Forgive my skepticism, Major, but if we were to accept your claim and your offer, then our lives, our ruler's life, and the fate of our realm would ultimately rest on your shoulders. And I think you will agree," he gave a small smile, "they are not very broad shoulders."

This drew a vast snort from Kryp. Sullyan spared him one piercing glance before turning back to Anjer. Aware that he was humoring her, she kept her tone neutral.

"My Lord, you are right to be cautious, and I concede that I am untried in your eyes. I do not wonder that you doubt me, considering the status of women in this realm."

Both Kryp and Vanyr bridled, and even Ephan frowned. She swept on.

"Therefore, my Lords, Majesty, I ask that you give me a

command. I am more than happy to prove my abilities in the field."

Kryp leaped his feet, joined this time by Vanyr. The General's grating voice was indignant with anger.

"That's a monstrous idea, quite disgusting! She's a woman, a girl! Whoever heard of such a travesty? It might be acceptable in Albia where they're scarcely even intelligent, let alone civilized, but here? Really, Majesty, I must protest!"

Pharikian eyed him. "Must you, Kryp? Exactly what are you objecting to? I grant you she's a young woman, but she is also a Major, a leader of men. Do you think her own command would follow her if she couldn't do as she claims? She's won an impressive array of battle honors, almost as many as you! Don't you think that trial on the field of combat is an excellent way to gauge the skill and success of a military leader, whatever their age or gender? Or are you perhaps afraid that the Major might prove to be more skilled in her command than you are in yours?"

The barb shot home. Shaken by this personal attack on top of Sullyan's earlier comment, Kryp gaped like a snared rabbit. Deflated, he sat. Pharikian stared at him in distaste. Ephan remained silent, keeping his thoughts to himself, but Anjer was more practical. Eyeing Sullyan, he said, "I have no sound reason to object to the Major's request. However, finding men prepared to follow her might be a problem."

Vanyr raised a hand. "Perhaps I might make a suggestion, Majesty?"

His diffident tone didn't fool Sullyan and her eyes narrowed. This was what she had been waiting for. The Hierarch gestured for Vanyr to speak on, and the Lord General raised his brows.

Vanyr smiled. "Give her Ky-shan."

Anjer rolled his eyes and Ephan looked as though he might protest. Kryp, however, beamed and clapped Vanyr soundly on the back.

"An excellent suggestion, Commander! I, for one, would be happy to accept the Major as his Majesty's Champion if she proves her skills by leading Ky-shan's men."

Ephan stirred. "Majesty ...."

"Ky-shan?" Sullyan's musing tone interrupted him. "A man from the eastern seaboard, by his name. And a pirate, unless I am mistaken."

Kryp's smirk disappeared and Vanyr scowled. Ephan's protest died on his lips, but his mouth stayed open. Anjer relaxed back into his chair once more, arms folded across his chest.

Kryp leaned forward, his wheezy voice rising with astonishment. "How on earth did you know that, girl?"

"I travelled extensively through Andaryon in my youth, General. I sailed the eastern seas once or twice."

The phrase 'in my youth' made Kryp's eyes bulge. Sullyan saw Robin close his own mouth. This was a tale even he hadn't heard before. She turned once more to Anjer.

"I would appreciate a little more information, Lord General, if you please."

Caught out in his enjoyment of Kryp's discomfiture, Anjer rallied quickly. "You seem remarkably well-informed already, Major."

She didn't react to the compliment, merely waited for his explanation.

"Well, you're correct. Ky-shan is the leader of a band of men hailing from the eastern seaboard. I think he might object to the term 'pirate', though. Free traders, I believe they call themselves. Technically, eastern seaboarders come under his Majesty's direct rule, but in practice they take little notice of the affairs of land-dwellers. Our recruiting officers went to the area, as they often do in search of suitable fighting men, and Ky-shan's band was attracted by the pay, the general amnesty, and the promise of bounty should Rykan be defeated. Such men are often skilled and ferocious fighters, but they are little used to fighting on land. This particular group has proved difficult to handle and unreliable as regards following orders. They have had several commanders already, yet none have been willing to take them into battle."

He paused, glancing pointedly at Vanyr. "Torman, weren't you their last commander?"

The white-eyed man shot Sullyan an evil look. "I was indeed, Lord General. Ky-shan is a conscienceless rogue who respects no one and follows no discipline but his own. My own men distrusted him and refused to take the field with his band."

"Yet you think they're a suitable command for the Major?"

At the Hierarch's interruption, Vanyr paled, realizing he had gone too far. "I only suggested them, Majesty, as all the other units are settled. Ky-shan's band is the only one without an officer. What better way for the Major to prove herself than with such an untried company? As my Lord General has so rightly pointed out, it would be impossible to convince an established force to follow her."

Pharikian's lip curled. "That was your reasoning, was it?"

To forestall any further unpleasantness, Sullyan turned back to Anjer. "My Lord, how many men does Ky-shan have?"

"Around sixty, Major."

"A discreet yet useful number. Are any of them Artesans?"

Anjer gestured to Vanyr, who answered sullenly. "Ky-shan and his son both have some power, but they are raw and untrained. Hardly surprising, as such ruffians set no store by discipline."

She raised her brows but made no reply. "Are they well-armed and mounted?"

Anjer frowned. "You sound as if you're considering taking them on, Major."

"In the absence of any other suitable candidates, Lord General,

I believe I am."

Vanyr exchanged a smug look with Kryp, and Sullyan also caught a glimpse of Robin's concerned expression. He wouldn't be feeling confident about this band of 'free traders' and she had to admit they sounded like a handful. However, he would back her in whatever she decided.

Anjer shrugged. "They have what they came with, Major. I imagine they are armed well enough, but as to the rest, you will have to see for yourself."

"May I have your authority to requisition what I might need, my Lord?"

Anjer twitched a hand at Gaslek, who hastily wrote on a parchment. "You will have my authority, Major." Gaslek passed him the parchment, which he signed with a flourish. He pressed his ring to the wax Gaslek dripped on it, and then the secretary came around the table to hand the parchment over. Sullyan scanned it quickly before laying it on the table to dry.

"I thank you, my Lord. I have one more question. Where are they quartered?"

Ephan answered. "They have a compound in the northern quarter, Major. I will have someone show you the way."

"I appreciate the offer, General, but it will not be necessary. The Captain and I will find them."

Ephan shrugged.

Satisfied with the outcome of the meeting, Sullyan bowed. She was about to retreat to her seat next to Robin when the Hierarch motioned for her to take one of the chairs at the oval table. Humbled by the honor, she took the chair directly opposite him, deliberately placing herself in the lowest position. This wasn't lost on either Pharikian or Anjer. She then gestured for Robin to come and stand behind her, which earned her a hard stare from Kryp. She chose to ignore it.

Anjer spared her one last glance before turning back to his commanders. "Very well, gentlemen, I propose we adopt the Major's strategy. Ephan, Kryp, I want to see you both in my office in one hour with full details of your companies' strengths. I want suggestions as to which units will carry out strikes on Rykan's column with the aim of distracting and splitting his men."

Sullyan sat in silence, observing the play of emotion across the warleaders' faces as Anjer outlined her strategy. Now and then she crossed glances with Kryp and Vanyr which Anjer noticed. While he didn't remark on it, the expression in his eyes was hard.

Sullyan was pleased to learn that she would be reporting to Ephan rather than Kryp. The Hierarch thanked and dismissed them, and the warleaders rose to leave. As they approached the door, Sullyan saw Anjer throw a massive arm across Kryp's heavily padded shoulders. Kryp looked none too pleased by the intimacy. They left the room together, and she stifled a laugh when she heard Anjer say, "So remind me, Kryp, when was the last time you used your sword in the field?"

Vanyr shot her a venomous look as he left, but she affected not to notice, busying herself with folding Anjer's authority and stowing it inside her jacket. Ephan passed behind her on his way to the door, and he was the only one who spoke.

"It seems we'll be seeing more of each other than I thought, Major. I wish you good fortune in your new command."

She flashed him a brief but genuine smile. "I thank you, General. Let us hope for a swift and favorable outcome to this conflict."

"Indeed."

The Hierarch also dismissed Gaslek, and the little secretary hurried after the others. Pharikian remained behind, alone but for his page and the guards by the door. He watched Sullyan quietly for a few moments, studying her face now that the ordeal was over.

She held his regard and he shook his head.

"That was very cleverly done, Brynne. You did well to get Anjer on your side so quickly."

She looked down at her hands, trying to conceal their trembling. She was wearier than she wanted to admit.

"He was not as prejudiced as he might have been, Majesty. You are fortunate to have such a man at the head of your forces. He is not so blinded by tradition that he cannot see or consider new ideas."

"Hmm. Not like Kryp, eh, Brynne? He couldn't see a new idea if it sat on his nose and bit him!" They exchanged smiles. "But he will bear watching, child, as will his protégé, Vanyr. The man hates you, although why he should, I don't know."

She sighed. "I am unnatural in his eyes, Majesty. He sees me as a threat. I outrank him in both military and Artesan skills, and he will never have encountered a woman in such a powerful position before. He is eager to prove that his weapons skills are superior to mine, as they may well be. He looks like a dangerous man."

"You are right, Brynne, he has a notorious and well-deserved reputation. So let me warn you. Don't get trapped into fighting him. Not only is dueling forbidden within my forces, but in wartime it is punishable by death. I can make no exceptions."

"I will remember that, Majesty. Let me assure you, I have no intention whatsoever of dueling with Commander Vanyr." She cast a sly glance at Robin, who colored at her tacit reference to his fight with Parren.

The Hierarch watched the exchange, but said nothing. Suddenly he laughed, causing Sullyan to start.

"Oh, Brynne, you are a dose of spring water, and no mistake! It might have been your father standing there today, playing my generals as he played his harp. It was a joy to watch."

He sobered. "Ah, but you look weary. Go and rest before commencing your duties. I'll send Deshan to you. He tells me he has found something that should strengthen you."

He turned to go, and then paused by the door. "Oh, I nearly forgot. I am hosting a small dinner party tonight, to give us all some relief from this uncertain situation. I would take it as a personal favor if you and your Captain would attend."

She inclined her head. "We would be honored, Majesty. I thank you for your kindness."

Then he surprised her again. "Count Marik will be joining your command in the field. Bring him to dinner too."

Chapter Seventeen

Taran made his way back to his shared quarters, reflecting that this would be a memorable day for Cal if what he was planning went well. He had been working on it ever since their return to the Manor, but Cal had no idea. He smiled. Even Rienne seemed a bit more cheerful this morning, and considering how uncharacteristically listless and preoccupied she had been lately, it was a relief. Being forced to leave Sullyan had hurt Rienne deeply even though Taran and Cal had done everything they could to comfort her. Until today, her sorrow hadn't lifted.

Following Sullyan's request, Rienne had taken charge of the Major's harp and guitar. Entering her abandoned quarters to fetch them had affected the healer profoundly. Taran could see how the memories of the happy evening the two women had spent there brought tears to Rienne's eyes, and Cal had told him that she passed the rest of that day in their sleeping room, just staring at the guitar in her lap. Rienne hadn't touched either instrument since.

Bull hadn't been much help. He was even more melancholy than Rienne. He sat either in his rooms or in Sullyan's silent office with a half-empty glass of firewater by his elbow and a bleary look in his eye. Worried that he was drinking too heavily, Taran had spent some time alone with him. Finally, the big man seemed to have thrown off the worst of his misery.

Since returning from Andaryon, Taran and Cal had spent

much of their time working on their Artesan skills. Now that he had gained Mastery over Water, Taran's next task was to learn how to influence Fire. He would also have to initiate and control Powersinks, whatever rank the other participants held. Cal was working toward Apprentice-elite, which meant strengthening his communication skills and learning how to identify unknown Artesans just by the pattern of their psyche. Taran had been training him hard and was pleased with Cal's progress.

That particular morning Taran had risen early, telling Cal he was going to talk to Bull. The Apprentice would be alone in their suite, as Rienne had resumed her duties in the infirmary. Cal didn't mind, as it was the only activity that could prod her out of her sadness, if only for a while. He told Taran he would spend the morning playing his longwhistle or practicing his Artesan skills. Now, as Taran approached, he could hear the strains of a folk tune coming from the suite. He smiled and pushed open the door, feeling genuine pleasure in the day. Cal looked up from his whistle, his brows rising in query.

"Come on," said Taran, "I told Rienne and Bull we'd meet them in the commons for a bite." He turned without waiting for a reply, leaving Cal to pocket his whistle and follow.

There was a lively hum of conversation in the commons. Since the cessation of Andaryan hostilities, the Manor had become quite crowded. The various companies stationed there took turns at guard duty, exercises, and patrolling the countryside, but there were always two or three units resting. The commons always filled up at mealtimes and was a noisy, friendly place.

As he and Cal entered, Taran could see Bull sitting at his favorite table. The big man was talking to Sullyan's company sergeant, Dexter. Taran and Cal had become acquainted with Dexter during their time fighting the invasion, but over the past few days they had gotten to know him much better. Dexter had quick wits and a cheerful disposition, and was thoroughly enjoying his spell as temporary commander of Sullyan's company. With luck and hard work, he knew it could be his passage to promotion.

The two men had their heads close together, and from what Taran could see Bull was sober. As he and Cal approached, Bull looked up and smiled. Taran nodded with relief. The big man's eyes were clear of the effects of drink. He took the chair Bull pushed toward him, and Dexter shoved one at Cal.

"Tad!" called Bull, over the din of conversation. The young lad sprinted over from the kitchens and took their order. Taran and Cal settled into their chairs, Cal appraising the big man openly.

"You seem more cheerful today, Bull."

Bull grimaced. "I suppose I've not been the best company lately."

Dexter snorted and leaned back in his chair, hands clasped behind his head. "That's a fact! You've been a morose old lush, mate."

Bull lunged forward and swatted his arm. "That's enough of your cheek, my lad. I may be retired, but I could still teach you a thing or two."

Dexter grinned and rubbed his arm.

The commons door opened again and Rienne entered, accompanied by Chief Healer Hanan. The two women had grown close through working together, and Taran was glad Rienne had someone of her own gender to talk to. They parted at the door and Rienne came over. She looked tired and careworn, her grey eyes clouded, her long hair dull. She rarely smiled these days, which wasn't like her, and Taran was pleased to see her face lighten when Bull got to his feet and kissed her cheek.

"You look better, Bull."

He ducked his head. "Yes, I know I've been hitting the bottle a little too hard recently."

She smiled. "You're not the only one."

Tad and two other boys arrived, deftly balancing plates of food, and Rienne spared the youngster a grin. They had all grown fond of the eager lad who never missed an opportunity to ask for news. Everyone knew he meant news of Robin, and Cal had remarked early on that the young lad had a terminal case of hero worship.

Now Tad hung back when the other lads returned to the kitchen, hopeful eyes fixed on Bull. The big man took a forkful of meat and chewed appreciatively. He looked round at the others, catching their attention.

"I've had some news."

They all stopped mid-chew and Rienne dropped her eating knife. "It's alright," he added hastily, "it's not bad news."

Rienne retrieved her knife with a hand that shook, and Bull continued. "I finally sobered up enough to receive a message from Robin this morning."

Rienne stared at him, her heart in her eyes. "How is she?"

"She's fine … well, as fine as she can be. Listen, I'm going to tell you all an incredible tale. You might find it hard to believe. I know I did. Robin assures me it's true, though, and it might just give us some hope."

Eyes wide, Rienne urged Bull to continue. While they ate, he related everything Robin had told him about the journey to Caer Vellet, their reception at the Citadel, and Sullyan's subsequent collapse. When he reached this part, Rienne's face went pale. "I thought you said it wasn't bad news!"

He patted her hand. "Wait till you hear the rest." He went on to tell them what the Hierarch had revealed about Sullyan's parents.

Taran was stunned. "That's incredible. She can really claim kinship with the Hierarch?"

"It seems so, although it's more of a blood bond than true kinship."

Rienne's face relaxed as she took in Bull's words. "Brynne," she murmured, trying the sound of it. "It's an unusual name. I don't think I've ever heard it before. I have to say it suits her."

Bull grinned. "Knowing Sully, she won't know what to do with it. She's lived with just one name for so long it'll take some getting used to."

She nodded. "What did you mean about giving us some hope?"

He leaned forward and lowered his voice. "According to Robin, the Hierarch says that it's possible for Rykan to remove the poison from Sullyan's body, undo the damage it's done. His power put it there, so his power can remove it."

Rienne gasped and Bull held up his hand. "He has to do it of his own free will, though. He can't be coerced."

She slumped, her optimism dashed. "What kind of hope is that, Bull? There's no way he'll do it."

He shrugged. "I agree, it looks unlikely. But would any of us ever have thought she would end up related to the Hierarch or find out about her parents? Come on, Rienne, there's a bit of hope here, surely?"

She gave a wan smile.

Taran thought it was time to change the subject. "Bull, have you thought any more about what we discussed a couple of days ago?"

"Going back, you mean? I'm still thinking about it. I didn't mention it to Robin when we spoke. I think we should wait a little longer and see how things turn out. Now that Robin is reporting more often—or will do if I remain sober—we can monitor the situation and make a decision when we know more."

Tad went back to the kitchens, and they finished their food, relaxing with cups of fellan and mulling over what they had heard. Dexter left them to attend to his duties, and slowly the commons emptied. Taran saw Cal glance at Rienne, expecting her to return to the infirmary, but she let Hanan leave without her. A subdued air of expectancy hung about the place.

Taran scraped back his chair. "Come on, Cal, I feel like doing some work. Let's go into the arena. It's not too cold out there yet."

Bull stood too. "I might come with you. I could do with a workout myself. Get some of that firewater out of my system."

Rienne shot him a sideways look. "It's about time."

He grinned sheepishly and threw an arm about her shoulders. Cal merely smiled, no longer threatened by Bull's protective behavior toward Rienne.

They collected their cloaks, for despite Taran's words it was frosty outdoors, and made their way to the arena. Some men from the Major's company were already there, and Cal looked surprised. Taran hid a smile. He and Cal were on nodding terms with most of these men since the invasion, but they had rarely seen so many training in one place at the same time. A few gave them friendly waves. Even Dexter was there, talking to one of his corporals.

Taran found a free space for them to work in. The regular swordsmen, accustomed to Artesans, knew to keep well away, and Taran soon had his Apprentice building portways by himself, anchoring them, and then dismantling them. Once he had done a few to Taran's satisfaction, he moved on to shielding. He was fast becoming strong and proficient.

Taran was impressed. Cal was working well, totally engrossed in what he was doing. He told Cal to go over his psyche, looking for weak spots and strengthening them. The younger man was concentrating so hard that he didn't notice General Blaine's arrival. The man walked quietly to the benches, sat down, and nodded to Taran. Had Cal seen him, he would have been amazed by the swordsmen's lack of response to their highest-ranking officer. He might even have realized they had been expecting him.

Taran ended their session by having Cal compare his psyche with Taran's. He asked him to identify the differences between them, and point out where Taran's was stronger. Again using his Apprentice's distraction, Taran glanced at General Blaine. He noted Cal's puzzlement as another glowing pattern suddenly insinuated itself into his consciousness. The younger man frowned at Taran, but he only gazed back in silence. Understanding grew in Cal's eyes and he grinned. The swordsmen around them had ceased their sparring, and both Bull and Rienne wore smiles.

Taran planted himself squarely before Cal, arms folded across his chest. "Apprentice Tyler, are you feeling strong today?"

He sensed the thrill that ran through Cal as he recognized the ritual phrasing. The young man's grin widened. "Yes, Adept Elijah, I am feeling strong today."

"Then your final test before becoming Apprentice-elite is to identify the Artesan behind this pattern."

Cal paused. This wasn't as simple as it sounded. He knew there were only a few Artesans at the Manor, but it didn't follow that this complex and subtly glowing pattern belonged to someone he knew. It could be someone from Taran's past. It could be someone Bull had once known. It certainly wasn't anyone Cal recognized.

Taran watched as Cal set to work, sensed him examining the pattern's component parts, getting glimpses of its owner through its characteristics. He knew Cal would think it might belong to Rienne, for although she was an empath rather than a full Artesan, she still had a pattern of psyche. On his first pass through it, though, Cal realized its owner was male, and silently Taran applauded his skill. Gradually, Cal built his picture. Male, middle-aged, maybe a touch older. Fairly powerful, Master-level at least.

He smiled as the Apprentice suddenly caught an echo of infrequent use and saw him snatch at the clue. After one more pass Cal was convinced. He grinned at Taran, and reaching out to the person behind the glowing pattern, touched the mind it belonged to. They both felt the congratulatory response.

General Blaine dampened his psyche, came over to Cal, and clapped him on the shoulder. "Well done, Apprentice-elite."

It was the first normal smile Taran had ever seen the General display. Cal managed a hasty "Thank you, sir" before the men in the arena surged around him, all wanting to slap his back in congratulation.

Blaine turned to Taran. "Well done to you also, Adept. You've done a good job with him."

Taran inclined his head. "It was the Major who showed me what to do, sir. She really deserves the credit for this."

The General's face clouded and he turned abruptly to Bull. "I believe you have some news for me?"

"Yes sir. I heard from Captain Tamsen earlier today …."

The two moved off together, and Taran stared after them, contemplating the change in the General's demeanor. Then Rienne came over, put her arms around him, and leaned her head on his shoulder.

"Thank you, Taran. This means a lot to Cal, and to me. I wish I could feel happy for him, but I seem to have forgotten how."

Taran's heart lurched. "I know what you mean. I wish there was more we could do."

"So do I," she murmured. Releasing him, she stared at the throng surrounding Cal. "So do I."

⁜ ⁜ ⁜ ⁜ ⁜

Sullyan and Robin made their way back to their suite. Once he was sure no one could overhear him, Robin asked, "How on earth did you know this Ky-shan was a pirate? I've never even heard you mention the eastern seaboard, let alone anything about sailing."

She gave him a straight look, but there was a sparkle in her eyes. "Lucky guess, Robin." He hissed in shock and she shook her head. "No, you misunderstand. What I told them was true. I have been to the eastern seaboard and I did spend time aboard a vessel whose captain and crew turned out to be free traders. It was Ky-shan's 'profession' I guessed at. The style of his name gave it away. It abounds among sailors in that region. Besides, the man is obviously someone who has given much trouble. Vanyr would not have suggested him otherwise. That told me he was not just a minor noble, but someone with his own authority. There was only one obvious possibility left, so it was not really much of a guess."

Robin didn't look convinced. "But if he's given so much trouble, why are you so keen to take him on?"

She sighed. "'Keen' is not the word I would have chosen. I knew I would not be given much choice, and I would rather accept a command of my own free will than have one forced upon me. And there is another factor here, something Vanyr probably does not know, which might make all the difference."

He waited but she didn't continue. "Well? What is it?"

She grinned. "Unlike the rest of this bigoted realm, it is not unusual on the eastern seaboard to find women working alongside men. Sailors, particularly legitimate traders, often spend many months at sea, and some take their women with them. It seems that easterners are more practical than these western types and can appreciate a woman's merits."

Robin's troubled expression cleared and Sullyan lifted a warning hand. "Do not assume that this will make them easy to sway, Captain. It is still rare to find a woman in a position of authority, and this Ky-shan is obviously a man full of his own importance. We must be very careful. I may have to resort to a dangerous tactic in order to convince him."

"What do you mean? What tactic?"

She refused to enlighten him and continued toward their suite. On reaching Marik's rooms, she stopped to inform the Count of the meeting's outcome and to extend the Hierarch's invitation. He was pleased to learn that he would be included in her new command but was terrified of attending the dinner-party. She was aware that most of the Hierarch's court regarded him as an enemy, even a traitor, so she could understand his nervousness. She said casually over her shoulder, "You just have to convince them of your loyalty, Ty."

Marik didn't say a word, and her apparent indifference gained her a sharp glance from Robin. She ignored him and returned to their suite, where she stripped off her dress uniform and indulged in a relaxing bath. At one point she heard Robin answer a knock at their door, and soon he appeared in the pool room, bearing a covered jug.

"Deshan left this for you. He said to drink it all—he'll send more later."

She grimaced. The drink was bound to taste foul. Healers seemed incapable of making their potions taste pleasant. However, when she emerged from the pool room and tasted the brew, she discovered that it was actually quite refreshing.

There was some food on a tray by the settle, and once they had eaten, Robin clearly expected her to rest until the dinner engagement. Sullyan had other plans. She pulled on her combat leathers and Robin frowned, watching her attach the Hierarch's rank-badge to those she already wore.

"Where are we going now?"

She looked up. "To see Ky-shan, of course." At his worried expression she pursed her lips. "Oh, you thought I would rest on my achievements today, did you? Well, may I remind you that this realm is at war and we came here to ensure that Rykan does not win? I intend to take the field tomorrow, so we have no time to waste. Does that not suit you, Captain? Would you rather spend your time relaxing here? You only have to say the word."

His surprise turned to chagrin and he held up his hands. They were back on a military footing, their old working relationship re-established. Knowing she needed his wholehearted support, he replied briskly.

"Of course not, Major, I'll be ready when you are. You can rely on me."

Her smile warmed him. "I know I can."

Half an hour later, they were walking through the snowy streets of the lower town, heading for the northern quarter. Alone, dressed in combat leathers and cloaks trimmed with the Hierarch's purple, they attracted much less attention than when they had arrived three days earlier. Her weatherproof cloak concealed Sullyan's gender and also hid her sword. She was on surer ground now that she had a clear purpose. The potion Deshan had brought her had certainly improved her vitality, and she moved with her usual grace, her gaze missing nothing.

Although they saw no one they knew on their journey, they found Ky-shan's compound easily enough. Sullyan stopped and took in the scene. The pirate band might not be officially captive, but their freedom was certainly being restricted. There were large numbers of Velletian Guard drilling conspicuously nearby, and Sullyan noted their presence grimly. Taking a breath, she strode past them and approached the pirates' courtyard, its entrance guarded by two huge fellows in breeches and greatcoats. Both men carried long pikes and sported thick beards, a rarity among Andaryans, who mostly went clean shaven. The two were so alike that they had to be twins. At Sullyan's approach they stepped together, barring her way.

She halted before them and flicked back the corner of her

cloak, letting them see she was armed. The two men were clearly puzzled and glanced mutely between her and Robin.

"I am Major Sullyan," she said. "I wish to speak with Ky-shan."

The giants fixed her with identical blank stares and remained silent. Sullyan sensed Robin preparing for trouble, but then another man appeared, strolling through the compound toward them. Medium height and powerfully built, he walked with a sinuous gait. His large, calloused hands were thrust through a thick leather belt, from which hung a heavy sword with a curved tip. Clean shaven except for a thin mustache, his eyes were very blue in his tanned and weathered face. He halted just behind his men and regarded the two Albians down a large, rudder-like nose.

Sullyan immediately gave him her attention, while he studied her with disparaging interest. Robin shifted uneasily and Sullyan was careful to keep her hands away from her sword hilt.

"Ky-shan," she said pleasantly. "How blow the winds across the Triple Sea?"

The man called Ky-shan frowned. When he opened his mouth to reply, he displayed large and very even, white teeth. His voice was deep and he spoke slowly. "They blow westerly, steady and strong."

She held his gaze. "Then it will be a broad reach over to Tallimore."

From the corner of her eye she caught Robin's bemused look. He had no idea what was going on. Thankfully, the pirate found meaning in her words and turned to the giants by the gate.

"Almid. Kester."

Both men put up their pikes and stood aside. Ky-shan gave a dramatic flourish with his hand, inviting the Albians in. Sullyan inclined her head and stepped past him, into the pirates' compound. Robin followed, shaking his head.

Chapter Eighteen

Men were lounging about the compound in attitudes of boredom and more came strolling out of the buildings on either side. All were strong and swarthy, some darker of skin than others. Their eyes were mainly blue or grey and of a greater intensity than most Andaryans'. They were stocky rather than tall, the two by the entrance being exceptions. Their ages ranged from twenty-five to fifty-five, Ky-shan being one of the oldest. Two were much younger than the rest, younger than either Sullyan or Robin, and one of these, judging by his features, was Ky-shan's son.

The men crowded silently around, surrounding the two Albians. Sullyan felt her Captain grow nervous and took care to hide her own discomfort. Standing confidently at Ky-shan's side, she openly assessed his band. Most of them stared right back at her, but a few wouldn't meet her gaze. Eventually, her eyes came to rest on Ky-shan's son, and she probed his mind delicately. She caught the aura of raw, untrained talent and the promise of strength. The youngster didn't respond and sullenly avoided her gaze. Withdrawing her attention, she turned to face Ky-shan.

He raised his brows. "You wished to speak with me, Lady?"

Hands on hips, she stared pointedly. "I came to see if you and your men have had enough of the easy life, Ky-shan, but by the looks of this lot, they have lost sight of what they came for. Perhaps they are content to laze here in comfort while others do the fighting and collect the bounty? I am disappointed. I thought eastern seaboarders were doughty fighters, but these do not look at all fearsome to me."

There were gasps of outrage, the loudest coming from Ky-shan's son. He took a step forward, his hand on his sword hilt. Ky-shan frowned deeply. Robin's hand strayed to his own sword, and Sullyan could feel his tension. She understood. He had never heard her speak so rudely to a stranger before and had certainly never known her to goad a man so deliberately.

Contempt showed on Ky-shan's face. "We came here to fight, Lady! It's hardly our fault they sent us bilge-bailers instead of officers."

"Ah, I see. Your men are unruly and cannot take orders. Yes, that is what I heard. I did not believe it because I thought the men of the eastern seaboard were disciplined and successful, but it seems I was wrong. I regret disturbing you, Ky-shan. Clearly, I am wasting my time."

She turned on her heel, preparing to stride away, but a shiver of drawn steel brought her up short. She was now facing Robin and saw the frozen look on his face. His voice sounded in her mind.

What on earth are you up to? He's drawn on you!

Trust me, Robin. I know what I am doing.

She spoke without turning. "Any man who draws steel on me had better be prepared to use it."

A metallic snap broke the brief silence as the partly drawn sword was rammed back home. Then Ky-shan snapped, "Pah! I don't fight women."

She turned with a smile on her lips. "You prove at every turn what they say in the barracks. They are right to keep you netted like fish. What is it they call pirates—your pardon, free traders—in the east? Sea wolves, is it? Ha, I think not! Just look at the state of your men, Ky-shan. Sea slugs would be more fitting. No wonder the officers here do not want you." She turned away again.

This time she had gone too far. Ky-shan snarled, drew his great sword, and sprang across her path, leveling his blade at her breast. Abruptly she halted and stared into his eyes, ignoring the dangerously waving sword.

"Well now," she murmured, "what is this? Would you challenge me?"

Despite having most of her attention on Ky-shan, she sensed that Robin was beginning to understand. Despite the Hierarch's express warning about dueling, and her own opinions on the subject, she meant to cross swords with Ky-shan for the right to lead his men. She knew Robin would trust her.

She almost smiled. Unlike the twin giants and Ky-shan's son, all of whom had their hands clenched upon their sword hilts, Robin was showing great restraint. He stood unmoving with his arms folded across his chest, watching the scene before him. His expression was calm. She wanted to hug him. It was at moments like these when she loved him the most.

Ky-shan was anything but restrained. He was roaring.

"Take back your discourteous words, girl. No one speaks to Ky-shan like that! What gives you the right to come in here, offering the traditional words of friendship and then insulting us? You're not even of this realm. You're human! I don't take insults from my own kind, let alone inferior creatures like you!"

His men bellowed their support. Sullyan saw Robin cast an uneasy glance at the soldiers outside the courtyard. They had heard the altercation and were gathering to watch.

"'Inferior creatures'?" she echoed, the sneer never leaving her face. "Is that the best you can do? I have heard better insults from children. If your sword arm is as weak as your wit, Ky-shan, I will have no trouble besting you."

Now the man was dancing with rage, his face suffused with blood. The tip of his sword trembled with the force of his anger.

"You wouldn't stand a chance, girl. I'm the best swordsman in the east! I've killed real fighters twice your height and strength. If you were a man I would make you regret your words."

"Oh, come now, my sex is a poor excuse. But I suppose if you have no stomach for it, then that is an end."

His son surged forward, sword in hand. "I'll fight her, Father!"

Ky-shan slapped the youth away. "Stay out of this, ignorant pup."

The boy subsided, looking sullen, and Ky-shan rounded on Sullyan. "Very well, girl, if you want a fight you can have one. I don't usually bother with the likes of you, but you need to be taught a lesson. You'll learn some manners and respect before I'm finished with you, and then my men can have you. They'll teach you much more than respect, believe me!"

Robin gasped and Sullyan felt her heart clench with fear before she controlled herself. "Very well, Ky-shan, I accept your terms. But I warn you, when I defeat you, I shall demand a forfeit."

"Ha! You can demand whatever the hell you like! If you can defeat me, I'll pay any forfeit you care to name. But when I defeat you, you're ours."

"Agreed. Captain!"

Her voice jolted Robin, who fortunately realized what she wanted, although his voice was a croak.

"Witnessed."

Sullyan removed her cloak and jacket, handing them to Robin. Ky-shan's eyes widened when he saw her rank insignia and battle honors, and wariness showed on his face. He waved his men back to the walls of the compound to make space for the fight. This hid them from the soldiers outside, and Sullyan noticed Robin eyeing the Guardsmen. He would be wondering how long it would be before news of the duel reached the Hierarch. Sullyan could hardly deny inciting Ky-shan. Knowing Robin trusted her, she pushed the thought to the back of her mind, waving him to a position not far from the compound entrance.

As she drew her sword, Ky-shan positioned himself across from her, his heavier blade already balanced in his right hand. Poised on the balls of his feet, he looked angry and dangerous. Sullyan chose a double-handed grip. It wasn't her usual style, but when the pirate attacked with no warning, she was glad she had. She blocked the mighty swipe and let Ky-shan's blade shiver off hers, the two-handed grip giving her stability against his heavier weapon.

He came back at her at once, and she allowed him to make contact with her sword, jumping away without striking back. She would test his skill and strength and let him spend the first flush of his anger. Moving easily around the space, giving ground as necessary, she made him do all the work. Yet he was not without subtlety and soon realized what she was doing. After a few testing passes which she parried cleanly, she saw him begin to re-evaluate her. She gave him her full attention, anticipating the real start to their duel.

The pirate lunged at her and she switched to a single, left-handed grip, parrying his thrust and following up with a lunge of her own. The very tip of her sword parted the sleeve on his right arm and she saw a thin trace of blood follow the blade.

His men saw it too and erupted, roaring their anger. It was only a flesh wound and could hardly have stung, but seeing first blood go to her refueled Ky-shan's rage. He bellowed and pressed her with a flurry of furious strokes. Sullyan parried smoothly, forcing him to circle, trying to tire him out. Where she could, she sidestepped his lunges, letting him spend his strength on empty air, and then followed up with a lightning-fast attack of her own.

Ky-shan's was the stronger weapon, but it was heavier and slower. His thick, meaty fingers weren't as flexible as Sullyan's and his control over his blade not as sure. His was a slashing weapon and his style reflected this, more suited to shipboard skirmishes than the finer art of dueling. Soon he began to tire, his breath coming in gasps. She guessed that her level of expertise had both surprised and infuriated him. Sustaining his anger was sapping his strength. As he fought, he gave a series of grunts and cries, whereas Sullyan fought in silence, only exhaling hard during a particularly vicious cut.

His men were jeering her, yelling encouragement to their leader. Ky-shan altered his tactics and advanced hard on her, attacking with a series of cross-body strokes so powerful they turned his torso from side to side. Each slash was punctuated by a heavy grunt. Sullyan blocked, backing away before him, his men parting to give her room. She was still using a left-handed grip and Ky-shan had the measure of that now, compensating well for the unusual angle of her blade. He was grinning. She moved sideways, parrying awkwardly, sliding away when she could. Ky-shan pursued her relentlessly, pressing home his advantage. His men roared and he swung his sword round to attack her unprotected right side.

Flicking her sword into her other hand, she ducked his violent swing, thrusting swiftly at his completely undefended left flank. Her blade opened a long, bloody cut down his side.

Ky-shan staggered, gasping in pain. As his men swayed forward, yelling their anger, Sullyan pursued him across the courtyard, opening two more superficial cuts before he recovered his balance. Enraged beyond thought now and egged on by his band, Ky-shan chased her back, beating down on her sword, raining blows as fast as he could. He drove her backward on the icy ground where the footing was treacherous, pressing her so fast that suddenly—she went down. With a roar of triumph echoed by his furious men, Ky-shan raised his blade.

"NO!"

As Robin's cry echoed across the courtyard, Sullyan whipped her weapon upward, catching Ky-shan's on the shaft. Shivering up under the hilt, it twisted the heavier sword out of the pirate's hand. The blade flew sideways, ringing across the compound until it came to rest at his stunned son's feet.

The men fell silent, crowding in a tight ring around their leader. Robin surged through them, shoving urgently, but then stopped, dumbfounded.

Sullyan lay on the frozen ground, breathing heavily. Above her, Ky-shan stood immobile, staring down. He too was gasping for breath, perspiring freely. His face was grey with fear, for the tip of Sullyan's weapon rested lightly against the artery inside his right thigh. One tiny thrust from her and the vessel would be severed, ending his life. Ky-shan couldn't afford to move a muscle and Sullyan's sword didn't waver.

She stayed where she was while her breathing slowed. Her eyes never left the pirate's, and his stayed locked on hers. Robin didn't move either, unsure what would happen next. The men around them were intent on the scene, hands clenched into fists. They were, Sullyan knew, one step away from tearing her and Robin to pieces. One word from Ky-shan was all it would take.

Her breath restored, she disengaged her gaze from Ky-shan's. Delicately giving her sword-tip a tiny push, she reminded him how close he had come to death. Then she lowered it, keeping it ready nonetheless. Her left hand was behind her, supporting the weight of her upper body. Now she brought it round and wordlessly held it toward him.

Silence.

Ky-shan's breathing slowed. He was still studying her, and she hoped he could see the respect in her eyes. She had tricked him more than once during their fight, and she knew that if they fought again she wouldn't be able to use the same tactics. She had used his anger, prejudice, and disbelief against him. The cuts she had given him were all designed to heighten his rage while not doing him too much harm. But had she judged him right? Would he recognize what she had done?

His frown deepened and she experienced a pang of doubt. Then he gave a huge snort, took her proffered hand, and hauled her roughly to her feet.

With the tension broken, sound returned. One of his men retrieved Ky-shan's sword and handed it to him. He took it by the blade, sheathing it with a ringing snap. Sullyan wiped her blade clean and did the same. The pirate regarded her, one hand clamped to his bleeding side. She placed her own hands on her hips and returned his speculative gaze.

His voice was rough. "You tricked me, girl."

"You allowed yourself to be tricked."

He snorted. "It wouldn't happen twice!"

"Irrelevant, my friend."

Ky-shan's eyes narrowed. "Very well, you have won your forfeit. What will it be?"

His men muttered and he gestured sharply for silence. They subsided, but Sullyan felt their resentment. She gazed around at the sullen faces before replying.

"The right of command."

They erupted, roaring in protest. Ky-shan shouted them down, wincing as his wound stung. He turned on her, disbelief plain in his eyes. "The right of command? Have you lost your wits?"

She stood her ground. "Do you really so enjoy being cooped up in this compound that you are willing to pass on the chance of gaining respect and battle honors? Think carefully before you reply, my friend, for this is your last chance. You may have his amnesty, but the Hierarch cannot let you return eastward now, not with battle imminent. Nor will he permit you to take part in the fighting without an authorized officer in command. I tell you this, Ky-shan, and hear me well. I am your last hope."

Ky-shan didn't immediately reply, and his expression was pensive. Then he frowned. "If you'd told me this from the first there would have been no need to goad me into fighting you."

She inclined her head. "That may be so, but would I have won your respect? I think not. It was worth the exercise, my friend."

"Exercise? If that was exercise, then I'd hate to see what you call work!"

"Our Witnessed agreement means that you will see exactly what I call work." She held his gaze, repeating, "I claim the right of command over your men."

That provoked another outpouring of dissent, especially from Ky-shan's son. Sullyan, unmoved, assessed the loudest protestors and noted their faces.

Ky-shan glared them into silence. "I gave my Witnessed word and I stand by it! Anyone who disagrees is welcome to take it up with me personally." To emphasize his meaning, he placed his free hand on the hilt of his sword.

Sullyan faced his angry men. "I understand your resentment and I am prepared to make you a bargain."

Ky-shan cut across her. "That isn't necessary, Lady. I agreed to the terms and I will fulfill them. This rabble will obey me, at least!"

She turned back to him, speaking for his ears alone. "Maybe, Ky-shan, but the right of command is not enough. I desire your loyalty, and I know that loyalty must be earned. We are going into battle and will be risking our lives. I will not hazard my safety or my Captain's on a company unwilling to obey me."

She raised her voice. "The bargain, gentlemen, is this. You will afford me your total obedience for the next seven days. Total obedience, mind! If at the end of that time I have failed to gain you success and honor on the battlefield, I will personally guarantee that you will be paid off and allowed to return to your homes with your amnesty intact. There will be no disrespect or dishonor." She paused to let that sink in, noting the discontented mutters.

"You can't seriously expect us to take orders from a woman."

The voice came from the back of the group. Sullyan didn't see who had spoken. Ky-shan was about to reply, but she got there first. "Do you have a wife, friend?"

The voice was grudging. "Yes."

"Then you already do."

It was a gamble, but it paid off. A few sniggers ran round the group and there were no further comments.

"Well?" she prompted. "Do we have a bargain?"

Ky-shan favored his men with a black look, but Sullyan knew she had them. No one would demur. Ky-shan's son certainly wanted to, but he was the only one who might have dared.

Ky-shan lost his patience. "Have you lost your tongues?" he roared.

"We agree," was the multi-throated reply, although some spoke with more conviction than others.

The pirate turned to Sullyan, bowing stiffly. "It seems you have your bargain, Lady."

The men dispersed, drifting off in groups to mutter about the agreement and the validity of Sullyan's victory. As they did so, she heard the soldiers outside the compound being ordered back to their drilling. She thought she caught sight of a venomous smile and the dead, white eyes of Commander Vanyr. Beside her, Robin shivered.

Sullyan ushered the wounded pirate toward one of the doorways leading off the compound. When he protested, she said, "You need my help. It is the least I can do. I gave you the wound, now let me deal with it."

He shrugged and led her to his private quarters. With a barked command, he sent his sullen son running for hot water and cloths. Sullyan helped him remove his sweat-soaked shirt, and then explored the long cut with expert fingers. When the water arrived, she cleaned the wound thoroughly before glancing at the pirate.

"This needs stitching."

"Just bind it. Stitches will pull and I can live without that."

She straightened up. "I can do better, if you will permit."

He didn't understand. Allowing her gaze to rest on him, she slowly dilated her eyes. Untrained as he was, it took him a while to realize her meaning. Then he gasped in comprehension.

"What rank?"

"Master-elite."

His mouth hardened before his expression cleared. Then a strange noise rose in the room and Sullyan smiled. The pirate was chuckling.

"By the Triple Sea, girl, you're full of surprises!" He gasped with pain between snorts of laughter. "You didn't need to use that sword of yours at all, did you? Go on, then. I've had no training, but I don't suppose that'll make any difference to you."

As Sullyan placed her hands gently on the man's muscled chest where the long, red slash gaped, she probed for his psyche. Ky-shan sat still, his eyes wide, while she used his strength as well as her own to stop the bleeding and encourage the flesh to seal. When it was done she eyed her work critically, Ky-shan squinting at the half-healed welt in amazement.

"It will still need binding and treating carefully for a couple of days until the flesh is stronger. But it should hold for now."

He looked up at her, the first glimmer of friendship twinkling in his eye. "My thanks, Lady."

She grinned, watching him accept a fresh shirt from his son

and slide carefully into it. "Now, will your men be ready to take the field tomorrow at first light?"

His head came up in surprise. "Tomorrow?"

"Unless you need a day to rest, of course."

Her innocent smile didn't amuse him. "First light it is!"

"Are your men armed and mounted?"

He turned his head and spat. "We are all well-armed, Lady, have no fear of that. But Vanyr, that misbegotten spawn of a sea snake, requisitioned our horses for his own men."

"Let me take care of that. I will stop by the horse lines and pick good mounts for your men. Be sure to have them ready by dawn, Ky-shan. I do not care to be kept waiting."

She turned to leave and Robin made to follow. Ky-shan caught at his arm and she barely heard his question. "Can she keep her side of that bargain?"

Robin's reply was sure. "The Major never makes promises she can't keep. She won't have to, though, I can assure you. Just make certain your men know the meaning of the word 'obedience'. It holds a special significance in any company under Major Sullyan's command."

The pirate remained silent and Sullyan smiled.

Chapter Nineteen

They were approaching their suite, Sullyan anticipating a cup of hot fellan and a bath before dressing for dinner. The smell of horses clung to her clothing, the result of an unsatisfying but ultimately successful interview with the Hierarch's horse master. The man hadn't known who she was, and it had taken Anjer's note of authority to gain her what she wanted. While there, she had also checked on Drum and Torka, as well as Marik's warhorse.

Intent on her bath, she wasn't happy at being waylaid by a member of the Velletian Guard, especially when the man planted himself stiffly in front of her and performed a barely respectful salute.

She glared at him. "Yes?"

"Your pardon, Lady, but the Lord General requests your presence in his office."

She waited, making him fidget. Finally deciding not to be difficult, she said, "Very well."

As he led the way, she cast a glance over her shoulder at Robin. He aimed a thought at her, showing her Vanyr's expression as he drew his men away from the pirate's compound. Grimly, she threw an image back, showing the vindictive Commander in an uncomfortable and life-threatening situation involving her sword. Robin stifled a snort. He knew how serious this could be.

The guard led them through the Palace to a door which opened into a comfortable and spacious office. The room contrasted starkly with the sparseness of Sullyan's own office back at the Manor, which was never used to impress as this one obviously was. The carpeting was rich and expensive, military banners adorned the walls, and the table was varnished to a high luster. There was gilding everywhere, and the faint scent of polish hung in the air. Sullyan wrinkled her nose.

The guard ushered them inside, announced them, and left.

Lord General Anjer stood at a huge window overlooking the inner Palace courtyard, his hands clasped behind his back. He didn't speak or turn round, and Sullyan and Robin waited before the table in silence. The Major recognized the tactic.

Eventually, Anjer turned and they both accorded him a respectful salute, Robin even remembering the correct style. Anjer smiled faintly before schooling his features, and moved to stand behind the table.

"Major Sullyan."

"My Lord General."

Anjer sat. "I believe you have been to see the pirate, Kyshan?"

"You have been well-informed, my Lord."

Anjer's eyes narrowed. "I have also been informed that you were involved in a duel."

"Have you, my Lord?"

His lips thinned and his voice betrayed tension. "Well, Major? Is it true?"

She couldn't afford to push Anjer's patience too far. Looking him full in the eyes for the first time, she replied firmly. "As dueling in wartime is punishable by death, my Lord, I hardly think so."

"Then what did Commander Vanyr see?"

She permitted understanding to show on her face. "Ah. Commander Vanyr." Her pause made Anjer frown. "What the

Commander saw, my Lord, was a simple training session."

Anjer surged to his feet. "Don't play games with me, Major. I'm not a fool! Training session? With a pirate?"

She held his black gaze. "Ky-shan and I have come to an understanding, my Lord, whereby his men will accept my command. But if you cannot take my honest word on what transpired, perhaps you will take Ky-shan's?" Deliberately, she lowered her eyes.

After a tense pause, Anjer barked for the guard. "Fetch Commander Vanyr. Bring Ky-shan too." As the man left, Anjer pointed a finger at Sullyan. "If I find you've been dueling, Major, then no matter what the outcome, the consequences will be serious. It will reflect very badly on his Majesty, who has placed his trust in you. I presume you realize that?"

"Of course, my Lord."

Anjer subsided into his chair, his expression thunderous. While they waited in silence for those summoned to arrive, he studied her with what seemed to be a mix of exasperation and admiration. Sullyan remained calm and impassive, hoping Anjer was regretting summoning her on Vanyr's say-so.

Soon the guard returned, bringing a self-righteous Vanyr and a bemused but wary Ky-shan. The pirate's wound was invisible to someone who didn't know it was there, and Sullyan's healing meant that he could move freely. She saw Vanyr staring at the pirate, his expression puzzled.

Once the guardsman left, Vanyr snapped a salute. Ky-shan just stood looking from Anjer to Sullyan, who accorded him not one glance. She was radiating ease, but sensed Robin's tension as soon as Vanyr entered the room. She wouldn't give much for the Commander's prospects if Robin ever came across him unarmed.

Anjer stared at Ky-shan, but soon realized he would get no acknowledgement from the pirate. Pursing his lips, he addressed

Vanyr.

"Commander, repeat what you told me you witnessed earlier this afternoon."

Vanyr was only too eager to oblige. "My men had abandoned their exercises near the pirate's compound, sir, and I went to see what had distracted them. The Major had entered the compound and I saw her and this ... this ruffian ... engaged in what was obviously a duel for leadership of his band."

He stopped, smiling smugly.

Anjer heaved a sigh. "Ky-shan, what is your version of events?"

Sullyan heard Robin's uneasy shift. Ky-shan's reply was crucial. She didn't allow herself to react and saw Ky-shan's eyes shift briefly from her own nonchalance to Vanyr's insufferable righteousness. A nasty smile appeared on the pirate's lips and she allowed herself to breathe.

"My Lord, the ... Commander was mistaken. There was no duel to decide who leads my men. I lead my men, as always. But Major Sullyan and I have come to an agreement, and we will take her orders on the field of battle."

Vanyr rounded on him. "What a pack of lies! Do you expect us to believe that you just let her walk in there and sweet-talk you into following her? We're not all fools, you know! I saw you, and you weren't holding a dignified discussion. What the hell were you doing if not fighting a duel?"

Ky-shan frowned. "Fighting? We weren't fighting. Oh, you must mean our little fencing session. Really, Vanyr, you could hardly call that a duel. I was simply showing the Major some of the more useful strokes we practice on the eastern seaboard. I thought she might find them interesting."

Robin coughed to cover a snort of laughter and Sullyan could barely control the quirk of her lips. Vanyr's face was a picture of outrage, his ire heightened by Ky-shan's lack of respect. He opened his mouth to continue the argument, but Anjer rose to his feet.

"Enough! Commander, go about your duties, and in future, keep your attention on your men. Leave the senior officers to conduct their own affairs."

Vanyr reacted as if slapped. He stared at Anjer with his mouth open. Then he made a sullen salute and a noisy exit. Robin shuddered, and Sullyan knew he had also felt the malice emanating from the man.

Dismissing his humiliated subordinate, Anjer turned to the pirate. "Ky-shan, I trust you and your men will follow the Major's orders implicitly over the coming weeks? Your future here depends on it. I hope she has made you fully aware of this."

Ky-shan stared back. "My men will do as they're told." His rough respect had clearly departed with the vengeful Vanyr. "We don't have any objection to officers who give sensible orders."

Anjer wisely decided not to prolong the interview. "Very well, Ky-shan, you may go."

Once the pirate's heavy footfalls had faded, Anjer spread his hands toward Sullyan. "I'm sorry, Major, I should have trusted you. The Hierarch has told me the reasons that brought you here, and Ephan revealed what he knows of your reputation. I wouldn't normally have taken Commander Vanyr at his word without consulting you, but these are troubled times. Dissention among our own I can do without."

"I understand, my Lord. Never fear, I will be taking Ky-shan's band into the field at dawn tomorrow, so we will be out of the Commander's way."

"So soon? Tell me, Major, how did you manage to gain that ruffian's respect so quickly?"

She gave him a winning smile. "Ky-shan may have shown me

some useful strokes, my Lord, but believe me, I know a few of my own."

He held up his hands. "I don't think I want to hear any more! I've taken up quite enough of your time. You must have duties to attend to if you're going out at dawn. Do you have the equipment you need? Good. There'll be supply trains in the field. Their runners will be told to watch out for you. I wish you good hunting for tomorrow, Major. No doubt I will see you at supper tonight."

Back in their rooms, Sullyan immediately shed her clothes to relax in the huge bathing pool. Robin joined her, and they spent a pleasant hour indulging their love, not thinking of the future at all, immediate or longer term. Once they were spent, Robin laid back, Sullyan cradled in his arms.

"Brynne?"

She was almost asleep. "Mmm?"

"How much of a risk was that little episode this afternoon?"

She smiled into his chest. "Which episode in particular, Robin?"

"I'm serious! I meant the duel, of course."

"What duel? You heard what Ky-shan said."

"Sullyan!"

She sighed. "Oh, it was a fair risk, Robin. You know my opinion of dueling. What occurred this afternoon was not an example I wish you to follow, but I could think of no quicker way to gain their respect. There was no time to win them over. I knew Ky-shan would never admit to dueling with a woman, no matter who won, and I was fairly sure I could defeat him. I must confess, though, he had me worried once or twice."

"He had you worried? I nearly had a seizure when you slipped at the end."

She frowned. "I did not slip! Have you ever seen me lose my footing? No, love, it was a carefully calculated move to put him off balance. My only worry was wounding him too deeply. I did not want to put him out of action."

Robin stared down at her, not sure if she was being truthful. She returned his gaze and he changed the subject. "Alright then. What was all that 'Tallimore' stuff?"

She smiled in memory. "Years ago—I was about nine, I think—I spent a whole summer exploring the east coast of Andaryon. It was easy to pass myself off as a boy, and as the ports were all teeming with strangers, no one took any notice of me. I was fascinated by the many vessels coming and going and soon found myself yearning to see what sailing was like. I offered myself as a cabin boy and was accepted on board the third ship I tried. By sheer chance, this vessel—a much racier craft than the heavy cargo ships, although at the time I had no idea why—turned out to be a free trader. By the time the captain discovered I was a girl we were too far out to put back into port, so he let me stay. He was pleased he did so, for I made myself useful. I used my senses to find the shoals of fish they trawled for—and they did fish, although fishing was not their most lucrative means of obtaining gold—and I also managed to warn them of a serious storm. The crew was convinced I was a storm-seer and did not want to part with me. They thought I was 'lucky', and I did not explain. Seamen are such a superstitious lot!

"In the evenings, I entertained them with songs and also learned a few of theirs. The one they sang most was *The Ballad of Tallimore*. Tallimore is where seamen believe they go when they die, and it is found far across the mythical Triple Sea. To wish someone a 'broad reach to Tallimore' is to give a seaman's blessing. I knew Ky-shan would recognize it and be curious."

She smiled up at him. "Come, love, pleasant though this is, we must dress for dinner. I do not want to be late." Sliding her slender form out of his arms, she left the pool, water sheeting off her smooth, tawny skin.

Their clothes were waiting, having been laid out by a servant. Pharikian had provided a gown for Sullyan. Made of pale lavender velvet, it caught the light attractively. It was plain and simple in design with a close-fitting bodice, a scooped neck, sleeves that clung to her arms, and a full skirt falling almost to the ground. She slid into it, liking its soft, warm feel. There was also a gold girdle which sat low on her hips, accentuating her flat belly. Once she had dressed, she partially braided her hair, leaving a long mass of it to flow down her back.

Robin's clothing was equally plain, yet elegant. Soft, black breeches with a white lawn shirt subtly trimmed with gold, and a black sleeveless tunic. Sullyan eyed him admiringly when he was dressed, and he smiled invitingly back.

Ruefully she shook her head. "Come now, Robin, duty calls. There will be time for that later."

A servant appeared at the door to escort them. The Count, although clearly nervous, had dressed with care. A long mantle of maroon velvet was shown off by a black sleeveless tunic and white shirt and breeches.

Sullyan smiled approvingly as he joined them in the corridor. "The ladies will be all over you tonight, Ty."

His melancholy expression lifted at her compliment and he fell into step beside them.

On entering the small hall where the dinner was being held, they saw that most of the other guests had already arrived. Pharikian, who had been talking to Anjer and two ladies, was watching for their arrival and came to greet them immediately.

"My dear Lady Brynne," he said, loud enough for all to hear, "I'm so pleased you could attend." Taking her hand, he raised it to his lips, then smiled conspiratorially and lowered his voice. "According to Anjer you've already made your mark in my service, child."

She curtsied deeply. "Just being practical, Majesty."

He chuckled as he went on to greet Robin, who managed a respectable, courtly bow. Marik was next, and he stuttered over his greeting, but Pharikian merely addressed him as 'My dear Count,' and acknowledged his reverential bow.

As he ushered them further into the room, Pharikian led the introductions. Anjer stepped forward, his huge frame elegantly handsome in unrelieved black. His eyes found Sullyan's in amusement. He presented his wife, the Lady Torien, who was a small, slim woman about Sullyan's age. The Major eyed her, thinking she would be crushed beneath Anjer's weight in bed. Yet Torien obviously adored her husband, and she gave Sullyan a friendly smile.

Next was Ephan, dressed in a dark blue that emphasized his grey hair and white eyes. His lady was more his own age. Her name was Hollet, and she regarded Sullyan coolly, although her eyes rested easily on Robin. Gaslek stepped out from behind her and took Sullyan's hand. He seemed to be unattached, and his fussy manner was absent in such relaxed company. Having greeted her, he touched Pharikian's arm and they moved away, deep in conversation.

General Kryp approached reluctantly, showing his unwillingness to greet Sullyan as an equal even in this informal setting. However, once his eyes had roved over her slender curves and more appropriate attire, his expression changed. Sullyan felt a shiver of discomfort. She preferred his hostility to this speculative stare. It reminded her too much of Rykan.

Prodded into his duty by a light cough, Kryp introduced his lady. Falina was a woman of ample girth to match her husband's, although her height was less than his. Her grey eyes were cold and she held out just her fingertips to Sullyan in a condescending fashion.

Sullyan inclined her head. "Lady Falina."

"So you are Brynne Sullyan." Falina looked down her nose and her voice was high and thin. "I barely recognized you out of those awful things you were wearing when we passed you in the Citadel."

Sullyan kept her tone pleasant. "Oh, were you there, Lady? I am afraid I did not notice you among the crowd."

Falina went pale and Sullyan saw Robin hide a smile. He knew very well that she had identified Falina as one of those simpering, gaudy peacocks who had sniggered behind her fan.

Determined to score a point, Falina said, "Will you take some advice, my dear? That lavender velvet does your complexion no favors at all. You really ought to ask an expert to go through your wardrobe."

Sullyan smiled sweetly. "Do you think so, Lady? Then I must remember to pass your opinion on to his Majesty. He will have to discipline his chatelaine, since it was she who chose this gown."

Falina's mouth closed with a snap. Kryp rescued her from further embarrassment by pulling her away to talk to Lady Hollet.

So far all the guests had pointedly ignored Marik, despite the Hierarch's greeting. He trailed disconsolately behind Sullyan and Robin as they moved farther into the room. They were about to find their seats when Pharikian approached them once more. On his arm was a woman who appeared to be in her early thirties. Sullyan guessed immediately who she was by her resemblance to her father, and made her a deep obeisance.

She heard Pharikian say, "Lady Brynne Sullyan, I would like you to meet my daughter, the Princess Idrimar."

As she rose, Sullyan studied Idrimar. The young woman was attractive in a pale sort of way, but she had a listless manner that wasn't entirely healthy. She seemed friendly as she greeted them, but Sullyan thought she probably had a gloomy nature. Of course, she reflected, the woman had lost her twin sister at birth and her mother soon after. She was also unmarried, unusual enough for an Andaryan woman of her age, but virtually unheard of for a ruler's daughter. It seemed she had every right to her sorrow.

Despite her underlying sadness, Idrimar chatted easily with them and even included Marik, which clearly unsettled him. As the servants announced supper, Sullyan noticed Marik watching the Princess out of the corner of his eye. She hid a private smile.

The meal passed pleasantly. Sullyan sat with Robin and enjoyed light conversation with Gaslek, Ephan, Anjer, and their ladies. She had been wondering where the Hierarch's son was, but soon learned he was currently staying in Morvaigne, the province of Tikhal, Lord of the North. Tikhal was Pharikian's premier noble, senior to Lord Rykan. As powerful as Rykan, Tikhal lacked the dark lord's brutal ambition, having no desire to overturn the Hierarch's rule. Should Rykan succeed in his challenge, Pharikian's Heir would be Rykan's next target, so the Prince had been sent to the safety of Tikhal's mountain stronghold. He wouldn't return until the war was over, when he would either congratulate his father or prepare to fight for his life.

Musicians played softly throughout the meal, and when it was over, they struck up a dance tune. Sullyan could hardly help remembering the last banquet she had attended as she danced in the Hierarch's arms, and judging by the look on Robin's face, he was remembering too. However, the handsome young man had little time for somber reflection, for he was soon claimed for dances by Anjer's young wife Torien, Ephan's Lady Hollet, and once, to his utter amazement and honor, by the Princess. Idrimar came alive when she danced, and Robin soon found himself entering into the spirit of the evening.

Sullyan also had her share of partners, and once saw Robin

trying to suppress outright laughter at the expression on Falina's face as the portly General Kryp escorted Sullyan around the floor. He was also highly amused by the look on Sullyan's face as she was forced to dance with the unwieldy General.

When they were finally able to dance with each other, Robin asked her how she had enjoyed Kryp's attentions. She shot him a look and was about to voice an acid reply when she spotted something that both amazed and amused her.

"Oh my, Robin," she murmured, "will you look at that."

Turning in the dance, she let him see the incredible sight of Count Marik and Princess Idrimar dancing closely together. Oblivious to the other guests, they were gazing deep into each other's eyes.

Robin chuckled. "I do believe our dear Count is making an impression."

Sullyan smiled and glanced at Pharikian, who was watching the pair with an unreadable expression.

The dancing finally ended. Sullyan had intended to excuse herself and Robin as they had an early start the next morning, but the Hierarch had one last surprise for her. Rising from his seat next to his daughter, who was still gazing down the table toward the Count when she thought her father wasn't looking, he turned to Sullyan. He was holding out a sheaf of papers, and as she stood to take them, she saw that they were musical scores. Her heart started to pound.

"I promised you the music your father wrote, my dear, and while I wouldn't presume to ask you to play it now, as you've only just seen it, might I prevail upon you to play something else?" His eyes were pleading. "I know you intend to take the field tomorrow, so I won't keep you from your rest. But it has been too many years since this was played, and I thought—I hoped—you might care to have it."

He gestured, and a servant approached Sullyan, bearing something covered with a blue velvet cloth. As soon as it was set on the table before her, she knew what it was. Fingers trembling, she drew the cloth aside and gasped with delight.

The harp was exquisite. Its rich, highly polished red wood was decorated with intricate gold and nacre inlay. The strings were gold and silver wires, and tiny diamonds adorned the tuning pins. It had been lovingly cared for and was in perfect tune when she ran a light hand over it. Tears standing in her eyes, she looked up at the Hierarch.

"It belonged to your mother," he murmured, "but it was your father who played it. If you are not too overcome, I would love to hear it again."

What could she do but take it in her arms? Robin placed a chair in front of the high table and she sat with the harp nestling into her lap as if it belonged there. She tried the strings, as much to compose herself as to test its tone.

Softly, she played a melody with no words. The last time she had played a harp was at Marik's mansion before Bull, Taran, Cal, and Rienne had left, and the melody was a subtle lament which brought back painful memories. She changed the tune and the Hierarch sat straighter in his chair, recognizing what she played. It was the air she had played for Rykan at Marik's banquet, and when she began to sing the words, the Count covered his face with his hands. He too associated the song with pain and loss.

Pharikian sat enthralled as Sullyan sang the words in the old High Language of Andaryon, a tongue no one spoke now. As the song shivered to a close, she felt a serene sense of completion, as if finally laying the bad memories to rest. She placed her hands on the strings to still their quivering, and the room resounded with applause. Even the sour Falina had found nothing to criticize in the Major's skill. Sullyan didn't react, simply sat with her head bowed over the harp while one hand stroked its wood. It wasn't until Pharikian came round the table and put a hand on her shoulder that she raised her face, her eyes full of emotion.

"Where did you learn that song, Brynne?"

"I cannot say, Majesty. I feel as if I have always known it."

His face showed wonder. "Maybe you have, child, for Bethyn used to sing it to you before you were born. The melody is very old, ancient even, but those words were written by your father, as a loving tribute to his wife."

Suddenly, Sullyan couldn't breathe. Everywhere she turned here she found reminders of what she had lost. This was just too much. She laid the harp aside and covered it with the rich velvet. In a choked voice she said, "I cannot tell you what it means to have this, Majesty, but may I beg you to keep it safe a while longer? There is no place for it where I am going. And now, if it does not offend you, might I ask that you release us? Robin and I have much to arrange for tomorrow, and the hour grows late."

Pharikian's eyes clouded as he took her hand in farewell. He escorted them to the door and reluctantly let them go.

"Stay safe, Brynne," he whispered. "I couldn't bear to lose you too."

Chapter Twenty

The early morning air was chill and Taran shivered as he drew his cloak tightly around him. He looked up, noting the glitter of the frost-spangled trees. It promised to be a beautiful day, but Taran wasn't looking for beauty. His thoughts lay elsewhere as he strolled aimlessly, eyes unfocused and heart uneasy.

He had slept poorly the night before and had come out to clear his head. Too many thoughts were crowding his mind and he couldn't stop their nagging. Uncertainties still plagued his life, and this dreadful waiting for bad news day after day was dragging him down. Cal's elevation to Apprentice-elite had brought things to a head, and Taran had felt unsettled ever since. Not that he was unhappy for Cal. Quite the contrary, he was proud and delighted. He clearly remembered his own euphoria on gaining such a prize, and Sullyan's recent ceremony confirming his Adept status still swelled his heart.

No. It was the future that bothered Taran.

The relative ease with which he had attained the rank of Adept after only a few hours' guidance had brought forcibly home to him just what he might be capable of. It wasn't something he had dared consider before. Sullyan's masterly touch and confident air, even Robin's forthright instruction, contrasted sharply with Taran's memories of his father's blunt and condescending comments. He couldn't recall receiving a single word of praise from Amanus, who had obviously considered goading and humiliation to be the best forms of encouragement. At the time, Taran knew nothing else and did his best to progress. Now, he realized he had been trying to please his father rather than identifying and acting on his own strengths and weaknesses.

Sullyan's method was to lead and encourage. Instead of highlighting failures and dampening spirits, she fostered understanding through experiment, praising each achievement on its merits. Taran knew he could only flourish under such gentle instruction.

That only made it harder to lose.

"Dammit to hell!"

He couldn't believe he had discovered such talented people only to have their support snatched away just when he was making progress. His love for Sullyan, which refused to die despite his knowledge of her commitment to Robin, would make losing her distressing enough. To be also denied the training he so desperately desired would only deepen his misery.

Taran knew that once Sullyan was gone and Robin came back to the Manor, he, Cal, and Rienne would be forced to return to Hyecombe. They were only here on sufferance, and that was because of Rienne's healer skills. Despite Sullyan's parting words at Marik's mansion, Taran knew that once things were back to normal neither Robin nor Bull would be free to spend much time with him. He would be right back where he started—only worse, because now he would truly know what he had lost.

He really didn't think he could bear it.

Eventually, cold air and a sad heart drove him to seek warmth and company. Rienne and Cal should be up by now. Perhaps he could persuade Bull to part with some of his time. It might help take their minds off what was happening beyond the Veils.

As he began the walk back, the sound of voices made Taran raise his head. One of the voices was Blaine's, and Taran frowned.

Why was he up and about so early?

He soon found out. Two men appeared from the direction of the training ground, and one of them was indeed Mathias Blaine. The General was more casually dressed than Taran had ever seen him, in a plain linen shirt and loose, black breeches, his sword belted at his side. His companion was the Manor weaponsmaster, Falkerk, and the two were strolling together, deep in conversation. Judging by their flushed faces and sweat-dampened clothing, they had been fencing.

Taran was mildly surprised to learn that Blaine still actively trained, but then reminded himself that the man was no great age. Bull was older, and he still trained regularly. As he thought more about it, Taran realized the General must have come out early to escape the curious eyes of his men.

He walked on, intending to greet Blaine politely as he passed. Before he got close enough, however, the General turned to Falkerk and made a comment. The weaponsmaster glanced briefly at Taran and nodded. He walked off down another path while Blaine came on, eyes fixed on Taran. He wanted to talk, Taran realized. What could be on his mind? Perhaps he had already had enough of them and wanted them to leave. After all, the reason they had come, the Andaryan artifact buried in the ruins of Taran's cellar, had lost its significance in the tragedy of Sullyan's fate. No one would be spared to deal with it until this sad business was over.

Schooling his features to hide his fear, Taran slowed.

Impassively, Blaine approached. His expression was as stern as ever, his demeanor gave nothing away. Taran often wondered whether he fostered this façade deliberately or whether it was natural to his character. He couldn't decide. When the General stopped in front of Taran, he inclined his head.

"Adept Elijah."

Taran returned the greeting, trying to suppress the urge to salute. He wasn't under this man's authority, yet Blaine's natural air of command seemed to demand respect. Taran thought he caught a glimmer of amusement in Blaine's hard blue eyes.

"Has that Apprentice of yours calmed down yet after his success?"

Taran was surprised. The General's tone was conversational, his opening subject casual. This wasn't what Taran had expected. Though Blaine was an Artesan and hadn't taken much persuading to participate in Cal's testing, Taran had always accepted that Blaine had no real interest in them. He was General-in-Command, personally responsible for all matters pertaining to the High King's military forces. He had far more important concerns than three troublesome civilians. Yet, thought Taran, perhaps he was wrong? He decided to put his impressions aside and take this unexpected moment at face value. No doubt Blaine would get to the point before long.

"It took a while, sir, but I think so. It meant a lot to him to have a Master confirm his status. Neither of us has had much in the way of support or encouragement in recent years."

"So I gather. It must have been very hard for you."

Taran frowned. This conversation felt surreal. What was the man after?

"Yes, sir. Harder than I care to remember."

"Still, you've made good progress, both of you. Neither of you took long to reach the next rank. It takes more than a talented teacher to bring powers along that fast."

"We did our best, sir."

Taran's puzzlement continued to grow. He was sure Blaine was fishing, but for what, he couldn't think. If there was something the General wanted to know, why didn't he come right out and ask? He didn't seem like the diffident type. Studying his face in the growing sunlight, Taran tried to read behind the expressionless eyes. The General's next statement stunned him.

"So your father must have done something right."

Taran gaped. He never had the slightest suspicion that Blaine knew who he was, and Sullyan had said she hadn't told him. So had the General known all along, or had he since remembered his interview with Amanus and his reaction to the man's request?

Blaine smiled at Taran's reaction, his entire demeanor changing. Now Taran felt companionship radiating from him, and it threw him completely off-balance. This was turning out to be a strange conversation indeed.

"Ah," said the General. "You thought I didn't know who you were."

Taran reddened. "You're right, sir. How long have you known?"

"I have many responsibilities, Adept, and my attention is necessarily spread over many areas. One of the consequences of my position is the development of an excellent memory. I rarely forget a face or a name, and your family name is not common."

Taran lowered his eyes. "You've known from the start, then. Major Sullyan gave me the impression you didn't."

There was a slight pause.

"Then she should have known better."

Blaine's voice had hardened and Taran glanced at him. The General's eyes were bleak and cold and he turned his face away. The Adept remembered this same reaction when he had mentioned Sullyan's name after Cal's testing. He also recalled what Bull had told them of the General's leave-taking at Marik's mansion. Taran guessed that Mathias Blaine was a man who scorned to show his emotions. Perhaps it was another consequence of his post.

The General sighed and faced him once more. "I have to say you're not much like your father."

It was such an obvious avoidance of a painful subject that Taran's opinion of the man underwent a radical change. He smiled. "I'm glad to hear you say so."

"If you had been, I doubt I'd be so willing to allow you and your friends to stay."

Taran's heart skipped and he shot the General a look, not wanting to take his meaning for granted. Blaine correctly interpreted the look and smiled again, although coldness still lingered in his eyes.

"I don't suffer fools gladly, it's true, but neither am I completely insensitive. I am aware of your feelings, Taran Elijah, and I'm not just talking about your desire for training."

Heat rose in Taran's face. He hadn't imagined that Blaine would know anything at all about his personal feelings. The General carried on, ignoring Taran's discomfort.

"We also have unfinished business in the matter of your artifact, and I wouldn't have asked you to leave until it's been resolved. With Captain Tamsen absent"—his voice caught, but he plowed on—"we can't make headway there, so I wanted you to know that you're all welcome to stay until he returns. The Major told me you'd be concerned about the future. It seems she was right."

Taran stared, stunned yet again. "She said that? When was this?"

Blaine's eyes clouded, and Taran knew he was forcing down painful memories.

"The last time I saw her." He moved swiftly on before Taran could speak again. "Be free with our facilities while you're here, Adept, and don't hesitate to ask Hal Bullen for guidance or instruction. Your Healer Arlen has more than compensated us for any costs your stay might incur. She's very talented, so Hanan tells me."

"But she's being paid, sir. She's drawing a captain's pay."

"I am aware of that, Adept! The offer stands. It's up to you how you use it. Now I must go. It's cold out here and I need to wash. No doubt we will speak again."

The General stalked away and Taran stood staring after him, his thoughts chaotic. He shivered. The rising sun had stirred a bitter wind. The movement brought him back to himself and he shook his head, mulling over what he had heard. The General's words might not have solved the problem of his long-term future, but at least his mind could rest easy for the present.

Eager to tell his friends the good news—and to see Rienne smile again—Taran hurried back to their rooms.

�֍ ֍ ֍ ֍ ֍

Dressed for combat and wearing heavy cloaks against the freezing wind, Sullyan, Robin and Marik carried their packs down to the horse lines. The lower Citadel was buzzing with activity. Theirs wasn't the only company leaving that day. Lord General Anjer had come up with a strategy to cause maximum damage to Rykan's marching troops with minimum losses to the Hierarch's. Sullyan and her band were to head out toward the southwest flank of Rykan's forces and stay there as long as they could. Three supply trains were already in the field, although each band would carry as much as they could.

On arriving at the horse lines, Sullyan was pleased to see Kyshan and his men already there. There seemed to be an argument going on, so she and Robin strode over to see what was wrong. The stocky pirate was swearing at the horse master while repeatedly jabbing a thick finger at some of the beasts selected for his band. He turned furiously to Sullyan as she approached.

"Lady, this idiot has let Vanyr take back some of the mounts you selected for us. He won't listen to me."

The horse master, a small, slight man with a receding hairline and harassed demeanor, spread his hands. "I can't gainsay the Commander, Lady, not without a direct order from the Lord General."

Sullyan faced him coldly. "You have already seen the Lord General's authorization, man. What more do you want?"

"I want you to be here when Commander Vanyr comes looking for his horses!"

She rolled her eyes. She didn't need obstructions like this. "Where are the horses I chose?" When the horse master indicated a corral, she realized that the horses in question were the largest of those she had selected, large enough to carry Almid, Kester, and Ky-shan himself. "Saddle them," she said. When the horse master opened his mouth to protest, she snapped, "Send Vanyr to me if he complains! That is, if he knows where the front lines are."

Ky-shan's men sniggered, but the Major ignored them. "Mount up," she called. "We have wasted enough time."

She handed her pack to Robin and adjusted her sword belt so that the longsword rode at her back. Then she walked over to Drum and swung herself into the saddle. The huge warhorse pranced and snorted, and the pirates eyed him warily. "This beast is battle trained," she warned them, "as is the Captain's. Do not ride too close behind or you will feel the steel of their shoes."

When they were all mounted, she directed Marik and Robin to flank her. Then she urged Drum to a canter and led her band out of the Citadel gates, passing a furious Commander Vanyr on the way. As they rode round the perimeter wall, they drew shouts of encouragement from the guardsmen manning it. More used to being reviled than hailed, the pirates' mood slowly lifted. Sullyan kept a stern eye on them, concentrating on identifying those she already knew and fixing in her mind those whose names she had yet to learn. By tomorrow night she wanted to be able to address each one by name and know something of their character. It would deepen their respect for her and was part of the reason why her Albian command followed her so readily.

She led them across the Plain in a southwesterly direction. The wind was bitter and the ground semi-frozen, but the light cloud cover presaged no rain or snow. They made good time, and after a couple of hours of hard riding Sullyan called a halt to breathe the mounts. As she moved round the men, talking to them and telling them what she intended, she noticed that some of them were drinking thick, brown liquor from stone jars. She nudged Drum closer to Ky-shan's horse and pointed to the jar in his hand.

"What is that?"

He wiped his mouth and grinned. "Brine rum, Lady. Try some?"

"I thank you, Ky-shan, but I do not drink. I do not object to your men doing so, but let me warn you. If I ever find one of your men incapable of fighting due to intoxication, I will send him back in disgrace. Our success as a company depends on each man's skills and obedience, and I will not tolerate less than total commitment. Remember the terms of our bargain."

He heard the threat in her tone and glanced severely at his men. There were some scowls, but they all stoppered their jars. "Have no fear, Lady, they won't let you down."

"See to it, Ky-shan. You are responsible."

Sullyan led them at speed for the rest of the afternoon, and they entered the forests bordering the Citadel Plain as the light began to fade. Under her instructions, Robin sent out scouts, but none returned with news of the enemy. Having already asked the Captain to use his metasenses, Sullyan wasn't surprised. She already knew roughly where Rykan's men were. She kept her own powers shielded. The last thing she wanted was for Rykan to catch a glimpse of her presence. She also concealed her knowledge from Ky-shan, as a test of his men. So far, she was content. The pirates were behaving themselves, happy to be out of the Citadel and doing what they had come for.

As the failing daylight made further progress through the trees too risky, she gave the order to make camp. Among the bustle and noise of settling the horses and lighting fires, she could hear some of the pirates commenting on the fact that she, Robin, and Marik were seeing to their own horses and gear. It gave her grim amusement. Ky-shan's men were used to Andaryan officers, who did nothing for themselves. There was an even greater stir when she and Robin made their rounds, something Sullyan always insisted on, before making a fire or seeing to their own comforts. They went round separately, talking to the men individually or in groups, seeing that they had all they needed and that there were no complaints. Many puzzled eyes and low mutterings followed them.

As they made their way back to where Marik was sitting with their gear, they passed Ky-shan's campfire. The pirate leader was eating with his son, Jay'el, the twin giants, Almid and Kester, and the other young lad, who was called Ki-en. Ky-shan invited the Albians to share his fire, and as Sullyan sat, one of the huge twins wordlessly offered her his flagon.

"I thank you, Kester, but I do not drink."

Surprise crossed the huge man's face, and Sullyan guessed that most people couldn't tell the twins apart. She grinned. "I was right, then?"

He smiled back with a shy expression which was strange to see in such a large, brawny man. Something about his manner caught Sullyan's attention and she frowned. "You cannot speak, can you?"

Wariness came into his eyes and he gave a curt shake of his head. His brother shot her an apprehensive look before turning his eyes on Ky-shan.

The pirate leader leaned back on one elbow. "They've had

their tongues cut out. Happened years ago when they were boys. It was Relkorian slavers. They often do that, the bastards, to stop their victims crying out. Triton knows how, but the boys managed to fight their way free, even young as they were. But they were useless then, with their tongues gone, so their kin cast them off. I found them begging on the foreshore one day, half-starved, ragged, and homeless, and took them on. You don't need tongues to sail a ship, you need brawn. And they've got that in shoals."

Kester watched Sullyan closely, uncertainty in his eyes. Discerning his worry, she grinned. "Have no fear, Kester. It is of no importance to me. My only care is how well you use that huge meat cleaver you carry."

He showed surprise again, then grinned back and traded a glance with his brother. It confirmed a suspicion for Sullyan, and she placed her hand on the huge man's arm. Kester leaped up as if he had been struck and stood there, staring wildly round. Ky-shan and the others jumped too.

Sullyan laughed. "I am sorry, gentlemen, I seem to have startled our big friend here. Kester is used to hearing only his brother's voice inside his head. Hearing mine was clearly a shock. Kester, would you like me to show you how I did that?"

Ky-shan frowned at her as they all settled back down. "You spoke to his mind, Lady? But they're not Artesans."

"Almid and Kester might not be Artesans in the usual way, but they are twins. Twins often share a bond of the mind. It is not always possible, but sometimes a skilled Artesan can tap into that bond."

The giants regarded her with awe. Then they glanced at each other and Kester slowly nodded. After a few moments, his brother Almid did the same.

Sullyan spent some time with them, only standing to leave when both twins could speak to Ky-shan and Jay'el, as well as

Robin. Fascinated and excited by their new skill, the two giants watched her with something akin to adoration in their fire-lit eyes.

"Ky-shan," said Sullyan, "we must set watches tonight. Divide your men into three groups, please. You will lead the first watch. The Captain here will lead the second, and I want Almid and Kester included in his group. I will lead the dawn watch, and I want your son and Ki-en in my group."

Jay'el started to protest, but his father shot him a quelling glance. "You're going to lead the dawn watch, Lady?"

"Do you have a problem with that, Ky-shan? No? Good. Let me remind you, I expect all your men to be alert and thoroughly sober, no matter what shift they are assigned. I leave their distribution to you, apart from those I have already mentioned. I am going to rest now. I suggest you give your orders and deploy your sentinels. Be sure to wake the Captain at the appropriate time."

Chapter Twenty-One

The night watches passed peacefully. Dawn found them breaking camp and mounting up, and Sullyan rode round the men, greeting them all before leading them off. Jay'el, who had sulked through his entire watch, stuck close to his father and his friend. Ki-en was a year younger than the twenty-year-old Jay'el, and clearly felt none of his friend's resentment of Sullyan. During their watch, he had asked her about Drum and Torka and seemed fascinated by the finely trained beasts. She answered his questions willingly, amused yet exasperated by Jay'el's obvious disapproval. She could only hope that Ki-en's more mature attitude would rub off on his sullen friend.

She led them southwest once more. The night had been bitter cold, and they moved at a steady pace to warm the horses. Once they were thoroughly limbered up, Sullyan increased the pace to a ground-eating canter. Around midday, they saw the first sign that Rykan's troops were near when they came across a team of field medics from the Citadel. Sullyan halted her band and rode over to talk with the Chief Healer. He was also a Master-elite, which pleased her as she rarely met others of her rank. He accorded her easy courtesy, grateful for her offer of metaphysical help should he require it. Before parting they exchanged knowledge of each other's psyche so they could communicate.

After a brief meal, they continued on. The going beneath the trees was getting rougher. Many men and horses had been that way. From the elderly Master Healer, Sullyan had obtained information of where Rykan's main forces were the day before, and she asked Robin to send out teams of scouts with strict instructions to report, not engage. She was gratified when one group, a team of six including Almid and Kester, rode in at the gallop, saying they had located a small force of the enemy off the right flank of Rykan's main column.

As soon as the other scouts returned, Sullyan called the whole band together. This was an important moment, and it was crucial that this first attack succeed. If it failed, it was unlikely she could continue to lead the band. She shared a look with Robin, making sure he understood. Then she turned to address the pirates.

"Gentlemen, our scouts have found us our first target. A small unit of enemy horsemen has strayed too far from the main body of troops. They have no scouts, and Kester reports that they appear disorganized. If we can surround them, we can kill them. We will advance in close order, following Kester's lead. Keep your progress as silent as possible to maintain the advantage of surprise. Once the order to engage is given, strike swiftly and strike hard. Do not get separated from your fellows. If the enemy succeeds in breaking back toward their fellows, we will retreat. There will be no waiting for stragglers. We will have other opportunities to strike at Rykan's men, but only if we take no unnecessary risks."

There were no dissenters. The pirates who had crossbows eagerly began to arm them. Robin loosed his crossbow from its straps on the saddle. It was a one-shot weapon, impossible to rearm in such close quarters, but one well-aimed bolt meant one less enemy to fight. The rest of the band drew their swords, holding the blades at their sides.

"Form up into your watch teams," called Sullyan. "Jay'el, please ride on my right."

The young pirate refused to meet her gaze, but he did sullenly kick his horse up beside her. Ki-en was just behind him, and he grinned nervously at Sullyan. She put Jay'el's childish resentment out of her mind and accepted Robin's and Ky-shan's nods of readiness.

"Ride on," she called, nudging Drum with her heels.

The pirates were plainly astounded when she didn't fall back behind them, but rode at their head as before. Despite her instructions for silence, she heard one man hiss at another, "Do you think she knows what she's doing? She'll likely get herself killed ...."

She ignored him, too intent on the outcome of the raid. They moved forward at a steady trot, following Kester's lead. After a few minutes, she felt his unpracticed touch on her mind. He and the other scouts had the enemy in sight. Her heart began to pound, and she felt the familiar rush of trepidation and excitement fill her, as it did at the start of every fight.

She gave a prearranged signal, sending Ky-shan's group off to the left. They would circle round and cut off the enemy's line of retreat. A few minutes later, she heard yells and the ringing of steel. Kester's group had engaged Rykan's men.

"Charge!" she called, and the pirates surged forward, moving as fast as they could through the trees. Then she could see Kester dead ahead, he and his men battling a small group of enemy horsemen.

The forest filled with shouts of warning and rage. The distinctive *thunk* as the pirates loosed their crossbows was alarmingly loud. As the enemy realized they were surrounded, they clustered together, but they were too slow. Horses screamed as the pirates plunged into their midst. Metal rang on metal, followed by the screams of men. Figures flashed in and out of Sullyan's vision, and her entire attention narrowed to what was immediately before her. Drum bore her powerfully forward, and her sword flashed as one of Rykan's men engaged her. She ran him through.

She felt Drum kick out and heard the dull thud as his steel-shod hoof met flesh. There was no scream. Then he reared, and she cut downward as an unhorsed rider ran past, fleeing Jay'el's curved blade. The man collapsed and Drum bore her onward, toward her next target.

She cut down two more men before realizing her band was gaining control. "Ky-shan," she yelled, "finish them!"

Within twenty minutes, it was over. Sullyan dealt her final opponent a vicious cut to the head and looked round, seeing only familiar faces. "Pull back," she called, and Ky-shan echoed her shout, gathering the pirates round him.

They returned the way they had come and found a suitable site to rest. Sullyan walked among the euphoric men, congratulating them and checking for injuries. Incredibly, they hadn't lost a single man in this skirmish, and their few wounds were minor. She had them retreat further into the forest, looking for a suitable campsite. Some of them muttered against this, wanting to strike the enemy again, but Sullyan insisted they rest. The short day was already beginning to fade, and the going would soon become impossible within the confines of the trees.

She and Robin did their rounds as usual, astounding the men once more as they stopped to check the wounded. Sullyan even helped heal a few. The whispers that followed her round the camp that evening were even more appreciative than the night before.

She came to Ky-shan last and spent some time with him, praising his men and discussing their next move. She also enquired how his own wound did and used her power to speed him back to full strength.

He tried to protest. "You shouldn't use your energies on us like this, Lady. You need your strength for yourself."

She looked him squarely in the eye. "Out here among the enemy, I am only as strong as the weakest of my command. Now, please deploy your watch teams as last night."

As she walked back to Marik and Robin, she could feel the stocky pirate's eyes on her. She hoped he was considering her words and what he had seen that day.

The next two days passed in similar fashion. Thanks mainly to Almid's and Kester's scouting skills, they located and destroyed many groups of stragglers who had become isolated from Rykan's main forces. The Lord General's strategy was working well, and Robin linked with General Ephan to report their success.

On the evening of their fourth day, they relaxed as usual after yet another successful attack. The troops they had ambushed that day proved to be the toughest yet, and Sullyan's authority was tested to the utmost as she directed her men in the most effective maneuvers. Used now to seeing her fight alongside them and respecting her skills, the pirates instantly obeyed her orders in the heat of battle. There were few serious injuries to deal with that night.

The only complaint she could make of her new command concerned the way they addressed her. She couldn't convince any of them to call her Major. They all insisted on using Lady. It galled her, but she had to let it go. That night as she did her rounds, she was intrigued to hear some of the pirates referring to Robin as 'Skip,' so she asked Ky-shan about it as she spent her usual hour with him before retiring for the night.

They drank fellan round his campfire. The pirate had laced his own beverage liberally with brine rum against the night's chill, so he said. He grinned at Sullyan where she sat opposite him, wrapped in her cloak against the cold, leaping flames playing on the gold of her rank insignia.

"The thing is, Lady, in our eyes 'captain' means the master of a sea-going vessel, and of course that doesn't apply here. The closest term my lads could come up with was 'skipper,' which is an informal version of the same word. They mean no disrespect by it. In fact, it shows they're comfortable with him, so don't you worry about it. It's just their way."

Sullyan had no intention of trying to change things; they were working out well as far as she was concerned. Robin was feeling more at ease with the men too, now that they had accepted him as one of their own. Fondly, she watched him moving among the pirates, exchanging pleasantries or insults depending on the individual. She went to her rest that night satisfied with their success.

The next day, things went terribly wrong.

⁜ ⁜ ⁜ ⁜ ⁜

The night watches passed peacefully as usual. Sullyan had come to terms with Jay'el's smoldering resentment and resolved to ignore it as long as he followed orders. Putting him in nominal charge of the dawn watch hadn't mellowed him as she had hoped it might, and she didn't know how else to win him over.

After breaking camp, they scouted for more of Rykan's men, soon discovering a large band of his troops moving their way. Once again, they managed to split the band and kill most of the men, but the band sustained many more injuries in this fray. It was something she had feared—their successes so far were making the pirates over-confident. It was mid-afternoon and they were far out on the right flank, so Sullyan ordered them to rest. She and Robin did what they could for the injured. The Captain had sent scouts to keep an eye on the enemy. An hour before dusk, one of them rode in at speed. He headed straight for Sullyan.

"Lady!"

She looked up, recognizing the man. "What is it, Xeer?"

He grinned, his teeth flashing white in his dark-skinned face. "It's Count Marik, Lady. He says, will you come?"

Leaving the remainder of her men to their rest, Sullyan called

Robin and Ky-shan to her, mounted Drum, and followed Xeer back the way he had come. They concealed the horses where he indicated and moved cautiously through the trees to where Marik and the other scouts lay. They were watching a clearing where a large number of Rykan's men were settling in for the night. Sullyan crept close to the Count and touched his arm. He glanced at her and she could just make out his eager expression in the deepening gloom. He gave a nod of his head, indicating the main body of troops, and Sullyan studied them. There were around a hundred men bunched together in the middle of the campsite, the rest of the force ranged in a ring around them. Most of those in the center sat hunched on the ground, morose and dispirited. Only a few were talking among themselves.

There was no doubt that the men in the center were being watched, guarded even, by those on the outside. A predatory smile appeared on Sullyan's lips.

"Now here is an unexpected opportunity!"

Marik grinned back, and they withdrew to a safe distance. When they had gone far enough not to be overheard, Sullyan turned to her Captain. "What do you think, Robin?"

"We can't miss a chance like this, Major. It'll need a good plan, though."

Ky-shan frowned and Sullyan explained. "The men in the center of the camp are Count Marik's retainers, members of his court who were conscripted into Rykan's forces when the Duke took me captive."

The pirate's face cleared and he chuckled. "Ah-ha! And you want to liberate them?"

Sullyan nodded.

"Shall we sneak up on them at dawn, before they're fully awake?"

"Dawn?" she echoed, looking hungrily over her shoulder

toward the enemy camp. "No, Ky-shan, I will not wait that long. We will attack them tonight."

He snorted. "Tonight? You can't attack in darkness!"

She gave him a challenging stare. "When will they least expect an attack? When will they be least capable of responding? When can we maximize our greatest weapon of surprise? No, my friend, it has to be tonight. There are too many of them to risk it in daylight." She turned to Robin. "Do you think you could get in there?"

"To warn them, you mean? Yes, I think so, if I can slip past the sentries."

"Leave that to me. No, Ty," she added, forestalling Marik's protest, "Rykan's troops might recognize you, and they know you are not with your men. Do not forget the price the Duke has set on your head."

Marik clearly had forgotten it. Ky-shan, who hadn't heard about it, regarded the Count with renewed interest.

Sullyan laid a hand on Marik's arm. "Robin will go in and alert your men. Who will be leading them?"

Marik shrugged. "Nazir, if he's still alive."

"Very well, gentlemen, let us return to the men. Once it is dark, we will approach Rykan's camp and surround it. On my signal, we will rush them from all sides. With your men fighting from within, Ty, the resulting confusion should enable them to escape Rykan's troops. You will regain your men, which should earn you the Hierarch's favor." She eyed him slyly. "It will also put you in a good light with the Princess."

Marik colored to the hairline.

Once more, Sullyan and Robin edged closer to the camp. Robin pulled up the hood of his cloak and wrapped its folds tightly around him. Then he nodded at Sullyan.

"Wait for my diversion, Robin, and then move as swiftly as

you can. We will stay close by until we know you are safe."

She moved away from him, watching as he wormed his way toward the nearest guards. There were six of them, standing close beside their campfire. Sullyan touched his mind, warning him to be ready. Suddenly, a stray flutter of breeze blew sparks from the fire onto the thick wool of two of the sentries' cloaks. In no time the men were ablaze, and their fellow sentries had to swiftly pull them down, rolling them on the ground to put out the fire.

Go, Robin!

Unseen, Robin flitted past the frantic guards and melted into the main body of troops. Once she was sure he was safe, Sullyan asked Xeer and the other scouts to keep an eye on Rykan's men. Then she led Marik and Ky-shan back to camp. Swiftly, she split the band into groups with Ky-shan commanding one section, Marik another, Kester and Almid the third, and she the fourth. Like Ky-shan, the pirates were a little dubious about attacking at night, but they all liked Marik, considering him an outcast like themselves, and were keen to help him. They soon had their horses saddled and mounted, waiting on Sullyan's command.

As she led them forward at the head of her section, her sword in her left hand, she caught the sound of muttering. It was Jay'el, whispering to Ki-en and two other men behind him. She flashed him a look and he fell silent, his expression morose. Irritation rose and she forced it down. She needed her whole attention on this night's work.

It didn't take them long to reach their positions. Sullyan had left Robin's horse with the scouts' mounts, and now she checked that he was free to move. The big chestnut was trained to come at Robin's whistle and would fight to reach his master's side at need. When all were ready, the men fanned out, following Sullyan's directions. Despite her earlier confidence, she was uneasy about Robin and didn't want to leave him vulnerable for a moment longer than necessary.

She was vaguely aware of Jay'el, still murmuring rebelliously beside her. She didn't know whether he was irritated by the delay or scornful of this risky night raid. Whichever it was, she would have to deal with his insubordination once this attack was over. She ignored him and reached for Robin's mind. Sensing his eager response, she smiled.

Mindful of Rykan somewhere in these woods, Sullyan felt deep within for the pattern of her psyche. Controlling her metaforce tightly, she isolated the element of Fire. Tendrils of power uncurled, snaking through the substrate, reaching out and blending with the many watch fires around the camp perimeter. A slight pulse of metaforce made them flare brightly. Her own men, ready for the move, were shielding their eyes, but the sentries were caught by surprise. As a man they turned to the flames in alarm, instantly compromising their night vision.

"Go!"

Marik's men, briefed and encouraged by Robin, immediately rose up to attack the sentries from behind. Simultaneously, all four of Sullyan's units charged the camp, throwing the area into confusion. Despite their surprise and the ferocity of the attack, Rykan's men gave no ground. The clashing of steel and the neighing of horses shattered the peace of the dark woods. Marik's men, freed at last from the restraints of Rykan's grip and finding their own lord in their midst, fought hard for liberty. Men fell on both sides.

Sullyan yelled encouragement and plunged deep into the fray. Drum kicked and bit, trampling men under his hooves. Sullyan's sword flashed, maiming and killing. The pirates fought hard around her, harrying Rykan's men, leaving room for Marik's to escape.

Eventually the Count's men won clear and ran for the trees.

The pirates steered their horses close so the fleeing men could grab their stirrups. This way, each horse could carry three men. The remnants of Rykan's band were in disarray and showed no signs of wanting to follow, so Sullyan ordered the few pirates still fighting to disengage. She sent Drum galloping round the fleeing group, checking on the men. She had seen a few of them fall, but most had survived. Two of those absent made her heart clench in fear.

She urged Drum closer to Ky-shan. "Where is your son?"

The pirate scowled and twisted in his saddle. "Jay'el!" His furious roar received no response.

Sullyan counted heads. "Ki-en is not here either. Nor are Iskel and Sh'iye."

Ky-shan swore and wrenched his mount to a skidding stop. One of his men came up to him, yelling, "I saw the young idiot go off with the other three. There was a small pocket of men still fighting. I think he wanted to finish them off."

Cursing, Sullyan spun Drum on his haunches, sending him plunging back the way they had come. Robin flanked her. Ky-shan roared at his men and dashed off in the same direction.

Soon, the ringing of sword blades and the yelling of men guided them back to the clearing. In the dimness of the deserted watch fires, Sullyan spotted Jay'el, Ki-en, and the other two pirates surrounded by a group of Rykan's men. All four were now on foot and fighting back to back. One of the older pirates was bleeding heavily. Without a thought, Sullyan sent Drum charging into the massed warriors, barging through them and sending them running. Her sword flashed out with deadly accuracy. Robin followed her, Ky-shan and his men still some way behind.

As she fought her way toward the four, the wounded pirate, Iskel, went down. Sh'iye tried to defend him, but one of Rykan's men thrust with his sword, opening a deep gash down the pirate's thigh. Blood spurted and Sh'iye screamed. He wouldn't last long with such a serious injury. Jay'el and his young friend were now in deadly peril. Sullyan yelled at Robin, and pushing herself to the limit, fought her way through to the two lads.

As Drum surged up on Jay'el's left, Sullyan kicked her right foot free of the stirrup. Fending off his attackers with deadly blows, she caught the frightened young seaman's attention. "Jay'el! Hold the leather!"

Jay'el looped his left arm around the stirrup leather and held on desperately as Sullyan urged the battling stallion out of the mêlée. Robin was already doing the same for Ki-en, who was bleeding and stumbling due to a badly wounded leg.

Seeing them burdened, Rykan's men closed in for the kill. Hampered by the weight of the boy on his right, Drum couldn't lunge and slash effectively with his hooves. Sullyan's sword arm was tiring as she beat off attackers from her left, Jay'el hacking desperately on her right.

Then Ky-shan and his men crashed into the enemy flank and took a little pressure off. Sullyan heard yelling. Someone was rallying Rykan's men, driving them on, and she and Jay'el found themselves facing an impenetrable wall of warriors. A crossbow thumped and Sullyan felt a wave of agony as a bolt sliced through the muscle of her right arm. She moaned in pain and dropped the reins, her right hand suddenly nerveless. Kicking Drum, she yelled at Jay'el.

"Hold on!"

The powerful stallion plunged forward. Sullyan cut and slashed as Drum squealed, barreling through the wall of men. She heard Robin yell somewhere off to her right and hoped he was winning free. A large body of warriors surged toward her and she groaned. She couldn't hold out much longer. She nearly sagged with relief when she saw they were Marik's troops. Suddenly she was free of attackers and running for the trees. Jay'el, still desperately gripping the stirrup leather, was carried bodily forward by the racing stallion. Sullyan risked a little power to stem the blood flow from her wound and numb the pain, and then she grabbed the boy by the back of his jacket, hauling him up to sit behind her. Terrified and exhausted, he clung to her waist with both arms. She looked dizzily round for Robin, but it was Marik who came up behind her.

"Go on," he yelled, "we'll finish them!"

She rode hard and fast for the camp, trusting Marik to rout any pursuit. As she rode, she looked anxiously about, but although she saw many of the pirates, there was no sign of Robin. When she reached the campsite, she slowed Drum to a walk. Ignoring the trembling boy behind her and her own throbbing arm, she rode about the men, searching frantically for Robin. He wasn't there.

He rode in a few minutes later, escorted by Almid and Kester, who were trying to keep him on his horse. Ki-en lay like a dead weight across Torka's withers and as the horse slowed and halted, one of the pirates came forward to take the unconscious boy. Relieved of his duty, Robin slowly slid from his stallion's back and collapsed in a heap on the ground.

"Robin!"

Sullyan leaped from Drum and ran over. She kneeled beside Robin, hastily examining him for injuries. His chest heaved raggedly, his face was grey and lined. Someone brought a brand from the fire, and its light revealed the red and spreading stain on Robin's side. As Sullyan touched it, he briefly opened his eyes, gazing into her agonized face. "Sorry," he breathed, and fainted.

She yelled for help and tore open his jacket and shirt. When she saw the nasty sword slash in the flesh of his side she gave a hiss of shock. Heedless of the dangers of using her metaforce yet again so close to Rykan's position, she placed her trembling hands against the tear, using her power and slowly willing the blood to stop. Almid and Kester remained beside her and others crowded round to see what was amiss. Ky-shan rode in and she heard him curse and shove someone roughly out of the way as he came to kneel by her side.

"What can I do, Lady?"

"Fetch brine rum and water. Quickly, Ky-shan!"

He ran. When he returned, she used the strong liquor to cleanse the deep gash in Robin's side, examining it minutely for signs of dirt. Then she rinsed it. Finally satisfied it was fully clean, she laid her hands on it again to begin healing. A movement beside her caught her attention as Jay'el, trembling and frightened, pushed past the twins to kneel on the bloody ground.

She heard his gasp of fear. "Will he be alright, Lady?"

His face was pale and his eyes flicked from her to Robin, unable to hold her gaze. She rounded on him, her anger blazing brighter than the watch fires earlier that evening.

"If he is, it will be no thanks to you, you thoughtless little fool!" Her snarl was savage and Jay'el reacted as if slapped. "What were you thinking? You have brought about the deaths of at least two good men tonight, both of whom were worth twenty of you. You have caused grave injury to my Captain, and if he suffers a fever—or worse—I will personally see you pay dearly. You put the entire company in jeopardy and compromised your father's promise to me. You have been surly and intractable from the start, and I have had enough of your adolescent behavior. You think you are a warrior? You are a child and a liability, and I will not tolerate it!

"Now I have extra work to do tonight before I can rest. Your friend Ki-en is gravely wounded, and if he dies of it, I hope you will remember who is to blame. Get out of my sight before I am tempted to remove you permanently. You have no place in the company of men!"

Jay'el lurched to his feet, tears of shame running down his cheeks. He tried to appeal to his father, but Ky-shan shoved him roughly away before stooping to pour brine rum over the awful gash in Ki-en's upper thigh. The young lad was out cold from a blow to the head and had lost a lot of blood.

Sullyan turned back to Robin, striving to calm her mind enough to work more healing on him. Just then, Marik and his freed retainers arrived, euphoric from their liberation and the slaughter of Rykan's troops. They congratulated their lord, speculating how much the price on his head might have risen because of their night's work. Sullyan barely heard them, intent on Robin's wound.

Someone knelt down beside her, his arm brushing her right shoulder. She gave a yelp of pain and turned to see Marik, the pleased smile fading from his face when he noticed the blood saturating her sleeve.

"Sullyan, that needs attention. Robin will be well for the moment. Let Almid and Kester care for him. You need help too."

She wanted to protest, but lacked the strength. Instead, she allowed Marik to lead her over to their fire where he stripped off her jacket and shirt in order to examine her wound. Fortunately, the crossbow bolt had not embedded, but it had torn a nasty hole in the muscle. Damping the pain, she allowed the Count to use brine rum to clean the tear and bandage it. By the time he was done, Almid was carrying Robin, still unconscious, over to the fire. The giant laid the Captain down and Sullyan saw that his side had been bandaged. His color was a little better, but she would be happier when he woke. Gently, she touched his mind, but he was deeply unconscious.

After shrugging a spare shirt carefully over the chemise she wore as an undergarment, Sullyan accepted her heavy cloak from Marik. She huddled into it. Blood loss and the shock of her wound, coupled with fear for Robin, was making her shiver. She rose and crossed to where Ky-shan was still tending Ki-en. The young lad's face was bloodless and he lay very still. The pirate took one look at Sullyan and tried to persuade her to go and rest, but she expended a little power on Ki-en first, trying to stabilize him so he could survive the night. Then she left him in the twins' charge. They laid him beside Robin so they could watch over both of them during what remained of the night.

She did her rounds, Ky-shan protesting all the way, but she had to satisfy herself of the men's condition. Apart from the two who had died trying to defend Jay'el and Ki-en, they had lost five other good men. There were many injuries, but none as serious as Ki-en's. Sullyan advised, congratulated, and commiserated with the band, noting the looks of gratitude and respect they accorded her. That last act of selflessness—putting her own life and her Captain's at risk in order to rescue two of her men—had won the pirates over.

Finally, she made her way to Marik's campfire. The Count was very worried by her pallor and sent her summarily back to her rest, saying that he and his men were well and they would speak in the morning. Dizzy and weary, leaning on Ky-shan, she complied.

Once back at her own fire, she checked that Robin and Ki-en were comfortable and warm. Drum had been curried and fed, a blanket tossed over his back. Her fire had been stoked and radiated a welcome heat. Ky-shan helped her sit and Almid pressed a mug of fellan into her numb hands. When she sipped it and tasted the rum, he prevented her from refusing it. Both twins sat watching her intently while she took every drop. Ky-shan organized the watches, and with no other duties to keep her, she rolled carefully into warmed blankets and quickly fell asleep.

Chapter Twenty-Two

The first thing Sullyan did when she woke in the freezing dawn was reach for Robin's mind. There was a weak but cheerful response. Rising stiffly, she went to kneel beside him. She examined his wound, relief flooding her when she found it clean and free of infection. His face was pale, but his eyes were clear, and he smiled at her concern.

"How do you feel?" she asked.

"Sore." He winced and she laid her hand on him to lend him some strength.

Almid and Kester were already busy by the fire, heating fellan and preparing breakfast. With a final caress of his cheek, she left Robin and crossed to where Ki-en lay. He was still unconscious. Carefully, she reached into him with her senses, finding a little fever and much weakness due to blood loss. By expending more power, she was able to damp down the fever, but could do little else. He was a fit and healthy young man apart from the wound, and his chance of survival was good.

Once more she did her rounds, telling the men they would rest that day. At Marik's campfire she gratefully accepted his offer to supply guards and sentries for the day and night. She acknowledged Nazir as he thanked her for her part in their liberation. When she returned to Robin, Kester had helped him sit. She folded herself down beside him and he suddenly noticed the dried blood on her jacket sleeve.

"You didn't tell me you were injured too!"

"Easy, Robin, it is only a minor wound. It has been tended and will heal well. I am much more concerned for you. I could not bear it if you became trapped here too."

There was a sudden movement behind her and Ky-shan stepped into view. "Trapped here, Lady? What do you mean by that?"

She frowned, annoyed he had overheard. The last thing she wanted was to explain her situation. She decided to give him a half-truth. "I have an … affliction, Ky-shan, which prevents me from travelling the Veils and returning to Albia. Hence my decision to join the Hierarch's forces."

He looked unconvinced. "And the Skip? I take it he doesn't share this affliction, so why is he here?"

Robin chuckled weakly and took up Sullyan's hand. "Why do you think?"

Ky-shan's face cleared and he gave his rumbling laugh. "Ah, you are spliced! Yes, we had wondered." He winked suggestively at Robin, who smiled.

Silently, Sullyan thanked her lover for diverting the pirate's attention. His hand tightened briefly on hers. They sat companionably, eating breakfast and drinking fellan. Robin's mouth fell open when Sullyan accepted Ky-shan's offer of a tot of brine rum in her drink, and watched in amazement as she savored every drop.

When the pirate surged abruptly to his feet, Sullyan glanced up, noting his thunderous expression. She followed his gaze to where Jay'el stood fidgeting a few feet away, his head hanging, his face ashen, his sword held naked in his hands. Beside her, she felt Robin go tense.

Refusing to meet the young pirate's gaze, she said coldly, "What do you want?"

He jumped as if struck. His father stirred, but Sullyan raised a hand to stay him. Slowly, Ky-shan sat.

Jay'el hovered a moment longer to gather his courage. Finally, he came forward and kneeled at her feet. He placed his sword on the ground between them, and then sat back with his eyes downcast. The surrendered sword sent a clear message to Sullyan, yet she made no move toward it. She stared at the boy with hard, emotionless eyes.

"I ask again. What do you want?"

His head came up. He had obviously expected another tongue lashing, not a question. His voice was hoarse as he spoke. "Lady?"

She remained silent, offering no help. He licked dry lips in confusion, and after a few more awkward moments managed, "Lady, I want to apologize."

She looked away. "I am not the one you should apologize to."

His clasped hands trembled. "But I shouldn't have disobeyed your orders, Lady. I shouldn't have endangered your life, or those of the men. I was wrong to force Is-kel and Sh'iye to follow me."

Her reply was hard, unforgiving. "Your apology comes too late for Is-kel and Sh'iye. It may not be too late for Ki-en, I cannot say for sure. I ask you one more time, Jay'el. What do you want?"

He stared at her expressionless face. His eyes were full of shameful tears and his face flushed bright red. With shaking hands he slowly reached out, taking up his sword by the blade. He raised it and held it out to her, bowing his head. His voice was a choked whisper.

"I want to pledge to you, Lady. I want to atone for my willfulness. I want to serve you and the Skip. That is, if you'll have me after what I've done against you. I'll pay for my mutiny, Lady. I'll take whatever punishment you think I deserve."

He fell silent, still holding the sword out while tears rolled down his cheeks. Sullyan regarded him, gauging his sincerity. She ignored the pleading look on Robin's face, begging her to forgive the young man's rashness. Ky-shan's face was closed, holding no clue to his feelings. He was obviously content to leave his son's fate in her hands.

She sighed and grasped the sword, which Jay'el released to her. She spoke his name, forcing him to look her in the eye before she would continue.

"Jay'el. I hear your words. My Captain has forgiven your disobedience and asks that I do the same. I cannot deny that my heart argues against it. What I said yesterday still stands, but today I will grant Robin's wish. You are pardoned. I cannot speak for Ki-en, and no one can speak for Is-kel or Sh'iye. Your heart will bear that burden forever."

His head dropped and he nodded, tears still welling from his eyes.

"Take back your sword." She held the blade out and his hand closed on the hilt. When she didn't immediately release it, he started, his eyes leaping fearfully to hers. Her voice was low and menacing as she held his frightened gaze. "Let me warn you, boy. If you ever do anything so damaging again, you will find no forgiveness left in me. Greater men than you have crossed me and learned to regret it. Now, I suggest you devote your time to your friend there. If he survives—and only if—I might reconsider your place under my command."

She released the sword so abruptly he almost dropped it. Ignoring his stammered thanks, she rose. His father rose to follow her and she heard him growl to his son.

"That was more merciful than you deserve, you worthless chunk of shark-bait. I'd have strapped you to the mast and flogged you."

* * * * *

Despite the healing Sullyan had given him earlier, as the morning wore on it became clear that Ki-en was going to need more intensive care. His fever had lessened due to Sullyan's touch, yet he showed no sign of waking. Jay'el sat beside him, talking to him, holding his hand, keeping the wound clean and his skin cool. The younger lad's face remained bloodless and unresponsive, and Sullyan grew concerned for his survival.

Robin spent the morning using his metaforce to heal. By midday he had gained enough strength to sit his horse without going grey, so Sullyan made the decision to move Ki-en to the field medics' camp. The pirates made him a litter, which they slung between Almid's and Kester's horses. Jay'el rode close behind.

By late evening they arrived at the field medics' camp and Sullyan conferred at length with the elderly Master Healer. Linking together, they probed the young man, dismayed when they found that the shock of his wound and the blow to his head had caused a blockage in his brain. When Sullyan gave him the news, Jay'el reacted with anguish and reeled away from the tent where Ki-en lay. Sullyan let him go. Through the cold night hours, she and the Master Healer labored over the young lad. By dawn they had managed to disperse much of the clotted blood and swelling that was pressing on Ki-en's brain. Sullyan returned to her fire exhausted and immediately sank into sleep.

Ky-shan and Marik took charge of the camp. Robin concentrated on healing and gaining strength, as he was desperate to avoid being left behind when she and the pirates rode out again. He also spent time with the distraught Jay'el, who was convinced that Ki-en's condition meant he would be sent away in disgrace.

It was mid-afternoon before Sullyan woke. She smiled over at Kester, who crouched beside the fire brewing fellan. His sheer bulk, coupled with the fellan's distinctive aroma, reminded her forcefully of Bull and she had to fight down a sudden lump in her throat.

A commotion on the edge of their camp caught her attention and she looked up in surprise as General Ephan rode in. She watched him dismount and ask a question of one of Marik's sentries. The man pointed her way, and Ephan strode over to her. She was about to rise when he gestured at her to remain seated. Foregoing the usual formalities, he seated himself by her fire, wordlessly accepting Kester's offer of fellan.

While he drank he glanced appraisingly round her well-ordered camp, noting the men who were resting, seeing to the horses, or cleaning gear. He studied Robin, who was moving more fluidly now that the soreness of his side had eased, and he watched Marik, who was doing his rounds of the sentries with Nazir.

Finally, he turned to Sullyan. "So, Major, I see that the tales of your military expertise were correct. The Lord General was right to trust in you. I received the Captain's reports of your success, but I wanted to see for myself."

Pleased with his praise, Sullyan inclined her head. "What is the position of Rykan's main force now, General?"

Ephan gazed at her. "That is the other reason for my visit, Major. In the light of yours and other units' successes, and the arrival of more of the Hierarch's reserves, Anjer has called a war council. You are required to attend."

She nodded.

"Leave your men to continue their strikes, and present yourself to the Lord General at dawn tomorrow. He has set up a field command ... here."

Anjer's location appeared in Sullyan's mind. Then she noticed Ephan regarding her narrowly and sharpened her attention.

"Bring an honor guard, Major, and also ... Count Marik."

She raised her brows. "So he can pledge his allegiance?"

Ephan nodded.

"I will bring him, General."

The tall man rose and returned his cup to Kester. "I must congratulate you, Major. You have done well so far. Anjer is impressed. His Majesty is also pleased, though I know he will be concerned to hear of your injuries. He charged me to tell you to be careful."

She smiled at him. "They were only minor wounds, General. I would contact his Majesty myself and reassure him, but I dare not risk alerting Lord Rykan to my presence. That could be disastrous."

"Of course," said Ephan. "Never fear, Major, I will be your messenger. I will see you at dawn tomorrow. Don't be late." Turning, he strode back to his escort.

Sullyan spent the rest of the day organizing the men and planning more raids. Ky-shan would lead in her absence, although he surprised her by being torn between the desire to kill more of Rykan's men and what he saw as his duty to her. At his request, she accepted Almid, Kester, and Xeer as an honor guard, along with Robin. Unable to refuse her Captain's whispered plea, she also reluctantly accepted Jay'el. The young seaman had been intensely relieved to hear that Ki-en should eventually make a full recovery and hadn't left his friend's side since. He was nervous when he learned he was to be a part of the Major's honor guard, but he left Ki-en's side in a happier mood.

Marik was also nervous, but he understood the necessity of making the trip. He hadn't yet formally pledged allegiance to the Hierarch and was a loose horse in Anjer's eyes. His men cheered when they learned why he was going, each one eager to take revenge for their involuntary conscription into Rykan's forces. They knew they would ultimately gain by Marik's declaration of loyalty, and readily accepted Nazir as second-in-command while Marik was away.

Sullyan led the small group out before dawn and they arrived at the command camp, along with many others, just as daylight broke. Jay'el and Xeer were left to care for the horses and Marik to await his summons. She and Robin, with the twins flanking them as ostentatious bodyguards, made their way to the Lord General's tent. Ephan and Kryp were already there and both greeted Sullyan, although the portly General's nod was grudging. Sullyan honored them both with a respectful salute, as did Robin. Almid and Kester waited outside.

As soon as Anjer arrived with the commanders of the other field units, the council was convened. Sullyan and Robin were regarded with unveiled curiosity, but the Major was relieved to see no obvious resentment. Anjer afforded her a smile of greeting as she and Robin participated in the general salute, and Sullyan returned the grin.

They spent a long morning discussing the state of the war. The Duke had been prevented from spreading out to throw a ring of men around the Citadel, and his orderly columns were now scattered and disorganized. The Hierarch had called in all his reserves, most of which were now mobilized. They were only missing around two thousand men, and these would arrive within two days.

Anjer proposed that they now begin moves to ensure that Rykan had to fight the Hierarch's forces on equal terms. All the generals and commanders had their own ideas as to where the decisive battle should take place, and these were put forward with their relative merits.

Sullyan sat quietly throughout the discussions, not contributing, merely listening. Anjer glanced her way more than once, inviting comment, but she held her peace. As they began chewing over the merits of the various sites, he addressed her directly.

"Major Sullyan, have you no comment to make?"

All heads turned her way. She met Anjer's black gaze calmly.

"My Lord General, the plans for the next phase of the battle are well enough. My command will play its part as before. However, this discussion over where the final meeting of the two forces should take place is irrelevant."

There was a restless stir. Few of the men in that tent would care to use the word 'irrelevant' to Anjer. Yet the huge man merely raised his brows and gestured for her to continue. "Why irrelevant, Major?"

"Because, my Lord, there is only one place where the Hierarch's challenge may be made, and that is on the Plains before the Citadel gates."

Voices were raised in protest, Kryp being loudest. Anjer sat back with folded arms, studying her calm face while he waited for the noise to die down. When he finally had silence, he said, "Would you care to explain to us why, having spent the last week preventing Rykan's men from approaching the Citadel, we should now invite them onto the Plains like guests?"

She smiled faintly. "We will not 'invite' them, my Lord. In fact, we should do just the opposite. As we all know, the purpose of our tactics over the last few days was first to prevent the Duke from besieging the Caer, and second to allow the Hierarch's reserves time to deploy. In this, we have succeeded. Our next task is to convince Rykan that the Plains are his choice for the final confrontation, not ours."

Anjer frowned. "Please explain, Major."

"What we must not do is let Rykan realize he is being manipulated. If he does, he will pull back, retreat to a place of safety, and formulate another strategy. He must continue to believe that he has the superior force, as he would have were we not aware of his numbers. This means concealing his Majesty's reserve troops and feigning a withdrawal. Retreat before Rykan's supposedly superior numbers so that he pursues us right to the Citadel gates."

"That's unnecessarily dangerous, Major! Why on earth should we allow Rykan that close to the Caer?"

Her voice dropped as she held Anjer's gaze. "Because the Hierarch must make his challenge in person."

Protesting voices rose once more, and even the Lord General reacted angrily. The commanders were clearly horrified at the thought of exposing their ruler to such danger, and Kryp appeared to be on the verge of drawing on her. Robin rose to his feet, his hand on his own sword hilt, but Sullyan touched his arm and he relaxed. He still kept a wary eye on Kryp, though. Sullyan sat calmly through the storm of outrage, and eventually Anjer regained control. He rose to his feet, his huge frame towering over her.

"Does his Majesty know of this ridiculous plan, Major?"

She kept her tone mild. "Of course, my Lord, but it was no idea of mine. I believe it was Baron Gaslek who unearthed the protocol. His Majesty is fully aware and prepared to fulfill the terms of the challenge. It is vital that the proper customs be observed in order to bind the Duke to acceptance. This has to be definitive, my Lord. If we are to remove Rykan's threat to the throne, we cannot allow the plan to fail because of concerns for his Majesty's safety."

Anjer gave an exasperated sigh. "I wish his Majesty had seen fit to inform me of the plan!" He threw Sullyan an irritated glance, but she didn't react. He subsided. Resuming his seat, he began issuing orders to initiate first a push on Rykan's troops, and then a staged retreat which would bring them all to the Plains below the Citadel walls.

Sullyan took no further part in the discussions, merely accepted her orders as they were handed out. When the meeting broke up and the other commanders departed, leaving only Anjer,

Ephan, and Kryp, the Lord General called to her as she was about to leave.

"Major Sullyan, would you do us the courtesy of remaining to witness Count Marik's Oath of Allegiance?"

She was both flattered and surprised by the invitation. "Certainly, my Lord, if you wish."

"This is your doing, after all," said Anjer. "It is only right that you witness it." He turned to Robin. "Captain, would you ask Count Marik to attend us?"

✢ ✢ ✢ ✢ ✢

Robin found the Count waiting nervously with Jay'el and Xeer and relayed Anjer's request.

"Don't look so worried, Ty! Anjer's not so bad. It's the fat one you have to watch out for. If he takes a dislike to you, you'll know all about it."

Marik grimaced. "Thanks for the optimism. It's alright for you two. You're heroes of the hour. Everyone's talking about you and the Major." He suddenly lowered his voice, making Robin frown. "I'll tell you now, though, I've heard some ugly stories circulating concerning what Rykan did to her. I don't know how it got out, but you might want to warn her."

Robin's heart fell as he watched Marik stalk toward the tent where he would pledge his allegiance to Andaryon's Crown. He knew how adamant Sullyan was that the true reason for her being here should remain concealed. She would be furious if someone had let the information slip. In uneasy contemplation, he strolled back to the giants, who were sitting with Xeer and Jay'el. Kester was brewing fellan while Jay'el polished Sullyan's sword. None of them commented, but Robin thought he caught a glimpse of something in Kester's eyes as the man passed him a steaming mug.

The Major appeared after half an hour and told them that Marik was in talks with Anjer. They would leave now, and the

Count would follow later. By mid-afternoon they were back in the field medics' camp, but Robin still hadn't mentioned Marik's concerns. Sullyan was preoccupied with her orders and he let her be. They wouldn't meet up with Ky-shan and the rest of their company until tomorrow, so he hoped there would be time to broach the subject later that night.

✣ ✣ ✣ ✣ ✣

As soon as they arrived at the medics' camp, Sullyan went to check on Ki-en. Jay'el trailed her like a whipped puppy, convinced she would leave him behind. When she entered the tent, she saw the injured lad was fully conscious and drinking from a mug of spice-tea. His face lit up when he saw them both, and he turned adoring eyes on Sullyan.

She sat on the edge of his bunk and took his hand. "How are you feeling, Ki-en?"

He grinned, a lopsided look full of pleading. "I am very well, Lady. My leg is a little sore, but nothing that won't come right after a bit of exercise."

She frowned and his young face paled.

"Lady," he begged, leaning forward and clasping at her hand, "please don't leave me behind. I am well enough to ride a short way. I can sit double behind Almid or Kester. They said I could. Even if I can't join the fighting for a couple of days I can still be useful round the camp. I can look after the horses. I'll look after your horses, Lady! You and the Skipper saved my life. I want to thank you by serving you. Please, please don't leave me here!"

She studied his face in silence, her eyes dilating as she verified the truth of his words. Satisfied, she gave him a small smile. "Very well, Ki-en. When we leave tomorrow morning you can ride with one of the twins. Jay here will look after you and see that you take no further harm."

She gave Jay'el a hard look. Ky-shan's son looked relieved,

and her familiar use of his name gave the lie to the firmness of her tone. Grinning at Ki-en, he remained behind as Sullyan left the tent.

It was nearly dark by the time Marik returned from his swearing, and he immediately sought Sullyan out. She and Robin were sitting with the twins and Xeer, but she rose to embrace the Count as he approached. He was smiling, exuding a new air of confidence, and she was glad to see it replace his former gloom.

"I take it all went well with Anjer?" she asked, releasing Marik and settling back down beside Robin.

Marik sat too and exchanged a brief look with Robin that Sullyan didn't understand. Robin made no remark, and Marik launched into an account of his meeting with Anjer, so she soon forgot the odd look.

"He wants me and my men to form a separate company," finished Marik, his eyes intent on Sullyan's face. "One of Kryp's commanders was badly injured and has had to return to the Citadel. Anjer's asked me to take the leaderless men and incorporate them into my own command."

Sullyan smiled in genuine pleasure. "That is exceptionally good news, my friend. Anjer is showing his trust in you and giving you the opportunity to win the people's respect."

Marik nodded, yet his long face didn't reflect the pride she expected him to display. In fact, his melancholia suddenly returned.

"What is it, Count? Surely you do not doubt your ability to lead these men?"

He shook his head and raised clouded eyes to hers. "I've been ordered to take my command over to the southeastern flank, if I can work them between Rykan's lines. I won't be able to guard your back any more."

There was naked emotion in his gaze, and Sullyan felt her

heart contract. "Oh, Ty."

Marik clasped his hands together and took a deep breath, as if gathering his courage. "Sullyan, I've been meaning to say this for a long time now. Your faith in me and your support have meant so much over these past few weeks. After what happened at my mansion—after I betrayed you to Rykan—"

She opened her mouth to protest, but the Count rushed on.

"No, don't say it. I should never have let him intimidate me like that. I should have stood firm and resisted him. I did betray you, no matter what the circumstances. But you didn't hold it against me, and I've never really told you how grateful I am. Now you've been the means of me regaining not just my self-respect, but also my future. I've won the chance to impress Anjer, and if I can lead my company even half as well as you've led yours, then maybe I'll also get the chance to repay Rykan for all his years of oppression. Maybe I'll even get Cardon back! I owe all this to you, Sullyan, and I couldn't begin to express the depth of my gratitude."

Sullyan reached out and gripped his hands, too choked to speak. Marik's eyes filled with tears and he smiled at her. Then he rose, looking embarrassed, and held out his hand to Robin.

"I thank you too, Captain, for not running me through when you found me in Rykan's palace."

Robin stood and clasped the Count's hand. "We'd never have got Sullyan out without you. And I never really apologized for doubting you, and behaving so stupidly at the drovers' hut."

There was a brief and awkward silence, both men thoroughly embarrassed by the show of emotion. Then they dropped each other's hands and Marik stepped away. He faced Sullyan, saying formally, "I wish you good hunting, Major. I'm sure we'll meet again once Rykan's forces are defeated."

He inclined his head and walked briskly away.

Sullyan watched him go, pride and fear warring in her heart.

She didn't want to part with him, but she knew that his destiny lay apart from hers now. He had his loyalty and skills to prove, and she would never deny him that chance. She sat in introspective silence after Marik had left, and twice rebuffed Robin's weak attempts to engage her in conversation. Xeer and the twins showed no signs of wanting to talk either, and she was thankful when Robin eventually gave up, leaving her to her thoughts.

Chapter Twenty-Three

The haunting sound of Cal's longwhistle always had the power to soothe Rienne's soul. She smiled to see him lost in his music, the silver instrument held lightly to his lips. His eyes were half closed and his fingers moved almost of their own volition, the notes like threads of silk weaving into a rich and wonderful tapestry of sound.

The tune was one she had always loved and she could not resist its allure. Her hand moved, caressing the wood of the guitar she held, her long fingers finding the strings. Her other hand formed the first chord of the song and she strummed, softly at first, and then with more confidence as Cal played the melody over the guitar's rich thrum. She almost held her breath, half expecting to hear Sullyan's sweet tones. Her vision blurred and her throat stung, but the guitar sang on.

Taran sat opposite her in their shared apartment, and she saw his eyes close as he immersed himself in the music. It was a balm to them all, soothing hearts and souls worn out by worry and care. Rienne could almost imagine a time when their spirits would be free of sadness and they could laugh and sing once more.

The apartment door crashed open and the guitar strings twanged harshly as Rienne jerked with shock. Bull burst into the room, his face white and pinched and his forehead damp with sweat. Rienne felt her heart shrink and thought it would stop with fright.

"Gods, Bull, what is it? What on earth's happened?"

The big man didn't answer. He was staring at them strangely, as if he had never seen them before. Then his normally florid face regained its color and even flushed a deeper red, causing Rienne to fear for his heart. She propped the guitar against the settle and rose to take his arm.

"Come on, sit down. Please tell us what's wrong."

Bull allowed her to lead him to the settle and collapsed onto it, shaking his head.

"Rienne, I'm so sorry. It's nothing. It was just hearing you play that guitar. It has such a distinctive tone, I thought for a moment Sully was—"

He broke off and gulped a breath, composing himself with difficulty.

"I just didn't think. I'm sorry. It was an instinctive reaction. I know damned well she's not here. I shouldn't have burst in like that."

Rienne felt the tension rush from her body, leaving her weak. She laid a trembling hand on his arm.

"It's alright, Bull, we know how you feel. Cal, get the man some fellan."

Bull drank one large mug straight off and Cal poured him another, rolling his eyes at Rienne. Then he refilled hers and Taran's mugs, finally pouring one for himself. He sat down opposite the settle, while Taran leaned back in his chair by the fire.

"I've rarely felt as helpless as I have these past few days." Bull's voice was rough with emotion and Rienne patted his arm. "When it became obvious a few years ago that I wouldn't be able to stand for Sully much longer, I made myself a promise. I vowed that no matter what, I'd always be there for her. I've been a part of her command ever since she won it under Major Anton, but our relationship began earlier than that, the first day she arrived at the Manor, a tiny bit of a thing sitting on Blaine's saddlebow. That's thirteen years ago now."

He stared at his mug, absently swirling its contents.

"She's gone on campaigns without me before, but she's never been beyond the Veils without me there guarding her back. She's so far away, Rienne! The thought that I'll never see her again—never speak to her, or feel her warm and generous spirit—is slowly destroying me."

Rienne felt tears sting her eyes and her throat closed tightly.

Bull glanced at her. "Now that I know what's been happening these past few days and what she's planning next, the knowledge that I can't help her is getting too much to bear."

"You've heard from her?" Rienne's voice was a harsh croak.

"From Robin."

"And they're both alright? Is Brynne … alright?"

Bull nodded. "They are now." Seeing Rienne's look of anguish, he took a steadying breath. "I'm getting ahead of myself. Let me tell it from the beginning, as Robin told me."

Cal once more refreshed their mugs and Bull launched into Robin's account of their initial meeting with the Hierarch's generals and Sullyan's method of persuading the pirates to follow her. Even Rienne managed to smile at some of Robin's descriptions—especially those concerning General Kryp—but her amusement faded when she heard the account of the duel with Ky-shan.

"Was it really necessary to take such a risk? She'd already been warned against dueling by the Hierarch."

Bull shrugged. "I've never known her to take an unnecessary risk. I think the Hierarch was probably aware she'd have to do something drastic. He wasn't warning her against dueling so much as telling her to be careful how she went about it."

"Oh." Rienne frowned.

"If only I'd been there instead of Robin. He's never heard the full story of her travels as a young girl. She's done far riskier things than sail with a bunch of pirates! I'd have known what to expect, but poor Robin probably thought she was mad."

He went on to relate the rest of Robin's news, ending with the Captain's account of the recent field council. Rienne's face went white when she heard about the injuries he and Sullyan sustained. What frightened her more, though, was the fast-approaching confrontation with Rykan.

"How long do you think it'll be before they entice him onto the Plains, Bull?"

"I don't know the terrain, so I only have Robin's guess to go on. He thinks a week, maybe less. Depends on how quickly they draw him—that is, if they can get him to take the bait."

Rienne gasped. "As soon as that? Brynne must be feeling very nervous. I'd be terrified."

Bull snorted. "If she is, she'll not be showing it."

Rienne sat in silence while they finished the fellan, leaving Cal and Taran to quiz Bull further. The big man was obviously feeling much better by the time he rose to return to his quarters, but his lighter mood hadn't transferred to Rienne. She closed the door behind him with a trembling hand, careful to conceal it from both Taran and Cal.

✣ ✣ ✣ ✣ ✣

The next afternoon, Taran went looking for Bull. The big man wasn't always easy to find, for although he had no fixed duties now that the Major wasn't running her office, he still took care of applications from young hopefuls who wanted to join the King's forces. Part of the Major's duties was to screen cadets for latent powers. She had always been hopeful of finding more untrained Artesans and convincing them to develop their talents. According to Bull, she hadn't had much success. The current prejudice against the craft meant that any youngsters showing even the slightest hint of 'unnatural powers' were likely to be forcefully dissuaded from using them by their parents. Yet Sullyan had still considered the process worthwhile. Some people didn't show signs of the gift until their late teens.

Robin had often helped with this task, but with the two of them gone, it now fell to Bull. He had also resumed his training of the youngest cadets, the job he had done before retiring. Blaine had apparently recognized Bull's need to keep busy, and the various masters at the Manor appreciated any help they could get. So during the day, Taran knew, Bull could be almost anywhere within the Manor house or grounds.

This time, though, Taran found him in his rooms, the last place he had expected Bull to be.

He knocked on the door, and after a moment's silence he heard the big man's footfall. The door opened only slightly and Bull peered round it, a decidedly shifty look in his eye. When he saw who his visitor was he ushered Taran inside, closing the door swiftly behind him. Taran immediately noticed the two full packs lying on the floor and stared at his friend in suspicion.

"What's going on, Bull?" The big man had the grace to color slightly and Taran rounded on him. "I hope you weren't planning to go off alone!"

Bull walked over to the table, where he sat and picked up a mug of fellan. He gestured toward the fire. "There's more in the pot."

Taran pursed his lips but played along, pouring a mugful and sitting down opposite his friend. "Well? Rienne's been going out of her mind with worry for Sullyan and fretting to go back. It would destroy her, you know, if you went off without telling us."

"What do you take me for, Taran? Of course I was going to tell you. It's Blaine I haven't told. My guilty conscience must be pricking me. I thought it was him at the door just now." Bull stared down into his mug. "I know I'm not strictly answerable to him now—not in a military sense, anyway—but I do want to return here … after. I've been with him for more years than I care to remember, Taran, and old habits die slowly. I still jump when I see him."

Taran had to chuckle, remembering his own urge to salute when meeting Blaine the other morning. "He does have that effect, doesn't he?"

Bull gave a lopsided grin. "It's been very carefully cultivated. He does it to cover up his sensitive side."

Taran snorted. "So what's the plan? Does Robin know you're intending to go back? Does the Major?"

"Hell, no!" Bull's face flushed a deeper red. "If I tell her, she'll only curse and order me back. I might tell Robin once we've gotten as close as we can, but it'll be up to him whether or not he tells Sully. Personally, I don't think he will." The big man closed his eyes and sighed deeply. "She ordered me not to follow her, Taran. I hate disobeying her, but I need to know I've done everything I can. Even if it's only to be there at the end …." He swallowed painfully. "I can't just abandon her now. I've known her for thirteen years, since she was a tiny girl of ten. I've trained her, helped her, worked with her, fought by her, nursed her, healed her, and learned from her. How can I let her down now?" He fell silent, memories blurring his eyes.

"Rienne feels the same," said Taran. "She's eating herself up with guilt thinking she could still be of some use. It's not like her, and Cal's been quite concerned. What worries me, though, is the possibility we'll get in the way, or be attacked, or even end up being taken hostage if Rykan's men discovered us. Think what would happen if he found out who we were."

Bull nodded. "You're right to consider that, of course, but I don't think it's a risk. Rykan will be fully committed to fighting the Hierarch's troops, and I don't propose to go looking for his men. According to Robin, they've been contained within the forests to the east of the Plains, and we'd be coming at the Citadel from the northwest. We would be well away from the fighting. I simply have to go, Taran. I need to know I'm near her if she needs me at the end."

That evening, Taran told Cal and Rienne what Bull was proposing. Both were keen to go, although Cal's reasons leaned more toward giving Rienne something to ease her aching soul.

Taran smiled at them. "That's settled, then. Bull's going to see Blaine tomorrow to let him know. You'd better inform Chief Healer Hanan, Rienne. They're going to miss you in the infirmary."

"I'll miss them too," she said. "It's been wonderful working with them all, and I've learned so much. But this is more important, Taran. There'll be time enough after ... to resume our lives. Mine's been at a standstill these last few weeks, and it'll never be the same again. At least let's see this through to the end and decide where we go after that."

The next morning, Taran woke to a knock on his door. He was surprised to see Bull standing there, smiling sheepishly at him.

"I thought you were going to see the General this morning, Bull?"

"I am, Taran, and I'm sorry if I woke you, it's just ... oh gods, look, would you mind coming with me? I know it sounds feeble, but I'm dreading facing him. If he gets difficult and starts arguing with me, you can stop me from losing my nerve."

Taran smiled. "Of course I'll come. Sound military principle, eh? Safety in numbers."

Half an hour later, the General's valet, Hyram, ushered them back out of Blaine's office. Taran turned to Bull, seeing his own amazement mirrored on the big man's face.

"That wasn't quite what you expected, was it?" he said.

Bull slowly shook his head. "No. I really thought he'd do his best to stop me going. I never imagined he might be wishing he could go himself. Sully would never believe it. Hell, I'm not sure I believe it! Do you know, Taran, in all the years I've known him that's the most humanity I've ever seen him show?"

They walked slowly back through the Manor, Taran playing the emotional yet successful interview over in his mind. Blaine had immediately known why they were there, and hadn't bothered to conceal his envy over Bull's freedom to do as he pleased. There hadn't been the slightest suggestion he would try to prevent their going, only good wishes and admonitions to be careful. Bull's dumbfounded expression was the funniest thing Taran had seen for a long time.

"Private joke?"

Taran's head jerked up. "Oh, hello, Dexter, I didn't see you there."

Sullyan's Sergeant grinned at him as he fell into step beside Bull. "Been applying to the General to join us, have you?"

Bull snorted. "If that were true, it wouldn't be as incredible as what's just happened, Dex." The Sergeant raised his brows. "We've just been telling Blaine we're going back to Andaryon, to try to help Sully. What do you think he said?"

"Fifty days in the cells for insanity, or insubordination?"

"That's more or less what I expected. How about 'good luck and I wish I could go with you'?"

Dexter's jaw dropped. "That's not even a good joke, Bull."

"That's because it isn't a joke. It's what he said. Ask Taran."

Dexter whistled. "Do you suppose his good wishes would extend to the lads if they asked him the same question?"

"I wish I could say yes, but we both know it's not possible. Taran, Cal, and Rienne are coming, and that's about as large a group as I can manage. Even if we could take the lads, we'd never get near the Citadel unnoticed. If we make it, we'll be sure to let Sully know you wanted to come."

"Make sure you do. Any one of us would die for her if we thought it would do any good."

Bull clapped Dexter on the shoulder and the Sergeant left them. Bull and Taran carried on toward the Adept's shared apartment. When they arrived, they found that Cal and Rienne had already packed their things, including Taran's, and had even thought to send for supplies. Yet this foresight brought its own problems, and Rienne was currently trying to calm down a tearful Tad. The young lad was desperate to go with them. Taran knew he wouldn't have had a clue how to dissuade Tad, and watched in admiration while Rienne, her usual good sense surfacing once more, used the two arguments the boy couldn't refute.

"First," she said reasonably, "we'd never get Goran to agree to release you. You know how much he depends on you. And second, this will be a very dangerous trip. You wouldn't want Captain Tamsen to be distracted from his duties by worrying about you, now would you?"

Tad scrubbed at his tear-stained face, plainly struggling to find a way out of agreeing with her. Finally, he sniffed. "No, I suppose not."

Bull patted his shoulder. "Good lad. We need people we can trust to stay here and keep things in order for when we return. Robin will be very proud of you, lad, when I tell him how brave and helpful you've been."

Rienne smiled gratefully at Bull as the young lad's expression lightened. She saw him off while Taran took a last look round the apartment. He closed the door behind them as they headed down to the horse lines.

✠ ✠ ✠ ✠ ✠

The day following the command meeting, Sullyan and Robin tracked the rest of their band to where they had camped for the night. Robin was pleased to see that Ky-shan had followed Sullyan's instructions, and their party was challenged by the sentries before he saw the campfires' glow. They rode in to enthusiastic greetings from the entire camp. Any residual resentment had clearly been wiped away by their selfless bravery on behalf of Jay'el and Ki-en. The injured young lad, who had ridden double with Kester, endured his fellows' ribbing with a shy grin.

While Sullyan went to make a quick round of the men, Ky-shan pulled Robin aside. "Skip, is it true what they're saying about what Rykan did to her?"

Robin went cold. "Why, what have you heard?"

The pirate gave him a terse and accurate account of the abuse Rykan had inflicted. "Is that why she can't return to Albia, why she's here with the Hierarch's men? To take revenge?"

"Something like that. How many people know, Ky-shan? She really didn't want this getting out."

"Too late, Skip, it's all round the men. They're furious because of it. She'll be finding out about now, I reckon, just how mad they are."

Robin sighed. "Be prepared for her being in a foul mood then. She hates pity or sympathy."

"She'll get no pity from us." Ky-shan shook his head. "But it's made me feel bad about what I said to her when she goaded me into challenging her at the Citadel."

Robin frowned, trying to remember.

"I said I'd throw her to the men or something like that," the pirate reminded him. "Now I know why she fought me so hard! I just hope she doesn't hold it against me."

The Captain grinned. "Oh, don't worry on that score. If she

was holding a grudge against you, you'd know it, believe me!"

As Robin feared, Sullyan returned from her rounds hard-eyed and pale. She had obviously heard exactly what the men thought of Rykan for what he had done to her. Robin took one look and wisely decided to keep his peace on the matter. He hastily briefed the giants and the two younger men to do the same.

Ki-en handed her a mug of fellan and she sat down stiffly by the fire. She drank wordlessly, and no one else spoke. Robin never heard any of them mention the subject again, but neither he nor the Major ever had to see to their own horses, gear, campfire, or food again during that campaign. Almid and Kester, alternating with Jay'el and Ki-en, saw to everything for them.

During the week that followed, Sullyan and her company were kept busy using their skills to harry the enemy and drive them forward, sometimes even feigning retreat to lure them nearer and nearer the Citadel. Their tactics seemed to be working according to the news they received from the other sections of the Hierarch's forces.

✤ ✤ ✤ ✤ ✤

Also during that week, and with no word of warning to Robin, Taran, Cal, and Rienne followed Bull through the Andaryan countryside. They moved cautiously, taking their time, scouting ahead to avoid any possibility of running into enemy forces. As they rode through Cardon, Marik's province, they found his people still wary and unwilling to leave the security of their homes. Rumors of war had spread throughout the realm and the countryside was largely deserted. This suited the little group, as it made their journey easier. On Bull's advice, they passed wide to the west of Marik's abandoned mansion, adding a few extra miles to their journey but avoiding the possibility of meeting any of Rykan's men who might still be seeking the Count. The nearer they came to the Citadel, the higher Rienne's anticipation grew.

✣ ✣ ✣ ✣ ✣

Sullyan's company had just returned from yet another successful attack when a dispatch rider galloped into camp. He made straight for Sullyan. The men were tired, dirty, and hungry, and there were injuries to be dealt with, so the Major left Robin organizing the camp while she spoke with the messenger. His news came as no surprise. She had been expecting it for at least two days.

Nevertheless, her expression was somber as she joined Robin on his rounds. They passed through the men together, seeing that they cared for their horses first before cleaning themselves up. Then she dealt with the more serious wounds. Two men had taken crossbow bolts, and these had to be drawn. Her own wound had healed well, although there would always be an indentation in the flesh where the bolt had damaged the muscle. Robin let her work without bothering her with questions. She was grateful—he knew she would tell him what the dispatch had said once they were seated round their own fire.

A couple of hours later, with watches set and men resting, Sullyan called Almid, Kester, Ky-shan, Jay'el, and Ki-en to her fire to tell them the news. She regarded them from the comfort of her cloak, the firelight leaping gold before her eyes, and watched for their reactions.

"A dispatch rider arrived earlier, gentlemen. The Lord General has recalled me. I leave for the Citadel at once."

Robin didn't react, but Ky-shan frowned and Jay'el looked worried. "Why, Lady? Why should we go back? We're doing everything they asked of us."

She smiled gently. "You did not hear me, Jay. It is I who has been recalled, not the whole company."

Ky-shan shifted uncomfortably. "What's happened? Has something gone wrong?"

"The campaign is proceeding according to plan. Rykan's men

are approaching the Plains. The main body of the Hierarch's forces is preparing to meet them before the Citadel, and all companies—including ours—will be required to engage them."

"But you won't be leading us."

She inclined her head. "That is correct."

Jay'el was indignant. "Why not?"

She turned to him. "Think, Jay. You know what we have planned for Rykan's defeat. If I am to be the Hierarch's Champion, I cannot risk myself in the kind of pitched battle that will be fought on the Plains. If I was killed, or even severely injured, our scheme would fail. It was only to gain the trust of the Hierarch's generals and troops that I was permitted this much freedom. So, Ky-shan, tomorrow you are to begin a withdrawal from this area. Your instructions are to meet up with Count Marik, regroup under General Kryp, and do as he directs you. Robin and I will return to the Citadel."

Almid stretched out his hand, requesting contact. Since she had shown the mute twins how to communicate with those who had the power to hear them, they had become proficient, speaking regularly with their fellows. Yet they never failed to ask permission before bespeaking her. Sullyan smiled at the huge man and his rough, untutored voice echoed in her mind.

Kester and I will come with you.

It wasn't a request. She briefly considered refusing him, but quickly let it go. Gratefully, she squeezed his huge forearm.

"I thank you, Almid."

Ki-en might not have heard Almid's voice, but he immediately guessed what had been said. "I'm going with you too."

Ky-shan nodded, grinning when he saw the expression on Sullyan's face. "All five of us are going with you, Lady." He held up a hand as she began to protest. "Don't waste your breath. Refusing will do you no good. We've fulfilled our part of the bargain, and we've seen what you are. Now that we understand why you're here and what you're doing, we want to help you. All of my men would follow you wherever you led them now. Indeed, it will be hard to make them accept someone else, even someone like Marik, who they know. But my mind's made up. Most of the band will go with the Count to swell his numbers, but the five of us," he swept the twins, Jay'el, Ki-en, and himself with a gesture, "are staying with you."

His gaze never wavered, and Sullyan felt her heart contract. She lowered her eyes, unable to speak for the moment, and shook her head at their obstinacy. When she raised it again, Ky-shan was smiling.

It was a strange moment the next day when Ky-shan summoned the band and told them what was to happen. Sullyan couldn't help but contrast their reactions to this news with the scene back at the Citadel when they had first learned they must go into the field under a woman's command. They had railed long and hard against that; now they railed against her leaving.

Ky-shan swiftly lost patience with their protests and was about to rebuke their lack of discipline when Sullyan stopped him. Coming forward to where they could all see her, she faced the men. They fell silent. Looking round at their familiar faces, she found a smile for them.

"Gentlemen, I thank you for your loyalty and support these past weeks. You are brave and fearless fighters. Count Marik will be glad to have your strength among his men. I will commend you highly to the Hierarch, and I know you will continue to play your part. If I can, once Rykan is defeated, I will speak with you again before you depart for the east. If I cannot … well, I want you to know now that I am proud to have fought alongside you and I wish you every success."

She paused, and then raised her lilting voice in song.

"May the westerly breezes blow you
Safe across the Triple Sea,
To Tallimore, to rest evermore,
Where we may meet once more,
If our charted course is true."

Her ritual leave-taking brought tears to many of the seamen's eyes, although they scorned to show it. They cheered her loudly and long, and her emotions soon forced her to withdraw to her own campfire where she sat wrapped in silence, wordlessly accepting fellan laced with brine rum from Kester.

She left Ky-shan to organize his band's departure, setting Xeer at their head as they rode out to join Marik. The Count was leading the columns of the right flank, under General Kryp. Once they had gone, Sullyan gathered up her belongings and prepared to return to the Citadel.

Chapter Twenty-Four

Taran had taken the dawn watch that morning and he still had some time to go before he could rouse his companions. It was dark and he was cold, despite the small campfire keeping the frost off his back. The blanket folded beneath him was beginning to feel lumpy and he reached down to pull it straight. A sound caught his hearing and he stopped mid-gesture, his fingers moving toward his sword hilt.

He let out a breath of relief as he watched the dark bundle that was Bull unfold itself. The big man stretched, yawned silently, and climbed to his feet. His eyes met Taran's and they exchanged a nod, the Adept's hand relaxing away from his sword. Bull moved over to Taran's side of the fire and sat on the edge of his blanket.

"What on earth are you doing awake at this hour, Bull?"

Like Taran, Bull kept his voice low so as not to disturb Cal or Rienne. "I thought it might be a good time to try for contact with Robin. I've been putting it off because I'm not sure how he'll react. The last thing I want is to distract him from his duties, but I've found it hard not keeping in regular contact. The discipline is drummed into every Manor swordsman from our earliest days as cadets, and that time is many years in the past for me."

Taran sat in silence while Bull ordered his mind and quested for contact with Robin. Once he achieved it, he threw a questioning look at Taran. The Adept accepted the offer to be included in the exchange. He hadn't seen anything unusual on his watch, and there was no reason to believe anything would go wrong over the next few minutes. However, as Bull's solid, symmetrical psyche melded with his, Taran still managed to keep a part of his mind on his duty.

Robin's mental tone was unsurprised as he returned Bull's diffident greeting.

So you've crossed the Veils, big man? I thought you might.

Bull's relief at the Captain's lack of censure was reflected in his tone as he replied.

We couldn't stand it any longer. The waiting was killing us. Where are you?

On our way back to the Citadel. Anjer recalled Sullyan yesterday.

Did she resist him?

Of course not. She knows how vital it is that she stays safe.

I'm glad. I was worried she might risk herself in the main battle, but I suppose I should have known better. So what do you think, Robin? Should we tell her we're here, or keep it from her?

There was a pause while Robin thought it over.

I think she's better off not knowing. She's got enough on her mind at the moment. She'd be mad at you at first, and then she'd either order you back to Albia or tell you to head straight for the Citadel. Either way, she'd be concerned until she knew you were safe, and that would take her mind off this meeting with Rykan.

Bull nodded, and the gesture made Taran smile. It was redundant because Robin couldn't see it.

Alright, if you're sure that's best. I know she's going to be mad at me, and the last thing I want is to worry her. If we're going to keep out of the way, where's the best place to camp? We don't want to run into patrols from the Citadel any more than we want to meet Rykan's troops.

*Keep well away from the southeastern side of the Plains.
There are some woods to the west and southwest of the Citadel, but
they're a bit far away. There's only one place I know where you'll
probably be safe. It's ... here.*

An image appeared in Taran's mind, and he sensed Bull
carefully studying it, memorizing the location.

*Thanks, Robin. That looks as good a place as any. I'll let you
know when we get there. Now, how is Sully's health holding up?*

Robin's mental tone changed and sadness suffused his voice.

*The Hierarch's physician has given her a potion which seems
to be helping. Most of the pain is controlled now. At least it's not
incapacitating her like it did before. But it's still there, Bull, eating
into her soul and slowly destroying her. I've been able to forget
about it during this campaign, but now that the final meeting is so
close, I can't get it out of my mind.*

Taran felt his heart sink at the despair in Robin's tone. It was
too much for Bull to bear, and he broke contact. Without a word to
Taran, he went back to his blankets.

✢ ✢ ✢ ✢ ✢

When Sullyan and Robin rode back into the Citadel later that day,
the Lord General came to meet them. He had clearly been waiting
for them. Grooms stepped forward to take their horses, and
servants relieved them of their packs. Ky-shan and the rest of
Sullyan's escort were amazed when they were included in this
courteous treatment. They had even been assigned a small suite of
rooms within the Palace. Before he left them, Anjer passed on a
request that they all present themselves to the Hierarch, although
Sullyan begged permission for a bath before fulfilling that
obligation.

Anjer laughed. "You didn't think his Majesty would make you
forego that pleasure, did you?"

She smiled with relief. "How long do we have, my Lord?"

"Long enough. A page will come for you."

Leaving Ky-shan and the others to settle into their suite, Sullyan and Robin made their way to their own rooms. Sullyan stripped off her soiled clothing and made straight for the bathing pool. She was accustomed to doing without when on campaign, but it only heightened her appreciation of clean hot water. A chance to scrub off the accumulated grime was most welcome.

Slowly divesting himself of his own clothes, Robin regarded her critically. "You've lost weight again."

She didn't reply, but she did hold out her arms to him as he joined her in the pool.

Two hours later, scrubbed and refreshed, Sullyan, Robin, and their escort followed a page through the palace corridors. Each person they passed, whether servant or noble, bowed courteously in Sullyan's direction. She acknowledged them all with a nod of her head. As they approached the private areas of the palace, Sullyan was surprised to see a familiar figure walking toward her. The Princess Idrimar halted, obviously intent on speaking, and Sullyan accorded her a deep curtsey. The men following her bowed.

The Princess stood with her hands tightly clenched. Her face was pinched, her pale grey eyes red-rimmed. They flicked uncertainly over the faces before her.

Sullyan regarded her with some concern. "Can I help you, Highness?"

Idrimar's air of anxiety deepened and she dropped her gaze. "Please forgive me, Major, I know you've only just returned from battle. You must be on your way to see my father, and I don't want to hold you up. It's just ...."

"Please, Highness, ask. I will tell you anything you want to know."

"I wanted to ask you ... do you have any news of Count

Marik?"

It took all Sullyan's will not to smile, and she sincerely hoped the others were being as circumspect. The Princess was trying hard to hide her true feelings, but her heart could not have been plainer had she held it in her hands.

"Highness, let me assure you that the Count is quite well. He leads his men on the right flank, under General Kryp. He has acquitted himself admirably so far, and I believe your father will be pleased with his contribution to this conflict."

Idrimar's cheeks took on a faint pink bloom. A shy smile curved her lips and she clasped one of Sullyan's hands. "Major, I thank you. You have eased my mind. I'll let you go now. We mustn't keep my father waiting."

The older woman departed, and Sullyan glanced meaningfully at Robin. "It seems the Count really has made an impression. Who would have thought it?"

Robin grinned. "Do you think anything will come of it?"

"Who knows? But the Princess is smitten, that much is clear."

The page led them to the door of the Hierarch's small audience chamber. Before they entered, Sullyan spent a few moments reassuring Ki-en and Jay'el about the forthcoming interview with their monarch. None of the pirates had met him, nor thought they ever might, and were understandably nervous. The older men hid it well, but the younger two could not. Once they had entered and lined up facing the oval table, the fanfare announcing the Hierarch's arrival made both boys jump.

Pharikian walked in, accompanied by guards and pages. He looked older, more careworn, and Sullyan frowned as she studied his face. He made his way to the table and halted beside the throne. When his eyes met hers he smiled, and his face shed years. Shyly, she returned the gesture.

Once the guards and pages had stepped back, Sullyan and her

escort kneeled to honor the monarch, she and Robin making the obeisance due to a Senior Master. Pharikian beckoned them to rise and come forward. When Sullyan approached he enveloped her in a loving hug, and she heard Jay'el gasp in astonishment.

Releasing her at last, Pharikian stood back, his gaze scrutinizing her thoroughly.

"You're thinner, Brynne."

She answered with a smile. "If you had been in the field for weeks, eating trail rations and fighting Rykan's troops, Majesty, you would be thinner too." Her familiar tone drew startled glances from Ky-shan and his men. "But you do look tired."

Pharikian gave a small shrug. "We are nearing the end, Brynne."

Rejecting the gilded throne, he drew them to a collection of easy chairs at the side of the chamber. Before permitting them to sit, he had her conduct the introductions and commended Ky-shan especially for his services to the Crown. He then eyed Jay'el, causing the young man to fidget nervously.

"I have heard of your little foolishness, boy. I hope you have learned your lesson and decided to behave like a man."

Jay'el swallowed. "Y-yes, Majesty."

Pharikian invited them all to sit. He and Sullyan spent some time discussing the past weeks, as she was keen to know how the rest of his troops had fared against Rykan. The monarch told her what he knew, but what interested her most was that no one had encountered the Duke in person.

Pharikian waved a dismissive hand. "I'm not surprised, Brynne. He'll be keeping himself safe somewhere far to the rear with his personal guard around him. He won't even risk his generals in the real fighting. If you were hoping he would commit himself, you'll be disappointed."

"Then we must devise a plan to make him do so, Majesty.

With your permission, I have a few ideas that I would be happy to put to the Lord General."

He smiled. "I'm sure Anjer would appreciate any advice you care to give."

Pharikian then turned to Ky-shan and asked the pirate about his band. His curiosity satisfied, Pharikian dismissed them, but once Ky-shan and his men had left, he called Sullyan back. Robin remained by the door at a gesture of the Major's hand.

The monarch drew her to him. "How are you, Brynne?"

Holding his yellow gaze, she replied honestly. "I will be better for a rest, Timar."

He frowned. "I'd heard you were wounded rescuing that foolish boy."

She gave him a small smile. "It was a flesh wound and has healed well. Robin's was worse, but he is also fit now. Never fear, Timar, it will not affect my ability to confront Rykan."

Pharikian was stung. "That isn't why I asked!" His tone was so sharp that Robin glanced over. Sullyan touched Pharikian's arm in tacit apology and he accepted with a shake of his head. "How are you apart from that?"

She knew what he really wanted. Out in the field, she had almost been able to forget the poison in her system. Deshan, the Master Physician, had done a good job in re-sealing it and slowing its advance. The potion he had given her had numbed the pain and allowed her natural vitality to reassert itself. Yet she couldn't fool herself into thinking she was well. Deshan had bought her a little more time, that was all.

Not trusting herself to speak, she opened her psyche to Pharikian's senses and invited him to see for himself.

The concern that flooded his features told her what she had guessed but hadn't wanted to acknowledge. He sighed sadly.

"We need another meeting with Deshan, child. I'll send for

you later. Go and get some rest, if you can. If there are any developments outside, I'll see that you hear of them."

Deshan and the Hierarch came to her rooms a couple of hours later. Sullyan had had some sleep and was feeling stronger. She had stretched out on the couch by the fire, leaving Robin still slumbering in the sleeping room. He woke at the page's tap on the door and came yawning into the living area as the Major admitted the two men.

The Master Healer took one look at Sullyan and frowned.

"Timar, she really shouldn't have been allowed to spend herself in the field like that. It wasn't a sensible thing to do."

Pharikian spread his hands. "We had no choice, Deshan. There was no other way to convince the generals to accept her."

Grumbling about the mental capacity of generals, Deshan gestured for Sullyan to lie on the couch. He sat beside her, one hand on her brow, the other holding her left hand. She allowed him access to her psyche so he could monitor her condition. When he saw how the poison had spread, the worry lines around his eyes deepened. Resignedly, he glanced up at the Hierarch.

"We can only do this once more, Timar. The poison has gone very deep, and if we delve too deeply to seal it off, we risk sealing her powers away too."

Sullyan gave a gasp. She knew that Pharikian hadn't told Deshan the entirety of her plans for Rykan. Indeed, she hadn't told the Hierarch everything. Much depended on the circumstances of the meeting, but she knew she would need every vestige of her powers if she was to defeat the Duke. Physical strength was only one part of the equation.

Pharikian understood her fear. He glanced from her worried eyes to those of his physician. "We will do as much as we can without impairing your energies, Brynne."

Robin approached, not wanting to be left out. "Can I help?"

Sullyan held out her hand to him and he came to the other side of the couch. She closed her eyes, opening her psyche fully to the three men around her. She sensed both Robin and the Hierarch giving control of their powers to Deshan, who used them, together with Sullyan's own fathomless, amber energy, to capture and encapsulate the invasive, black well of poison in her soul.

She could tell how repulsed Robin was by the texture and feel of the poison; he was staggered by how vast it had grown. So was she, although she fought not to show it. It seemed that every fiber, every corner, of her being was infected with it. Only one area was free, one tiny, pulsing, crystal clear star right at the core of her soul. Robin struggled not to show his despair, but they were each so completely interlinked that their senses and emotions could not be hidden. Sullyan couldn't bear to see him so crushed and sent out her love to surround his heart. Yet she couldn't soothe away his sense of failure, and when the work was done and the three men released their meld, Robin's face was damp with tears of shame.

Exhausted by the expenditure of power, Sullyan lacked the strength even to open her eyes. She sensed Robin moving away from the couch, his feet unsteady, and knew when Pharikian put an arm around his shoulders. She heard Deshan leave the room. Robin was trembling, giving way to his fear of losing his love. Sullyan yearned to comfort him, but her body wouldn't obey her. She was so thankful when she heard the Hierarch take Robin into a close embrace. Leaving Pharikian to help her lover work some of the pain out of his system, she slipped into a deep, restorative sleep.

✤ ✤ ✤ ✤ ✤

In his habitual curt manner, Lord General Anjer summarized the action so far.

"Our various companies in the field, under the direction of Generals Ephan and Kryp, continue to harry the flanks of Lord Rykan's troops. Forcing small battles where they can, they draw his men ever nearer the Citadel. Ephan controls the movements of the left flank while Kryp commands the right. Between them, they are herding Rykan's men into closer and closer formation, denying them the chance to slip around behind our forces and cut our supply lines.

"His Majesty's extra troops have now arrived in full, and while we're holding the majority of these in reserve so they'll be fresh for the final confrontation, some have been deployed to drive the enemy from behind to ensure Rykan doesn't fall back. Our tactics seem to be working, as neither Kryp nor Ephan has reported signs of retreat. It appears he's committed to following his challenge through. He always was an arrogant man, he'd never risk losing face with his commanders or subject lords by backing down."

Sullyan nodded and resumed her pacing. She, Anjer, and the Hierarch, accompanied by Robin, Almid, and Kester, had climbed to the roof of the Palace Tower where they had a panoramic view of the Plains to the east, the forests to the west, and even the small knoll where Sullyan, Robin, and Marik had had their first view of the Citadel. On emerging from the Tower doors, Sullyan's gaze had rested briefly on that insignificant hill, recalling their journey. The weak winter sun glinted off the frost coating the stone battlements.

She stood looking eastward, as if she could see the two opposing forces already drawn up in their battle lines.

"Still no one has seen the Duke himself?"

Anjer hugged his heavy black cloak tighter around him against the bitterly icy wind, his black eyes roving the countryside. "No. Most of Rykan's commanders have been sighted, driving their units from behind as usual, but so far no glimpses of either his generals or the great man himself. I shouldn't have thought you so eager to see him again anyway, Brynne."

They were on less formal terms now, at least when none of the other ranking officers were about, and Anjer had taken to using her given name. Despite this, Sullyan reacted forcefully to his casual statement, the barely controlled power blazing from her eyes causing him to step back in alarm.

"I should be very pleased never to set eyes on him again, Anjer! But it seems I have to be intimate with him one more time, whether I will it or no."

Anjer traded a worried look with the Hierarch and Robin, both of whom gazed back helplessly. Chastened, the General was about to apologize, but Sullyan got there first.

"Forgive me, my Lord, you did not deserve that. I ask your pardon."

He smiled wryly. "There's nothing to forgive, Brynne. It was a stupid thing to say."

She resumed her pacing, the outburst forgotten as her mind returned to their problem. "How soon before the main body of Rykan's troops reaches the Plains?"

Anjer glanced at the Hierarch, who nodded. "About three days, if they keep up their present rate of advance."

She turned to face him. "Could we hold them back now, if we chose?"

"Possibly." He frowned. "But why would we want to?"

Sullyan rested her hands on the parapet, heedless of the frost coating the stone, and gazed out over the Plains. "We have to know for sure where Rykan is." Her voice was a murmur, as if speaking to herself. "Force him to halt, make him regroup and rethink. Yes. Send units to attack the rear of his columns, see if they can flush him out. If so, well enough."

In the silence Pharikian shifted, as if reluctant to disturb her train of thought. "And if not?"

She didn't immediately respond. The watery sunlight shone

into her eyes, sudden moisture blurring her view of the Plains.

"If not ...." She paused and drew a shaky breath. "If not, then there is only one course of action left."

The Hierarch moved to stand before her. Taking her shoulders in both hands, he looked sternly into her misted eyes.

"No, Brynne! I won't risk you again."

Her breath came out as a sigh. "Ah, no, Timar, that was not my thought. I am not so eager to confront the Duke that I wish to ride out and find him myself." She gave Anjer a small grin.

He stared back at her. "What then, Brynne? What more could we do to entice Rykan out?"

She glanced guiltily across at Robin, seeing her Captain's sudden understanding. He knew what she meant and why she was so reluctant to suggest it. He couldn't help her, though, and gazed sympathetically back.

The Hierarch's grip on her shoulders tightened. "Well?"

She turned her eyes once more to the frozen Plains. Softly, she said, "There is someone else whom Rykan would be keen to recapture. Someone who has the Duke's price on his head for rescuing me. Someone for whom he may well be tempted out of concealment. But it would be asking much of one who has already risked himself for me and who even now strives to recover what he has lost."

She fell silent, disliking herself intensely for the suggestion. It was too late now, though. Anjer and Pharikian understood.

Anjer's tone was kind. "It may yet prove unnecessary, Brynne. But under the circumstances, I think it would be wise to prepare." Glancing around for a member of the Velletian Guard, who were never far from his presence, he snapped, "Send for Commander Vanyr. We need a runner to go into the field and recall Count Marik."

✤ ✤ ✤ ✤ ✤

Evening was drawing on. Taran sat watching a pan of water heating over the campfire. Cal and Rienne had nearly finished feeding the horses, and Bull, who had dug the latrine, was already sitting on the other side of the fire, wrapped in his thick, warm cloak. He stared deeply into the flames, his eyes unfocused as he communed with Robin.

They were nearly there, thought Taran. According to Bull, they were now less than a day's ride away from their destination, a small hill overlooking the Citadel Plains. From there, provided they were careful, they should be able to watch the final battle.

Bull had made them skirt several villages on this final stage of their journey. They had kept up a strict watch in rotation for any signs of either Rykan's or the Hierarch's men, but the woods were deserted. Bull had said that in such troubled times peasants and villagers kept as near to their homes as possible, so it hadn't been hard to avoid detection. The big man was not as fearful for their safety as he was for secrecy; it wouldn't do for rumors of a small group of Albians heading toward the Citadel to reach enemy ears. Despite the fact that it was winter and no one was working in the fields, Taran had seen some laborers out and about. Bull told him this meant the area hadn't been disturbed by fighting and so they should be safe.

Given the reason for their journey, thought Taran as he poured steaming water onto the dried fellan seeds, they were all in surprisingly good spirits, even Rienne. Just being on the move had given her the sense of purpose she had lacked since leaving Sullyan. And Bull's regular but short contacts with Robin were helping them feel included in what was happening. They now knew that the final day of battle, when the future of both realms would be decided, was drawing near.

Whether it was the fellan's rich aroma or the natural ending of his conversation with Robin, Taran didn't know, but Bull suddenly shifted, stretching his back and rubbing his hands. He smiled as Taran handed him a mug of fresh brew.

"What news, Bull?"

The big man glanced up as Cal and Rienne approached the fire. "Come and warm yourselves," he said, "while I tell you the latest piece of gossip."

They arranged themselves as close to the flames as they could, Cal throwing an arm about his love. Taran handed out more mugs and then placed some cuts of wild pig over the fire. The meat's gamey smell began to rise into the air.

Bull had a playful expression in his eyes. "Alright. Judging by what Robin's told us so far, who would you say was the least likely person to take on the role of hero?"

Rienne frowned. "What do you mean, Bull?"

"Well, no one's seen tip nor tail of Rykan since the fighting started, and apparently it's vital that he be present on the Plains in person. So who would you choose to go and flush him out?"

"Someone who knows what they're doing, that's for sure," said Cal. "But from the look on your face, that's not what they've done."

Rienne reached out and turned a piece of meat in danger of burning. "Who is it, Bull? Not that young seaman, the one who caused such trouble?"

Bull shook his head. "No, not him. It's Marik."

The healer sucked in a breath and Taran raised his brows. He said, "Is that wise? Didn't Rykan put a price on his head?"

Bull nodded. "That's precisely why Sully suggested him. Apart from her, Marik's the one person the Duke might be tempted out of hiding for. They're hoping to use him as bait."

"But what if Rykan kills him?" said Rienne. "Poor man, he's lost so much already. Has he agreed to do it?"

"I doubt he has much choice, dear heart. But they haven't

asked him yet, the messenger only left today. And it might not be necessary—Anjer's still hoping his troops can flush Rykan out. They'll only send Marik if everything else fails. You know, it's funny, really. A short time ago, Robin didn't have a good word to say for Marik. Yet now they're on first name terms and Robin speaks of him like a friend."

Rienne's voice carried an acid edge. "Then let's hope Rykan doesn't kill him. There's far too much talk of death at the moment as it is."

Her sobering words silenced them all.

✤ ✤ ✤ ✤ ✤

Vanyr's runner found the Count's command easily enough once Kryp had told him Marik's location. The Lord General's dispatch was placed in Marik's hands, and the Count was on his way back to the Citadel within the day. The other dispatch, the one addressed to both generals requesting them to do all they could to force Rykan's columns to halt, was being implemented before Marik and his escort reached the Citadel.

They rode in to general acclaim around noon the next day. The Velletian Guard saw to their horses and gear, and the Count was given time to refresh himself before being summoned to the Hierarch's presence.

All this Sullyan learned in an interview with the Hierarch that morning, an interview she had requested and during which she voiced a particular wish. When he heard what she was asking, Pharikian granted it willingly, though he failed to see her reasons.

"Why do you wish to speak privately with Count Marik before he comes to me, Brynne?"

She regarded him openly, her dislike of the situation plain in her eyes.

"I want to give him the opportunity to turn us down, Timar. He would never refuse you or the Lord General, and I want to make sure he thinks very carefully about what we are asking before he accepts."

Robin, by her side as always, made to comment, but she forestalled him. "Yes, I know, Robin, he is unlikely to refuse me either, but at least in private, between the two of us, I can do my best to dissuade him."

"Dissuade him?"

Pharikian frowned and Sullyan smiled sadly. "It is a gesture only, Timar, a sop to my conscience. Yet it will help me through the next few days if I know I have done all I can to keep him safe. Ultimately, it will be the Count's decision, but I am not the only one who values his safety."

The Hierarch pursed his lips, clearly understanding her meaning. She gave him an impish grin which he mirrored. He was aware of his daughter's unexpected feelings toward the Count.

Later that afternoon, Sullyan sent a page to show the Count into the small room she had chosen for their meeting. When he walked in, he was clearly surprised, confused to find himself facing her rather than the Hierarch. However, his pleasure at seeing her again soon took over.

"Sullyan!" He crossed to where she stood and embraced her warmly.

She looked him over. "How are you, Ty? I have heard glowing reports from Anjer of your successes. You are gaining quite a reputation."

He ducked his head and grinned. "I owe you a deep debt of thanks for the opportunity to do so."

"It was the least I could do, after what you gave up for me."

They stood looking at each other in sober silence before she drew him to the two easy chairs by the blazing fire. While he made himself comfortable, Sullyan poured fellan for them both.

Marik took a few mouthfuls, savoring the bitter richness. "So what's all this about, Sullyan?" When she didn't immediately reply, he glanced at her sharply. "What is it? What's wrong?"

She faced him, letting him see her discomfort. "I have something to ask of you, Ty, but I want you to understand that it is only a request. There is no compulsion for you to undertake this. No one will think less of you if you refuse."

He gave a wry smile. "Alright. Now that you've ensured my interest, tell me what you need."

She laced her fingers round her cup and leaned back. Briefly, she outlined the problem concerning Rykan's position and the necessity of enticing him onto the Plains.

"It is essential that he be there in person to receive the Hierarch's challenge. The Lord General has ordered his commanders to halt Rykan's advance and is sending units to the rear of the columns where we suspect Rykan to be hiding to force him into the open."

"And if he doesn't oblige?" Marik cocked his head when Sullyan didn't immediately reply.

She flicked him a guilty gaze. Never one to back down from an awkward situation, she was finding this harder than she had imagined. Luckily, comprehension dawned and Marik rescued her once again.

"Ah! I understand. You need to offer him a reason to show himself. You want me as bait."

She cringed at his frank choice of words. The fact that he obviously relished the prospect did nothing to lessen her guilt.

"You are not to feel constrained in any way to accept this, Ty," she said. "I wanted to be the one to ask you, to give you the chance to refuse if you wished. This is a serious matter, my friend. We both know what Rykan is capable of, and should he manage to capture you, your life would be less than worthless. You have been through enough already, and you are very dear to me. I would not see you endanger yourself unnecessarily."

Marik sat staring at her throughout this speech, his expression grave. When she was done, he put down his cup, kneeled on the floor beside her, and took one of her hands. Gazing into her eyes he said, "My dear, there's nothing I wouldn't do for you. You should know that by now. You have already repaid me ten times over for my help when you needed it, but friendship isn't about giving and receiving favors. It's about being there for someone whatever the circumstances. You knew very well I wouldn't refuse to do this, but I appreciate your giving me the choice. Don't forget, I have scores of my own to settle with Rykan, and this is just the chance I need. Come on, take me to the Hierarch. You can tell him I've been reluctantly persuaded to be his hero."

"Oh, Ty!"

She laughed, rose, and embraced him once again. "It is good to have you back."

Chapter Twenty-Five

The interview with Pharikian was short. Afterward, Marik left to brief his men and Sullyan took her leave of the Hierarch. She felt restless and troubled, and there was only one thing that gave her any ease when she felt that way. She went in search of Ky-shan, hoping to convince the brawny pirate to fence with her.

On her way through the Palace's private section she caught a momentary glimpse of the Count, who had been waylaid on his return to his men. The Princess Idrimar was currently engaged in showing Marik how deep her feelings for him had become and was encouraging him to be careful. She seemed to be employing her lips and hands rather more than her voice, and Marik was proving a good listener.

Sullyan smiled as she moved on, feeling lighter for that privileged glimpse of someone else's happiness.

Wrapping her heavy cloak around her, she emerged into the frosty air and headed for the barracks where the seamen were most likely to be found. When she located them, Ky-shan seemed suspiciously reluctant to accede to her request.

"I don't know, Lady," he said. "We don't want to fuel any more speculation about dueling, do we?"

She stared in disbelief. "Oh, come now, Ky-shan. That is not the real reason, is it? Has someone said something to you about protecting me?"

His reluctance to answer told her the suspicion was correct.

She spat a vicious barrack room obscenity, causing Ky-shan's eyes to widen, Jay'el to blush, and the twins to grin. Then, a smooth, clipped voice behind her made her freeze.

"Well, Major, if these men won't oblige you, I'm sure I can. No one's said anything to me about protecting you."

She turned slowly, seeing the tall form of Commander Vanyr. He stood loosely, one hand resting on the hilt of his sword. His stance suggested unconcern, but she read his eagerness in the lines of his body and the avid look in his eyes.

She clamped down on her irritation. She could not let him goad her. Vanyr was a man to take seriously. One didn't become the commander of the Hierarch's personal guard without being a consummate swordsman. Nonetheless, total concentration on an unknown but skilled opponent was just what Sullyan needed. This confrontation was inevitable, so why not conduct it before witnesses?

Vanyr was waiting. Slowly, she removed her cloak and jacket, handing them to Jay'el. His eyes on the commander, he said, "Be careful, Lady."

She smiled. "There is no call for concern, Jay'el. We are only fencing for exercise." Glancing at Vanyr's faintly superior expression, she added, "We are not in competition here, and there is no intent of bloodshed. Is that not so, Commander?"

"Of course." Moving economically, he stepped back into the larger space of the barracks training ground.

Sullyan observed how he moved and placed his feet, realizing immediately that he would be a difficult opponent. He was much taller than she was and had a greater reach. His lithe body might well cancel out any advantage her smaller size and agility usually gave her. Briefly, she entertained the notion of starting with a right-handed grip, but then remembered he had observed part of her fight with Ky-shan. A man like Vanyr wouldn't forget such talent. She abandoned the idea and slipped her sword free of its scabbard using her stronger left hand. She would watch for an opening to change grip if one presented itself.

The pirates moved to one side so they could watch the bout. Ky-shan was clearly uneasy. A couple of off-duty Velletian Guardsmen also strolled over to see what their commander was up to. Ignoring them all, Sullyan concentrated on the lithe man before her.

Vanyr stood lightly balanced, his gaze assessing her. He was probably the most dangerous fighter she had yet to meet. The prospect of learning his fighting style and testing her skills against him suddenly made her smile. It was what she wanted, to feel the purpose of her life again, to pit her strength and cunning against a worthy opponent, to be able to block everything else from her mind. It was what made her come alive, and she loved it.

This change in her demeanor clearly puzzled Vanyr. She saw his momentary confusion and used it to make the first strike. He failed to anticipate the move and was forced to parry. It was a clumsy stroke and was also, she thought, what he had intended to force out of her. His eyes showed a flash of ire, yet he was too fine a swordsman to allow irritation to affect him for long. Soon, they were fencing in earnest.

✤ ✤ ✤ ✤ ✤

Robin was growing restless. During Sullyan's interview with Marik and subsequent meeting with Pharikian, she had asked him to remain in their suite. He didn't mind. He knew what she was doing and appreciated the chance to rest. After a couple of hours he began anticipating her return. When she didn't appear, he started to worry that the meetings hadn't gone well. Another uneasy half hour passed before he finally decided to go look for her. First, he made his way to the small office where she would have spoken with the Count. As expected, the room was vacant, all signs of occupation removed by the servants. Thinking she might be discussing the battle with Pharikian, he walked through the corridors toward the Hierarch's more intimate audience chamber, the one he used for less formal interviews. Yet the Captain quickly realized the room wasn't in use as there were no guards outside. Even within his own Palace, the Hierarch was constantly shadowed by the Velletian Guard.

Robin was puzzled and stood a moment in thought before shrugging and turning back. Sullyan would either have returned to their rooms by now or perhaps be up on the battlements with Anjer. However, just as he began the walk back he saw the Lord General emerge from a corridor ahead.

Anjer saw him and turned. "Captain!"

Robin waited for Anjer to approach and accorded the huge man his due salute. Anjer had no time for formalities. "I need to find Brynne, Captain. Where is she?"

"I don't know, my Lord. Isn't she with the Hierarch …?"

"Their meeting ended over an hour ago. Can you find her, Captain? There have been developments and I need to speak to her."

Closing his eyes to aid his concentration, Robin searched for her familiar pattern. Finding it immediately, her total lack of response told him what was happening. He opened his eyes and grinned.

"I might have known." Seeing Anjer's puzzlement, he added, "She's having her mind diverted. She always does this when she's worried. I just pity the poor man she's chosen to distract her. She's out on the training ground, my Lord."

Anjer scowled. "Who with?"

Now it was Robin's turn to look puzzled. "I don't know. She's too committed to let me see, and I don't want to risk disturbing her. It must be someone very skilled or it wouldn't take up all her attention."

Anjer's face darkened, his whole body radiating anger. "Come with me." Turning, he strode toward the Palace's outer doors, moving so swiftly that Robin had to trot to keep up.

✤ ✤ ✤ ✤ ✤

Vanyr and Sullyan circled each other warily, looking for weaknesses. To Sullyan's delight and the Commander's clearly displayed annoyance, they were evenly matched. Vanyr had tried several times to disarm her or slip through her guard, but instead of proving easy to vanquish, Sullyan had forced him to employ every defensive maneuver he knew in order to avoid her lightning-fast strikes. She was lighter and more agile than he thought, and as he had never fought a woman before, he hadn't expected her strength. Sullyan had also developed other, subtler techniques to overcome her lack of height and mass, and she never allowed Vanyr into a position where he could use his greater weight against her. Instead, she kept him on the move, forcing him to spend his energy in lunge, parry, and dodge, while she danced lightly around him, looking for openings in his defenses.

Had he been less annoyed, she thought, less frustrated, less eager to humiliate her, he might have enjoyed the bout. Sullyan herself was enjoying it greatly. Her muscles felt strong and alive and her skin tingled with the energies flowing through it. She never felt as vibrant as when using her physical skills against a competent opponent and in the pure pleasure of the moment she completely forgot the animosity between them.

When Anjer's battlefield voice suddenly reverberated around the training ground—"Commander!"—Vanyr's reaction took her completely by surprise.

Sullyan broke off her attack instantly, but Vanyr did not. Intensely annoyed by his failure to master her, he neither retracted his lunge nor attempted to turn aside his blade. As Sullyan lowered her guard and stepped back, the tip of Vanyr's sword laid her left forearm open almost to the bone. Gasping in pain, she clamped her right hand over the wound and sank to one knee.

Robin sprinted over to help her. Vanyr stood towering over them both, a nasty smile playing on his lips. Anjer strode furiously up to him, black eyes blazing.

"I saw that, Commander, it was a deliberate strike! You heard me call you, man. Why didn't you put up your sword?"

Vanyr stood sullenly, unwilling to answer. Anjer turned to Sullyan, who had risen shakily with Robin's help, her hand still clamped about the bleeding wound. Her face was white and her eyes dilated wide as she expended power to slow the bleeding and ease the shock.

"I'm sorry, Major." Anjer's voice was gruff with concern. "I'll see he pays for that."

Sullyan dampened her power and turned some of her attention on Anjer. Calming her breath, she allowed a small, humorless smile to quirk her lips. "Never mind, my Lord." Her eyes turned hard as she regarded Vanyr. "You must not blame the Commander. He was overpressed and mistimed his stroke. Is that not so, Commander Vanyr?"

Vanyr's eyes narrowed angrily. She had backed him into a corner. He had to either admit a mistake, which would gall him intensely, or reveal that his last action was deliberate, in which case he would suffer Anjer's wrath. Either way he was shamed in front of both her men and his, and she knew he would never forgive her. The fact that his predicament was entirely of his own making wouldn't sway him.

Anjer was waiting, clearly not believing Sullyan's version. He stared Vanyr in the eye. "Well?"

The Commander shot Sullyan a malicious glance and gritted his teeth. "The Major is correct, my Lord. A mistimed stroke, that's all."

Anjer wasn't satisfied. "And?"

Color flared on Vanyr's pinched face and he sheathed his sword with an angry snap. "Major. Please accept my apologies."

She glanced up from hooded eyes, her hand still clamped about her injured arm. "I hear your gracious apology, Commander. We will say no more about it."

Anjer studied her before turning back to Vanyr. "Commander, I suggest you spend more time in practice if you are mistiming strokes." Vanyr clenched his fist on the hilt of his sword, but Anjer didn't notice. "Go about your duties, man."

Vanyr turned on his heel and stalked away. The pirates stared angrily after him. Jay'el came forward and slung Sullyan's cloak about her shoulders, keeping her heated body from chilling with the shock and freezing wind. Robin put his arm about her and led her away, Anjer falling into step beside them.

The Lord General accompanied them back to their suite and sat waiting while Robin and Sullyan saw to the cleaning and dressing of her wound. By expending power between them they had it half-healed already. The dressing was mainly for protection. Sullyan stripped off her shirt and breeches, which were damp from perspiration, and quickly washed. Dressed in a clean white shirt and plain black breeches, she joined Robin and Anjer by the fire. Robin handed her the fellan he knew she would need. Anjer frowned as he saw how shaky her grip was.

"I'll have Vanyr's miserable hide for this," he growled.

Sullyan hadn't spoken since the incident. She suddenly rounded on Anjer, startling both him and Robin. "My Lord, did you give orders to the men that I was to be protected?"

Anjer flushed and had the grace to look away. "We—that is, Pharikian and I—were concerned for you, Brynne. It was to prevent just such an occurrence that we did it. We didn't want you exposed to unnecessary risks."

Her heart pounded with anger. "As you can see, it worked very well!"

Robin shot Anjer a look. The Lord General wasn't sure quite how to deal with this. Sullyan, however, wasn't finished.

"For nearly twenty-four years I have relied on my own skills and strengths, my Lord. I am well used to protecting myself. I neither want nor need your interference. I am fully aware that you are more concerned for the wellbeing of the Hierarch's Champion rather than Brynne Sullyan, but you will do me the courtesy of allowing me to worry about my preparations for the day."

Anjer's flush deepened and he began to protest, but Sullyan continued furiously.

"I will decide what I need and will conduct what is left of my life as I choose. When I need your intervention or protection, my Lord, I hope I shall have the sense to ask for it. Until that time, pray keep out of my affairs!"

She turned abruptly and sank into one of the easy chairs by the fire. Her hand shook as she downed her fellan. Anjer remained silent, clearly taken aback by her outburst. Robin, who was used to her temper, gestured for the huge man to wait. They sat in awkward silence.

After a few minutes, Sullyan sighed.

"Gentlemen, my apologies. Lord General, I ask your pardon. I did not mean to speak so harshly. It is not easy being a woman among so many men, and I do not take kindly to cosseting."

Anjer gave a rueful smile. "So I see. I will remember that in future." He leaned forward. "How's the arm?"

She grimaced. "Two days should see it right. We are not likely to encounter Rykan before then, I think." She raised her eyes to his. "My Lord, it might be politic not to mention this incident to the Hierarch. I do not want to worry him."

Anjer's expression was grim. "I doubt I'd have to mention it to him. There were too many witnesses for it to remain a secret. Your … seamen in particular were most displeased. But that aside, there was a reason why I sought you out. There's been news from Ephan. Our forces have successfully brought Rykan's troops to a halt and have engaged them directly. The units sent round to the rear of the columns have encountered fierce opposition in one particular spot. Their commanders have reported seeing some of Rykan's personal guard among the defenders, but there's still been no sign of the man himself. It seems we were right, Brynne. The Duke of Kymer is skulking at the rear, protected by his elite guard. He has no intention of showing himself before he's ready."

Sullyan's heart fell and she bowed her head. She had been hoping desperately that Marik wouldn't need to endanger himself to flush Rykan out. She was very much afraid now that he would.

Later that evening, the Hierarch, the Lord General, Sullyan, Robin, and Marik gathered in one of Pharikian's private drawing rooms to discuss Marik's best strategy. The Count was eager to play his part, but Sullyan pleaded caution, begging him not to put himself in any unnecessary personal danger.

Marik shrugged. "But in order to be effective, Sullyan, I'll have to place myself right under his nose. Otherwise he'll just send out his elite guard rather than coming after me himself."

Sullyan glanced at Anjer. "My Lord, I have a suggestion. If we keep up the current pressure on Rykan's front lines, drawing them on toward the Plains, the rearguard will move forward also so as not to be separated."

Anjer nodded. "Of course."

"Then I think we should deliberately try to separate them."

He cocked his head, considering.

"My Lord, the units sent to the rear of Rykan's columns should move up to the point of fiercest resistance. Our right and left flanks would then coordinate to pinch the column between them, as if attempting to sunder Rykan from the rest of his command. Such tactics would surely force the Duke to act."

Marik butted in. "Yes! And once the movement's begun, my men can become the wedge in the break, so to speak, driving in as if trying to herd Rykan away from the bulk of his troops. If I let myself be seen, that should get his attention."

Sullyan added, "And if our forces keep harrying the main column, drawing them onward, the Duke will want to deal swiftly with Marik so he can rejoin his men."

Anjer frowned. "But what if the separation ploy fails? What if Rykan refuses to chase the Count?"

Sullyan shrugged. "He will not refuse, my Lord. He was so enraged on discovering my disappearance and Marik's defection that he almost put off mobilizing his troops in order to give chase. It was fortunate that he did not, for there were only seven of us and I was no use at that time."

Pharikian leaned forward. "Seven? Your other friends did not stay with you, then?"

She closed her eyes against the pain of the memory, thinking especially of Bull and Rienne. "I thought it best that they return to Albia. We did not know what we would find when we got here."

"A pity. I would have liked to meet them. You must miss them."

"I am happier knowing they are safe. My Captain keeps them informed, and he will return to them once this is over."

Anjer folded his arms and leaned back. "Very well, Brynne. I will communicate with Ephan and order the units sent to the rear of Rykan's lines to begin a pincer movement designed to separate his column of troops. Kryp will take control of the forces engaging the front of the column and step up the pace, drawing them on toward the Plains. Count Marik and his men will attempt to slip around

Rykan's flanks and coordinate with Ephan, driving into the breach made by Ephan's units while ensuring that Rykan sees who is responsible. Marik will then run for the Plains, hopefully drawing Rykan with him. Once he's in the open, Ephan and Kryp will pull back, allowing the split forces to rejoin. This tactic should fool Rykan into thinking he still commands superior numbers. Only when it's too late will he see our full complement of troops, ranged on the Citadel Plains. He will realize he's been matched in strength, and once he understands he can't win, he'll be forced to capitulate."

Sullyan nodded. "That is the trickiest part. As formal challenger, Rykan must either defeat his opponent or withdraw his challenge. Only by a withdrawal will the Crown be free to challenge on its own behalf."

The discussions over, Sullyan didn't stay to see the Count depart. Exhausted by her concern for Marik, her earlier exercise, and the shock of Vanyr's malice, she retired early. On entering their apartment she surprised Robin by not bathing, as she had done every evening since their arrival at the Citadel. Instead, she went straight to her rest. He followed and held her close while she slept, trying not to worry over what the next few days would bring.

Chapter Twenty-Six

As his horse followed Bull's onto the crest of the small hill, Taran finally had his first view of the Citadel and its surrounding Plains. It was an hour before noon and the day, although cold and frosty, was bright with sunlight from a pale blue sky. The horses' breath plumed in the air before them and their coats steamed faintly. Taran, with Bull to his left and Cal and Rienne to his right, sat gazing across the few miles separating them from Sullyan and Robin. It might as well have been hundreds, he thought, for all the chance there was of crossing them.

Bull roused himself. "Yes, this is the place Robin showed me. He said the fighting's been contained in those forests over there," he pointed eastward, "but now they're hoping to draw Rykan onto the Plains. We won't be able to see the finer details from here, but if the Hierarch's challenge is successful and Sullyan has to confront Rykan, we should be able to link with Robin and watch from his perspective."

Rienne paled at the thought of Sullyan meeting Rykan, and Bull hurried on.

"I suggest we set up camp and make ourselves as comfortable as possible. We'll need to post watches. Although the burden of scouting for the enemy will be taken by me and Taran, we must all be vigilant. Rykan's men are the main threat, of course, but I don't want to be found by the Hierarch's either. That would be highly embarrassing. I can just imagine what the Major would say if we were escorted in under armed guard."

319

Even Rienne smiled at that, and although Taran knew Bull was serious, the humor lightened the tension. He had expected to feel better once they arrived at their destination, yet he was actually feeling more restive. Knowing they were so close to Sullyan yet still unable to help her was galling. He suddenly noticed Rienne staring at him and wondered if the empathic healer had caught an echo of his thoughts. He shivered and she looked away. Taran didn't mention it to her. There really wasn't any point. Instead, he busied himself seeing to his horse. There would be time for reflection later.

As soon as the basic tasks were done—horses picketed and fed, latrine sited, fire started—Bull asked Taran to help search the woods around the campsite. Taran readily agreed. Using their metasenses, both men made sweeps of the area. Neither found signs of recent activity by either faction, although there were indications that patrols from the Citadel had passed that way before the war began. It was, after all, one of the obvious routes to the few small villages close by. Taran had learned that the majority of the population lived further northwest. According to Robin, and fortunately for the locals, Rykan's troops were concentrated in the Haligan Forest to the east, which was largely uninhabited save for some charcoal burners' and hunters' huts.

Bull set about showing his companions how to make the camp, and their occupation of it, as invisible as possible. Everything was organized with a swift departure in mind, in case they should be discovered. He asked Cal to gather kindling and firewood and showed him how to store it so that it looked natural but was near enough to the fire to dry. Taran helped Rienne drag pine branches closer, for screening the fire as well as their sleeping places. The latrine was sited a good distance from the main camp, and there were plenty of dead leaves nearby to cover it. Such precautions wouldn't fool a practiced eye looking for a camp, but they would be effective against any locals brave enough to come foraging this way.

Once the watches were organized, Bull asked Cal to take his crossbow and go hunting. The young man went on foot and returned an hour later, just as the last light was draining from the sky. He had managed to bag a couple of the small wild pigs that roamed the woods. That amount of meat would last them some time. Each of them had brought a fair amount of dried fruit, cheese, and some corn meal in their saddlebags. Bull wasn't anticipating being there for more than a few days, so Cal's contribution ought to see them through.

Taran took their water jars down to the stream running not far from the bottom of the hill. It was frozen over, but he found a deeper section where the ice was thin, the water flowing just fast enough to resist the freeze. He broke through and filled the jars, trusting that the ice would reform overnight.

Once Bull was satisfied with their precautions, he advised Cal and Rienne to get some sleep. Then he joined Taran, who had drawn first watch, by the fire.

"I'm going to try for contact with Robin before I sleep, Taran. Do you want to listen in?"

The Adept nodded and melded his psyche with Bull's once again. Robin noticed the big man's questing thought almost immediately and indicated that it was safe for them to talk.

What's been happening, Robin?

We're entering the final stages now, Bull. Anjer's best efforts to flush Rykan into the open have failed. The Duke's hiding behind his commanders, letting them direct his men. Anjer doesn't want to reveal his true strength, so he can't send any more men to force Rykan out. He's also worried that Rykan will find out on his own about the Hierarch's extra troops. It would only take one quick-witted scout to evade Ephan's patrols and discover the reserves. If Rykan realizes too soon that we've matched his numbers, he might decide to retreat, give himself time to come up with another strategy. It's vital that he doesn't learn he's lost his advantage before he has committed to the final battle. If he does, our efforts will be wasted. I can't imagine what that would do to Sullyan.

Taran could clearly sense Robin's distress and knew that Bull felt it too.

So what about Marik? the big man asked.

He's our final arrow. He's leaving tomorrow. All we can do is hope he succeeds.

✠ ✠ ✠ ✠ ✠

The dawn light woke Sullyan as usual, and she and Robin breakfasted in their suite. They took their time. Neither felt like talking. After a while a page arrived, bringing an invitation from the Hierarch to join him and the Lord General on the battlements. Once they had bathed and Robin had changed the dressing on Sullyan's arm, she opened the door and stepped out into the passage. She stopped, astonished to find both Almid and Kester stationed on either side of the door, looking as if they had been there all night.

"Why—?" she began, but stopped short when she noticed the deep bruising on their faces and the bloody knuckles on their hands. With hard eyes she studied them, waiting for one of them to explain. Neither spoke. While she debated whether to press them, Ky-shan, Jay'el, and Ki-en arrived, all three also bearing the unmistakable signs of having been in a fight. The pirate leader grinned at Sullyan and nodded to the twins, both of whom left. It was so obviously a change of guard that Sullyan stared in exasperation. Ky-shan merely raised his brows, daring her to comment.

She growled under her breath, "For the Void's sake!" and stalked off, heading for the Palace Tower. Robin shook his head and fell into step beside her, the pirates shadowing them.

When she reached the Tower roof, Pharikian and Anjer were already there. They were standing side by side, both gazing over the parapet down toward the lower town. Pharikian turned when he heard her approaching and held out his hand.

"Come stand by me, Brynne. It's nearly noon and Count Marik will soon be leaving with his men."

As she leaned on the parapet beside him, following his downward gaze, she saw the tiny figures moving around in front of the Citadel's southern gates. Men and horses together; the sun glinting occasionally off harness and weapons. A brave sight, she thought.

Anjer, on the other side of the Hierarch, turned to regard the pirates. None of them replied to the directness of his gaze, and Anjer's brows drew down over his snapping black eyes.

"Would those bruises and cuts have anything to do with why Commander Vanyr is unable to rise from his bed this morning?"

Ky-shan shrugged. "I know nothing about Vanyr's sleeping habits. Perhaps he isn't as fit as he should be. Or maybe his little fencing session with Major Sullyan yesterday took more out of him than he thought."

Anjer opened his mouth, but then shut it again. His lips thinned and he shot Sullyan a look. She gazed back. There was nothing she could say. They both knew that once Ky-shan had set his course, nothing short of a full-blown gale would make him veer. He had clearly meted out his own form of justice, and she now had a bodyguard rather than companions. In the light of Vanyr's malice, she didn't feel like refusing them.

Turning her back on Anjer's irritation, she concentrated on the scene below. Another friend was about to hazard his safety, and she wasn't sure how she would cope if he didn't return. Her heart offered silent prayers to the gods.

✥ ✥ ✥ ✥ ✥

Count Marik walked down to the lower town lighter of step than he had felt for years. No thoughts of death troubled his mind. He had absolutely no intention of sacrificing himself. Just an hour earlier he had taken an emotional farewell of the Princess Idrimar, and was still in a state of shock at finding that her feelings for him were not just a passing fancy. Indeed, he was having trouble coming to terms with his own emotions. He had been more than half in love with Sullyan for some years, despite knowing it was hopeless. His melancholy nature was well suited to thoughts of doomed love. Yet this love—the Princess' love—might actually be attainable, and he was finding such good fortune hard to understand.

When the Princess had waylaid him in the Palace, she had made it clear that she would not tolerate him dwelling on the past. He quickly understood that she was determined to have him when the war was over, and if in the meantime he covered himself with glory, well, so much the better. As he walked out into the sunlight with Idrimar's blessings in his ears and her kisses on his lips, Marik's soul soared like a tangwyr. Suddenly, he felt capable of achieving whatever his heart desired.

On joining his small escort in the lower town, Marik mounted his horse. Followed by his men, he galloped through the Citadel's southern gate. Cheers from the battlements sounded in his ears as he led his little company back toward the forest. Once under the trees, he quickly met up with Nazir and the remainder of his command. They were waiting for him where Anjer had told him they would be. They flocked around him, greeting him, eager to learn their orders. Marik explained the new strategy and the role they were to play.

"Remember, lads, we are not to engage Rykan in combat. Our purpose is as decoys. We will only fight if absolutely necessary, to retain his interest and fuel his anger. We are not to engage him before he reaches the Plains. The Hierarch has other plans for him—vital plans—and we're here to help them succeed. Is that understood?"

They roared their agreement and Marik grinned, wheeling his horse to lead them deeper into the forest. They would have to strike southwest for quite a way in order to skirt the main troop column and avoid the skirmishes that frequently broke out on its flanks. For Marik to succeed in his task, he would have to be quick. Anjer didn't want news of the Hierarch's reserves reaching Rykan before this maneuver had a chance to work. Knowing this, the Count and his band made all possible speed through that day, resting only briefly. They made a late and hasty camp, and before he slept, Marik quested for contact with Ephan.

His Artesan skills were scarcely even Apprentice strength, so Marik had to rely on Ephan recognizing his psyche. As soon as the General realized who it was, he immediately accepted the link. Ephan wasted no time on pleasantries.

Count Marik. How soon can you and your men join us?

Sometime before nightfall tomorrow, General. I'm pushing as hard as I can, given the terrain, the weather, and the bad light.

Make sure it's no later or we risk losing this chance. Kryp's troops are holding Rykan for now, but they can't do it much longer. I can spare you fifty men, Count, but I'll need to send the rest to reinforce Kryp. Otherwise Rykan could break through and destroy our advantage.

I understand, General. We'll be moving before first light. I'll contact you again tomorrow.

Ephan broke the link and Marik checked his sentries. Then he went to get what rest he could.

He and his men were moving before the sun was fully up, the forest dark and still under a covering of snow. The going was tricky, treacherous for the horses, and they had to skirt sporadic outbreaks of fighting between small units of Ephan's men and outriders from Rykan's forces. By midafternoon, however, Marik was nearly ready to position himself for his risky but essential undertaking.

Using his feeble Artesan powers, he contacted Ephan, showing the General where he was. The pale-eyed man rode into the camp at nightfall, bringing Marik his extra men. He was accompanied by the commander of one of the units detailed to effect the pincer movement. The three leaders, plus those Marik had chosen to help him coordinate his swelled forces, sat down to discuss the minutiae of their strategy.

The temperature was dropping and a light snowfall began. Marik hoped it would last. A good covering of snow would conceal his troops and aid their surprise move on Rykan. Ephan's units would begin their push just after dawn, as soon as there was enough light to see by, hopefully catching the enemy before they were fully alert. A good overnight freeze would slow everyone's reactions, so it was essential for Marik's and Ephan's men to be up and limbered well before dawn. Warm men and horses would move faster than those still cold from their blankets.

"Drive your men in fast and sure, Count," said Ephan as he took his leave. "Force Rykan as far south as you can. My units will harry the rest of the column northward, where they'll naturally run to close ranks with their fellows. A good, fast execution should see Rykan well out of touch with his men inside a couple of hours. Then let him chase you back toward the Plains. Kryp and I will give you all the support we can. I wish you good fortune."

Marik grinned and flipped Ephan a salute. He had a good feeling about this and went to his rest well content.

He had his men up long before dawn. They were tense with anticipation and quickly had the camp dismantled and the horses saddled. Marik rode through them, as much to keep warm as to give final instructions. Xeer was at the head of Ky-shan's band, and Nazir was in charge of Ephan's troops. All knew their place in the general plan. Marik and his own men, each one a trusted retainer, were the spearhead. They would drive deepest into the enemy in search of Rykan.

Finally, Marik received Ephan's instructions to proceed to their positions where they would await his signal telling them the drive had begun. The snow had continued to fall during the night, but dawn brought rising temperatures and the wind was noticeably warmer. This meant melt water dripping off trees and down necks, and the going underfoot would turn slushy. Those on horseback wouldn't have much trouble, but the majority of the enemy was on foot and would find the going treacherous.

As he moved his men into position, Marik did his best to keep warm. The grey light slowly penetrated farther into the trees, and finally he heard the sounds that told him the assault had begun. Screams and roars and the clash of steel echoed through the forest. His men were fidgeting, anticipating the command to move, and Marik's own stomach curdled with tension. He was more excited than afraid, more avid for revenge than fearful of the consequences.

He signaled his men to draw swords, waiting impatiently for Ephan's command. When it came at last the sun was well up and so was Marik's blood. Eagerly, almost joyfully, he yelled, "On, lads!" and his entire unit forged ahead, the horses straining at the rein. The forest resounded with the clamor of fighting and it all seemed horribly close. The cold air conducted sound well, and Marik kept his eyes alert as he rode toward his goal.

When they caught sight of men fighting, Marik gave a prearranged signal. Smoothly, his own unit surged to the fore while Nazir's split left and right. Xeer's command brought up the rear. Putting heels to their mounts in this diamond formation, they charged at full speed into the gap between Rykan's men and Ephan's. The commander in charge of Ephan's units now turned his men northwest to herd the column after their fellows. Marik was left to complete the sundering and force Rykan to turn southwest.

As expected, there was fierce resistance. Rykan's elite guards, identifiable by their black and silver uniforms, were experienced warriors, trained by the Duke himself. Fearlessly, they came at Marik's men, determined to beat them back. Once or twice during the mêlée, Marik caught sight of an officer in black and scarlet, but he saw no sign of the great lord himself.

Marik and his spearhead concentrated on driving their wedge deeper into Rykan's position, leaving the other units to distract and engage his men. Marik fought hard while his warhorse helped with hooves and teeth. His men crowded close around him, protecting him, more intent on advancing than killing the enemy. Although resistance was stout and continuous, they made good progress, and suddenly Marik caught sight of someone he had been watching for, as his presence was a sure indication that Rykan must be nearby.

The man was dressed in the black, silver, and scarlet of a general, but his cloak bore a pale blue trim. Ungainly and fat, he sat astride a powerful, stocky warhorse. He was wheeling the animal about, trying to see what was happening. Although he held a naked sword in his hands, Marik knew he wasn't much of a swordsman. He drove straight for him, roaring his name.

"Sonten, you slimeson! Stand and fight, you miserable coward! Where's your master, running safe somewhere? Tell him I've come looking for him. Tell him I've a score to settle!"

Even as Marik roared his challenge, other members of Rykan's elite guard converged on him. Madly, he drove them off, still heading directly for Sonten. He saw the General turn pale at the sight of him and spur his horse away, running from Marik's onslaught.

Not quite as reckless as his words suggested, Marik checked he was not alone before kicking his horse after the frightened General. His other units were doing their work, forcing Rykan's guard further away from their fellows and preventing them from hindering Marik. This left the Count free to follow Sonten, who was sure to lead him straight to Rykan.

Sure enough, through the press of trees Marik soon made out a core of men, all mounted, all wearing the colors of Rykan's elite guard. Sonten galloped straight for them, yelling, "Your Grace, your Grace! We must ride, we are surrounded!"

You miserable excuse for a man, thought Marik, remembering Sonten's condescending manner when they had spoken in Rykan's palace. He had been so superior, so confident, when Marik was trapped and in fear of his life. *Now the sword is in the other hand,* thought Marik. *Now we'll see what sort of general you are!*

The men Marik could see were huddled together, gathered around a central figure mounted on a fiery bay stallion. He heard a deep, commanding voice yelling orders and recognized those silken tones. He smiled grimly. Then he saw the bank of crossbows leveled at him and his men and abruptly yanked his warhorse to a squealing, dirt-showering halt.

He screamed, "Back, BACK!" and his command veered away, scattering wildly as the multiple *thunk* of bows sounded, heralding the deadly bolts. One grazed Marik's sleeve, tearing the fabric but missing his skin. He heard the harsh cry of a stricken horse and saw one of his men go down. Unable to help, he left the man to fend for himself, knowing he would sell his life dearly.

Desperately gambling that there was no second bank of bowmen, Marik roared at his men to wheel and charge before the bows could be re-armed. They abandoned their flight immediately and followed the Count as he reversed direction and came at

Rykan once again.

Marik's other units were now approaching from two different directions, driving the enemy before them. Rykan saw them and yelled to his men, suddenly advancing to meet Marik. Unwilling to engage him directly, Marik swerved his horse, drawing Rykan's guard with him and forcing the Duke to follow or be left unprotected. He caught the malevolent yellow glitter of Rykan's eyes as the Duke briefly locked gazes with his most despised foe.

He was yelling something, but there was too much noise for Marik to hear what it was. The Count let his warhorse run before the enemy, not getting too far ahead. He was relieved to see Xeer and the pirates veering right and left through the trees, harrying Rykan's guard and even cutting some down. The shrieks of the fallen and the roars of his pursuers filled Marik's ears. He forced his attention back to Rykan and caught another glimpse of that dark, predatory face as Rykan urged his guard to capture the Count.

Taking a brief moment to check his direction, Marik found he was heading too far southwest. He needed to turn now and run farther north while not letting the Duke close too soon with the rest of his troops. He hoped that Ephan's commander had shepherded the column far enough north by now so he would have room to play cat-and-mouse. The last thing Marik wanted was for Rykan to lose interest or suspect an ulterior motive, so he swerved his men aside and had them melt into the trees, hoping to see Rykan and his guards go pounding past.

To Marik's annoyance, the Duke hadn't entirely lost his caution. He had counted heavily on Rykan's eagerness to capture him and hadn't fully considered the man's natural cunning. Rykan, it seemed, suspected a trap and was holding back.

Marik now pinned his hopes on Nazir. His men were farther behind and wouldn't have seen what had happened. They would only know that the enemy had faltered and would see their chance to wreak havoc among the rearguard. Soon, more screams and ringing steel told Marik his luck was in. By the sound of it, Nazir's units had crashed full-tilt into the back of Rykan's, scattering them like windblown leaves.

Marik grinned in satisfaction and began leading his company back to where he thought Rykan might be. He circled to the south, as quietly as possible, his men riding cautiously through the woods. Those with crossbows held their weapons ready.

A movement in the trees ahead caught Marik's attention and he barked a command. The bowmen let fly and leaped forward. In that instant, Marik found himself to the rear of his group, but as he urged his horse onward to catch up, the animal gave a bubbling scream and crashed to the ground, a crossbow bolt embedded in its ribs. Marik was flung from the saddle, but the rest of his men went flying ahead, unaware what had happened to their lord.

Marik hit the ground hard and bounced, coming to rest against a tree. He lay still, stunned by the fall. Slowly, his head cleared and he rolled groggily to his hands and knees, hoping some of his men were within call. There was silence all around as he kneeled in the slushy snow. The light was already beginning to fade as the short winter day waned toward evening. The mission had taken longer than he thought.

A horse snorted close by and he heard its rider dismount, hopefully coming to his aid. Instead, to his everlasting horror, he heard a familiar, gloating voice, its deep, silken tones deceptively mild.

"Well, well, if it isn't the treacherous Count Marik. Who would have thought it, eh, Sonten? Only a few weeks ago this man was parading about my palace, taking my hospitality, and enjoying the entertainments I provided. Trying—quite successfully—to convince us he was a pathetic, whining coward. Yet all the time he was plotting to stab me in the back by ruining my plans and liberating a valuable captive.

"Look at him now, Sonten, already on his knees before me, hoping, no doubt, to beg my forgiveness. What do you think? Should I forgive him for betraying me, his rightful overlord, and for depriving me of my quarry and throwing my careful plans into chaos? Should I welcome him back with open arms and allow him to help me obtain my victory?"

Marik's heart sank and he retched. Trembling in every limb, he raised blurred vision to the cruel, dark face towering above him. Looking his death full in the eyes, he vowed to follow Sullyan's example and never give in to this monster, no matter what he did. In that terrifying moment, Marik fully appreciated how Sullyan had felt, lying naked and helpless at this brutal man's feet. His admiration for her increased tenfold.

Sonten, who hadn't dismounted, sniggered. Marik saw Rykan smiling down at him, white teeth gleaming in the murk.

"No, I don't think I should, Sonten. I think I should just cut out his craven, treacherous heart and stuff it in his lying mouth. I think I should kill him where he kneels."

Marik spat bile onto Rykan's boots. He never saw the kick aimed at his head, but he did feel it connect with his temple. It floored him instantly, drowning him in pain and darkness.

Chapter Twenty-Seven

Sullyan paced the Tower battlements constantly during the daylight hours following Marik's departure, never resting, pausing barely even to eat, and then only when forced to by Robin or Pharikian. She knew both men despaired of easing her throughout this time, but couldn't shake her looming sense of doom. Her inability to use her powers to watch over the Count only increased her frustration.

This profound unease had manifested long before he had ridden out to play his part, full of confidence. Had she been able to contact or watch him she wouldn't have felt so helpless, yet it was vital that her presence be concealed from Rykan. She couldn't risk him catching so much as a hint of her psyche. Even using Robin was a risk, as his pattern possessed a uniquely Albian aura. She felt thwarted, restrained as never before, save only when under the numbing effects of Rykan's spellsilver.

Anjer was still at the Citadel. He wouldn't take the field until the final battle was joined. As his pattern of psyche was already known to Rykan, he had offered to relay the sequence of events. Having learned Marik's pattern before the Count left, the Lord General was subtly tracking it, staying in the background so as not to disturb him. However, as he was in overall command, Anjer was also coordinating with Ephan and Kryp and couldn't concentrate solely on Marik. After telling Sullyan of Marik's successful engagement of Rykan's elite guard, he had broken off to deal with a query from Kryp. By the time Sullyan's hand on his arm urged him to regain contact, all he could sense was blackness.

"Please, my Lord," she begged, "try again."

Her heart beat frantically while she waited. When his eyes regained their focus and he reluctantly shook his head, she froze, a sense of helplessness overwhelming her. It was all she could do to restrain herself from running to the horse lines for Drum and riding out herself. Eyes filling with tears, she hugged her cloak tighter. Desperately, she whispered, "Can you tell if he lives?"

Anjer nodded slowly. "Yes, his pattern's still there. He's unconscious, I think."

She bowed her head. "He should never have been allowed to do this. I knew something dreadful would happen."

✣ ✣ ✣ ✣ ✣

Robin watched Sullyan turn and move stiffly away, lost in sadness. Anjer glanced at Robin. "She's not prescient, is she?"

The young man shot him a look, dark eyes full of worry. "The truth is she's been deeply unhappy about asking Marik to do this from the start. Just don't go reminding her it was her idea, my Lord. You may regret it."

Anjer grunted and turned back to the battle. Robin followed Sullyan along the wall at a discreet distance, Almid and Kester doing the same. The twins were constantly on duty as bodyguards, although if the state of Vanyr's face when he finally appeared was anything to go by, he had been taught a harsh lesson. He stayed well away from Sullyan, and Robin was thankful for this small mercy.

✣ ✣ ✣ ✣ ✣

By the time Marik regained consciousness the light had faded fully from the sky. He ached in every limb and there was a dreadful throbbing in his skull. He felt sick, immediately regretting a rash movement which only served to tell him he was trussed like a felled boar. He stifled a groan, reflecting dismally that things could only get worse.

As if to confirm this, a sharp kick in the ribs made him gasp.

"Ah," said a satisfied voice. "He's awake, your Grace."

Marik heard soft footfalls and a pair of long legs, clad in black breeches trimmed with silver and scarlet, appeared before him. Raising his eyes to Rykan's, he held the Duke's gaze. Rykan smiled, showing his teeth, and crouched beside his captive. "Tell me, Count," he said idly, "what did you do with her?"

Confused, Marik tried to think around the sickening throb of pain. Sonten's boot landed once more, encouraging him to lucidity.

"Gently, Sonten," reproved Rykan, "he'll remember in a minute."

The Duke held a naked dagger and he brought its point round to caress Marik's throat. The Count swallowed compulsively, the movement causing the blade to nick his skin.

"Oh, dear," purred Rykan, "I seem to have drawn your blood, Count. Now, would you like to answer my question or shall we play a little first?"

Staring up at the Duke, Marik forced a small, hard smile onto his face. Rykan's frown was his reward. "You can do what you like to me," he rasped, "but at least you can't do her any more harm."

The frown deepened. "What do you mean?"

Marik let his disgust at what this brutal man had done to the helpless Sullyan color his reactions. His eyes filling with tears, he spat, "She died of your cruelty, Rykan. Yes, I rescued her. Yes, I took her out of that awful cell you threw her in." His voice rose, anger fuelled by the fear of death. "You'd more than half-killed her anyway, but I wasn't going to let you complete what you started. I only wish I'd had the courage to do it sooner. Perhaps then I could have saved her life. But at least I saved her from having to give her powers to you!"

Gathering his strength, he spat in Rykan's face.

The Duke cursed and reared back. Curtly, he motioned to Sonten and the stocky General laid in with his boot again. In despair, Marik felt his shoulder blade break under the repeated vicious kicks. His breath was forced from his body and he was unable even to scream as the toe of Sonten's boot thudded home again and again. Rykan stood watching, his expression thunderous.

Too badly injured for lucidity, the growing commotion in the trees didn't mean much to Marik, but he did see Rykan's head snap round and heard him barking orders at his men. Hastily, they ran for their mounts.

"Finish him!"

Rykan flung the words at Sonten. Already halfway to his horse, the command forced the General to turn back. Drawing his sword, he lumbered toward Marik, only to stumble to a halt as a large group of yelling men burst into sight, crossbows thumping as they came.

Barely conscious, Marik saw Rykan wheel his bay stallion, cursing Sonten's hesitation. Still swearing, he spurred the nervous animal toward Marik, deliberately setting the horse at the Count. Yet despite the raking spurs and dragging reins, the battle-trained stallion leaped over the Count instead of trampling him. Roaring his fury, Rykan yanked cruelly on its mouth before kicking the beast away.

Forcing his eyes wider, Marik recognized the pirate Xeer leading Ky-shan's men in pursuit of the Duke. Desperate to stop Rykan escaping, Marik gathered his waning strength and yelled hoarsely at the top of his lungs.

"She'd never have given her powers to you, Rykan, but before she died, she passed them on to me! And I intend to see that you never win this war."

Dimly, Marik registered Rykan's furious face as he spun round in the saddle to glare at him.

Caught on the ground as Xeer's men rushed closer, Sonten heard Marik's words. Drawing his dagger, he threw it as hard as he could at Marik's prone body before scrambling clumsily onto his horse. Even as the blade thumped home, ripping an agonized scream from his throat, Marik heard Rykan's enraged roar.

"Sonten, you lackwit! NO!"

His vision red and blurred by pain, Marik was only vaguely aware of horse hooves trampling next to his head. Spiking agony prevented him from protecting himself. Fortunately, the horse belonged to Xeer, who had stayed behind while the others engaged Rykan's guards. Slithering down, Xeer grasped the hilt of Sonten's blade and yanked it from Marik's back, throwing it after its retreating owner. Then he roughly hoisted the helpless Marik and slung him over his horse's withers. The violent movements tore at the Count's wounds and he shrieked, close to passing out.

Xeer leaped into the saddle of his curveting horse yelling, "I've got him, lads! Quick, follow me!"

The pirates abandoned their attack and crowded after Xeer as he turned and galloped for the Plains. Marik felt the pirate's hand gripping the back of his jacket, steadying him as best he could over the horse's neck as they pelted dangerously fast through the dark forest. The yelling of men and pounding of hooves was loud in Marik's faltering ears.

For all his agony and fear, Marik felt a strange satisfaction. He had managed to taunt Rykan with the one thing guaranteed to make the Duke pursue him. Thoroughly enraged by Marik's resistance and convinced that he had now been twice deprived of the power he so obsessively desired, Rykan's pursuit showed he was determined to take the Count at all costs. Marik had convinced him that if he could just recapture the Count he could still have

Sullyan's powers, and their acquisition would set the seal on the outcome of his challenge. This, Marik felt, was worth dying for.

In total darkness, it was a nightmare ride. They were all riding blind, although Rykan's men would have the slight advantage of hearing their quarry ahead. Fading in and out of consciousness, praying to die while pain tore at his body, Marik was aware of the pirates forging on at whatever speed they could hold, only their sense of direction guiding them. As the yawning chasm of the Void finally came to claim him, Marik vaguely heard them yelling for reinforcements. He desperately hoped the rest of his command was nearby as they galloped recklessly toward the Plains.

✤ ✤ ✤ ✤ ✤

Sullyan couldn't leave the battlements. Robin, Almid, and Kester stayed with her the whole day, but with the final battle so close now, Anjer had gone to rest while he could. He needed to be fresh for the following day when he would personally lead the Citadel's defense.

Pharikian replaced him as Sullyan's eyes. She protested at Andaryon's Supreme Ruler acting as her liaison, but he brushed her objections aside, saying he was as concerned for the Count as she was. He stayed by her as darkness fell and was able to tell her that Marik had regained consciousness as Rykan's captive. Her heart shriveled inside her, hope for the Count's survival diminishing fast. Yet Pharikian also sensed the pirates come charging into Rykan's camp, and they realized all was not yet lost. When he relayed the words Marik yelled at Rykan, Sullyan smiled grimly.

"We could not have thought of a better way to convince him to follow."

Pharikian nodded and tightened the arm he had placed around her shoulders. "If the Count comes out of this alive, I'm going to make him a Lord of the Realm."

She stared up at him, a proper smile slowly forming. "That should please your daughter."

He grinned, glad to see her somber mood lifting. "It would rather neatly solve the problem, wouldn't it?"

"He has to reach the Citadel first," said Robin, and Sullyan sighed.

Turning to his guard, Pharikian instructed that Anjer be fetched from his rest. "Alert the Velletian Guard to incoming troops," he added as the man hurried off.

When Anjer learned what had occurred, he swiftly ordered Kryp and Ephan to give the pirates every support. It would be a delicate balance, because they couldn't afford to lose Rykan now. With the enemy so close to the Plains, darkness had not brought the usual cessation to the fighting, and the Hierarch's hitherto secret reserves were readying themselves to form the Citadel's last line of defense. Both generals reported fierce fighting and a savage push by Rykan's men to force their way onto the Plains. Anjer gave the order to slowly fall back and encourage them on. Dryly, Ephan remarked that encouragement wasn't necessary. He had only just been able to hold them that extra day as it was.

Pharikian relayed all this to a tight-lipped Sullyan. They remained on the battlements, anxiously awaiting the pirates' and Marik's arrival. Xeer was no Artesan, and Marik seemed mercifully to have lost consciousness, so they had no contact with them. After about an hour of constantly scanning the darkness, Sullyan stiffened. Robin felt it and leaned forward, straining to see in the darkness. They could just make out movement through the closest trees.

The Hierarch saw it too. "Here they come," he said, and sent a command through the substrate to Vanyr, who was waiting with a full contingent of Velletian Guard to shepherd the pirates home. Sullyan watched intently as Vanyr's well-trained men charged the pirates' pursuers, causing them to veer back into the protection of the trees. Xeer on his overburdened horse, followed by the remnants of his band, thundered on toward the Citadel.

Sullyan didn't wait to see them in. She was already running for the Tower stairs, leaping recklessly down them, desperate to tend to Marik's hurts and see him safe. Robin followed.

Knowing that Xeer would reach the Palace courtyard and be relieved of his burden before she reached the Tower base, Sullyan made straight for the infirmary. As soon as she burst through its doors a Healer waved her to one of the smaller rooms. With Robin shadowing her heels Sullyan entered the room, seeing the Count's body already laid on the bed. Coming straight to his side, she took in his grey, sweat-sheened face, blue lips, and slack features. Deshan was bending over him, removing the Count's bloodstained clothing. Silently, Sullyan helped. When they had finally stripped the Count, the extent of his wounds became clear. Sullyan sucked in a breath.

The right shoulder blade was broken clean in two, one half sticking out through mangled flesh. Rykan's boot had made a mess of the left temple, where there was a huge and spreading bruise. Sonten's enthusiastic kicks had also broken and cracked a few ribs, and Deshan suspected a punctured lung. The worst wound, however, had been inflicted by Sonten's knife. The serrated, nine-inch blade had entered Marik's back and lodged against the spine, and Xeer's hasty removal had done yet more damage. They would need to probe deeply to assess the extent of the harm, but Sullyan already knew by the look in Deshan's eyes that he feared the Count might never walk again.

Master Physician and Master Artesan regarded each other over Marik's body. Sullyan's look was challenging.

"I will not accept an outcome in which the Count is crippled," she said.

Deshan eyed her grimly. “It will take much time and effort. We must find the extent of the damage, lessen the swelling, check for severed nerves, mend broken bones, and that is all supposing his spine is intact. If it is not ….” He paused, shaking his head.

Sullyan looked down at Marik’s face. He lay on his stomach, his head turned to the left. Reaching out, she gently stroked his discolored cheek.

“He risked so much for me. He kept me alive when no one else could. He undertook this mission for me, and I will not fail him now. I care little how long it takes, Deshan, but while I have breath, strength, and power within me, I will not rest. This is your area of expertise, Master Healer, so I give you control of my power. Direct it and use it as you will. But let us waste no more time. We need to know what we are dealing with.”

Deshan drew a deep breath and Sullyan felt his offered psyche. Accepting the contact, she melded with him, and together they began working to repair Marik’s wounds.

Robin didn’t disturb them. He sat by Sullyan’s side, mutely offering his strength if she needed it. Without acknowledging him or diverting her attention from the delicate work Deshan was performing, she accepted and made use of her Captain’s power. No one else entered the room, but Sullyan was vaguely aware of a tall, lonely female figure keeping an anxious vigil outside the door that long night through.

✣ ✣ ✣ ✣ ✣

As grey light streaked the dawn sky, General Sonten emerged from his tent. He stood in silence, regarding the two great armies drawn up facing each other on the Plains. He grimaced. Contrary to his expectations, the Hierarch had been able to summon sufficient numbers from his supporters to confront and hold Rykan’s swelled forces. Constrained by the rules of formal combat, Rykan was now compelled to engage the Hierarch’s troops in an all-out battle for supremacy. If he lost, he would have to capitulate. To say that he was unhappy about this was a gross understatement, and he had spent much of the previous night taking his displeasure out on Sonten.

The General glared at the distant Palace towers, reaching like bared fangs into the new light. No one in the Citadel could possibly be aware that Rykan's failure to secure Sullyan's powers was not the first, but the second blow to his far-reaching plans. The Duke's total confidence in her eventual surrender had not only led him to issue his challenge prematurely, but had also given her friends the time and opportunity to spirit her away. However, taking her captive and forcing her to give up her vast strength had not been part of the Duke's original plan.

"That bloody Albian Baron!" growled Sonten. "Why did Rykan ever listen to him?"

His scowl deepened. It was the Baron who had given Rykan the Staff, the terrible weapon that would have made taking the human witch's power possible, and because of this, he felt entitled to make demands of the Duke. Quite why the Baron was so eager to see Sullyan destroyed, Sonten didn't know, but Rykan was quick to see the merits of the fanatic's proposal. The subsequent loss of the weapon and Sullyan's escape had taken the Duke's fury to new and terrifying levels. Sonten still found it hard to believe that such a fragile and defenseless young woman had resisted the brutal Duke for so long. Yet despite Rykan's fury at her defiance in the face of considerable pain and torment, Sonten knew he had conceived a reluctant respect for her, doubtless an uncomfortable sensation for one who habitually treated women like disposable playthings. It was something Rykan would never admit, not even to Sonten, and Sonten would certainly never dare mention it.

"Still," he muttered, "she's dead. That should please the Void-damned Baron. Now all we have to do is win this bloody war."

Despite the shock of being confronted by more men than he had expected, Sonten retained his confidence that the Hierarch had no idea of Rykan's true strength. The outcome of the Duke's personal challenge didn't necessarily depend upon metaphysical prowess, so Rykan could still emerge the victor. Sonten assumed that Anjer, a man he both hated and respected, had been unwilling to rely on what he knew of Rykan's strength and had ordered some of the Hierarch's closest reserves to mobilize. Even so, Sonten didn't believe they could stand against the true strength of Rykan's forces. He consoled himself with the thought of Anjer's shock when Rykan's own reserves entered the fray.

Marik's claim that he had been gifted Sullyan's power had planted a worm of doubt in Rykan's mind. Sonten had managed to calm the Duke by assuring him that the Count had been mortally wounded by his desperate knife throw. His actions had initially enraged the Duke, just when it seemed that Sullyan's coveted strength might still be his, and Rykan had been apoplectic when Marik escaped him yet again. No one but Sonten had dared approach him since, and it had taken the General some time to convince Rykan there was no chance of Marik surviving such a deadly wound.

Sonten was aware that much of Rykan's rage stemmed from the shock of realizing that Marik was fighting for the Hierarch. His initial outrage at the Count's daring rescue, when they had all thought him a puling, spineless coward, had cooled, set aside to be dealt with later. The Duke had been convinced Marik would hole up somewhere in terror of his life, so his incredible reappearance at the head of a well-trained band and his audacity in attacking Rykan's supposedly protected position had inflamed the Duke beyond measure. Rykan simply couldn't believe Pharikian's actions. Far from slaying the traitor out of hand, or at the very least incarcerating him, the Hierarch had actually recruited the lackwit, and set him against his former lord. To Rykan, this was another indication of Pharikian's failing faculties, one more insult for which both he and Marik would pay.

Sonten shook his head and sighed. As the light of the new day grew, showing him more and more of the Hierarch's forces, doubt formed in his heart. Not because of the potent Artesan powers Marik had supposedly acquired; even if Sonten was wrong and the Count survived, he wasn't concerned about that. It would take the Count many days, if not weeks, to recover from such serious wounds, and Rykan had always derided Marik's pitifully weak Artesan gift. Even if the human witch had passed her vast store of knowledge on to him, he would be hopelessly untutored in its use. Rykan would easily crush the worm.

No. What troubled Sonten was the niggling worry that the Count might somehow know about Rykan's plans. There were already more men facing them than Sonten had bargained for. What if Marik had heard something that led him to suspect Rykan's true strength? What if last night's wild chase through the forest hadn't finished him off? What if he had reached the Citadel alive and managed to whisper his suspicions to Anjer? Anjer would certainly have sent runners through the night to demand more men from his supporters.

Sternly, Sonten shook himself and thrust the doubts aside. No, it wasn't possible. Marik couldn't have known. Not even the Duke's regular troops knew of his reluctant conscripts. They had all been kept well away from the palace by trusted commanders, drilled separately under harsh routines. Marik had been watched while in the palace, and although he had managed to keep his mercy visits to Sullyan secret, neither he nor his men had ever left the palace compound.

These extra forces drawn up in readiness on the Plains had simply been brought in by a nervous opponent—one uncertain of victory. This would work in Sonten's favor. The Duke's forces would press forward with determination and their officers would drive them from behind and spend their strength extravagantly. His Grace would win the day, and Sonten would gain his reward.

He gave a hard smile. The Duke's towering ambitions and the plans of his despised yet powerful Albian supporter were about to be realized. Turning on his heel, the General went to inform Rykan that battle was about to be joined.

Chapter Twenty-Eight

Pharikian and Anjer paced the battlements in the early morning breeze. The slight thaw of the previous day had continued overnight and the wind had lost its bitter teeth. Yet it was still strong enough to snap and stream the banner flying impudently above the Duke of Kymer's tent, well to the rear of his battle lines.

Wrapping his heavy purple mantle even tighter about his lean frame, the Hierarch stared over the ordered ranks of his reservists and regular troops. Anjer stood massively beside him, studying the battlefield and the deployment of Rykan's men. A movement by the Tower doors drew their attention. Almid and Kester appeared, both scanning the battlements. When they saw the two men standing by the wall, they moved aside to allow Sullyan to pass between them. Dwarfed by their stature, she seemed even tinier this morning, and as she came closer the pallor of her face caused Pharikian to gasp.

She was clearly exhausted. Enormous in the grey light of dawn, her golden eyes were accentuated by the dark rings beneath. She moved with less than her usual grace, and Pharikian remembered that she had been up all night helping Deshan with the wounded Count. He frowned. Surely she should have gone to rest before now?

Seeing his disapproving expression, she raised a defensive hand. "Do not reprove me, Majesty. I need to see this before I can rest."

She sounded heartsick, and Pharikian's rebuke died on his lips. Fearing the worst, he said, "How is the Count, Brynne?"

Pain creased her brows and her golden eyes darkened with worry. "He lives, Timar. We have repaired the shoulder, although it will be many weeks before it is strong. The punctured lung and broken ribs mended well. The surface swelling will heal with time. His spine was thankfully intact, but there is severe bruising. Deshan has tended the area and reduced the swelling as much as he can, but the nerves may have suffered irreparable damage. Until he wakes, we cannot know whether he will walk again. He slept throughout, and Deshan has administered a strong sedative to keep him unconscious. It is essential he remains still for as long as possible."

She fell silent, and Pharikian saw her tremble as exhaustion and worry took their toll. Wordlessly, he gathered her to him and wrapped her warmly in the folds of his cloak. Feeling the gauntness of her beneath his hands, he said, "When was the last time you ate, Brynne?"

She wasn't listening. Her eyes ranged out over the massed ranks of the two great armies. Pharikian felt her stiffen when her gaze fell on the standard of Rykan, Duke of Kymer. Her hands strayed unconsciously to her belly.

"He succeeded then?"

The Hierarch switched his gaze to the Duke's men, leaving Anjer to reply.

"Oh yes, Brynne, the Count succeeded very well, as you see. Now it is up to us to continue his work, to engage Rykan in battle, fight him to a standstill, and force him to surrender."

"And then …." Her whisper trailed off.

Pharikian glanced down at her. She had looked exhausted before, but now she looked ill. Irritated by her stubbornness, he turned her face with one hand.

"You need rest, Brynne. Where is the Captain?"

She had the grace to smile wryly. "I sent him to bed, Majesty. He sat with me all night and I used his strength as well as my own."

He stared in exasperation, expelling his breath in a huff.

"Very well," she said, throwing up her hands, "I will go. But you must promise to wake me if there is any change in the Count's condition or any developments out there."

"You have my word, Brynne. Anjer is leaving now to oversee the battle, and I think we can leave that in his capable hands. I'm sure Deshan has stationed healers by the Count's side who will call you if need be."

She gave a sidelong smile. "Yes, Marik has the best of healers, Majesty."

She turned to go, Anjer placing a comforting hand on her shoulder as she passed him. She made her unsteady way to the stairs, Almid and Kester following, and cast a last worried glance over her shoulder at the vast enemy army.

Pharikian watched the doors close behind her, Anjer silently studying his face. After a few moments the Lord General said, "She's so small and frail, Timar. While I have the greatest respect for her tactical skill and don't doubt the word of those who've fought with her these past few weeks, I confess I'm finding it hard to credit the truth of her reputation. Will she be capable of fighting Rykan when the time comes? You know how skilled and ruthless he is. Might it not be better to choose another Champion?"

The Hierarch sighed deeply, his expression anguished. "You're watering a dead tree, my friend. I can't choose another Champion, no matter how much I might wish to. I gave her my word and I can't take it back. Besides, the reasons for accepting her are still valid. Would you trust that man to adhere to the Codes? Even if we had someone capable of matching his skill with the blade—no offence, my friend!—there's still the question of his metaphysical rank. As I am prohibited from meeting my challenger in person, there is no one else qualified to face him. Like Brynne, I have no doubt he would use his metaforce if he found himself losing the duel. As she pointed out, why should he feel constrained by the Codes if he plans to put us all to the sword? None of his followers would dare task him for it. No, Anjer, I'm afraid there's no other way. Brynne Sullyan is my chosen Champion and she will meet Rykan on the day of the duel. But I wish to all the gods she didn't have to."

"Is there truly no other way to end this man's threat?" Anjer's question was rhetorical, and he returned to his scrutiny of the battlefield, his large hands braced on the wall.

"I can't see one," said Pharikian. "I can't break the Codes, and even if I could, an arrow through the heart would only end Rykan's ambition. Others would take his place. And killing him won't help Brynne. Don't forget, Rykan's her only hope of cheating death now. We can't deny her the chance of persuading him to undo the damage he's done."

Anjer snorted, his black glare fixed on the Duke's streaming banner. "How realistic is that chance? Even if he could be ... persuaded to help her, could she physically stand the strain? Deshan seemed to think the damage irreparable."

The Hierarch groaned and bowed his head. In the short time they had known her, they had both come to deeply respect—and in Pharikian's case to love—the slight, tawny-haired young woman. Pharikian felt very close to her due to his special relationship with her parents. He still missed Morgan's support and strength, the only person who had ever been his metaphysical equal. To finally find the man's daughter, grown so beautiful, so skilled, so accomplished and confident, only to lose her to the spite and brutality of one of his own subjects, was a pain he wasn't sure he could bear. The one thing keeping him from despair was the fragile hope that Rykan's power could undo the damage. Despite Sullyan's own determination never to place herself at his mercy by asking for it, Pharikian was going to make damned sure Rykan knew he must help her or die.

Raising his head, yellow eyes glittering dangerously, he said, "We must make sure she can. Come, Anjer, the sun is well up. We will not allow the Duke any more leisure to plot against us. The sooner we best him, the sooner this will be over."

The two men and their escort made their way back down the Tower stairs. Within thirty minutes Anjer was galloping through the Citadel gates, riding to join his men on the Plains.

❖ ❖ ❖ ❖ ❖

Robin woke midmorning. No one had disturbed their rest since Sullyan came in, and now he stood looking down at her sleeping under the goose down comforter. She had unbraided her glorious hair before undressing, and the tumbled mass of it about her sleep-smoothed face made her look very young.

As silently as possible, the Captain dressed and left the suite. He was hungry, but he wanted to check on Marik before finding breakfast. Nodding to Ky-shan and Jay'el stationed outside the door, Robin made his way to Marik's sickroom. There he found the Princess Idrimar still sitting in the huge chair someone had found for her last night. She was fast asleep, her hand still clasping Marik's. The Count lay in drugged slumber on the bed.

Seeing one of the healers, Robin drew the woman aside. "How is the Count?"

She glanced at the pair over her shoulder. "There's no change, I'm afraid, sir. We're keeping him deeply asleep and so have no way of knowing whether there's any improvement. Only Deshan, the Hierarch, or the Lady Brynne could tell if his nerves are recovering at this moment. We just have to hope."

Robin looked at Marik's face, which was turned toward him. The Count was lying on his left side to ease the shoulder blade and keep his spine aligned. Robin frowned in concern. Having long put aside the guilt, jealousy, and rage which had colored his earlier dealings with the man, he now counted him a friend and was as worried for him as he would have been for Bull. Sighing, unable to do any more, he left in search of breakfast.

Once he had eaten he felt stronger, more capable of coping with what was happening outside. Passing the suite on his way to the battlements, he noted wryly that Ky-shan and his son were no longer at their station, meaning that Sullyan was up and about. He had hoped she would sleep for longer, but he wasn't really surprised she hadn't.

He was also unsurprised to find her on the battlements. What did surprise him, however, was that one of her companions was Commander Vanyr. Vanyr stood stiffly on the opposite side of the Hierarch, who stood next to Sullyan, and the atmosphere between the two was decidedly cool. Not so strange, thought Robin, considering that Vanyr's face still bore evidence of the pirates' justice. Barrack gossip said he had also been thoroughly chewed out by Anjer and threatened with demotion should he ever do anything so vicious again. Robin wondered why he was here. Over by the Tower doors, he could see both Ky-shan and his son watching the Commander as a tangwyr watches a dying beast.

If Pharikian had noticed any frostiness in the air, Robin thought, he had probably put it down to the animosity he knew Vanyr bore the Major. The Commander remained firmly on the Hierarch's other side, keeping what distance he could.

With a perfunctory nod to the sullen man, Robin moved to Sullyan's other side. Gazing out across the Plains, he was amazed at the size of the two armies and began to have serious doubts about the Hierarch's ability to force Rykan to surrender. Sullyan smiled wearily at him and briefly touched his arm. Placing it around her shoulders, he held her close.

The preliminary moves of the battle were being played out before their eyes. The archers and crossbowmen on either side were currently trying to reduce their opposite numbers while the foot and mounted troops behind them stirred restlessly. Robin could see Anjer in his dark, gold-trimmed uniform, sun glinting off his rank insignia and array of battle honors as he rode to and fro along his lines, encouraging, planning, and bestirring his men to action. The Captain could also make out the forms of Kryp and Ephan, both rallying their men and holding them in readiness for the main assault.

Guiltily, Robin's eyes strayed southwest over his shoulder, toward the knoll where Bull, Taran, Cal, and Rienne had made camp. He wondered if he could get away with a tight link to Bull without Sullyan's knowledge. His skills were sufficient for the task, he just wasn't sure how focused she was at present and whether she might notice his distraction. Regarding her closely, seeing how intent was her concentration, he decided to risk it.

Bull?

The call was as soft and tight as he could make it, and there was an instant response from the big man. He must have been aware of the start of the fighting and was waiting for Robin's call.

Robin! What's happening?

The Captain swiftly told Bull about Marik's heroic venture and its consequences. Bull's concern was plain through their link, but there was nothing Robin could do to alleviate it. He gave quick details of the Count's care and treatment, and then told Bull how the battle was shaping. But Bull had more immediate concerns.

How's Sully?

Robin glanced at her as she stood talking quietly to the Hierarch. She was very pale, and the way she kept pressing her belly worried him. It was as if the old pain was gnawing at her. He was deeply afraid that the poison in her soul would claim her life before she could fulfill her self-imposed task.

Bull clearly felt Robin's fear despite his shielding. *Can't the Hierarch and his physician do anything more to help her?*

They've done all they can, said Robin sadly. *They're afraid that if they try again they'll impair her own powers, and that would be disastrous. I'm terribly worried for her, Bull.*

Then let's hope this battle is over sooner rather than later. Remember, lad, don't hold the wake before the bloody funeral!

Bull broke the link abruptly, but Robin sensed his despair. Smiling a little at Bull's favorite phrase, he hugged Sullyan to him.

✣ ✣ ✣ ✣ ✣

The Major stood encircled by her lover's strong arms, his warmth easing the tension in her belly. Presently, she noticed Vanyr stirring. The man had remained silent unless asked a direct question by his monarch, and now he made his excuses to Pharikian and turned to depart. In Ephan's absence, he was in full command of the Velletian Guard and he had duties to attend to. Before he could leave, however, she stepped away from Robin and addressed him.

"Commander Vanyr, would you do me the courtesy of granting a private word?"

He froze mid-stride. Both Robin and the Hierarch turned their heads, as startled as the white-eyed Commander, but they made no comment. Unable to refuse in their hearing, Vanyr replied stiffly.

"As you wish, Major."

She moved farther away from the other men and he followed at some distance. Ky-shan and his son still watched his back like hungry sharks, their glances as piercing as daggers. Seeing this, Sullyan imagined Vanyr's shoulder blades crawling with tension. She stopped just out of their earshot and faced him, raising her open gaze to his pale, hard eyes. Refusing to come too close, he stood staring, balanced lightly on his feet as if expecting attack.

She sighed. "Commander, I know you bear me no love, nor would I expect it. I wish you to know, however, that I hold no grudge against you for your actions the other day. Nor did I have anything to do with, or knowledge of, the beating you received. I do not condone it and would certainly have stopped it had I known."

If this little speech affected Vanyr, he showed no sign.

"Yes, Major, so I was told."

She raised her brows. At least Ky-shan had made sure Vanyr knew exactly who was responsible for the retribution he had received.

Coldly, he added, "Was there anything else?"

She might have said more, but his tone forbade her. "No, Commander, I will not waste any more of your time."

He stared at her for an instant before turning on his heel and stalking to the Tower stairs. The pirates made a show of watching him depart, but he studiously avoided their eyes. Returning to her study of the battlefield with a closed look on her face, Sullyan chose not to respond to either Robin's or Pharikian's enquiring looks.

The battle proper commenced later that day. The archers and crossbowmen had done their work, and now both sides let loose their mounted troops and infantry. The noise of the two forces coming together was clearly audible for miles around.

By nightfall, little progress had been achieved. The fighting was fierce but tactical, neither side committing to an all-out push, merely trying each other's strengths and employing subtle feints here and there to draw out pockets of men where they could be surrounded and cut off. All that day, the watchers on the Tower saw no sign of Rykan himself. The Duke stayed concealed in his command tent, issuing orders through his general, Lord Sonten.

As night fell and the battlefield slowly vanished under the smothering winter darkness, both armies retreated to their own lines. All that could be seen from the Citadel were the thousands of flickering campfires dotting the Plains with their firebug glow. Briefly, Sullyan entertained a wicked desire to tamper with Rykan's fire and set his tent alight, but there was no wind, and although she could influence Air, she did not yet have full Mastery. Pharikian did, but as Supreme Ruler he was constrained by the Codes not to interfere in a metaphysical sense in the outcome of this battle.

Exhausted by the constant worry, they went to rest, Sullyan deciding to check on Marik before she retired. On entering the infirmary, she and Robin found the situation unchanged save for the presence of Deshan, who was doing his rounds. There was a steady stream of wounded coming in to the healers, and they were overwhelmed. Seeing this, Sullyan offered an hour or so of her time. Robin worked alongside her, using his powers to soothe nerves, numb pain, and begin healing where he could.

Looking up from a gut wound she feared would not repair, Sullyan glanced at her lover as he worked. She smiled, knowing that his skills and strength of mind were well able to support Master Artesan status. It saddened and gladdened her both, for it was unlikely she would see him confirmed. At least she could rely on Mathias Blaine to accomplish that for her. The sudden blur of tears in her eyes brought her back to the task in hand.

Eventually, Deshan thanked them and shooed them away. Before leaving to rest, they looked into the small room occupied by Marik and the ever-present Idrimar. Bowing her head to the Princess, who looked pale and careworn, Sullyan crossed to the bed and looked down on the sleeping face of her friend. Idrimar stared at her pleadingly, hoping for some confirmation of improvement, but Sullyan was loath to probe Marik while he was drugged.

Gently, she bade the Princess be patient. "You can call me any time of night or day, Highness," she added. "If you are worried or need anything, just send someone for me. I will always come to you."

"Thank you, Lady Brynne," said Idrimar, her deep voice tight with tears. Her eyes were damp, but her face wore a wan smile. "If he doesn't fully recover, it won't be for lack of care."

"Of that I have no doubt," said Sullyan, stroking Marik's hand where it lay outside the covers. "We can only hope now, Highness. Deshan and I did all we could. The rest is up to the Count."

Trailed by Ky-shan and Ki-en, she and Robin returned to their rooms. Consoling themselves in each other's love, they eventually fell into an exhausted sleep.

Chapter Twenty-Nine

Taran woke with a start to find Bull standing over him. Taran squinted in the gloom, guessing it was just before dawn. Bull moved on to Cal and Rienne, shaking their shoulders urgently and hissing for them all to move.

"What is it, Bull?" said Taran, hurrying to draw on his outer clothes against the cold drizzle. It didn't take him long. They all slept fully clothed, wrapped in their cloaks for comfort.

"Company," rasped Bull, kicking over what remained of the fire and using a little water to make sure it was fully out. Stamping on the ash to stop the smoke, he pulled a small pile of dead leaves and twigs over the remains before covering everything with pine boughs left ready for the purpose. Then he ran for the horses and helped Taran saddle up.

They had kept the camp tidy and free of refuse for just such an emergency. Even the horses' droppings were scattered away from the site. Any evidence of their stay was quickly hidden, and the frozen ground bore few traces save what was there before they had arrived. Mounting swiftly, cold and tension making him tremble, Taran sent out his senses. Immediately he encountered what he guessed was a small party of Rykan's men, probably foraging. There were about ten of them, and they were carrying hunting bows as well as longswords. Hastily, he showed Bull what he had found.

"There's no point trying to kill them," hissed the big man. "Three against ten are bad odds. Leaving them alone is the safest option. We can't risk capture or discovery."

Beckoning to the others, Bull led them away from the foragers and into the dripping woods.

✣ ✣ ✣ ✣ ✣

The small band of Andaryan warriors moved stealthily through the bare trees. Commander Heron had given Lieutenant Arif orders to scout the area, but Arif was nervous this close to the Citadel and feeling vulnerable so far away from his fellows. He had no choice, though, as the meat ration allotted their section of the army was dwindling and the supply trains were either late or had been intercepted by the enemy. Commander Heron, unwilling to bother General Sonten with such trivial matters at this crucial stage of the campaign, had made the decision to send Arif and his group out overnight to bag what they could.

So far the pickings were lean—a couple of small pigs and one scrawny deer—and the Lieutenant wanted to try the area around this small hill before turning back. He needed to have his men back under cover by full light, so he made only a cursory examination of the knoll. As he had feared, there was no game in sight. Frustrated, he was about to give the order to return when the faint smell of smoke caught his attention. Cautiously, suspecting a unit of the enemy stationed on this ideal lookout spot, he ordered his men to search.

His eyes narrowed when they uncovered the doused fire, but there was no one in evidence and no sign of long term occupation. Eventually assuming that some village hunter had spent the night there, he called his men off. He would report the matter to Heron, but he doubted the Commander would pursue it. He led his band away, melting back into the forest.

✣ ✣ ✣ ✣ ✣

"Well," huffed Bull, his breath steaming in the chilly air, "that was a close call."

Nodding, Taran slid from his horse.

Rienne's worried grey eyes searched the trees. "Do you think it's safe for us here, now?"

"I think so." Bull gave his horse's reins to Taran and threw back his hood. "They were only hunting, and they won't have found much game round here thanks to Cal's success with that bow. I doubt they'll be back. We'll do the same as before, keep constant watches and make sure we can decamp at a moments' notice. Well done, everyone, we managed that very smoothly. Now, let's rekindle that fire. I need some fellan!"

✵ ✵ ✵ ✵ ✵

Sullyan was thinking the same thing and was about to put the kettle over the hearth when a rapid knock sounded at the door. Crossing swiftly to open it, she found one of the Princess' pages outside, hopping frantically from foot to foot.

"Lady Brynne," he panted, "Her Highness says please will you come?"

She didn't bother with questions. Luckily, she had thrown on a shirt and breeches before tending the fire so she didn't need time to dress. Leaving Robin to follow if he chose, she waved the page on.

Arriving at the infirmary, still in darkness and quiet from the night shift, she found the Princess in a rare state outside Marik's room. On seeing her, Idrimar broke into sobs, causing the Major to fear the worst. Taking the older woman by the shoulders, she sent her calming thoughts. Idrimar had no control over her own metaforce, but Sullyan's much deeper energies reached in to steady her.

"Slowly, Highness," she soothed. "Tell me what has happened."

Idrimar took a couple of deep, sobbing breaths. "He's in such pain, Lady! He woke about an hour ago, but he's been moaning and crying out for much of the night. The healers gave him pain relief, but it's not working. He doesn't know anyone and he won't keep still. I'm so afraid he'll damage himself. Deshan was here until the early hours, and I didn't want to wake him, he's so worn out. You did say you'd come, Lady, but I know you're exhausted too …."

"You were right to call me, Highness. I told you I would come if you needed me. Now, you say he has great pain. Do you know where?"

"What? No … no." The Princess was wringing her hands. "But he was muttering in his sleep about his legs hurting and I—"

"His legs?" Sullyan stepped quickly past Idrimar and entered Marik's dimly lit room. The healer by his bed was trying desperately to calm the Count, who was barely conscious. His body streamed with sweat and his face bore an agonized look. Despite the poor light, Sullyan could see that his skin was grey from pain and he was trying to thrash around, although a strapped shoulder and tightly bandaged torso made that difficult. Sullyan moved to his side.

The healer glanced up. "I'll have to send for Deshan, Lady. I've given him pain relief, but it's having no effect. If I can't calm him, he's going to damage himself."

"Let me try." Gently, Sullyan moved the woman away. Idrimar approached the other side of the bed, fingers gripped tightly together. Sullyan placed one hand on the Count's sweaty brow and took his left hand. She felt her eyes dilating as she reached to Marik's psyche. The Count's eyes, which were darting frantically about the room, suddenly ceased their movement and locked with hers.

"Easy, my friend, you are safe now. I am here and you are

safe. Be easy now, rest quietly."

Talking softly all the while, she eased some of his pain. It was impossible to tell where it was coming from, but hot agony was searing through him, and in his semi-drugged state he couldn't deal with it. The sedative the healer had given him was also blocking Sullyan to some extent, and she wished the woman had called someone before administering the dose. Finally, she eased Marik enough to allow his consciousness to surface. Retracting her mind, she sat on the bed and used a cloth dipped in cool herbal water to wipe some of the sweat from his face. Looking into his pale grey eyes, she smiled.

"Hello, Ty."

She said it softly, giving him time to recognize her. The Princess, watching anxiously, held her breath. The Count seemed to struggle for a moment. Then, weakly, he said, "Hello, yourself."

Idrimar immediately dissolved into tears and Sullyan was glad she wasn't a noisy weeper. Marik hadn't noticed she was there. His head was turned toward Sullyan.

"How is the pain now, my friend?"

He thought before replying. "Better, but it still feels like someone's pushing red hot needles into my legs."

She grinned and he glared. "It's nothing to smile about!"

"Ah, but it is." She rose. "I am sorry, my friend, this might hurt a little. Do you think you can bear it?"

A look of fear came over his face. "I don't know! What are you going to do?"

Idrimar stopped crying long enough to protest, "Hasn't he been hurt enough? Leave him alone. I'm not going to let you touch him!" Coming round the end of the bed, she advanced threateningly on Sullyan.

Marik saw her. "Idri!" He held out his hand and the Princess pushed Sullyan out of the way so she could take her place at

Marik's side. Unnoticed by either of them, Sullyan moved down to the end of the bed where she slid her hand under the bedclothes. Swiftly, she pinched each of the Count's feet. His squeak of pain told her what she wanted to know.

Idrimar rounded angrily on her. "What do you think you're doing? I said leave him alone!"

Deshan came into the room and stopped, staring at the infuriated Princess. Not noticing her father right behind him, Idrimar pointed at Sullyan. "Get her out of here!"

Both men looked at the Major, who grinned unrepentantly back.

"What are you smiling at?" snapped Idrimar.

Sullyan ignored the overwrought Princess. "Your pardon, Ty. It was the only way to test whether you could feel your feet."

The Count's eyes widened. "Feel my ...? Well, why wouldn't I?"

She came closer, keeping the bed between her and the Princess. "You have had a nasty spinal injury, Ty, and we were not sure whether it would permanently affect your legs. It seems it has not." Turning to Idrimar, she said, "I am sorry I frightened you, Highness, but it was necessary. At least we now know the Count will make a full recovery."

Dissolving into tears once more, Idrimar sobbed an apology. Sullyan stood smiling down at Marik, who was just realizing what a close call he had had. He reached out his good hand. It was shaking.

Sullyan clasped it. "Deshan did all the hard work," she said, ignoring the physician's snort, "and you must be patient, rest as much as possible. You have other hurts which also need to mend. We will leave you in peace. Her Highness will tell you the outcome of your bravery, but then you must sleep again. I will see you later, my friend, but right now I need some strong fellan."

✤ ✤ ✤ ✤ ✤

"Why in the Void are you telling me this now, Heron?"

Sonten glared at his Artesan Commander, who stood in the light of the spitting fire. "Don't you think I have more important things on my mind than some raw lieutenant's jumpy nerves?"

The penetrating chill, the constant light rain, and the tense anticipation of the day's events were playing on Sonten's temper. Knowing how the Duke's volatile mood had affected all his military leaders, Heron ignored the General's anger.

"Lieutenant Arif isn't given to nerves, my Lord. It would be a mistake to dismiss his information. He might not have seen evidence of prolonged occupation, but that doesn't mean Anjer hasn't stationed reserves nearby. The light was poor and he was pressed for time, but he saw enough to convince him that someone had been there recently. He said it was an ideal spot from which to observe the battlefield."

Sonten scowled, irritated by the delay yet unwilling to dismiss this incident completely. If Arif's suspicions were correct and Anjer had stationed reserves in the woods to the west of the Plains, then it was something to bear in mind. Yet Sonten was sufficiently familiar with the terrain to know that the land in question wasn't ideal for concealing troops. There was too much open farmland and the woods were far too sparse. Any reserves coming from Gwayeth in the west would be on a forced march and unlikely to waste time by circling so far round. Sonten couldn't imagine Anjer directing them away from the battlefield when the final offensive was in full swing.

Trusting his judgment, he made an instant decision. He was due in Rykan's command tent to receive his final orders for the day's battle and any delay would inflame the already irritable Duke.

"Keep a close eye on our western flank, Heron, and be alert

for the possibility. I can't spare a unit to investigate right now. Post a lookout to the west, that's the best we can do. If word arrives of a flanking attack, send some of our boys to deal with it. Don't rely on his Grace's conscripts, they're far too flaky. Now get back to your command and listen for the trumpets. There's precious little time before dawn."

Snapping a salute, Heron turned on his heel. The General heard Rykan's angry voice and hurried toward the command tent, his own nerves strung tight. He dismissed Heron and his suspicions to the back of his mind.

✠ ✠ ✠ ✠ ✠

Sullyan met with Robin on her way back from Marik's room. The young man had taken time to dress properly and carried both their cloaks over his arm. He fell into step beside her and smiled as she told him the good news. Steering her away from their apartment, he said, "There have been developments outside, Major. I knew you'd want to see so I've asked them to bring food up to the battlements. Doubtless the Hierarch will be along soon."

Taking the Tower steps two at a time, they emerged into a miserable, grey, drizzly morning. The clouds hung low over their heads, almost touching the tallest spire. The Hierarch's standard hung limp and dripping from its pole. There wasn't a breath of wind and it was depressingly cold. Servants brought braziers out to warm them, along with pots of fresh fellan and plates of hot food. They erected a canopy for shelter from the dreary rain, and Sullyan huddled gratefully beneath it, drinking from a steaming mug and eating warm bread dripping with honey.

The Hierarch soon joined them and raised his brows at the civilized arrangements. Robin glanced up at him. "I hope I didn't overstep the mark, Majesty."

Pharikian smiled. "No indeed, young man, it was a very thoughtful thing to do. We'll probably be spending much time up here over the next couple of days, so a bit of comfort won't go amiss." Glancing at the Major, he said, "Brynne, my dear, this is a very considerate young man you have."

She grasped Robin's hand as he blushed. "Yes, Timar. I think so too."

Moving closer to them beneath the purple canopy, Pharikian accepted fellan from Robin. He turned to Sullyan and cocked his head. "How are you, Brynne?"

"As well as I can be, Timar."

He pursed his lips at the pallor of her face and noted the hand that had unconsciously strayed to her belly. Flicking a glance at Robin, he put an arm about her shoulders and drew her closer. She didn't resist. "Maybe we should allow Rykan to withdraw his challenge after all. You don't have to do this, child."

She started beneath his hands and drew a sharp breath. "I wish your words were true, Timar, but it is my only hope. Even if the hope is forlorn, I would rather die knowing that Rykan is no threat to Albia and that I did all I could. There is no other way for me now."

She turned back to the battle unfolding on the Plains, just catching the Hierarch's glance at Robin, whose handsome features wore an expression of grief and pain. She was struck by sudden sadness as Pharikian reached to Robin's psyche, giving him what strength and comfort he could. Silently, Robin accepted.

Preliminaries over, the fighting on the Plains intensified. Anjer, Kryp, and Ephan could be seen directing their own battalions, and there were also other generals, unknown to Sullyan, commanding the Hierarch's reserves. The noise became deafening as the various units clashed, cavalry and foot troops all playing their part. The three on the battlements, joined after a short while by a taciturn, hard-eyed Vanyr, watched the struggle unfold before them.

✣ ✣ ✣ ✣ ✣

On their small hill, Taran, Rienne, Cal, and Bull also stood in the drizzle, watching the drama playing out on the Plains. Taran didn't need Robin's eyes to see that the war was now raging in earnest. He could clearly hear the cries of the dying, the wounded men and horses, and see the black carrion birds and huge tangwyrs circling the skies above. Occasionally one would land, only to flap clumsily aloft again, carrying some dripping morsel in beak or talons.

Sharing watches with Bull, on constant guard against the threat of capture or discovery, Taran awaited the outcome of this war.

Three days later, it came.

Chapter Thirty

The weather turned milder. The bitter easterly winds dropped and the temperature climbed a few degrees above freezing. The ground on the Plains turned to mud with the constant churning of horses' hooves and men's boots. The armies slogged through its clinging stickiness as they fought, neither side gaining the upper hand for more than a few hours.

Anjer and his generals were tiring, as were their men. From the battlements, the Hierarch sent encouragement and support where he could. The healers were stretched to breaking point, as there were terrible losses on both sides and there were always more wounded than healers. Sullyan and Robin helped where they could, the Major feeling ever more useless as time went by.

She was unused to watching events unfold from afar and disliked having to rein in her powers and stay in safety. Had she not needed his comforting presence and strength so badly, she might have released Robin to join the fighting. She knew he was torn between his desire to fight and his need to stay close to his love.

The days of constant fretting were also taking their toll on Sullyan's health. She tried hard to resist it, but she was losing vitality by the day. She set aside a few hours every morning for sword practice, and that helped to a certain extent. She even managed to cajole Ky-shan, Jay'el, and even Xeer into fencing with her, the challenge of new opponents doing much to engage her concentration. On Pharikian's strict orders they used training foils instead of steel blades. She knew this was just as well, for she was often distracted and there would have been injuries had they used edged weapons.

Marik continued to improve, thanks largely to Deshan's and Sullyan's healing sessions, but he wasn't yet well enough to rise from his bed. Idrimar was his constant companion, and there was a steady stream of other visitors when the infirmary wasn't too frantic.

On the fourth day since the two armies clashed, Sullyan went up to the Tower walls at dawn, Almid and Kester by her side. Robin had gone to visit Marik, as the Count became irritable and restless if he didn't receive constant updates on the battle's progress. Commander Vanyr was also pacing the battlements that morning, but he kept a healthy distance from Sullyan.

The fighting had recommenced at first light as usual, and despite the men's exhaustion, it was intensifying by the hour. This escalation puzzled Sullyan and she scrutinized the battlefield intently. When she saw the reason for the change she turned, intending to send one of the twins in search of the Hierarch. Abruptly, a sharp pain ripped through her belly. A cry escaped her lips as intense agony sapped her strength and she was obliged to lean against the wall for support. Kester stepped close to help her, and even Vanyr glanced over, reluctantly curious.

The agonizing pain left Sullyan gasping for breath. Dizzy and sick, she slid down the wall. With Kester's help, she rested her back against it while Almid ran to find either the Hierarch or Robin. Despite Kester's huge presence and forbidding expression, Vanyr approached, drawn by the intensity of her pain. He ignored the giant's looming hostility and eyed Sullyan.

"Major, is there anything I can do?"

Her utter amazement at both his concern and curt offer gave

her the strength for a gasped reply. "I thank you, Commander, but I will be well when Robin comes." She sat as quietly as she could, each breath coming at a price, her vast powers completely unable to numb the pain.

It seemed an age before Robin arrived, skidding to a stop beside her and going down on one knee. The Hierarch was right behind him, Deshan in tow. Vanyr moved back, but his awkward stance and stern mouth betrayed disquiet.

Lack of breath had turned Sullyan's lips blue and she was shivering violently. "Bring her inside," commanded the Hierarch, and Kester scooped her up before the distraught Robin could move. The giant carried her through the Tower doors to the top of the stairs, but as soon as the big double doors clanged shut behind him, Sullyan's pain vanished as if it had never been. The tension constricting her lungs disappeared, and she could speak again.

"Put me down, Kester."

The giant didn't respond.

"Down!" she commanded, so firmly that he nearly dropped her. Robin and the Hierarch stared in amazement as she turned to face them. "The pain has gone," she said slowly, a horrible suspicion growing in her heart. "There is something very strange happening here." She shook her head, recalling what she had seen just before the pain struck. "Majesty, I was about to call for you when the pain hit me. The Duke of Kymer has finally taken to the field."

"What?" Pharikian turned on his heel, pushing back through the doors to see for himself.

Robin took Sullyan's arm, looking her over. "Are you alright?"

Her lips were no longer numb and the shivering had stopped. Regarding him frankly, she said, "I am at present, Robin, but I very much fear a complication I had not anticipated. Will you come with me back to the wall? I may need your help if the pain returns."

"Is that wise, Major?" asked Deshan.

"Maybe not, but it is necessary. This could be very important. Kester, I might need you too."

The giant followed as she pushed through the doors. She could see Vanyr watching her from his place by the wall, his face unreadable. She forgot him once she had taken two steps, though, because the pain was coming again. The nearer she got to the walls, the worse it grew. Soon she stopped, breathing heavily, and Pharikian turned from his scrutiny to watch her, anxiety plain on his face.

"Robin," she said, her voice weak and fearful, "I need your help. I cannot use my metaforce to numb the pain."

She sensed his alarm as he reached out, enveloping her mind with his own. His dismay was clear, but so was his relief when his strength seemed to help. Sighing as the pain eased, she moved nearer the wall. She made it almost as far as the wall itself before agony doubled her over once more. This time Pharikian added his strength to Robin's, and after a few moments she was able to straighten. Leaning on Kester's arm, she continued to the battlements. Her face felt pinched and tight, but she was able to bear it.

She saw Pharikian share a worried look with Deshan. Vanyr regarded her closely, mixed expressions warring in his strange white eyes. Breathing deeply, Sullyan leaned against the wall, trying to calm the panic rising in her heart. This was a complication she hadn't even considered, and she was sure the Hierarch was ignorant of its cause. But she knew. Her eyes had fastened on Rykan's dark form as he emerged from his command tent, and she had seen him turn toward the Citadel and fix his gaze hungrily on the Hierarch's standard. As his glance brushed hers—

and she knew he hadn't even seen her, let alone recognized her at such distance—the agonizing pain had struck her down.

Rykan's insidious poison had reacted to its maker's presence.

Now, leaning against the cold stone, panic and fury in equal measure tearing through her heart, she watched the enemy lord brutally rally his troops for what had to be a final push. The Hierarch kept up a soothing cocoon of power around her, for her own vast store of energy seemed beyond her control. Robin helped direct both his and Pharikian's strength to where it would do most good, but she could still feel the monarch's dismay at this unforeseen setback. Bleakly, she wondered how—or even if—she could overcome it. If she could not, all their plans were lost.

As before, they spent the morning watching the two armies playing out the power struggle beneath them. It was soon obvious to Sullyan why Rykan had finally deigned to appear. He had kept some of his forces in reserve and now considered it necessary to deploy them. The dreadful losses sustained by both sides were testament to the valor of the men on the field, but it was also clear that despite the ferocity of the fighting, neither side could gain the upper hand. The morning wore on and Sullyan, who had managed to calm her earlier panic, became increasingly concerned.

Pharikian was beside her as he had been all morning, and Robin was still directing their flow of metaforce to shield her from Rykan's influence. Vanyr had also stayed, keeping his distance as usual. Sullyan glanced up at the Hierarch, trying to gauge his mood and guess whether he had seen and recognized Rykan's latest tactic. Anjer was on the battlefield directing his men. She was sure he was unaware of his enemy's latest move. He had runners and dispatch riders, but the field was in chaos and it wasn't easy for them to get through. Reluctant to interfere with the direction of the Citadel's forces while its ruler and one of its commanders were standing beside her, Sullyan kept her counsel.

Time passed with still no countermeasures from Anjer, and Sullyan could stay silent no longer. Pharikian didn't seem to have noticed the surge of Rykan's fresh troops, and Vanyr hadn't said anything either. If she didn't speak now, she feared the battle could sway dangerously in Rykan's favor. She felt very proud of Robin, who had nudged her arm some time ago to indicate that he had also seen the danger, although she had gestured for him to keep his peace.

Finally, she spoke. "Majesty?"

Pharikian turned, obviously thinking she was in trouble again. "Yes, child?"

"I trust the Lord General will not leave it too much longer before mobilizing his reserves?"

She saw Vanyr startle and the Hierarch stared at her. "What reserves, Brynne?"

She went cold. "He must have reserves, Majesty, surely?"

Pharikian frowned. "He does, but how do you know about them? They were kept a closely guarded secret to stop word of them reaching the enemy."

Some of her tension eased. "The secret is safe, Majesty, never fear. I only know because it makes sound tactical sense." Her gaze returned to the mass of men, struggling together on the Plains. "But if he does not deploy them soon, it will be too late." She pointed, drawing the Hierarch's eyes, and Vanyr craned over the battlements too, intent on the conflict below. "See how the Duke has worked those fresh units around to your left flank where General Kryp is weakest? If he breaks through your lines there, he has access to Anjer's rear and could conceivably cut him off. So if the Lord General is waiting for a signal, Majesty, may I strongly suggest that you give it?" She saw his stare and added, "With the greatest respect, of course."

Pharikian glanced back down at the conflict, verifying the

truth of her words. He shook his head. "You're wasted as a major, Brynne."

"Tell that to my General, Majesty."

She smiled, but the expression faded swiftly as she realized there would be no point.

Pharikian's face darkened and she heard him mutter, "Be sure that I will, child."

He concentrated, sending the information to Anjer. They all saw the start Anjer gave on receiving his ruler's message, and once he had instructed his runners he turned in his saddle to salute the watchers on the battlements.

"Anjer sends his compliments, Major, and thanks you for your timely observation," Pharikian reported. He grinned and Sullyan smiled faintly back, allowing him to lighten her mood. Vanyr stood watching her with what could have been reluctant respect.

Over the next few hours, Anjer's hidden forces came into play, countering Rykan's final surprise tactic. Clearly furious at its failure and unwilling yet to surrender, the Duke whipped his men to an even greater frenzy. The mud of the battlefield disappeared beneath fallen bodies as the Hierarch's troops surged forward to meet these desperate attacks, but as time wore on it became obvious that Rykan's men couldn't sustain this pace. They were exhausted and failing.

In the middle of the afternoon Princess Idrimar appeared, seeking the watchers on the Tower. She told Sullyan she had been sent by Marik, who had heard of the battle's progress and was desperate to see it for himself. Since the healers wouldn't let him rise from his bed, he thought Sullyan might be able to persuade them, knowing she would understand his need.

Sullyan left the battlements, taking Almid and Kester with her. She found Marik fretting in his bed. Glad of a reason to use her powers since they were useless on her own malady, she poured strength and stability into him as well as numbing some of his pain. The giants then wrapped him carefully in blankets and a huge cloak before lifting him into a solid padded chair. This they carried between them up the interminable stairs and out onto the Tower roof, positioning it so Marik could look over the walls and observe the scene below.

What he saw was total carnage. There were dead and dying men and horses everywhere. The noise of battle was loud and the smells of warfare spiraled on the torpid air. Generals and commanders on both sides could be seen exhorting their tired and dispirited men, but those on Rykan's side were having less success than those on the Hierarch's. As Sullyan knew, many of Rykan's troops were newly subjugated and had little or no stomach for this fight. Finding themselves on the losing side, they vanished from the battlefield like wraiths in the sun. Watching Rykan's forces dwindle by the hour brought a grim smile to Pharikian's face.

Eventually, just as the light was fading, a distinctive horn-call blared across the Plains. Sullyan traded a look with Pharikian. Rykan's heralds were signaling his intention to surrender. Robin hugged her tight and Commander Vanyr shook his sovereign's hand. Sullyan simply felt numb.

Suddenly, the Citadel's curtain walls were thronging with people, all cheering their victorious army. The fighting men, too exhausted to cheer, watched as Anjer and his honor guard rode forward to meet Rykan's emissary and receive the Duke's token of surrender. He reported the news that Rykan would formally cede victory to the Hierarch and withdraw his personal challenge one hour after dawn on the following day. Pharikian sent his acceptance.

To noisy acclaim from the populace, Anjer returned to the Citadel.

✤ ✤ ✤ ✤ ✤

So it's definite? He's surrendered?

It was evening, and Taran was listening in to Bull's conversation with Robin. They learned that the Captain had finally persuaded Sullyan to rest once the furor of congratulating Anjer had subsided, but they were due to attend the Hierarch later to discuss Rykan's formal surrender.

Taran and his companions had heard Rykan's horns without realizing their significance. On learning the truth, they shared mixed emotions; elation at the outcome of the war, but trepidation at the thought of what Sullyan must now face. Bull in particular was alarmed when he heard Robin's account of how the Duke's physical presence had affected her.

So how will she cope with fighting him? he asked.

Robin replied heavily. *I have no idea. She's going to have to tell the Hierarch tonight and I don't know how he'll react.*

Any idea when the duel will take place?

I'd imagine the day after tomorrow. The Hierarch will issue his own challenge in the morning, and I expect Rykan will be given a day to rest and prepare after the fighting. Not that he took much part in it. He only crawled out of his tent this morning.

What are the chances we can get closer to watch?

Robin paused to consider. *Not good, Bull. Both armies are still entrenched around the Citadel. You'd never get through Rykan's lines unobserved. Even if you did, I doubt the Hierarch or Anjer would approve of what you've done. Best keep your heads down and stay where you are. I don't even want to think how the Major would react to learning you've been there all along. She's got enough on her mind right now.*

Bull conceded the point, although his heart railed against it. He broke the link and left Taran to tell the others what they had learned. This he did with a heavy heart, knowing how distressed Rienne would be.

✣ ✣ ✣ ✣ ✣

Sullyan woke to Robin's gentle kiss a couple of hours later. He was sorry to do it. She had been soundly sleeping, which was a rarity in itself, and he knew how badly she needed the rest. Yet they had to attend the Hierarch, and it wouldn't do to be late. She gave him a soft smile and immersed herself in the bathing pool before accepting Robin's offer of fresh fellan as she dressed.

The meeting would be informal, attended by the Hierarch, Anjer, Ephan, Kryp, and Vanyr. Its purpose was to discuss the arrangements for hearing Rykan's declaration of surrender and the promulgating of the Hierarch's own personal challenge. It would be held in Pharikian's lesser audience chamber with its more comfortable seating and roaring fire. By the time Sullyan arrived, Ky-shan and Jay'el still shadowing her, everyone was there with the exception of the Hierarch.

Leaving the pirates by the door, Sullyan crossed to Anjer, intending to give her personal congratulations on his victory. Instead of waiting for her to speak, however, he startled her by sweeping her into his arms. He was smiling hugely.

"If it hadn't been for you noticing Rykan's sneaky little move, the battle might have had a very different outcome. Andaryon stands in your debt, Major Sullyan."

He set her on her feet again and she flushed, embarrassed by his praise. "I am sure you would have seen it for yourself, my Lord."

"Not soon enough, my Lady! Kryp wants to thank you as well, for his lines were weak on that side and Rykan might well have broken through if you hadn't alerted me."

To her deepening mortification, Kryp heaved himself to his feet and held out a meaty hand to her. Unable to refuse, she took it and he clasped hers to his chest as he added his heartfelt thanks to Anjer's. All traces of his former animosity seemed to have vanished. She noticed how he favored one leg and commented on it.

"It's only a flesh wound, Lady Brynne," he said. "I was one of the lucky ones."

Ephan was wounded too and sported a bandage over one eye, his left arm in a sling. His smile of greeting also conveyed his gratitude. Vanyr bowed his head to her, although he didn't speak. The Commander seemed to have put aside much of his former hostility, although he still seemed ill at ease in her company. She noticed his eyes on her more than once during the evening.

The chamber door opened and the Hierarch, preceded by two pages, entered the room. To the delight of all, Marik followed him, the twins once again carrying the Count in his chair. Deshan and the Princess walked behind him, and they took seats on either side of Marik once the twins placed him at the oval table. There were congratulatory remarks all round for the heroics of the Count and his men.

The meeting got off to a slow start as servants brought in a light meal. Anjer and Kryp devoured theirs as if they feared a famine, but the rest ate more sedately. The Hierarch watched Sullyan closely as the meal progressed, and she saw his lips purse at the small amount she ate. When the plates were finally cleared away, he turned to her.

"Brynne, before we discuss the real reasons behind this meeting, I think we need to establish exactly what happened to you this morning. Would you mind?"

Sullyan's eyes darkened at the memory, but she couldn't escape the necessity of his question. The fire opal at her throat leaped to the beat of her heart. Anjer, Kryp, and Ephan, all informed of the attack she had suffered earlier that day, turned concerned eyes on her. The Major took a moment to compose herself before speaking.

"It was the Duke's physical presence, Majesty. I never imagined it would cause such a reaction in me. My powers were useless against the pain, and I have no idea how to counter its effects. I very much fear it will compromise my efficiency in dealing with him on a personal basis."

Their concern was palpable and Anjer leaned forward. "Then what are we to do?"

Pharikian held up a hand to ward off further queries. Sullyan watched him, suspecting he had a plan. She was right.

"Yes, I thought that might be the case. Deshan and I have been discussing this, child, and we believe we have found a way to ensure your freedom from this pain when you face Rykan. On the day of the duel, just before you go to meet him, we will share life force with you. That should give you the physical strength, at least for a while, to ward off the poison's effects. Hopefully it will last long enough for you to defeat him."

This was an unprecedented offer and Robin's eyes widened. Sullyan shook her head. "I cannot take your life force, Majesty, it would be too risky! What if I should lose?"

The Hierarch regarded her, eyes hard. "If you lose to him, Brynne, it will matter little that you carry our life force. Do you think Rykan will allow any of us to live if he takes the crown? You and I both know he will put us all to the sword, regardless of rank or Code."

She expelled a breath, capitulation in her eyes, and he saw it. "Then it's settled. Tomorrow morning, when we ride out to accept his surrender and issue the challenge, I will shield you from his influence. Before you face him in the arena, those of us who are Artesans will share life force with you. We trust you, Brynne Sullyan, and if the fate of this realm is to rest with you, then surrendering life force is the least we can do."

She sat with her hands in her lap, her head bowed, not really listening to the rest of the conversation. She trusted Robin to relay the details later. She knew he appreciated how she was feeling and would realize the Hierarch was giving her time to assimilate his words.

Her thoughts were churning, assessing the offer. The sharing of life force between Artesans was an intimate and risky thing. Simply put, it was to give control of one's very existence into another's hands, and once given, it couldn't be taken back save by the willing release of the holder. It gave the holder, for a finite period, total access to whatever powers the donor possessed, both mental and physical. If the donor died before their life force could be returned, then their metaphysical powers became part of the recipient's psyche. But if the recipient should die, so would the donor. Understandably, it was a rarely proffered gift.

Sullyan knew that it often took a lifetime of practice for someone born with the Artesan gift to learn how to use it effectively. She was a rare exception in her level of Mastery at such a young age. To suddenly be given control over powers as mighty as the Hierarch's, however, could be extremely dangerous, even for her. One slip, one lapse of concentration, and lives would be lost. And that was not the only risk.

In this situation they were hazarding everything, gambling their lives and the fate of the realm on Sullyan's ability to overcome Rykan. If she defeated him, his threat disappeared and the Hierarch reaffirmed his sovereignty. Yet if Rykan won, he stood to gain much more than mere sovereignty. If victorious, Rykan would almost certainly stipulate access to Sullyan's intimate power as his prize, and with the donor life forces within her, he would instantly control more power than anyone had ever possessed before. He would become invincible, truly omnipotent.

Sullyan knew she couldn't allow it.

Should the unthinkable happen—should she fail to defeat

Rykan—there was only one way she knew of to prevent such a terrifying outcome. Unfortunately, it depended on the Duke's respect for the honor codes surrounding the challenge they proposed to issue. Like the Hierarch, she had absolutely no faith in Rykan's honor.

She was still brooding on the subject when the meeting broke up. The others were leaving and she stood, Robin beside her. Pharikian came over to her and held out his arms. Wordlessly, she entered his embrace and they stood motionless for a while.

Eventually, he released her and stepped back, looking closely into her small, pale face. "Never fear, dear child," he murmured, cupping her chin with one hand, "you will not fail if our strength and love can do anything to prevent it. Now go and rest, both of you. Tomorrow will be a difficult day, and you need whatever strength you can summon. Try not to brood, Brynne. What will be, will be."

Kissing her brow gently, he sent her away.

Chapter Thirty-One

espite her fears that sleep wouldn't come, Sullyan and Robin spent a dreamless night. Lying entwined and unmoving, exhaustion quickly claimed them. They were woken an hour before dawn by servants bringing food. The fire in their suite was stoked to a bright blaze and they took fellan together by its comforting warmth before Sullyan disappeared into the bathing room. A few minutes later she heard a knock on the outer door, followed by a surprised exclamation from Robin. She frowned—it clearly wasn't the Hierarch. Before she could call to Robin, the door of the bathing room swung open and Princess Idrimar strode in. She held a bundle of clothing over her arm, and she smiled at Sullyan before firmly closing the door behind her.

A short while later Sullyan followed the Princess from the pool room. She was pleased to see that Robin was now fully attired in his dress uniform, the one bearing the Hierarch's colors. He was sitting by the fire, eating bread spread with honey, and he stared admiringly as she approached him, appreciating what had been done. The Hierarch must have expressly ordered the clothes, as they fitted Sullyan perfectly. Her own combat leathers and the new jacket in the Hierarch's colors were too big for her now she had lost so much weight. The new uniform hugged her slight figure intimately and was obviously designed to assist movement.

The leather was soft and supple whilst still affording some protection. It was very dark purple—almost black—with gold buttons on the linen shirt and jacket, and a gold buckle on the soft leather sword belt. The shirt and jacket collars were trimmed with imperial purple, and Sullyan's array of rank insignia and battle honors gleamed above the jacket pocket. Lying across a chair was a flowing cloak, designed as much for show as for warmth. The Princess picked it up, draping it about Sullyan's shoulders. The Major was uncomfortable at having Andaryon's Princess serve her like a maid, but she accepted her attentions as best she could. Eventually, Idrimar stepped back to survey the effect. "Very good," she approved. She then gestured for Sullyan to sit and served her bread and honey, encouraging her to eat while they waited for the Hierarch's summons.

The light outside increased as a pale, watery sun nudged its way over the rooftops. A page appeared at the door and Idrimar turned to Sullyan. "Are you ready?" Sullyan inclined her head, not trusting herself to speak. She and Robin followed the Princess along the corridors, Ky-shan, Jay'el, Ki-en, and the twins walking behind. Clearly they weren't going to miss this if they could help it, and Sullyan couldn't refuse them. She nodded as she passed them but didn't speak.

When they reached the outer courtyard, there was already quite a crowd. Horses had been readied, their hides and gear gleaming, warm breath steaming faintly in the cool dawn air. Sullyan looked for Drum, but although she could see a groom holding Robin's chestnut Torka, there was no sign of her big black stallion.

The entire royal household had turned out to see the party ride off, and the ladies Falina, Hollett, and Torien were all in attendance on their lords. Kryp and Ephan, still sporting bandages, were dressed in their battle uniforms, but Sullyan suddenly noticed that Anjer wore clothing identical to hers. She frowned.

A stir by the doors to the royal apartments heralded the arrival of the Hierarch, who was followed by his secretary, Baron Gaslek.

Sullyan heard Robin's gasp of admiration and could scarcely blame him, for the tall, patrician ruler was dressed magnificently. His state robes were white, gold, and purple, and he wore a long, flowing cloak of gold gauze trimmed with white fur and purple velvet. It shimmered strangely in the watery sunlight as he crossed the courtyard. Coming over to where Sullyan waited, he beckoned Anjer to him. The two men halted in front of her and as she was about to make an obeisance, Pharikian took her hand.

"We'll dispense with the formalities today, child, there'll be enough of that outside very shortly. Now, Brynne, you will doubtless have noticed that your enormous warhorse isn't here. That's because we thought it best to keep your presence concealed from Rykan until we choose to reveal the Crown's Champion. You would be all too visible aboard that huge beast, so I have provided another mount for you today. Stay at the rear of the party, if you will, until we call you forward."

"As you wish, Majesty."

He turned to Robin. "As for you, young man, your duty this morning will be to direct the flow of my shielding toward Brynne, as I may well become distracted once we meet Rykan face to face. There's never been any love lost between us, and there's even less cause for it now. So don't allow your attention to wander."

Robin nodded and the Hierarch turned back to Sullyan.

"My child, the Lord General has claimed the right to be your second, both today and tomorrow. Under other circumstances, the Champion's lot would have fallen on him, so I think this is fitting. Do you agree?"

"Of course, Majesty. I would be honored." She smiled up at Anjer's massive, comforting form. He placed his hand on her shoulder.

"Then I believe we are ready."

A groom brought the Hierarch's horse forward. It was a stately golden mare with a nearly white mane and tail. Her coat was burnished and gleaming, her gear polished brightly and glittering with golden fittings. She was decked out with a cloth of gold trapper, and purple bunting adorned the reins. Belying his age, Pharikian swung easily into the saddle, his back straight and strong as he nudged the mare toward the gates. His generals mounted their warhorses and Sullyan settled herself into the saddle of the dapple-grey pacer the groom brought her. It was much smaller than her familiar Drum.

They formed up in the courtyard, Pharikian in the lead with Anjer by his side, Kryp and Ephan following, then Gaslek, and finally Sullyan and Robin. The pirates ranged themselves around her, and no one commented on their presence. A full contingent of Velletian Guard, all wearing purple and gold ceremonial uniforms and led by a brooding, hard-eyed Vanyr, surrounded the party. The Hierarch raised his arm and the many trumpeters stationed on the Palace walls brought their horns to life. To the resulting bellow of sound, the courtyard gates swung open and the party rode onto the Processional Way. With the pale sunlight gleaming off polished swords and gold cloth, they rode in stately fashion, acclaim from the populace ringing in Sullyan's ears. The noise was deafening as they entered the lower town, and flowers and petals were thrown under the horses' feet.

When they reached the perimeter road running the circumference of the Citadel's curtain wall, the cheers of the guards stationed there swelled the clamor. Robin nudged Sullyan's arm and she caught sight of the patrol commander who had escorted them to the Citadel gates so many weeks ago. She wondered what the man thought of them now. She soon forgot him as Pharikian looked back over his shoulder at Robin, indicating that he should begin concentrating on the shield protecting Sullyan. With an anxious smile, the young man complied.

At a nod from their ruler, the array of heralds on the curtain wall now began their fanfare. For some reason this made Sullyan think of Bull, and she suddenly longed for his comforting presence. Giving herself a mental shake, she turned her attention to the strong flow of metaforce coming from Andaryon's ruler. As the guards slowly cranked the enormous Citadel gates wide, Robin's strength was added to the shimmering web of power cast around her mind. His deft skill earned him her grateful smile, and he held her eyes for a moment to convey his loving pride.

As they rode through the gates, the townspeople's cheering faded into the roar of reverent greeting that rose from the massed ranks of the Hierarch's forces. Sullyan's heart turned in her breast as she remembered similar occasions when she and Robin, returning from a victorious campaign, had been the ones so lauded. Glancing at the young man beside her, she knew he was wondering what she was feeling right now.

Feeling, however, was exactly what she was trying not to do. She rode in silence, looking neither left nor right, trying to think no further than her horse's next pace. Her body's unexpected reaction to Rykan's physical presence had shaken her badly. She was not at all confident she could hide it today. The Hierarch's protective flow of metaforce was doing its job at present, but they still hadn't seen any sign of the rebel lord. Gathering what little strength she had left, she tried not to think what might happen over the next hour or so.

The party continued through the massed ranks of men, each commander saluting his warlords as they went. The Hierarch and Anjer acknowledged the acclaim with smiles and nods. They reached the edge of their forces and halted there, looking out over the no-man's-land between the two armies.

The Plains were littered with the dead and alive with carrion birds and rats. A few tangwyrs stretched their enormous wings, circling lazily overhead. They were too big to be comfortable on the ground so near to living men. The stench of death was appalling. Everyone was grateful the fighting had not occurred in the summer heat.

They sat waiting, and Sullyan could clearly see how angered Pharikian and Anjer were by Rykan's failure to meet them. There was no movement from his command post, although horses were ready, being held by grooms. Just as the Hierarch turned, no doubt intending to send Vanyr to demand the Duke's attendance, Rykan's escort emerged from the tent and mounted their horses. Riding the animals forward in line, they blocked the tent from view so no one would see Rykan mount his steed.

The Duke's heralds blew their own fanfare as the little cavalcade moved forward. Lord Sonten was at its head, lavishly dressed in black, silver, and scarlet with pale blue trim. He was accompanied by two other commanders sporting different family colors. An honor guard of twenty surrounded them, all Rykan's elite troops. As they drew nearer, the dark lord himself could be seen riding at the rear, mounted on a fine bay stallion. Peering between the pirates, Sullyan noted sourly that its sides were scarred from the spur, its mouth dripped red foam, and the veins stood out on its damp neck.

They advanced slowly, and as they neared, Vanyr rode forward with ten of his men. The commander of Rykan's elite guard did the same. Sullyan saw Robin glance her way and she nodded, trying to appear composed and serene despite the pallor of her face. He seemed satisfied that the shielding was doing its work. What he didn't see, because she was doing her level best to hide it, was the rising tide of panic she felt at the thought of meeting her ravisher face to face. Drawing desperately on years of independence and self-reliance, she schooled herself to calm. Despite her best efforts, she felt the fire opal at her throat jump erratically.

Having exchanged formalities, Vanyr and Rykan's commander now reined back. Pharikian, flanked by Anjer and Ephan, rode forward to accept Rykan's formal surrender. Halting their steeds a few paces in advance of their party, they waited for the Duke of Kymer to approach.

His men gave ground before him, opening a corridor between them down which he rode his nervy stallion. Robin was staring at Sullyan's nemesis, and she clearly felt the great surge of hatred welling up inside him. The darkly handsome Duke was dressed in black trimmed with silver and his sword belt was of scarlet leather. Tall, slim, and strongly built, he swayed easily with the stallion's paces, one hand tight on the reins, the other resting on his thigh, close to his sword hilt. He wore an expression of haughty arrogance, undimmed by the surrender he would be forced to submit. His pale yellow eyes were fixed on the Hierarch, his sensuous lips parted in a faint smile.

Rykan brought his stallion to a snorting stop before the Hierarch's mare. Hesitating just long enough for insolence, he inclined his head, causing the Hierarch to narrow his eyes. "Majesty," he said, his deep and silky voice flaying Sullyan's heart. The last time she had heard it she had been naked and helpless, lying torn and chained beneath his weight. Swallowing the bile rising in her throat, she struggled for calm.

"Rykan," said Anjer curtly. The insult given Rykan by the Hierarch's refusal to acknowledge his greeting caused the dark lord to frown. "Get on with it!" snapped Anjer, his massive frame towering over the slimmer man. The Duke's face darkened further and he glowered at Anjer. Then the insolent smile returned, and he directed his reply to the Hierarch.

"Majesty, before these witnesses I cede the field of combat." His ringing voice carried no hint of humility. "I withdraw my challenge to your right to rule, and with your permission will begin a retreat back to Kymer within the day."

No one spoke. Pharikian held Rykan's gaze so long that the Duke's eyes shifted uncertainly. The Hierarch waited long enough to unnerve him before saying coldly, "I think not."

The Duke started, clearly not expecting this development. Hooding his yellow eyes, he glanced around. Sullyan was suddenly grateful that she and Robin were at the back of the party, sheltered from his gaze. The pirates had closed tightly around them, hiding them from view.

"Majesty?" Rykan's tone made it clear he was unsure how to proceed.

Capturing his gaze, Pharikian stated, "Lord Rykan, Duke of Kymer, you have committed an act of treason by leading forces against the Crown. Your admission of defeat is noted and the withdrawal of your challenge accepted. However, the Crown chooses to deny you your right of retreat."

Rykan's face paled at the charge of treason, although it was just. But the last statement was unprecedented. Sullyan knew there had never been an occasion when a defeated challenger had been denied the right to withdraw.

Rykan knew it too. Drawing himself stiffly erect, he demanded, "Why?"

His rudeness caused Anjer's hand to drop to his sword hilt. Pharikian quelled him with a look. "Because, my Lord, the Crown chooses instead to issue its own personal challenge. Rykan, Duke of Kymer, consider yourself bound by the Codes of single combat."

Someone in Rykan's party gasped. Sonten recoiled in shock, and Rykan himself betrayed a momentary start of fear. But then the arrogance slipped back into place and he sneered. "Are you losing your wits, Pharikian? Both you and I know the Crown can't engage in single combat."

Smiling tightly, the Hierarch gestured to Gaslek. The fussy little secretary nudged his cob toward Rykan, a sheet of parchment in one hand. Clearing his throat under the Duke's hooded gaze, he announced, "This codicil to the Codes of Honor reads thus, my Lord. 'Subsequent to lawful challenge, and if it so desires, the Crown, on emerging victorious from the field of combat, shall hereby be empowered to likewise issue a challenge of single combat, said conflict to be conducted by a warrior designated by the Hierarch. This warrior shall be known as Champion of the Crown'."

Startling them all, Rykan snorted, and then gave a roar of mocking laughter. "Gaslek, you pompous old booksnout! Where did you dredge that one from?"

The secretary gathered his dignity around him like a cloak. He sniffed, his unruffled manner drawing approval from the Hierarch. "Seldom used and obscure it may be, your Grace, but this law is well recorded in the annals of our realm."

Rykan's mirth ceased abruptly. "Show me this ridiculous law!"

Gaslek handed his parchment to Vanyr, who carried it to Rykan. The Duke snatched it, scanning it quickly. Realizing its validity, fury flooded his face. "Majesty, I protest! Where is the precedence for this?"

"What's your problem, Rykan?" said Anjer. "His Majesty makes his own precedent, as well you know. It should be enough for you that the protocol exists. You have two choices. Accept the challenge or renounce your rank."

Rykan glared, trapped into a situation he had not foreseen. His rage at being thwarted yet again spiraled dangerously. Just then, Sonten leaned forward and whispered in his overlord's ear. Rykan's temper cooled visibly. He regarded Anjer, a calculating look in his eye. The unpleasant smile reappeared as he addressed the Hierarch.

"And what will you wager on this challenge, Majesty?"

Pharikian studied the arrogant man. His lips quirked. "Andaryon's throne, of course."

Eyes narrowing in hungry triumph, Rykan said, "Then I accept your challenge." He cast a satisfied glance at Sonten before turning to stare at Anjer. "So, Anjer, you and I are to meet under arms at last, eh?"

The Lord General shook his head. "Regrettably no, Rykan. Much as I would appreciate the chance to put an end to your arrogance, I must forego that pleasure. However, I declare your acceptance of his Majesty's challenge duly Witnessed."

Rykan frowned and Sonten's brow also creased. Sullyan felt herself tense and knew her face was white, her eyes huge as she anticipated the Hierarch's call.

Rykan stared round the party, dismissing both Ephan and Kryp with disdain. Then his eye fell on Vanyr and his assurance returned. "Well, well, Vanyr, don't tell me you volunteered for this position? I thought you stayed comfortably behind your Citadel walls these days after that last beating I gave you. As I remember, I sent you running like a whipped cur."

Vanyr's face paled dangerously and his whole body stiffened. Sullyan saw Robin's start of surprise. He glanced quickly at her, but she didn't react. Her thoughts were elsewhere.

Despite his anger at Rykan's taunt, Vanyr mastered himself enough to reply levelly.

"I'm afraid I must disappoint you also, my Lord, for there is one here more worthy than I to be your opponent."

His choice of words amazed Sullyan and she eyed him. But Rykan was losing patience with the game and he rounded angrily on the Hierarch.

"If not Anjer or Vanyr, then who? Who else in your forces has the skill at arms—not to mention the metaphysical prowess—to stand against me?"

The Hierarch spoke calmly and Rykan suddenly stilled.

"There is one among my court whom you have deeply wronged, Rykan. One who is your equal both in power and sword skills, one who is deserving of the chance for retribution, and one I am very proud to name my Champion."

This speech clearly puzzled Rykan, aware as he was of the skills of the men in the Hierarch's court. When Pharikian turned in his saddle to beckon Sullyan forward, both pirates and Velletian Guard parting to afford her passage, Rykan failed to recognize her. The dark uniform she wore and the hood of her cloak covering her tawny hair disguised even her sex until she came closer. With a veneer of serenity hiding the rising tide of panic within her, she rode forward to confront her most visceral nightmare.

She walked her horse toward the dark lord, her eyes never leaving his. Mercifully, the Hierarch's shielding held even this close, and she could concentrate on hiding her panic. Halting before him, she made herself relax, one hand lightly on the reins, the other resting on the pommel of her saddle. Drawing back her hood, her expression unreadable, she said, "My Lord Duke, I am the Hierarch's Champion."

The puzzlement on Rykan's handsome face changed swiftly through suspicion to recognition and fear. His eyes wide with shock, he glared from Pharikian to Sullyan. Hissing through his teeth, he snarled, "You, you little witch? That traitor Marik told me you were dead!"

She allowed herself a tiny smile. "As you see, my Lord, he lied."

Rykan gathered himself with an effort, barely controlling his fury at seeing her alive and still in possession of the powers he coveted so.

"Well, you obviously can't keep away! Did you so enjoy my hospitality and favors that you've come to beg for more? I know you never had a man before I took you, so is that it, girl? None of these men can satisfy you like I did, eh?"

She heard Vanyr's shocked gasp. The white-eyed Commander was one of the few who hadn't yet heard the truth of Rykan's abuse. His face went tight with fury and muscles jumped along his jaw. Although her own eyes darkened with remembered pain, she was able to hide her rising disgust.

"As you well know, my Lord, I experienced no pleasure whatsoever in the duress of your company, unless you count my extreme gratification at denying you what you so brutally tried to take."

Her words inflamed Rykan, and Anjer moved forward to protect her should the need arise. However, the infuriated Duke contented himself with words.

"You should have died at my hands, and I should have slaughtered that whining traitor Marik when I had the chance! You would never have escaped without his help."

"On the contrary, my Lord, it was your overweening confidence that allowed my friends to rescue me, and it has brought you to this pass. I shall take great pleasure in acting as his Majesty's Champion tomorrow."

This statement froze Rykan's temper. Glaring furiously, he decided to try another tack.

"Majesty, surely you can't be serious in appointing this ... this ... girl ... as your Champion? Look at her! She's not half my height, she's female, and she's not even from our realm!" Grasping at this loophole, he stated, "I'm sure I am not bound by Andaryan law to accept an opponent not of our race." He glared at Gaslek, daring him to refute this assertion from his parchment.

The Hierarch was silent. They hadn't discussed this valid objection and he had no ready answer. Sullyan saw Gaslek frown and knew Rykan was right. There was nothing in the Codes to cover this. It was up to her to save the situation. Forestalling whatever reply Pharikian might have given, she caught Rykan's attention again.

"My Lord, would you be so kind as to give us your definition of 'race'?"

He swung back to her, fury sparking in his eyes. "Well, obviously, someone who was born in this realm and has Andaryan blood running through their veins!"

Very deliberately, she leaned forward. "And you would accept a Champion who fulfilled those criteria?"

He laughed. "Of course!"

She turned to Anjer and he responded.

"Heard and Witnessed."

Rykan scowled, suspecting he had somehow been outmaneuvered but was unable to see the joke. Sullyan enlightened him.

"My Lord Duke, I fulfill your criteria on both counts. I was born here, in the Citadel behind me, and I have the blood of Pharikian's House running through my veins. I trust that satisfies you?"

There was deathly silence from Rykan, who stared at Sullyan in shock. Then he rounded furiously on the Hierarch.

"I refuse to believe this! How is it possible? She's Albian. It is a trick of some kind!"

"It is no trick, my Lord," snapped Sullyan, more confident now that Rykan's veneer of calm was shattered. "How it happened is none of your concern. What matters is that it is true. Your acceptance of my position as Champion has been Witnessed, therefore it remains only to settle the time and the place. My second will finalize the details. I bid you good day."

Wheeling her horse, she showed Rykan her back and rode stiffly through the ranks of Velletian Guard. The pirates once more closed around her, murmuring their approval. As she returned to his side, Robin gripped her arm, clearly worried by her pallor and the way her body trembled, but he was the only one who noticed. She turned to watch the final scene of this act.

Fuming and helpless, Rykan was left facing the mildly enquiring look on Anjer's face and the outright satisfaction on the Hierarch's. Once again, he was defeated and he knew it. But his eyes were coldly calculating as he allowed Anjer and his own second, Sonten, to set a time of one hour before midday on the morrow, agreeing to conduct the duel outside the Citadel's southern gates. Sullyan shivered as his gaze tore through her once more. Then, summoning Sonten, he viciously neck-reined his stallion and spurred it back to his tent.

Chapter Thirty-Two

Safely back inside the Palace courtyard, Sullyan dismounted and clung to her stirrup until her legs felt they might hold her again. The trembling reaction that had set in once the confrontation with Rykan was over hadn't abated, and she felt dizzy and weak. She saw Robin fling Torka's reins at a passing groom and hurry over to help her. Gently, his arm slipped about her waist.

"Are you alright?"

She shook her head, trying to stay upright as Anjer and Pharikian approached.

"That was very well done, Brynne," said the Hierarch, taking her hand and studying her face. "The shielding obviously worked." At Robin's unspoken protest he said, "No, Captain, she's only exhausted. Where are those huge twins?" He looked about for either Almid or Kester and beckoned one of them over. He could never tell them apart, but it was Almid who swept her off her feet and carried her toward the Palace doors. She vaguely heard the Hierarch telling Robin to let her rest, saying they would meet again that evening to talk over the preparations for the next day.

Almid carried her swiftly back to the suite and laid her on the bed. She was already nearly asleep, so the bearded giant helped her remove her cloak, jacket and boots. Then he covered her with the goose down comforter and retreated. She slept, not knowing whether he stayed or left.

*****

Rienne was sitting with her head tucked into Cal's shoulder, his left arm tight around her waist. A fit of hysterical sobbing had left her exhausted. Cal, frightened by the intensity of her crying, used his right hand to soothingly stroke her hair. Bull and Taran, both concerned, sat by their fire, huddled in their cloaks against the winter chill. Bull's face was somber and Taran stared into the flames, wishing there was something he could do. The nearer the time came to the meeting between Sullyan and Rykan, the more helpless they all felt.

Rienne sighed and eased away from Cal's embrace. She glanced across at Bull.

"So, this time tomorrow it'll all be settled, one way or the other. What realistic chance does she have, Bull?"

Taran winced. Rienne's tone was matter of fact, her exhaustion mysteriously gone. The big man beside him narrowed his eyes, clearly reluctant to answer.

"Of defeating Rykan by the sword?"

Rienne nodded.

"Normally I'd say pretty fair, unless he's extraordinarily good. And even then she'd stand a reasonable chance." He paused. "It all depends on what physical strength she's got left. These are not normal circumstances. I'm not sure I like the sound of this sharing of life force."

An hour earlier, Bull had communed with Robin. The Captain had told them everything that had happened that morning, as well as the previous evening. Taran listened in as usual, but as he couldn't understand much of what Robin said, it was left to Bull to explain. The Hierarch's offer to share life force had at first cheered Rienne, who thought it meant that Sullyan couldn't possibly fail. But then Bull revealed the full implications, and Rienne's hope died, sparking her fit of crying.

Taran was still confused. "But don't the rules of formal

combat forbid the use of metaphysical force? As I understand it, if they agree on swords, then it's swords and nothing else."

"You're right," said Bull, "she wouldn't be able to use metaforce once the bout commenced. I think the Hierarch intends for her to draw physical strength from what they give her, rather than metaphysical. There'll be no link with any of them once the duel starts."

"That's going to be very hard on Robin," murmured Rienne.

Bull nodded. "It won't be easy on any of us."

He fell silent, his right hand slowly massaging his left arm. There was an unfamiliar breathlessness about his voice as he spoke, and Taran thought his face, usually so florid, looked a little grey. He considered mentioning it to Rienne, but changed his mind. Maybe it was a trick of the watery sun. Rienne had enough to think about right now. Poking the fire with a stick, Taran kept his concerns to himself.

✣ ✣ ✣ ✣ ✣

Robin left Sullyan to sleep for as long as she could. The noon meal came and passed, and still she didn't stir. Unable to rest, the Captain went to sit with Marik. The Count was looking much better for being allowed out of bed, even if it was only to a chair by the window. His arm and shoulder were still strapped and he was under strict orders not to move his legs or twist his spine if he could possibly help it. Idrimar was usually on hand to ensure he obeyed the physicians' commands, but Marik had no desire to undo all their hard work.

He had received an unexpected visit from the Hierarch shortly after midday. Robin was incredulous when he heard the news. "He's making you a what?"

"I know, I know," said Marik, a huge grin on his face. "I can't believe it myself. He's only doing it for Idri, of course, but never in my wildest dreams did I think I'd ever be a Duke."

Robin eyed him slyly. "You do realize, don't you, that once you marry her, you'll be second in line to the throne?"

"Oh, gods!" Marik's face paled and his grey eyes darkened in shock. "I never even thought of that."

Robin let the idea sink in before asking, "Have you ever met Pharikian's Heir?"

"No! Bloody hell, Robin, what if he doesn't like me?"

"It's his sister you'll be marrying, Ty, not him."

Marik grimaced. "Well, if he's anything like her, we'll get on just fine. And she's a year older, so even if he is the Heir, she should be able to keep him in line."

Robin snorted. "It's what she'll do to keep *you* in line that you ought to worry about!"

Marik smiled maliciously. "Is that the voice of experience? Yes, I'll bet Brynne Sullyan keeps you on your toes."

Robin grinned, then sobered. He simply couldn't forget his fear of tomorrow's duel. He felt he was being disloyal if he allowed his doubts to surface, but the fact was Sullyan wasn't anything like as fit as she should be, whereas Rykan was hale, hearty, and twice as strong. A nightmare image of the darkly handsome lord abusing the tortured Sullyan kept surfacing behind his eyes.

Marik, who had witnessed it for real, understood what the younger man was feeling.

"Have faith in her, Robin," he urged, putting his good hand on Robin's arm. "Just as she had in you when she was waiting in that filthy cell. She never doubted you for a moment, you know, and you must do the same for her."

The young man raised pain-filled eyes and drew a deep breath. He poured fellan for them both and they sat in companionable silence, looking out over the inner courtyard while awaiting Idrimar's return.

✤ ✤ ✤ ✤ ✤

Sullyan woke around mid-afternoon and lay cocooned in warmth and comfort, fervently wishing she could stay there forever. Her brain kept replaying the morning's meeting with Rykan, over and over again, and she couldn't turn away from it. The effort of keeping her composure while forcing down the panic and revulsion she felt on facing him again had exacted a heavy price from her depleted strength.

Only a few more hours, she told herself. Only a few more, and then you can rest. Maybe forever.

Strangely, she was finding the thought of dying less terrifying than before. Her anguished struggles of the past few weeks now seemed as futile as trying to stop the sunrise. She suddenly realized she could actually welcome the thought of oblivion.

It wasn't the first time. She had felt this once before, after Rykan's final malicious rape. She had lain alone in the uncaring darkness, naked, broken, and strangely devoid of emotion. His triumphant revelation, grunting out his plans at the climax of his brutal passion, was the catalyst that finally pushed her over the edge. She had decided then that oblivion was preferable to this desperate struggle for survival. Now, knowing what she faced, it was once again an oddly soothing thought, and she let it flow through her mind.

Suddenly, unbidden, an image thrust this thought aside. It was an image of her mother, lying in this very room, fighting to give life to her child. Sharply drawn, it hung with startling clarity before her mind's eye. Her mother's face was ashen and etched with lines of pain, but her eyes held her daughter's firmly. Sullyan's lethargy began to recede and the thought that Rykan had already defeated her made her furiously angry. Who was he to hold such power over her? The image of her mother wavered and vanished as her skin grew hot with rage, and she stoked the fire of her anger with memories of Rykan's evil. Whatever the outcome of their duel, she would somehow exact retribution.

The decision galvanized her. Rising, she dressed in her normal combat leathers. She had to cinch her sword belt much tighter than usual, and this also fuelled her fury. She had always been proud of her trim figure, honed and smoothed by years of physical activity. Now she was aware of prominent hip bones and angular shoulder blades and knew what Robin thought when he looked at her thin body. The deep and powerful love they had allowed themselves to embrace was far too precious for a man like Rykan to destroy, and the knowledge that his evil had already touched her love heightened her ire still further.

Striding purposefully from the suite, trailed by the faithful Almid, she went in search of distraction.

Around the barracks, the Velletian Guard went about their duties. The forces still beyond the curtain walls were occupied in burning their dead, raising huge pyres for the corpses. The Plains before the Citadel would be scarred for months—maybe years—to come.

Unremarked by the swordsmen, Sullyan stopped and leaned her back against the barracks wall. Resting her hands on her sword belt, she let the familiarity of their bustle wash over her like a balm. The mere normality of the scene reminded her of the Manor. It calmed her and strengthened her resolve. She stared at the ground, half-listening to the swordsmen's chatter, lost in thought.

After a few moments, a sound made her look up. Commander Vanyr emerged from the barracks door and his white gaze swept over his men, checking they were not idle. Then he turned and his body stiffened as he saw her. Eyes narrowing, he seemed to struggle briefly with himself. Glancing round as if to check who was about, he made up his mind. With an eye to Almid, who stood some way off, he casually walked over to Sullyan. When he reached her, he turned round and leaned his own back against the wall beside her, careful not to come too close.

She didn't speak. Uncertain of his intentions, she gazed at the ground and waited him out. The silence dragged on for a while before he broke it.

"Major."

She raised her head but didn't look at him. "Commander."

There was another awkward silence, during which his eyes never left his men. Then he awkwardly asked, "Are you recovered now?"

Amazed that he should care, she answered as best she could. "I am well enough, I thank you."

Clearly he had something on his mind, but she couldn't begin to imagine what it was. This verbal maneuvering was a clumsy way of getting to the point and betrayed the history between them.

Vanyr stared at his hands. They were strong, long-fingered, browned from weathering, and marked all over with tiny, white scars, as were hers. He raised his eyes to his men again.

"So you'll meet Rykan tomorrow."

She stiffened. "It would seem so."

"Are you well prepared?"

She was tiring of the game and turned to look him full in the face. "Just what is your point, Commander?"

His lips thinned, but he took a breath before answering. "I have fought Rykan before. I'm the only one here who has."

Thinking he had finally revealed his thought, she said, "Ah! And you feel it should be you who confronts him tomorrow."

"Hell, no!"

His alarmed reaction caught her off balance. She frowned. "Then what is the point of this? I wish you would speak plainly, Commander. I have enough to occupy my thoughts without playing guessing games with you."

He stiffened, clearly offended, and she suddenly realized that incredible as it might seem—and clumsy as it was—he was actually trying to offer her something. She sighed and touched him lightly on the arm before he could stride away.

"Your pardon, Commander. I meant no offence. I was preoccupied and forgot my manners. Please, what did you wish to say?"

Her soft tone and frank apology mollified him. She imagined he was finding this interview difficult enough and probably had Anjer's vicious tongue-lashing uppermost in his mind. Her curt manner hadn't helped.

Tersely, he said, "Rykan is a superb swordsman, but he is not without flaws. I know his style and a few of his tricks. If it would help you, I could tell you of them."

Sullyan remained silent and Vanyr shot her a glance, worried she thought he was insulting her skills. Her amazement at his generous offer had softened her eyes, and her lips held a smile of unmistakable friendliness. Unable to help himself, he smiled briefly back.

"That would be helpful indeed, Commander, and deserving enough of my thanks," she said. "But I would appreciate it even more if you showed me."

Wariness came into his eyes. He was doubtless remembering their last fencing session. Sullyan, however, had already pushed away from the wall and was waiting for him to accompany her to the training ground. Unable to retract the offer, he nodded.

Watched carefully by Almid, the two sparred for half an hour or more, Vanyr remembering more and more of Rykan's favorite moves as they worked. Sullyan found him an excellent teacher, and in turn she impressed him by the speed with which she learned. Having fenced with her before and experienced her skill, he was expecting to find her arrogant and unwilling to take criticism. He was surprised when she had him show her each move many times over, and then asked him to assess her execution of them before she was satisfied with her competence.

They were working on the final, very complex, charging maneuver which enabled a skilled fighter to disarm and down an opponent of equal or greater skill when Robin came looking for her. The time had passed so swiftly she hadn't noticed the fading light. She could sense Robin's concern at finding her fencing yet again with the untrustworthy Commander, but before he could protest, she sent him an abrupt command for silence. Obediently, he stood beside Almid, watching.

Using Vanyr's momentary distraction at Robin's arrival, Sullyan put her learning into practice. She used Rykan's charging move against Vanyr, and it worked perfectly. The surprised Commander found himself lying in the dust at her feet, minus his sword, and with her foot resting lightly on his empty hand.

As she retrieved his sword, she asked, "Was that correct, Commander?"

He rubbed his wrist where the concussion of her blow had numbed it and looked up without rancor. "You know damned well it was."

She grinned and held out a hand to help him regain his feet. "I am deeply in your debt, Commander Vanyr. I cannot thank you enough. Your teaching could prove invaluable tomorrow."

Clearly embarrassed, he brushed her thanks and her hand aside, got to his feet, and stalked off. Robin watched him leave, a speculative look in his eyes.

"What was all that about?"

Raising her head, she stared after Vanyr, who was swearing loudly at one of his men.

"A peace offering, I think, Robin."

She turned to smile at the handsome young man. She could

see him studying her and was aware of the healthy flush to her skin, which was lightly sheened with sweat. Her whole body tingled with welcome vitality and she knew Robin could sense it. Something fundamental within her had changed, yet he was unwilling to be grateful to Vanyr. Hesitantly, he smiled back.

They made their way to their suite to change for dinner. The Hierarch had asked them to dine with him that night and Sullyan had been dreading it. Before, she had felt it was too much like feasting the doomed, but now, in the light of her more determined mood, she found she could approach it with pleasure. It was, after all, a gathering of friends, all of whom shared a common aim.

She and Robin, wearing more comfortable clothing, went to join the party. Everyone seemed determined to enjoy themselves, and for Ephan, Anjer, and Kryp, it was a chance to relax after their labors in the field. Their forces on the Plains were being relieved in rotation, and most were either on funeral detail or guard duty against the depleted ranks of Rykan's army. Despite the uncertainty over tomorrow's duel, a pleasant atmosphere prevailed.

All three generals had brought their ladies, and even Falina seemed disposed to be civil. Her husband had clearly told her that Sullyan had probably saved his life, so she was more gracious than before. Hollett was amiable, Torien as friendly as ever, and Idrimar was merry and laughed frequently.

The meal passed pleasantly, and even Pharikian could not complain about the amount Sullyan ate. Her new lighter mood had affected her appetite, and the tasty offerings of game, fish, and fowl were too delicious to resist. She even accepted a little red wine, much to Robin's amazement, and he whispered a warning in her ear. Laughing at his caution, she allowed him to taste her glass. It was almost half water.

"I do not intend to let anyone down tomorrow, my love," she murmured, "least of all myself." Then she drew him onto the dance floor with the others.

Later in the evening, Sullyan slipped away from Robin and spoke quietly to Almid. The bearded giant nodded once and left the room. He was back shortly with a small packet which he gave to Sullyan. She then accosted one of the Hierarch's pages—the one who reminded her of young Tad—and he grinned and scampered off. He too returned swiftly, bearing a covered object which Robin, who was puzzled by all these errands, now recognized as the harp that had belonged to Sullyan's mother.

After placing it on a table, the page went to speak to the musicians. Once they finished their set they laid their instruments down, the unscheduled silence making Pharikian look round in surprise. Sullyan, who had taken the exquisite harp into her lap, caught his eye. She had a few sheets of parchment spread out before her, and after testing the strings, softly began to play.

The melody was simple yet evocative and it brought tears to Pharikian's eyes. The room fell silent as all the guests found chairs in which to listen to the softly rippling music. Sullyan forgot them all, losing herself in the melodies her father had written. She played three pieces through, and then stilled the strings. There was no applause. They were all too deeply affected by the long-silent music.

His eyes shining, Pharikian rose and crossed to where Sullyan sat. Leaning down, he kissed the crown of her head. "Thank you, my dear," was all he could say. She laid the harp aside and stood, then motioned for the minstrels to strike up again. Thankfully, they played a completely different set of tunes, so as not to break the mood she had created.

The party broke up shortly afterward. The next day would be momentous for all, and no one wanted to keep Sullyan from her rest. As she and Robin made to leave, Pharikian and Deshan approached her.

"Will you be able to sleep, child?" asked the Master Physician gently.

She smiled, letting him see deep into her eyes. "Yes, Deshan, I believe I will. And if I cannot, well, I have Robin beside me. If anyone can help me, he can."

Pharikian looked sidelong at Robin, at the younger man's arm draped about her shoulders. "Yes," he mused, "I expect he can."

Robin flushed. Amused, Sullyan said, "He has many uses, Timar."

The two older men smiled. "We will send for you just before the appointed hour, Brynne," said Pharikian. He kissed her hand in farewell and clapped Robin gently on the shoulder. "Make sure you both take time to rest," he added as they left the room.

They obeyed, but not before reaffirming the depths of their love.

✣ ✣ ✣ ✣ ✣

It was nearly pitch dark inside the room, the soft glow of the banked fire barely visible. Robin woke abruptly from a deep sleep and lay quiet, trying to identify what had roused him. Gradually, and with a growing sense of unease, he realized that his was the only breathing he could hear. Sullyan was always a quiet and unmoving sleeper, but the regular rhythm of her slumbering breath was usually just audible. Turning carefully over in the huge bed, he put out a hand and touched nothing but cooling bedclothes. Alarmed, he sat up, every sense searching the lightless room. On discovering he was completely alone, he cursed and swung out of bed. With their military training, it was never easy for either of them to leave without waking the other, but they could use metaforce to cover their movements. She must have done just that, he thought. Annoyed, he cast farther out for her pattern.

He touched it but couldn't sense where she was. Her shield was down tight, a sure sign she didn't want to be disturbed.

Normally he would have respected that wish, but tonight was different. He couldn't leave her alone tonight. Dressing hurriedly, he grabbed both cloaks from the rail. She hadn't taken hers, and he was pretty sure where she was she would freeze without her cloak.

As he left the suite he saw that Ky-shan was standing guard alone. Softly he asked the pirate where Sullyan and Jay'el had gone, but the stocky man only shrugged and smiled. Irritated, Robin made his way through the sleeping Palace to the Tower and quickly climbed the steps. He knew his guess was correct when he saw the huddled form of Jay'el just inside the Tower doors. Nodding to the young man, who was shivering within his cloak, Robin cracked the door and slipped outside.

Despite the bitter cold it was a breathtakingly beautiful night. The air was still. There were no clouds, and a quarter-moon swung low on the horizon. Stars glittered in the sky's dark vault, and it was completely silent. Up here, the stench of the battlefield was undetectable. Watch fires flashed and glowed like firebugs on the Plains. The Hierarch's standard hung limp from its pole, and there was no sign of Sullyan.

Robin made his way over to the wall and began his search at the section overlooking Rykan's camp. She wasn't there. He couldn't see very far along the walls as there were buttresses at regular intervals jutting out onto the roof. She could be sheltering behind any one of them. He made his way around the roof until he saw a darker shape leaning against the south-facing battlements. Her arms tightly hugged her chest and her face was turned up to the sky. In the faint glimmer of starlight, Robin could see the tracks of tears on her cheeks. Momentarily unsure, he stopped, unwilling to intrude. Soon the sound of soft sobs compelled him to her side.

He wasn't shielding, so she knew he was there. Mutely, she turned to the comfort of his arms and he wrapped them about her, lapping her in the folds of her warm cloak. She rested her head against his shoulder and he felt the tremor of her body. They stood in silence until she calmed. Then, raising her head, she wiped at her eyes with a fold of cloak. He looked down at her and the only thing he could think of to say was, "What is it, love?"

"Oh, Robin." Her voice was rough, broken. "I could die tomorrow. I thought I was used to the idea after Rykan's ... abuse, but suddenly I find that I want to live so very much."

He couldn't stifle a sob of his own and tightened his arms about her thin body. Burying his face in her fragrant hair, he murmured fiercely, "You're not going die! You're stronger than that. There isn't anyone who can stand against you in a straight fight, not even Rykan. I don't care how good he is. I believe you're going to beat him, and so does Pharikian. And Anjer. And Kryp and Ephan. Even Vanyr does. I saw the look he gave you when you floored him this afternoon."

She drew away from him and gazed into his face. The faint starlight had turned her golden eyes black. She wore a grateful smile. Kissing him on the lips, she said, "You are my strength, Robin Tamsen, do you know that?"

"And you're my life, Sullyan. I can't imagine living without you. That's how I know you're going to survive this. You'll defeat Rykan. I don't know how you're going to beat the poison. I just know that you will. There will be a way. There has to be!"

His certainty, his absolute faith in her and in Fate, was so sure, so unshakeable, that he felt her begin to believe it. Her earlier mood of optimism suddenly returned in full. He felt her gratitude for his love and support and saw her loving smile. He held her close, fearing his heart would break. The thought of what they had gone through, what she had done for him, and what they had experienced during the two short years they had been together, brought tears to his eyes, but they were tears of love and happiness, not sorrow.

She lifted her head and now there was a faintly challenging look on her face.

"At least you managed to keep Bull and the others far enough away. I am glad they are safe."

Shock jolted through him. "Far enough away?"

The challenging look turned into a mischievous grin. "Oh, come now, Robin, you never thought I would not know they were here? My love, Bulldog and I have been together nearly fourteen years. I know his psyche as well as my own. Did you truly think I would not sense him? Bull could not hide from me even if he flew to the moon."

He was dismayed, and she laughed. "You should know better than to keep secrets from me, love. Where are they, up on that little hill to the south?"

He nodded, and she gave his hand a squeeze.

"I spoke to Bull," she said, "just before you came up to find me. I fear I gave him rather a hard time, but he deserved it for trying to deceive me." She shook her head. "Ah, my love, you are both forgiven. I know you only had my welfare at heart. If this goes as I hope, then we will all meet up again later. I would dearly love to see them again. But when we do"—her voice was stern despite the smile—"you are not to tell Bulldog he is forgiven until I have given him another piece of my mind. He disobeyed my direct orders, after all."

He felt her demeanor change and she gripped his arms, her large eyes holding his gaze.

"Robin, I want you to trust me tomorrow. Whatever happens, whatever is said or done, promise you will trust me."

He went still. "You know I will. But why do you say that? Is there something you're not telling me? What are you planning?"

She shook her head, starlight shimmering in her unbound hair.

"Maybe … it may be nothing. There is something at the back of my mind, Robin, nagging at me, something I need to remember, something I need to do. I came out here hoping it would surface, but it has not. Ah well, if I am meant to recall it, I will. Let us go in, my love. I am cold, and poor Jay'el must be frozen by now. There will be time enough tomorrow to think. Probably too much time."

✣ ✣ ✣ ✣ ✣

Over to the south, on the little wooded knoll, two men sat at watch. They lit no fire at night and so were wrapped in every piece of clothing they possessed. Only their faces were bare to the cold, and even these were partially hidden within lowered hoods. Nevertheless, Taran could see the tears glittering in Bull's eyes, eyes that never left the Citadel, faintly outlined against the starry sky. He could also sense the grief that constricted Bull's great chest, and see the way the big man constantly rubbed his left arm. Unwilling though he was to intrude on Bull's thoughts, Taran felt compelled to speak.

"It won't be long now, Bull. We just have to have faith in her. At least we're not sitting around the Manor, not knowing what's going on."

Bull started and looked round, as if he had forgotten Taran was there. Then he gave a sigh.

"Yes, I suppose you're right. But it's not just that." He looked down at his hands. "She knows we're here, Taran. She's known all along, damn her."

Taran frowned. "How? How could she have known?"

Bull gave a rueful grin. "It's my fault. I should have guessed she would sense me. She's been waiting for Robin to tell her. He'll get it in the neck now, like I just did."

Taran gaped. "You've spoken to her? What did she say?"

"I won't repeat her exact words, but she was furious. She

chewed me out at great length for putting myself, and all of you, in danger. Told me exactly what she thought of me for disobeying orders."

Taran's heart fell. "Did we really distress her that much? Rienne will be upset—she never wanted that."

Bull shook his head. "Don't worry. Once she had thoroughly worked me over and got the anger out of her system, she told me how much she loved me, and how pleased she was that we're here. That's always been her way. First the explosion, then the swearing, then the forgiveness."

He sighed sadly. "We should have gone to the Citadel straight away. We would still have had the dressing-down and the foul language, but it would have been done with soon enough. Now we're stuck here until it's over. She ordered me to tell you all this, though. If by some evil stroke of luck Rykan wins, we're under the strictest orders to get the hell out as soon as possible. And I had to promise on my oath to obey this time."

"But what about Robin?" asked Taran.

"Robin will have to take care of himself. There won't be anything we can do if he gets caught in the middle. We'd only get ourselves killed, and I don't intend to let that happen."

Chapter Thirty-Three

It was a rare and perfect dawn, the sun lifting effortlessly into a peach-colored sky. There was no wind and the air was mild. Sullyan, lying in Robin's arms, woke to a soft chorus of birds outside the window, celebrating this early promise of spring.

She freed herself from Robin's embrace and wrapped a robe about her body. Going to the window, she looked out over the inner courtyard, staring at the dawn. Why did it have to be so lovely? There was a very good chance that she would never see another dawn like this. Then movement behind her and strong arms coming around her stopped that train of thought, and she let Robin's love distract her from her gloom. Hand in hand, they went into the bathing room to prepare themselves for the day. This day would decide Andaryon's future and Albia's future too.

They had bathed, dressed, and were eating a light breakfast by the time the Hierarch's page appeared. Pharikian came behind him, smiling at their invitation to enter. A second page followed him, carrying a long, velvet-covered box which he placed on the table. He lifted the lid and Sullyan's eyes widened when she saw what it contained.

Pharikian cleared his throat. "I wasn't sure whether to do this or not, child. It was Ty Marik who convinced me I should give you the choice."

Sullyan rose and walked slowly to the box. She stood looking down at the fine blade nestled within, beautifully polished, honed to perfection, slim and strong. She put out her left hand and gently stroked the hilt. The blade was plain and unadorned, but the wrist guard was engraved with swirls, loops, and spirals. With a sudden shock, she realized what she was looking at. Her vision blurred as she turned to the Hierarch.

"Was this my father's blade?"

"Yes, child. It was my gift to him."

Wonderingly, her fingers lingered over the wrist guard. Part of the design she recognized. It was as much a part of her as her own skin. The rest was less familiar, but the whole made up a representation of the psyche belonging to the man for whom the sword was made.

"I have never seen this done before. Robin, look."

He came to stand beside her and gasped in admiration at the sword's beauty and workmanship. Yet he didn't realize the significance of the etched design.

"Look at the pattern on the hilt. It is a representation of my father's psyche."

It took a moment to sink in. Then Robin looked up in amazement. "How is that possible?"

Andaryon's ruler smiled. "The swordsmith was a man of rare talent who could see my projection of Morgan's pattern. He fixed it in his mind and engraved it onto the sword." He gazed at Sullyan, who was feeling strangely reluctant to take the weapon into her hand. "I thought you might like to use it today, child, and so I give it to you now, in case you need to learn its weight and balance. But I think you will find it comes easily to your hand. Morgan was neither tall nor heavy, so it was made light and strong. Try it, Brynne."

At his urging, Sullyan took the hilt reverently into her left hand and raised the shining blade from its box. "It balances better than my own weapon!"

The look on her face made Pharikian smile. "I thought it might. It will be good to see it used again, and I can't think of a better time for it to leave its box."

"Has it seen combat, Timar?" Her voice was soft. She was still admiring the beautiful length of steel.

"Many times, child. It didn't let Morgan down then, and it won't let you down now. Go and practice if you need to. You still have a couple of hours before we'll call you."

He turned to leave the room.

"Majesty?"

The formal address made him frown. "Yes, child?"

She lowered her eyes, suddenly diffident. "When we gather for the exchange of life force, may I ask you to ensure that everyone present is perfectly willing?" She raised her gaze to meet his. "This is not something that should be done lightly. I do not wish to meet Rykan knowing I carry unwillingly donated life force."

He inclined his head. "I understand, Brynne. You need have no worries on that score. We have all agreed and deem it an honor to help you in this way. There will be no forced participants, I assure you."

Her murmured thanks followed him as he left the room.

Sullyan spent some time out on the training ground with Robin, testing her father's sword. The balance and weight of it were so perfect for her that it felt like an extension of her arm. In that respect, practice was unnecessary. It was the weapon's emotional implications she had to come to terms with. The thought that her father's hand had gripped the hilt where hers did, that his muscles had flexed and contracted as hers did, that his body had moved and responded as hers did, was constantly on her mind. Nevertheless, she moved about the arena with her accustomed lethal grace. If Rienne, who had once doubted Sullyan's capacity to kill, had been watching her at that moment, she would have had no doubt whatsoever that her friend was an efficient and implacable killer.

Whatever else it did, the sword reaffirmed Sullyan's faith in her own skills. Robin, facing her attacks and trusting her not to follow through on the killing thrusts, smiled grimly as he recognized the look in her eyes. Pharikian had gambled well on her reaction to her father's sword.

Sullyan ended the session long before either of them tired, and they sat companionably in the sunlight. Joined by Ky-shan and his entire band, they engaged in weapons talk. Nothing too specific, just a commander and her unit discussing the finer points of sword play. It was just what she needed, and when the servant came to summon her for the ceremony of sharing life force, they were all amazed at how much time had passed. Sullyan found it incredible that she had actually forgotten for those few precious hours what was to happen that day. Gratefully, she smiled at her band.

"Gentlemen, I thank you for your time and your most agreeable company."

She rose and was about to follow the servant when Ky-shan also stood, followed by Jay'el, Ki-en, Almid, and Kester. They waited expectantly as she stared, bemused.

Ky-shan bowed formally. "Lady, we want to offer our life force also, to help you beat Rykan. I know we are untrained, but we are strong. We can do nothing else to help you now, and by this offer we hope to thank you for what you did for us, for getting his Majesty to accept us and for risking your life for ours. This is our wish, and we are all in agreement. Please, Lady, don't refuse us."

She had been going to do just that, but the look in their eyes stopped her. Shaking her head at them, she smiled. "Very well, gentlemen, you have outmaneuvered me. If the Hierarch agrees to your inclusion, I will not refuse you. And I thank you all."

Xeer led the rest of the men in a chorus of cheers that made her flush. The sound of it followed her as she left the arena.

✣ ✣ ✣ ✣ ✣

They had to change out of their sweaty clothes before meeting the Hierarch, and so split up to go to their respective quarters. Robin hung back for a final word with Ky-shan while Sullyan went on ahead, so he was alone in the corridor when he heard raised and angry voices.

He recognized Anjer's gruff tones immediately and frowned when he also heard Vanyr's voice. He couldn't quite make out the words, but through an open door he saw a long corridor which ended in a far room. There, the huge Lord General and the lithe Commander were facing each other, both clearly furious. Anjer was gesticulating and they were obviously in the middle of a heated dispute. Not wanting to be caught eavesdropping, Robin hurried on. He had the distinct impression that Vanyr was receiving another tongue-lashing, and from the tone of Anjer's fury, he didn't envy the man.

✣ ✣ ✣ ✣ ✣

A short time later, they gathered in the formal audience chamber. Sullyan and Robin hadn't been there since their first meeting with the Hierarch all those weeks ago. Pharikian, Anjer, Kryp, Ephan, Ky-shan, Jay'el, Ki-en, and the twin giants were all in attendance. Although the twins had no control over their metaforce, Sullyan's link with them meant she had access to their life force provided they were willing. They hadn't wanted to be left out.

Sullyan noticed the absence of the Journeyman-ranked Vanyr and pursed her lips. She was disappointed that the man hadn't felt able to participate, particularly since she had assumed they were now on easier terms. Still, he had made her a gift of his teaching, and it would prove invaluable. She suddenly wondered if that was why he had offered it, knowing he wouldn't be here today. She let it go, having no strength to waste on speculation.

The Hierarch brought them all to order and Sullyan tried to compose herself. The assimilation of life force couldn't be undertaken lightly. There were lives at stake, and she had never actually done this before. She hoped she was hiding her trepidation from the others better than she was from herself.

Pharikian gestured her toward a chair in the center of the room. Settling comfortably, she closed her eyes. She didn't need to see who was making the offer, and watching their reactions as she accepted would be a distraction she could do without. Silence filled the room.

She heard Pharikian stir and expected him to be first, but it was Robin who approached and kneeled before her. He took up her hands and they effortlessly established their familiar link. She felt no hesitation in Robin as he opened himself unreservedly to her. Very gently, so gently that had he not known her so intimately he wouldn't have been aware of her touch, Sullyan reached out and took what he offered. He felt no different, she knew. He already considered his life to be hers. Briefly, she opened her depthless eyes and smiled. Robin squeezed her hand and stood up.

Pharikian came forward then, and his experience was as gentle as Robin's. She sensed his amazement at the lightness of her touch. Assimilating his life force, however, was not as easy for Sullyan. The Hierarch was a Senior Master, a full level above her own skills, and his well of power was so vast that it took her breath away. She struggled to contain what he gave her and he stayed close, watching her carefully until she was stable. Then he broke their link.

Her face felt white with strain and she wondered whether she had done the right thing. But then her eyes cleared. Pharikian was still watching her closely and she smiled, allowing him to see how she had managed his vast store of power. Compartments had been created within her mind, her own and Robin's power on one side, Pharikian's on the other. They were linked by the bond of her Andaryan blood, blood which originated with him. He nodded in admiration, and withdrew to one side.

Anjer, a Master Artesan, was next, and now that Sullyan knew how to treat the Andaryan's power, it was easier on her. After him came Ephan, and then Kryp. Despite the Hierarch's earlier assurance, she insinuated a question into each of their minds, to satisfy herself that they were completely willing. The only one to experience a moment's hesitation was Kryp. She was about to refuse him when she felt him give himself fully to the task, and so his gift of life force joined the others'.

The pirates experienced less of the process than the rest due to their untrained status. They couldn't have shielded themselves from her consciously, but had they not been willing, a natural barrier would have rendered their minds inaccessible to a whole battalion of Senior Masters.

Once the process was complete, Pharikian indicated that everyone should remain quiet and still so that Sullyan could come to terms with what she had done. She had surprised herself in her ability to take them all. She knew she would have no trouble with Robin, and hadn't been too surprised at her capacity to accept Pharikian, despite the scope of his powers. She had, however, expected to reach her limit after accepting Anjer. The fact that she had then been able to assimilate three more Adepts-elite plus four untrained minds was something she needed to think about.

Finally, she came to terms, and only the fire opal pulsing in the hollow of her throat betrayed the rapid beat of her heart. Pharikian approached her and she sensed his dismay at the tears standing in her eyes.

"What is it, Brynne? Is the pressure too great?"

She shook her head, unable to speak. When her voice returned, it was husky with emotion. "Such selfless generosity, Timar. How can I possibly stand it?"

Smiling gently, he took her hand and raised her. "Think of it as a gift between friends, child. A gift freely given, to show how we love you."

His words hit her like a punch to the stomach and she gasped. She stared at him, wide-eyed and open-mouthed, and he stared back, clearly alarmed. Rooted to the spot, she struggled to breathe. They were all staring at her, confused, and Pharikian took her by the shoulders. Through the urgency of his touch she could feel his concern, his fear that she was suffering another attack like the one that had hit her on the Tower. In a way, she was.

Blindly, she stared at him. "A gift freely given!"

He frowned, uncomprehending. Robin stepped forward, also frightened by her demeanor, and she knew she wasn't making any sense. She shook her head to clear her thoughts and clutched at the Hierarch's arm. "Majesty, I must speak with you!"

Bemused, he let her lead him out of the audience chamber and she closed the door firmly behind them.

✣ ✣ ✣ ✣ ✣

Robin stood alone, completely at a loss. He had no idea what had just happened, and his feelings were in turmoil. The Major had clearly remembered something important, but whether it was good or bad he didn't know. All he could do was wait and trust she would tell him in time.

After a few moments, the door opened and he heard the Hierarch's voice summoning one of his pages. A young boy went to him and came back in seconds. He sped through the chamber and out into the opposite corridor. Five minutes later, he returned at a dead run, carrying something Robin thought he recognized but couldn't immediately identify. He could see that everyone in the room was watching him as if he knew what was happening, but like them he was totally baffled.

The blare of a horn from outside made everyone jump. Robin's heart thudded painfully. Surely it wasn't time already? But Anjer was rising and moving to the door, ready to inform his monarch if Pharikian hadn't heard the signal. The Hierarch reappeared immediately, Sullyan following. Both wore grim expressions, but Robin thought he detected a gleam of triumph—or at least hope—in Sullyan's golden eyes.

Pharikian was speaking to her as he strode into the chamber.

"... you'd have to be very careful. I don't like it, Brynne, and I can't publicly condone it, but if you think you can do it, then you have my blessing."

She gave him a brief glance. "I thank you, Majesty. That is all I need."

Robin kept his voice low as he fell into step beside her. "What was that all about?"

"Not now," she murmured, and squeezed his arm.

He heard the honor guard approaching down the corridor and his heart thumped sickeningly. Pharikian gave the box containing Sullyan's sword to Anjer, who as her second had the right of arming her. Surrounded by the honor guard, they left the audience chamber, Pharikian leading and Sullyan next, flanked by the massive Anjer, who dwarfed her completely. Robin and the others followed in their turn.

In the courtyard, the horses were ready. This time Drum was present, looking fit and sleek. He stood quietly awaiting his rider, but Robin could see his muscles quivering as he sensed the tension in the air. They mounted up, and once again the entire royal household turned out to watch them leave. This time the acclaim was for Sullyan, and she raised a hand in acknowledgement. Commander Vanyr led the honor guard, and Robin saw Sullyan regarding him closely. Vanyr steadfastly refused to look at her and his eyes were hard. Robin frowned. What was his problem? He let it go. He had more pressing matters to worry over.

On leaving the courtyard and emerging onto the white-paved Processional Way, Robin noticed a small carriage waiting to one side. Drawn by a single pony, it held two people, and he smiled when he saw who they were. Idrimar waved at Sullyan as she passed, and Marik lifted his thumbs in encouragement. She acknowledged their support gratefully, and Robin nodded their way.

Once again, the heralds' fanfare sounded and the Citadel gates swung open as the cavalcade reached them. The guards manning the walls, the sentries, the Velletian Guard, and the forces outside the gates all added their voices to the roar of approval that met ruler, warlords, and the Champion of the Crown. Robin felt a lump come into his throat and suddenly thought of Bull and the others up on their hill. As soon as he did so, the big man's presence flooded his mind, comforting, bolstering, encouraging. Robin thanked him silently and set his gaze firmly ahead as the party rode around the perimeter wall toward the south gate, the same gate that he, Sullyan, and Marik had entered by all those weeks ago.

A contingent of swordsmen had been hard at work creating the combat arena and arranging seating for those permitted to witness the duel. The arena itself was a large, flat, circular area of grass, marked out with gold and purple flags. A pavilion had been set up at the south gate end, draped in gold and purple cloth. Four standards bearing the Hierarch's tangwyr crest marked the corners of the pavilion, and seats were arranged within it.

Opposite this and facing it was a similar pavilion, this one draped in black and silver. As they rode closer, Robin could see the heavy figure of Sonten inside and a few of Rykan's elite guard. Of the tall Duke there was no sign. He heard Sullyan take a deep breath and knew she was drawing on her donated strength to ward her against Rykan's inevitable appearance. She would have to use it sparingly as the effects wouldn't last for long. Robin had no idea how soon they would fade, never having experienced this before. He could only hope it would be enough.

The late winter sun shone down out of a nearly cloudless sky. Following the Hierarch's lead, Robin dismounted by the pavilion and allowed a groom to take his horse. Pharikian drew Sullyan and Anjer aside and Baron Gaslek joined them. Robin watched them talking quietly, going over what was to happen.

Sullyan was dressed in the clothes the Hierarch had ordered for her, and Robin thought she looked calm and composed. It was more than could be said for him. Her eyes were hard when last he looked, and he hadn't dared disturb her by speaking to her. He had no part to play in this and stood at the rear of the group, trying not to feel alone and forlorn.

A movement close by drew his attention as Princess Idrimar brought her carriage up beside him, deftly handling the high-stepping little chestnut that drew it. Marik leaned down to grip Robin's shoulder and the younger man looked up at him gratefully.

"I'm glad you're here, Ty."

Marik's smile was grim. "I can't wait to see Rykan's face when he realizes I'm not dead."

Robin nodded. "Anything that puts him off balance acts in our favor." Silently, he cursed himself for not being able to keep the tremor out of his voice.

Marik looked sympathetic, but he didn't have time to respond. The Hierarch's herald blew three strident notes on his horn. Pharikian moved into the arena, followed by Sullyan and Anjer. Vanyr and the Velletian Guard flanked them. The Hierarch's elegant robes—gold, purple, and white—swirled around him. He halted in the center of the arena and the herald called for Rykan.

Robin craned his neck to see, an uncontrollable tremor beginning deep in his soul.

The rebel Duke was dressed in his usual black and silver trimmed with scarlet. He stalked into the arena, no expression on his handsome face. Sonten attended him as his second, and his elite guard escorted him. He stopped a few paces from the Hierarch, insultingly close, and Robin saw Anjer's face darken. Rykan saw it too and gave a small smile. Sullyan didn't react, but Robin noticed that her face was stony, her eyes fixed upon Rykan's.

Hands on hips, the Duke addressed his rival. "Well, Pharikian, shall we agree on terms?"

The Hierarch was furious at Rykan's dismissal of protocol. "You're here under sufferance, Rykan. Don't overstep your mark."

Rykan refused to be intimidated. "I have accepted your challenge in my right as an equal. Once I win this contest, Majesty," an insulting emphasis accompanied the title, "we shall see who is here under sufferance. Let's get on with it."

Anjer and Sonten stepped forward. As seconds, it was their duty to agree on terms.

"This trial of combat is for the right to Andaryon's throne," rasped Anjer. "The Hierarch, Timar Pharikian, hereby agrees to relinquish all hereditary rights due his House and his Heir should Lord Rykan win the day."

Sonten nodded once. "In his turn, his Grace, Rykan, Duke of Kymer, agrees to be bound by the Hierarch's rule and will submit to his command should the Crown's Champion be victorious."

Anjer paused before continuing. "As challenger, the Crown decrees that the challenge shall be settled by skill at arms. The chosen weapon is the sword."

Both Rykan and Sonten frowned. Given Sullyan's Artesan status, they had clearly expected a metaphysical duel. Rykan's yellow eyes narrowed and he whispered urgently to Sonten, who nodded before turning back to Anjer. "His Grace agrees."

The Lord General inclined his head and was about to step back, but Sonten wasn't done. "We have a condition."

Anjer glanced over his shoulder at the Hierarch. "A condition, Sonten? What gives you the right to demand conditions?"

Sonten looked smug. "It is written in the Codes."

Robin saw Pharikian confer briefly with Gaslek, who was holding a sheaf of parchment. The little secretary shrugged and nodded. "Very well," said Pharikian. "One condition."

"Well?" snapped Anjer. "What is it?"

The General's fat lips quirked. "His Grace, Lord Rykan, doesn't trust the Champion not to use her metaphysical powers once it becomes clear that she cannot defeat my Lord."

His arrogant phrasing brought an audible gasp of outrage from the Hierarch's supporters. Robin stiffened indignantly. Sullyan didn't react, but Robin saw her eyes dilate as she passed someone a message. Pharikian turned and stared at her. Rykan watched her intently, a predatory look in his eye. Robin knew he was trying to unsettle her.

"So what's the condition?" said Anjer.

Sonten smirked. "The condition, my Lords, is that for the duration of the contest, the Hierarch's Champion wears spellsilver."

That provoked a general outcry, the loudest coming from Marik, who leaned out from his carriage to yell, "Rykan, you evil bastard! Have you no courage? You're only doing this because you know you can't win!"

His voice carried easily, and Rykan's face flushed with fury as he suddenly noticed the Count. He turned and cast a venomous look at Sonten, who paled, clearly realizing his knife hadn't done nearly as much damage as he thought.

"Marik, you treacherous coward!" roared Rykan. "There will

be no hole deep enough for you to hide in once I'm the victor here. I'd start running now, if I were you."

"That's an empty threat," retorted Marik. "You've already lost. Give up now."

Rykan was about to make some foul reply when Sullyan's calm, clear voice cut through the uproar.

"Majesty, my Lords, I will accept the Duke's condition providing he grants us the right to propose our own."

This earned her a glance of alarm from Anjer and quiet resignation and a shake of the head from Pharikian. Rykan's attention snapped back and his face resumed its predatory smile. Robin, who once again was left out of Sullyan's plans and feeling useless, reached for Bull's psyche. He badly needed the big man's comfort and knew that he and his companions would be desperate to know what was happening. Contact came immediately and Bull's psyche flooded Robin's mind.

He could tell that Bull had his arms wrapped tightly around Rienne so she could share what he was seeing through Robin's eyes. Although she was no Artesan, the healer's empathic abilities would enable her to sense Bull's thoughts. Taran and Cal, also linked to Bull, were standing close by, Cal's hand resting on Taran's shoulder. Bolstered by their presence, Robin opened his mind fully to his friend and turned his attention back to Sullyan.

Anjer had moved closer to her and was whispering fiercely in her ear, the Hierarch at his side. Sullyan shook her head and replied firmly, but Robin couldn't hear what she said. It didn't please Anjer much, that was clear, but then she added something which mollified him a little. He drew back, glanced across at the overconfident Rykan, and smiled. The dark lord saw it and his yellow eyes tightened. Anjer stalked toward him.

"The Crown proposes a counter condition."

Rykan frowned, but he could hardly refuse if he wanted his

own terms accepted. He feigned indifference. "What is it, then?"

"The Crown proposes that the duel be conducted within the confines of a Firefield. This will be cast by his Majesty, who pledges not to break it until the defeated challenger yields. Whatever takes place within the Firefield is to be deemed valid within the terms of the contest."

Rykan scowled, looking for the catch. Robin was puzzled. He knew that a Firefield meant that no outside interference—whether physical or metaphysical—could reach the combatants while the field was active, but he failed to see what advantage it gave Sullyan. Unless, of course, she feared that one of Rykan's men would shoot her should she gain the upper hand. Rykan would know that Pharikian couldn't break his word. There were far too many witnesses for that. Robin watched him staring at Anjer and Sullyan—whose face was unreadable—before glancing at Pharikian. Andaryon's ruler stood conversing quietly with Gaslek, pointedly ignoring his rival. Rykan held a low, hasty conversation with Sonten, who nodded heavily before stepping forward again.

"His Grace accepts these terms on the understanding that it doesn't affect the personal claims of each combatant."

This puzzled Robin even more, but he was momentarily distracted by Bull's voice in his mind. Then he smiled, for the big man was clearly replying to someone who was as puzzled as he was.

I'm no expert on the intricacies of Andaryan combat codes, so I can only surmise that as Sullyan and Rykan are representing factions rather than acting on a personal basis—although in Rykan's case, of course, it's the same thing—they are entitled to personal claims on the outcome.

Robin could barely hear Cal's indignant voice. *That's a bit unfair on our side, isn't it? Rykan gets two benefits while we only get one!*

His smile widened as he caught Bull's acid reply. *You don't consider putting an end to Rykan benefit enough, my friend?*

Cal was wisely silent.

When Robin finally turned his attention back to the field, Anjer was Witnessing Rykan's agreement of the conditions. The two parties then withdrew to their respective pavilions to ready themselves for combat. Robin drew closer to Sullyan as they walked, concerned that the donated life force wasn't sufficient to protect her from the effects of Rykan's presence. By her clear, hard eyes he could see she was expending no metaphysical power and he realized she was already drawing on their gifts. She gave him a tiny, reassuring smile, but it didn't calm the frantic beat of his heart.

Chapter Thirty-Four

Despite his earlier flash of fear at seeing Marik alive and the knowledge that Rykan would make him suffer for the failure, Sonten felt confident as he turned to follow the Duke back to their pavilion. The two men who were clear candidates for Champion and who might, conceivably, have given Rykan trouble, had obviously stepped aside in order to give the human witch her chance at revenge. He snorted. Revenge! He could hardly believe that the Hierarch's advisors had even proposed this ruse, let alone that Pharikian would actually try it. Did they really think his Grace would fall for such an obvious trick? While it was just possible that the girl possessed some sort of skill with a sword—this abominable thought made Sonten shudder—no one would be fooled into thinking she could be a match for the superbly talented Rykan.

This, he thought, was the reason why the Crown had stipulated combat by arms rather than by metaforce. They obviously thought that the witch's presence, coupled with this ludicrous charade, would unsettle the Duke. They hoped he would be duped into believing he could defeat her easily. At which point, she would employ her Artesan powers and try to overcome him with metaforce.

The General smiled. How stupid did they think Rykan was? They had already made a serious error in allowing the witch to confront Rykan the day before, for it had given him and Sonten time to discuss the strategy and take countermeasures against it.

Rykan had easily negated the threat of her metaphysical prowess by demanding the use of spellsilver. The Crown's counter-condition of a Firefield was another desperate attempt to unsettle the Duke, but neither Rykan nor Sonten could see any real disadvantage in it.

Chuckling under his breath, Sonten threw one last satisfied glance over his shoulder at the retreating Hierarch. Pharikian's time on the throne would soon be at an end.

He was about to turn back when a figure caught his attention. Eyes narrowing in shock, he halted abruptly. His heart hammering, his feverish gaze leaped from the young man accompanying the human witch to scan the other members of the Hierarch's party. As he did so, a phrase, a parting remark, echoed loudly in his mind. It was Commander Heron's voice, reporting his lieutenant's suspicion of lookouts stationed on an ideal spot from which to observe the battlefield. Heron's concern over reinforcements stationed there was unfounded. The Hierarch's extra men had come from elsewhere, and Sonten now guessed that the witch had warned Anjer of Rykan's true strength. Nevertheless, those words held vital importance.

Suddenly, with uncharacteristic insight, the General knew who had left those faint traces on the knoll. His certainty was borne out by his failure to find the face he sought among the Hierarch's party. He was damned sure the cocky Albian who had murdered Jaskin wouldn't have stayed in the Citadel when everyone else was here.

Flushed with urgency, Sonten cast a furtive glance at Rykan's pavilion. The Duke was fully occupied within and Sonten hastened out of his line of sight. "You!" He beckoned to a soldier. "Find Commander Heron immediately. Send him to me."

When the Artesan Commander arrived, Sonten curtly issued explicit orders. Heron didn't like it and glanced swiftly at the preoccupied Rykan. "Get on with it, man!" rasped Sonten. "Do as I say!"

Heron left, vaulting onto his horse and galloping off toward the remnants of Rykan's army.

✣ ✣ ✣ ✣ ✣

Sullyan drew Robin aside so they could speak privately. She could see the anguish in his eyes and feel his terror for her. Taking his hands in hers, she smiled up at him, trying to give him some of her own calm strength.

"Be brave for me, Robin," she murmured. "I am ready for this now. I feel no fear and have no pain. I can do what I came to do, and it is thanks to you that I can. I could not have endured these past weeks if not for you, and I want you to know how much I love you."

He closed his eyes in pain and she took a deep breath. "Remember what I said. You must trust me, Robin. I will do whatever I can to destroy Rykan, and I will preserve my own life if at all possible. But you need to know, my love, I cannot let him win. He may well defeat me by might of arms—that is a separate matter and I cannot guess the outcome—but I cannot allow him to win the day. Do you understand me?"

He gazed down into her golden eyes. "I understand that I must trust you, love, though I can't pretend to know what's in your mind. I especially don't understand why you agreed to the spellsilver. I have to admit that I'm very frightened for you—I've tried not to be but I just can't help it—but you know that you have my total support in whatever you do. Every ounce of my strength and love is yours, you know that too, and I will be here for you whatever happens."

She smiled, feeling the tears that spangled her eyes. "Then do something for me, my love." Holding his gaze, she drew the gold band he had given her from her finger. "Keep this safe for me. I do not want it to be lost should things go awry. Never fear, I will claim it back from you later."

He took it wordlessly, trembling fingers closing about the band.

She turned her head and dropped her voice as Pharikian glanced toward her. "Now hold me tightly, Robin, and wish me good fortune."

He took her in his arms and hugged her tightly. Then he released her, and walked beside her back to the pavilion.

✢ ✢ ✢ ✢ ✢

Soon, far too soon for Robin, the page that the Hierarch had dispatched to the Palace once Sullyan had accepted Rykan's spellsilver condition returned. He was bearing a wrapped package which he gave to his monarch. If the expression on Pharikian's face was anything to go by, thought Robin, he was very much against this condition. Sullyan saw his discomfort and spoke privately with him for quite some time. Eventually, he sighed and turned away. She came back to stand by Robin, watching Pharikian with a calm, if slightly sorrowful, expression.

The Hierarch gestured and the heralds blew three strident blasts. With a final clasp of Robin's hand, Sullyan joined him, and together they walked out of the pavilion. Robin followed, halting by one of the arena's gold and purple flags. A deep bass voice echoed through his mind as Bull prepared his companions for what was to come.

Here we go.

Through the link with Bull's psyche, Robin knew that Rienne had a hard, tight knot in her stomach. She feared she might be sick. Taran and Cal seemed empty and helpless. He knew how they felt. All any of them could do now was watch.

His heart sank further as Rykan and Sonten, the latter bearing Rykan's sword naked across his hands, entered the arena. They marched to the center where they stopped. Rykan stood insolently, hands on his hips. His expression showed unconcern, but his yellow eyes were hot.

Sullyan, accompanied by Anjer, approached him slowly. The massive Lord General bore Morgan Sullyan's polished blade almost reverently in his large hands. The two of them came to a halt opposite the Duke, and Robin twisted his fingers anxiously. He moved closer to Marik's carriage, suddenly feeling in need of support and friendship. In a short while he might very well lose everything that made his life worth living, and he knew he wouldn't be able to bear it.

The Hierarch, escorted by Vanyr, approached the four in the arena. He came between the two combatants and studied their faces carefully. Rykan stared back at him but Sullyan's attention was riveted on her opponent's face.

"My Lord Rykan," said the Hierarch, "do you agree to be bound by the Witnessed terms and conditions of this contest?"

"I do," said Rykan, only adding an insulting 'Majesty' when Pharikian refused to continue until he did so.

"Should you emerge the victor in this bout, what is your claim over your opponent?" The Hierarch's tone was reluctant, already knowing what the rebel lord would say.

"I claim the right to her power," declared Rykan, everyone within earshot hearing his intent.

"Major Sullyan?" The Hierarch turned to her, inviting her to accept or refuse.

Her eyes never left Rykan's as she replied.

"Should my Lord Rykan be the victor today, I will accept his right of claim over my personal power."

With a grim smile, Robin acknowledged her clever phrasing. She had neatly avoided granting Rykan access to the donated life force within her. He saw Rykan's eyes narrow, pondering her words, but as he was unaware of her augmented state, he could find no reason to challenge them. Impatient to start the contest, he nodded curtly.

The Hierarch turned back to Sullyan.

"Major Sullyan, do you agree to be bound by the Witnessed terms and conditions of this contest?"

"I do, Majesty."

Pharikian then asked her the ritual question and Robin expected her to lay claim to the Duke's power should she win.

She didn't.

"Majesty, I claim this man's life, to do with as I will."

A ripple of exclamation ran round the arena and Robin clearly felt Bull's puzzlement through their link. Rykan was frowning. He knew that simply claiming his life wouldn't give her access to his power if he wasn't willing to surrender it. Robin couldn't imagine the circumstances under which Rykan would be willing, and felt his anxiety rise. If only she had confided in him ... but her face was closed, as was her mind, and Rykan had no choice but to agree to the claim.

Stepping closer to Sullyan, the Hierarch flipped the covering from the package he held. With a shudder, Robin saw that it contained a silver collar much like the one she had worn in Rykan's dungeons. Careful to hold it by the cloth, the Hierarch unclasped it in order to lock it about her neck.

Sonten's harsh voice stopped him.

"Majesty, we claim the right to inspect this collar as we would our opponent's weapons."

Robin immediately noticed the sudden paling of Sullyan's face. There was concern in her eyes that she was trying hard to conceal.

Rounding on Sonten, Pharikian said, "Do you insult me, General? Do you doubt that this is spellsilver?" He thrust the collar into Rykan's face. "Would your Lord care to handle it?"

The Duke's insufferable smile never wavered, although he did step back a pace.

"Of course not, Majesty." His voice was silky smooth. "It is a formality only. My second merely asks to observe the protocols."

Grimacing, Pharikian almost threw the collar at Sonten. The General weighed it in his hand for a moment before finally nodding to Rykan. The Duke's smile widened.

"Check the clasp, Sonten. We wouldn't want it mysteriously coming undone halfway through the duel."

The Hierarch narrowed his eyes but didn't speak. Anjer fumed silently at his side. Sullyan appeared relaxed. Finally satisfied, Sonten returned the collar and the Hierarch stepped up to Sullyan once more.

"I am very sorry for this, my dear," he said, and quickly fastened it about her neck.

Her face went white and her breathing faltered as she adjusted to the spellsilver's terrible numbing effects. Rykan watched her closely. Robin could see Sullyan drawing strongly on her donated life force as she slowly regulated her breathing. Her face regained some color, but Robin's hands trembled with tension. He gripped them tightly together.

Both seconds then made a show of examining each sword. Anjer moved in front of Sullyan and placed his hands on her shoulders, looking down into her eyes. She smiled at him and even Robin could see that she was now calm. Only the pallor of her face and the blue tinge to her lips betrayed her discomfort at the spellsilver's touch.

She shed her jacket, giving it to Anjer. Rykan did the same. After a moment, and despite the chill air, the Major also removed her shirt, leaving only the light, sleeveless chemise she wore beneath. Pharikian drew in a breath when he saw the long, red scar that marred her forearm. Under normal circumstances, Robin knew, she would have spent more time on it. Although it was healed, it hadn't faded. The Hierarch cast a grim glance over his shoulder at Vanyr, but the Commander wasn't looking. Robin knew that Anjer had convinced his ruler to say nothing about the incident, especially as Vanyr had already been disciplined. Once the pirates had taken out their rage on the man, Anjer felt there was nothing more to be gained by raking it over again.

Robin's attention switched to Rykan, who was watching Sullyan disrobe. He stood at ease, his sword point grounded before him. There was a leering look on his face and he suddenly leaned forward.

"Why stop there, witch? You have nothing I haven't already seen and used as I wished!"

Sullyan didn't grace him with a reply, didn't react in any way.

Rykan's lips thinned. "Once I have won this travesty of a duel," he snarled, "you know what to expect from me, don't you? I will have what I want, girl. Powers and pleasure both! There will be no friends to rescue you this time."

Slowly, she raised her golden eyes, her expression full of scorn. She spoke clearly and coldly.

"May I suggest you save your energy for your sword arm, my Lord? You may have some skill with that weapon, but before witnesses I declare that you have none whatsoever with the one between your legs."

There was a ripple of derisory laughter and even a few cheers. Rykan went purple with rage. He raised his sword as if to strike her, but Anjer whipped his weapon protectively across Sullyan's body before Rykan could lunge. Breathing heavily, the Duke forced himself to calm.

Sullyan didn't react, and Robin admired her air of control. He knew she was centering herself, drawing her skills and knowledge to the fore, and planning her strategy. In that state, she wouldn't have reacted had a whole swarm of tangwyrs come swooping through the arena.

Once calm was restored, Anjer presented Sullyan with her father's sword. The two seconds then withdrew, leaving only Rykan, Sullyan, and the Hierarch in the arena. Pharikian studied both combatants before speaking.

"You are about to commence combat for the right to Andaryon's throne. You have agreed to the terms of this contest and have been Witnessed by all present. Any deviation from those terms will incur the penalty of disqualification and defeat. In such an event, the victor's claims will be honored. Do you understand?"

They nodded and Pharikian stepped back. "The contest will begin once the Firefield is in place. I wish good fortune on you both."

Despite his words, his gaze was on Sullyan. She didn't notice. Her attention had remained fixed on Rykan since accepting her sword from Anjer. She brought it up before her face, the keen edge giving a shiver of steel song. Rykan locked eyes with her.

Andaryon's ruler moved to the sidelines and Robin felt the Hierarch's hands come to rest on his trembling shoulders. He could clearly sense Pharikian gathering his will and power and knew he was preparing the Firefield. Those with the Artesan gift gasped as the glittering, sparking cage of elemental energy crackled into life.

✣ ✣ ✣ ✣ ✣

Due to the spellsilver's leaching effects, Sullyan couldn't actually see the Firefield. Her skills and her power, however, were so much a part of her life, and her Mastery over Earth established for so long, that she could feel the echo and throb of the field where it emanated through the ground. Her nerves tingled with the proximity of Fire and she felt a stab of relief. At least one gamble had paid off. It would have been a severe handicap—although one she had been willing to risk—if her senses had failed her. Her earlier weeks of intimacy with Rykan's spellsilver had prepared her for what to expect. Still, it was reassuring to have those expectations confirmed. She had experienced a bad moment when Sonten insisted on inspecting the collar, but she had also gambled on Rykan's reluctance to touch it. That too had paid off. Rykan would have realized instantly, but Sonten had no way of knowing that the silver was actually Rykan's. Her hunch in bringing the collar from the drovers' hut had been borne out.

Capturing the Duke's predatory gaze, she concentrated on gathering the strength given her by those who had pawned their life force.

Rykan assumed a defensive posture as soon as the field became active. She never took her eyes from him and saw with satisfaction that he was unsure how to treat her. Vanyr's instruction had been invaluable and she intended to make good use of it, but she also intended to use her own judgment and not take anything for granted. It was some years since Vanyr had fought Rykan. A person's style could change.

They circled each other slowly. Rykan was right-handed so Sullyan was also using her right hand. She hoped that the long, red scar down her left forearm would give the Duke a false message. Watching him intently, she continued to gather donated strength until she felt her skin would burst.

Rykan watched her as a cat watches a rat, knowing its prey has teeth but thinking itself superior in strength and size. She saw his eyes flick to her hand, noting how she gripped her sword, and then to her feet, checking her balance. After a few moments of circling, she knew he was ready. His gaze sharpened and his lips parted in a faintly feral smile.

That slight change in expression was Sullyan's cue. It signaled a momentary distraction, a change in thought processes. It was what she had been waiting for. With a loud cry—"Hau!"—she gripped her sword in both hands and charged her opponent, allowing her gathered energy to explode in a flurry of furious strikes. Metal rang harshly on metal. Sparks flew from the blades. Her shocking scream, coupled with the sheer ferocity of her unexpected attack, caught Rykan off guard. Driving hard, her father's blade ringing incessantly on his, she forced him back relentlessly toward the sparking Firefield. Within two minutes she had drawn his blood, to the approving roar of her supporters.

✠ ✠ ✠ ✠ ✠

Watching from the sidelines, Robin gripped his hands tightly together. Through the touch on his shoulder he could feel the tremor of Pharikian's body as the fight began. He glanced up. Pharikian's eyes were wide as he witnessed the skill and fury that Sullyan's slight, fragile-looking body produced. Robin guessed he was realizing how deeply even he had underestimated her and finally understood what her General had meant when he recommended the Hierarch use her 'unique talents.'

His gaze travelled left to where Marik's white-knuckled hands clenched the rail of Idrimar's carriage. Robin heard the Count murmuring encouragement under his breath. Beside him, Idrimar watched with wide, pale eyes, shocked by the intensity of Sullyan's attack. Vanyr looked totally shaken by Sullyan's ferocity. Robin heard him mutter "Bloody hell!" two or three times and briefly wondered whether Vanyr was feeling thankful that Sullyan hadn't released this depth of rage on him. Behind Vanyr, Anjer, Ephan, and Kryp all watched with incredulity, clearly praying this unnatural strength would last.

✠ ✠ ✠ ✠ ✠

It didn't last, of course. Sullyan knew it couldn't. It did last long enough for her to force her opponent into the Firefield. Still trying to find his balance and gain an advantage, Rykan had forgotten how close the barrier was. Sidestepping a powerful thrust from her blade, his left foot moved too far and blundered into the raw element. Fire crackled viciously in response. Rykan snatched his foot away. Burned by the power and furious at the pain, his hoarse scream reverberated round the arena. He twisted, snarling, falling back under her incessant rain of deadly strokes.

"You'll suffer for that, witch! Yield now before I kill you."

Sullyan didn't waste her breath.

Favoring his left foot, Rykan kept the Firefield at his left shoulder and continued to fall back before her. She realized he was drawing her on, hoping she would use up her strength. Instantly, she changed tactics. Switching her sword into her left hand, she attacked his unprotected side, forcing him to parry awkwardly. He was still too close to the Firefield, and the tip of his sword just caught its edge. There was a sharp *crack!* as the metal of his sword flared red-hot. Fire shot up the blade, stinging his hand, and he cried out once more.

"Curse you!"

Sullyan immediately came after him, aiming more vicious cuts at his body, forcing him further back. It was a small victory, but she knew he was too good a swordsman not to rally. He had her measure now, and she could see his brain working. Suddenly, he broke away from her attack, giving himself room to breathe. She allowed it, her own first flush of strength nearly spent.

As they circled each other again, she noted that his hot yellow gaze never left her face. His underestimation of her was now completely reversed, and he was watching her with wary respect as well as anger. She registered this with a flash of unconscious intuition. Her mind was already planning how next to put him off balance, and she still had reserves of donated strength left before she must rely totally on her own.

Rykan decided to try her own tactics against her and rushed her abruptly, his grip double-handed. She had been waiting for something of the sort and sidestepped his powerful stroke, twisting to come up behind him before he could recover. Her low slash to the leg would have hamstrung him had he not been so agile. As it was, she opened a long, shallow cut on his left thigh, her success bringing a raucous cheer from her supporters. Rykan ignored the wound, pivoting swiftly to catch her before she completed her stroke. She swayed back, sweeping her blade round to meet his. The clash of steel on steel reverberated through the air.

✤ ✤ ✤ ✤ ✤

Rienne and Bull, his arms locked tight around her waist, her mind enmeshed with his, shared emotions as they watched through Robin's eyes. Bull had to use all his power to enable Rienne to see, as she couldn't consciously receive his thoughts. Due to her inability to shield, he was subjected to the full flood of her emotions, and this was uncomfortable for them both. She knew it took all his concentration and control to remain open for her, and her uncontrolled flow of panic, fear, terror, and love confused his senses. His admiration for Sullyan's skills helped in some measure to calm Rienne's nerves, but she was all too aware of the strain this was putting on him. His breathing grew ever more ragged and his heart limped in a chest tight with pain.

She was only vaguely aware of Cal and Taran standing a little way off, both lost in the contest unfolding below them. She imagined them analyzing every sword stroke, every footfall, as they tried to guess Sullyan's next move. So caught up in the duel was she that she didn't even wonder whether anyone had recently checked their surroundings.

✤ ✤ ✤ ✤ ✤

The longer Sullyan fought the Duke, the more familiar each became to the other. She knew he had finally recognized her skill. She could sense his grudging respect, his acknowledgement of the way she used her height and weight to her own advantage. She in turn had learned why he was considered the best swordsman in the land and was beginning to fear she wouldn't be able to defeat him unless he made a mistake.

Lithely, he avoided her latest feint, making her grunt with effort as she parried his counter swing.

Frustration gnawed at her. He was just too tall, too strong, and too good, she thought, whereas she was not at full strength, weeks of illness and abuse behind her. Yet this just made her more determined, and as he came at her again, aiming an overhead strike at her head, she called once more on her fading reserves of donated strength.

Switching hands yet again to keep him off balance, she got in a few more telling blows, flicking through his defense with the tip of her sword. She drew his blood once more and he gasped in pain. Although the wounds were superficial, psychologically they gave her an advantage. He had only managed to touch her once and she knew it galled him. Gathering her strength she rushed him, driving him relentlessly backward until his left hand once again touched the Firefield.

"Agghh, you wretched girl!"

Pain wrung the cry from him. The shame of being forced three times into the barrier ignited a powerful bloodlust in Rykan. He roared his rage, his face turning purple with strain and frustration.

"You've thwarted my plans long enough, you witch! I'm the most powerful lord in this realm and I'm too close to achieving my goal. No one—and certainly not a human witch—is going to stand in my way!"

Abruptly, heedless of injury or defense, he flung himself

against her, trying to use his vastly superior reach and weight to get past her guard. She fell back, letting him rush past her. As he did so, he pivoted, and the edge of his blade just caught her side, opening a long cut down her right flank.

She gave an agonized gasp.

The cut wasn't deep, but it bled freely. Normally she would have closed it with a thought, as Rykan had with his own wounds, but the spellsilver prevented her. Blood soaked her thin chemise and she steeled herself to ignore the pain. The gasp of horror that soughed round the watchers died away as she parried Rykan's follow-up and came back at him again.

Furious that his blade had failed to do worse damage, Rykan tried one of his tricks; a sly feinting turn to the left, followed by a thrust partially hidden by his body. Thanks to Vanyr's expert coaching, Sullyan recognized the move and sidestepped it neatly. She heard Vanyr's yell of approval as Rykan expended his strength on empty air.

✠ ✠ ✠ ✠ ✠

On the sidelines, Robin strained unknowingly against the Hierarch's hands. He was so intent on Sullyan and so inextricably linked to Bull that he barely had a conscious thought left. If Pharikian hadn't had both hands firmly gripped on his shoulders, he would have run to the Firefield and flung himself against it. He was willing Sullyan on so strongly that he was only vaguely aware of his surroundings. He knew that the Hierarch had passed Anjer a tense message, and that Anjer had come closer, but didn't give a thought to whether Anjer might be there to help restrain him.

In the carriage beside him, he could hear Marik fidgeting with worry. Idrimar constantly murmured to him, obviously doubting the wisdom of letting him watch, for he refused to keep still. She repeated her fears for his recovery, exhorting him not to rise to his feet. Yet he was totally focused on the duel and Robin knew he couldn't hear her.

His attention snapped back to the arena.

Something had changed.

✣ ✣ ✣ ✣ ✣

Sullyan was tiring and knew Rykan was too. They had been fighting for the best part of an hour, most of it short, sharp bursts of fury followed by careful circling and well-planned attacks. She was bleeding from innumerable small wounds which sapped her energy. Rykan had closed most of his wounds, but the expenditure of metaforce under such pressure had taken its toll even on him.

The Duke had tried all but one of his nasty little tricks and found each one countered by Sullyan's quick reactions. At first he had shown rage and surprise, but soon after her last success she had seen him cast a glance at the sidelines to where Vanyr stood watching the bout. Rykan clearly suspected Vanyr had coached her. She noted the cold, hard fury rising in his eyes and knew that murder would be its consequence.

Vanyr's fate could wait, though. Sullyan simply couldn't disguise the fact that she was coming to the end of her strength, and she was well aware that Rykan knew it. Her evasive moves were slower, her attacks less precise. Despite the fact that Rykan was tiring also, she was sure he would outlast her.

Despair flooded her heart. It was what she had expected, what she had planned for, but still the panic rose.

The end was very close now.

Chapter Thirty-Five

At the base of a small hill, twenty men crouched in the trees. Their leader gestured and three of them followed him as he began a slow, stealthy upward creep. All had knives in their hands.

On reaching the crest of the hill, they saw a group of four Albians oblivious to their surroundings and totally engrossed in the drama below. The one woman in the group had both hands tightly clenched and pressed to her mouth, the pressure of her huge companion's arms around her waist unheeded as she stared with blank eyes. Two younger men—one of them the target—stood apart from the other two, closer to the trees. They were far enough away that the man and the woman couldn't directly see them.

Silently, the leader indicated the two men. His three followers nodded. The Albians had heard nothing and remained ignorant of the danger behind them.

✤ ✤ ✤ ✤ ✤

Down in the arena, soaked in sweat, her breath coming in ragged gasps, Sullyan knew things were coming to a climax. She had exhausted her donated strength long ago and was fighting both Rykan and the effects of his poison completely unaided. It sapped her will, weakened her muscles, and slowed her reactions. She was running on instinct, on pure panic, and could afford no mistakes.

Rykan, unaware of the insidious creep of his poison within her, simply assumed she had come to the end of her endurance. Yet he too was exhausted, she could see it. Despite his superior strength, he was failing. Her lighter mass had enabled her to last as long as she had—that and her desire for revenge—and although none of Rykan's rage or determination to defeat her had diminished, she knew that he now held more respect for her than at any other time in the past. She had even seen a glimmer of something else in his eyes and wondered whether he was regretting his brutal abuse. Yet things had gone too far for such thoughts now. He was still pressing her hard, beating down on her sword, forcing her to parry, and subtly drawing her ever closer to the Firefield.

She was powerless to prevent it.

She didn't have the strength.

✤ ✤ ✤ ✤ ✤

Robin, remembering Vanyr's coaching session, watched intently for the one move Rykan hadn't yet attempted. Silently, desperately, he urged Sullyan on. He could feel everyone around him doing the same. The air fairly prickled with tension and fear. Although he was fully aware of her skills and her strength, even Robin was astounded by what he had witnessed today. In all his life he had never seen such a consummate display of skill and nerve, and it was all the more incredible when he remembered her physical state. His love for her had never been greater and his respect for her knew no bounds.

Then he gave a gasp of recognition. Rykan was preparing for his final trademark move.

✤ ✤ ✤ ✤ ✤

Sweat streamed into Sullyan's eyes, her breath rasped raw in her throat. She was ready for it all to be over. She had nothing left to give. Fully aware that all her skills and cunning had failed to overcome Rykan, she now accepted that he was her master. Defeat was inevitable. It was only a matter of time and she hoped it would be quick. She would have risked a glance at Robin had her training not kept her eyes locked on her opponent.

The Duke, breath heaving through lungs starved of air, suddenly lunged at her. She sidestepped as he intended she should, but was unable to complete the move due to the Firefield's proximity. Forced to veer awkwardly to avoid being burned, she was momentarily wrong-footed. Like a striking snake, Rykan made another lunge—a feint—to her unprotected side. At the last minute, he swerved and charged her, striking her shoulder, then slipped his sword under hers, twisting it violently out of her hand. Following through on the charge, he forced her to the ground.

As she fell, her hand struck the Firefield. Rykan stamped viciously on her wrist to keep it there.

The crunch of splintering bones was shockingly loud before her agonized shrieks filled the air.

Profound silence settled over the crowd. The only sounds were the combatants' heaving, ragged breaths, Sullyan's tinged with agony as her hand charred sickeningly in the Firefield. Rykan stood with one foot planted on her shattered wrist, the other against her waist. His sword point rested firmly between her breasts as he stared avidly down into her pain-filled eyes.

✣ ✣ ✣ ✣ ✣

Apart from one disbelieving gasp, Robin watched in silence. He was trembling violently. Behind him, hands still gripping his shoulders, Pharikian held his breath painfully tight. Even in his shocked state, Robin could sense the Hierarch's panic. He could also hear the generals muttering frantic denials and Marik openly weeping in the carriage. Idrimar had her arms wrapped around the Count, as much to stop him rising as for comfort.

Only one voice broke the appalled silence. Vanyr, incredulous and stricken on the sidelines, clearly couldn't believe what he had seen. His hands balled into fists at his side, he cried out in a great roar of anguish.

"NO!"

Vanyr stared back and forth between the tableau in the arena and the Hierarch at its edge. "But I showed her that move!" he cried. "We practiced it! She could do it better than I could! She should have seen it coming! Why didn't she see it coming?"

Staring at Robin, his voice harsh, he demanded, "Why didn't she see it coming?"

Robin didn't have any answers.

✛ ✛ ✛ ✛ ✛

On the hill, Taran heard Rienne's soul-rending cry as Rykan triumphed over Sullyan. She covered her face with her hands, unable to bear what she was seeing. Bull seemed to be having trouble breathing. His left hand clutched at his chest while his right rubbed his upper left arm. His eyes remained locked on the scene below, but his face had gone grey and his lips were tinged with blue.

Like Cal beside him, Taran was frozen. They stood locked together in disbelieving horror. Taran had lost contact with Bull's mind, but his attention remained focused on the arena. His every sense strained toward Sullyan, as if by sheer will he could alter what had just happened. He knew the spellsilver she wore would prevent him from reaching her psyche, but still he tried.

Until a cold, sharp knife pressed beneath his ear and the rancid smell of bad breath flooded into his nose.

✛ ✛ ✛ ✛ ✛

Robin was frantic. Sullyan's breathless shrieks as the Firefield burned her cut to his heart, and he would have fallen to his knees if not for the hands gripping his shoulders.

"Cut the field!" he cried, desperately struggling against the Hierarch's hold. "Can't you see she's burning? For pity's sake,

Majesty, cut the field!"

Pharikian's voice was rough with anguish. "I can't, son, I'm honor bound to maintain it until the victor is declared."

"But the bastard's won, hasn't he?" yelled Robin. "What more do you want?"

The Hierarch's grip tightened. "It might not be over," he hissed. "She hasn't yielded yet. Have faith in her, son."

Abruptly, Robin stilled. Pharikian's words echoed Sullyan's earlier plea and he rounded angrily on the elderly ruler. "You know something, don't you? Something she didn't tell me. What is it, what's going on? Tell me!"

Pharikian gazed into Robin's eyes, reading his pain and helplessness. He shook his head. "It's a gamble, son, nothing more. Just trust her and watch."

Anjer and the generals had also heard Pharikian's words and stared incredulously into the arena. Even Vanyr moved closer to the barrier.

✣ ✣ ✣ ✣ ✣

Sullyan whimpered as Rykan removed his boot from her shattered wrist. Slowly, she found the strength to move her badly charred hand from the Fire. The agony was overwhelming and the stench of burned flesh took her breath away, making her feel sick and disoriented. Loss of blood and the poison weakened her still further until it was as much as she could do to meet her tormentor's eyes.

Rykan towered over her, straddling her body, the tip of his sword still resting between her breasts. The fabric of her chemise, red and wet with blood, was torn from the sharp steel point. An evil smile twisted his lips as he gazed down on her.

"Well, my dear," he said, breathing heavily, "here we are again. You really didn't have to go through all that to gain my attention, you know. I'm quite willing to renew our acquaintance, and I can assure you that I, at least, will enjoy the experience."

His words froze her heart. She wouldn't wager against him raping her again, even now, in full public view. In fact, she thought, it would probably heighten his arousal, especially with Robin looking on. The Firefield, which she herself had proposed and which Pharikian could not, in honor, remove until she formally yielded, would prevent any interference.

Centering her fury, she let it strengthen her resolve. Anger was all she had left. She stared up at him, putting all her scorn and disgust into her eyes, hoping to infuriate him with her defiance as she had once before. He frowned and she felt momentary satisfaction. But then he leaned a little harder on his blade and it slipped beneath her skin, causing her to gasp with pain.

"You'll not escape me now," he warned her, his yellow eyes frigid. "You've been defeated and must abide by the terms of our agreement. Your powers are forfeit and I claim my right."

He shifted his feet, planting one on each of her wrists to pin her down. She shrieked again, unable to bear the pain as the shattered bones of her left wrist shot needles of agony up her arm. A ripple of anger ran round the arena at this unnecessary brutality, but Rykan ignored it. Once she was securely pinned, he removed and sheathed his blade.

Looking down on her, he said, "Well, witch? Are you ready to surrender? Are you ready to give up your power?"

Cold despair flooded her and she closed her eyes. Rykan's next words would seal her fate, and she was totally helpless, too exhausted even for panic. This was her worst nightmare come true, and she had sought it out all by herself. She felt great sorrow for the grief of her friends—especially Robin—and wished she could speak with them now. She desperately needed a friendly voice to help her through this.

Suddenly, almost as if he had heard her, Marik's furious voice rang clearly across the arena.

"Don't give in, Brynne! Don't give the bastard what he wants! Remember how you held out before? You can do it again, I know you can! We trust you, Brynne. We love you! Don't forget it!"

Rykan's face darkened in fury. His head came up and he screamed at Marik, his foot grinding on Sullyan's wrist, wrenching another agonized cry from her throat.

"Silence, traitor! I'm the victor here and I claim what's mine by right! I'll deal with you later, and when I do, you'll wish Sonten's blade had done its work properly that night!"

Sullyan barely registered his face as he glanced back down at her. The agony of her shattered wrist drowned her in nausea and she felt herself slipping away. Rykan's face blotted out the light as he leaned down, his voice a savage snarl.

"Don't you die on me before I get what I want, girl!"

His weight shifted from her wrists and he reached closer, his fingers circling the spellsilver collar, arm tensing as he prepared to wrench her to her knees. The collar blocked his power as well as hers, and despite his reluctance to touch it, he had to remove it before the transference of power could take place. Limp and spent, Sullyan hung in his grip.

✣ ✣ ✣ ✣ ✣

Taran's sight faded to black as the spellsilver knife pressed in below his ear, shutting off every sense he possessed. Shocked and frightened, he tried to cry a warning to Cal or Bull, but a hand clamped painfully over his mouth, making speech impossible. Weakened, sickened by the spellsilver's touch, he felt himself being hustled backward into the trees.

"The General wants a word with you," growled a threatening voice in his ear.

The words sounded oddly muffled, and all he could see were vague, dark shapes. Coldly fearful, he could do nothing as his captors wrestled him away, leaving his companions oblivious on the hill.

✣ ✣ ✣ ✣ ✣

She knew she had to be quick. As soon as Rykan's hand tightened on the silver collar, Sullyan gave in to her terror. Fuelled by desperation, determination, anguish, and shame, she made a heart-straining effort. Denied the time to realize that the collar was of his own making, Rykan was unable to stop her as her mind breached the spellsilver, slipping past its effects to fasten on his. At the same time, her right hand shot out and gripped his wrist, preventing him from releasing the collar.

Immediately, his senses flooded her psyche. Rykan's shock at her impossible use of metaforce nearly overwhelmed her. He roared in pain as her mind clamped down, desperately latching onto his awareness. He still hadn't realized the spellsilver was his, and so didn't know how to counter it. Sullyan took advantage of his disarray to shoot needles of force into his brain, making him scream. He struggled furiously, momentarily blinded, fighting the draining of his strength. Sweat beaded his brow and his eyes bulged with horror.

"But this is treachery!" His voice rasped with pain. "I defeated you! You accepted the agreement. You were Witnessed! You cannot break the Code!"

She speared him yet again with hot needles of metaforce. "The Code stands, my Lord, as does the agreement. Do I look defeated? Did I yield to you?"

He groaned as every portion of his mind was overwhelmed by her power. "Might of arms only, those were the terms!"

Pain roughened her voice. "But did you not also agree to the use of a Firefield, within which all would be fair?"

She felt his anger as he suddenly saw the implications of those terms. Slowly, his body gave way under her pressure and he fell to his knees. With her grip on his left wrist unrelenting, his right hand came to rest on the ground by her left arm. His white and sweating face hovered inches above hers.

"But the silver?" he croaked. "How have you breached the spellsilver?"

She held his stare. "I had plenty of time to learn about your spellsilver, my Lord."

"My ...?"

His eyes widened, seeing the trick.

"I had little else to do and so was forced to find new ways to resist you. I am afraid you underestimated me badly."

Merciless, she gave his captive brain another wrench, drawing a groan of agony from him. She held him immobile, pinned by her power to the spellsilver field. Slowly, painfully, she inched out from beneath him, ignoring the fresh flow of blood this brought from her wounds. Still gripping his wrist, as much for support as restraint, she raised herself to her knees. True to her vow, she would not lie helpless beneath him.

"Yield, my Lord."

His yellow eyes, screwed up with pain, glared back at her. She saw defiance that echoed her own, and smiled. Inexorably, she tightened her grip on his mind. The muscles and tendons in his neck bulged as he fought not to cry out.

"Yield!" she demanded, her gaze boring into his. The whites of his eyes slowly filled with blood at the pressure she was exerting. He wasn't far from passing out and she didn't want that. Easing her grip slightly, she sent hot needles into his nerves. This time, he couldn't bite back the agony which escaped in a raw scream.

Her voice hissed through clenched teeth, her own pain fuelling her fury. "One more time, my Lord. Will ... you ... yield?"

Huge tears welled from his eyes as the pain became too much.

She felt his spirit crumble. Almost inaudibly, he whispered, "Yes."

She gave him another wrench. "The Hierarch did not hear you."

Raising her voice as far as her waning strength allowed, she cried, "Rykan, Duke of Kymer, do you cede the field of combat?"

She stabbed him again and his voice escaped in a hoarse cry.

"Yes, damn you, yes! I yield!"

A vast, triumphant roar erupted from the watchers round the Hierarch's pavilion. Rykan's admission was the cue for the heralds to blow a prearranged fanfare declaring the Champion's victory. The resulting crescendo of sound from the assembled army and the Citadel behind was deafening.

✢ ✢ ✢ ✢ ✢

The instant he heard Rykan's words, Pharikian cut the Firefield. He ignored Robin's frantic pleas for release and instead ordered Anjer to restrain him. Robin was forced to watch and listen as Andaryon's ruler approached the pair on the ground.

His face stern with worry, Pharikian took note of the blood on Sullyan's body, the blue tinge to her lips, and the tremor of her hand which still gripped Rykan's wrist. His eyes skated over the ruin of her left hand, but the smell of charred flesh was unavoidable. Robin's eyes blurred with tears. He would never forget that stench.

Neither combatant registered Pharikian's approach. He had to touch Sullyan's shoulder to gain her attention. Without slackening her grip on Rykan's mind, she glanced up, and even Robin could see the feral hunger in her eyes. Pharikian reacted with shock. Sullyan dampened her fury, but Robin knew she couldn't release it altogether. It was probably the only thing keeping her from flying apart.

His metasenses fully functioning now that the Firefield had gone, Robin felt the Hierarch reaching out to Sullyan through the breach in the spellsilver. His soothing flow of metaforce relieved the pain of her wounds as well as Rykan's poison. With a sigh of relief, she slumped, dropping Rykan's wrist. The Duke's hand fell from the collar and Robin could clearly see where it had burned him.

Pharikian reached down and freed the collar from Sullyan's throat. She gave an agonized cry as it dropped away. Her head fell forward and he had to support her to keep her from falling. Using a little more power, he halted the flow of her blood, but Robin knew she had already lost far more than she could afford.

Gradually, he saw her rally until she was able to support herself. She remained kneeling, though, lacking the strength to stand. The Hierarch stood looking at Rykan, whose mind was still not his own. The Duke's yellow eyes glared hatefully back.

Pharikian raised his voice. "Rykan, Duke of Kymer, you have failed to resist my challenge and have yielded before witnesses. I hereby declare the Crown's Champion to be the victor. In accordance with the terms of your agreement, your life is forfeit. I hereby grant it to Brynne Sullyan to do with as she will."

There was another roar of approval from those loyal to Pharikian. Rykan glared venomously at Sullyan, but the Hierarch wasn't finished. Once the noise abated, he continued.

"If you wish it, you may yet have a chance to redeem your life, although your rank and lands will still be forfeit to the Crown. Will you hear the terms?"

Sullyan glanced at the Hierarch and slightly shook her head. A sly look crept into Rykan's eyes, and Robin guessed he had realized he might not be completely powerless. If the Hierarch was prepared to discuss terms, Rykan might yet have some leverage. He remained silent, however, pretending to consider.

Pharikian grew impatient. "Well?"

Through his pain, Rykan smiled. "I'll hear your terms, Timar."

Past caring about formalities, the Hierarch ignored the insult. "Your brutal and unforgivable abuse of the Lady Brynne has left a lethal legacy."

Rykan's gaze switched back to Sullyan and his eyes narrowed. She didn't react, her eyes dark with the strain of holding him captive. Robin's heart ached to hold her, to soothe that strain away.

Pharikian ignored the Duke's speculative look. "You have the power to remedy the situation, and this is the means by which you could redeem your life. Make no mistake, Rykan, Brynne Sullyan doesn't ask for this. She was ready to die if necessary and quite willing to take you with her. I have granted her your life, but if you agree to do this, she will agree to spare you."

The momentary flash of anger in Sullyan's eyes clearly stated her disapproval of this plea-bargaining. Robin's heart sank. *Rykan will milk this for all it's worth,* he thought. *After all, he has nothing to lose.*

"And what will my life be, Majesty, without the means for living?" snarled the Duke. "If my rank and lands are forfeit, what use is life to me?" Staring at Sullyan, he smiled nastily. "It might just be possible to persuade me to do this favor for you, but it will cost you more than my life!"

Sullyan's eyes turned black and hot as she sent agonizing needles of pain deeper into Rykan's skull. He screamed and cowered back.

Pharikian was furious. "How dare you bargain with me, Rykan? Those are the terms, accept or refuse. Your life for hers. That is what I offer. Give me your answer!"

Rykan gasped for breath, his burned fingers clawing the air. "I refuse!" he shrieked. "I wouldn't give either of you the dirt from under my feet, let alone save her life. You can both go to Perdition for all I care, and I'll be waiting for you! By the looks of her, I won't have long to wait."

He stared at them, chest rasping as he tried to laugh. The terrible sound tore through Robin's heart as he struggled in Anjer's arms. Tears poured down his face as his last hope for Sullyan disappeared. Slumping, spent and exhausted, he sobbed brokenly, arms clasped around his aching chest.

✣ ✣ ✣ ✣ ✣

Pharikian stared at the rebel lord and at the small, slight figure on her knees. Sullyan was holding herself stiffly upright by might of will alone. He laid a gentle hand on her shoulder.

"Forgive me, Brynne, I had to try. If you still think you can do it, if you still have the strength, use it now with my blessing. Do with him as you will."

Turning away, he came back to stand beside Robin.

From where he half-lay on the bloody ground, Rykan stared into Sullyan's face, his eyes filled with loathing. He was clearly expecting a swift, knifelike thrust into his brain, followed by oblivion. She could sense him preparing for it. She didn't oblige. Meeting the hate in his eyes, she allowed the pressure of her grip to slacken. Immediately, he shot out a probe to test her control.

She easily countered this sally. "Oh no, my Lord, you will not be released. Not yet, anyway."

Infuriated by her hesitation, he frowned. "Are you playing with me, witch? My life is yours. Have you the courage to take it or not?"

She cocked her head. "Ah, you were expecting me to kill you. Well, you may believe me or not as you choose, but I care very little whether you live or die. Killing you is not my purpose. I have claimed your life because I require utter and ultimate power over you and all that you possess."

His frown deepened, not understanding the distinction. She held his gaze, deliberately silent, while she began the process she had been planning. Gradually, almost gently, she insinuated her mind deep into his, gathering, stealing, working her way toward the intimate seat of his power. His psyche and the sum of his metaforce, right down to his spirit and ultimate essence; this was what she intended to suck from him, what she prepared to take into herself.

Suddenly realizing what she was doing, he shrieked, "NO!" and tried to clamp down his shield. Yet he couldn't force her out. She had twined her psyche around his innermost soul and was inextricably linked to him now. With the pain of her violation wringing a hoarse scream from his throat, he almost passed out.

Grimly, Sullyan held on to his consciousness. Denied the release of oblivion, Rykan began to struggle physically, as if that could help him. She let him use his strength, knowing he could hurt her no more.

Feeling the continuing leach of his powers, he cried, "But you can't do that! I'm not willing! I refuse to surrender my power! You can't do it!"

"Oh, but my Lord," she hissed, "I believe you will find that I can."

"How?" he groaned, the terrible pain growing as his inner being slowly tore apart. "How is this possible?"

She gazed at him, all the while drawing out the heart and core of his power, filament by agonized filament.

"Do you really not know? Why do you think I laid claim to your life instead of just the sum of your power? I knew you would never help me willingly, and your metaforce alone would not suffice if you refused the Hierarch's terms. No, my Lord, I need your very soul for this task, and it was you who gave me the means to take it. Do not think to complain. You would have been spared this pain had you acceded to the Hierarch's request, but it is too late now. Do you not remember the words of the ancient bargain?"

"Bargain?" he rasped. "What bargain?"

"I will explain. When someone willingly gives their essence to another as a gift freely given, they also give influence over their psyche. You are a Master-elite, my Lord. Surely you have heard this?"

"What are you talking about?" He was almost screaming. "I gave you no gifts, freely or otherwise!"

"Oh, but you did, my Lord. On four brutal occasions, as I recall. Count Marik even watched you. Surely you remember?"

His eyes bulged as understanding crashed upon him.

Her gaze was hot and vengeful, her voice a hiss. "By the power of your seed within me, seed that you gave with such savage pleasure, you gave me your essence. With it I was able to work past your spellsilver, and with it I am able to reach within you now and take what you would deny me."

She extracted another strand of his soul, causing him to gibber in horror and pain. The import of her words and the agony of this appalling rape sent shockwaves through Rykan. He trembled violently like a dog with ague. The consequences of her actions clearly terrified him, and with good reason. His body might not immediately die without its soul, but his mind would suffer irreparable damage. He would become a husk—a helpless, drooling, mindless husk—and she knew that to a vital, virile man like Rykan, this was a fate far worse than death. A swift, clean death by either sword or metaforce he could have borne, but to linger on for days, maybe months if she chose, as an object of scorn or pity to his enemies? No, that he could not bear.

Desperation entered his eyes and he pleaded with her. "I beg you, Lady, don't do this!"

"Oh, is it 'Lady' now, my Lord? Is it begging?" Her eyes were hot with remembered pain and shame. "I seem to remember begging you when you forced yourself upon me time and time again! My voice went hoarse with pleading, but what good did it do me? What mercy did you show?"

Rykan stared at her, seeing no remorse and knowing he was doomed. She had all but sucked him dry and he had no resistance left, no defenses against her taking that last fundamental spark of psyche that made him who he was.

Suddenly, her expression softened.

"Yet I will have mercy on you, my Lord. For I am not like you, and even now, after all you have done, I will not become like you. I will not leave you naked, helpless, and torn, the way you left me, to die shivering and terrified in the dark."

Slowly, gently, causing him no further pain, she extracted the final thread of his psyche. She knew that the watchers around the arena had no indication of the dreadful suffering she had to endure in order to absorb his soul. It was alien, strange, it did not fit anywhere inside her, and it made her feel foul. She wished she could cast it from her but she needed it, at least for a while.

Weakly, her left arm hanging by her side, she staggered to her feet. Rykan still lay half-slumped on the ground, his features slack, his eyes dull and staring. There was still a spark of intelligence there—she had left him a shred of his mind—but the shock of her violation rendered him numb.

She walked unsteadily to where her sword had come to rest.

"Now you understand how it feels, my Lord."

Reaching down, she took the blade into her right hand and approached him once more.

"I'm sorry," he whispered, his dull eyes unmoving.

Furious that he had the gall to repent after all he had done, she hissed, "How dare you! It is too late for rue, my Lord, far too late!"

Standing before him, she stared down at her father's blade, its bright edge stained with Rykan's blood.

"No," she murmured, "I will not dishonor this blade with yet more Andaryan blood."

Rykan's eyes flashed briefly as his terror resurfaced. He understood she was going to kill him and welcomed it, but this refusal to use her sword panicked him anew.

She laid the blade awkwardly on the grass and reached instead for Rykan's heavier weapon. She pulled him to his knees, his head hanging, his eyes closed. There was no resistance, no defiance or fight left in him. She had stripped him of everything.

Groaning with pain, she brought her left hand round, using her right to clasp the charred fingers around Rykan's sword hilt. She held them there by covering them with her other hand. Without a thought she damped the agony of shattered wrist bones, and raised the heavy sword high past her right shoulder. Taking a deep breath, she gathered what little strength she had left.

✤ ✤ ✤ ✤ ✤

At that precise moment, Taran was lying bound and gagged over his horse's withers, a knife of spellsilver thrust through the ropes against his skin. He saw nothing.

Had he seen it, he would have recognized the stroke Sullyan used to sever Rykan's head. It was the same stroke he had used to kill Jaskin. He would have approved of the way she handled it and the neat, efficient job it made of striking off the defeated lord's head.

But he didn't see it, and he had no idea how the contest had ended.

He didn't see the Hierarch, along with Robin, now freed from Anjer's arms, run to catch the exhausted woman who collapsed, shaking, in the gory aftermath of Rykan's killing. He didn't see her anguish as the two men supported her in their arms. He didn't hear the cry she gave as she summed up Rykan's power, the power that should have been equal to hers, the power that should have been sufficient to remove the poison eating into her soul.

"It is not enough, Timar, it is not enough! I took all he had to give, but it is not enough!"

He did not see her, defeated and despairing, sink into hopeless oblivion.

The End

Glossary

Albian Characters

Amanus Elijah. Taran's deceased father. An Artesan Adept.

Bethyn Sullyan. Major Sullyan's mother, now deceased.

Bull, aka Bulldog, aka Hal Bullen. Major Sullyan's aide.

Cal Tyler. Taran's Artesan Apprentice.

Dexter. A sergeant at the Manor under Captain Tamsen.

Elias Rovannon. Albia's High King.

Falkerk. Weaponsmaster at the Manor.

Goran. Master cook at the Manor.

Hal Bullen. See 'Bull.'

Hanan. Chief Healer at the Manor.

Hyram. General Blaine's valet.

Jessy. Sister to Robin Tamsen, now deceased.

Mathias Blaine. The Manor's senior officer and General-in-Command to High King Elias.

Morgan Sullyan. Major Sullyan's father, now deceased.

Parren. A captain at the Manor.

Rienne Arlen. A healer, and Cal's lover.

Robin Tamsen. A captain at the Manor under Major Sullyan.

Solet. The Manor's stablemaster.

Sullyan. A major at the Manor under General Blaine.

Tad Greylin. Young kitchen boy at the Manor.

Taran Elijah. An Artesan who is desperate to learn his craft.

The Baron. Mysterious ally of Rykan, Duke of Kymer.

Andaryan Characters

Aeyron Pharikian. The Hierarch of Andaryon's son and Heir.

Almid. One of a pair of giant twins, members of Ky-shan's pirate band.

Anjer, Lord General. General in overall command of the Hierarch's forces.

Arif. A lieutenant in Rykan's forces.

Arlow. An Andaryan Baron, chamberlain to the previous Hierarch.

Barrin. A lieutenant in the Hierarch's forces.

Calder. A jailor at Duke Rykan's palace.

Deshan. The Hierarch's Master Healer, also a Master Artesan.

Ephan. A general in the Hierarch's forces, overall commander of the Velletian Guard.

Falina (Lady). The wife of General Kryp.

Gaslek. An Andaryan Baron, secretary to the Hierarch.

Harva. Marik's elderly former nursemaid.

Heron. Sonten's Artesan commander.

Hollet (Lady). The wife of General Ephan.

Idriana. The Hierarch's wife, now deceased.

Idrimar Pharikian. The Hierarch's daughter.

Is-kel. A member of Ky-shan's pirate band.

Jaskin. Sonten's nephew, who was killed by Taran.

Jay'el. Son of pirate leader Ky-shan.

Kester. One of a pair of giant twins, members of Ky-shan's pirate band.

Ki-en. Younger member of Ky-shan's pirate band.

Kryp. A general in the Hierarch's forces.

Ky-shan. The leader of a band of pirates from Andaryon's eastern seaboard.

Nazir. A minor noble in Count Marik's court.

Reece. One of Duke Rykan's commanders.

Rykan. Duke, Lord of Kymer province, and aspirant to the Andaryan throne.

Selmar Pharikian. Timar Pharikian's older brother, Heir to the Andaryan throne before his death.

Sh'iye. A member of Ky-shan's pirate band.

Sonten. Duke Rykan's ambitious general. Lord of Durkos province.

Tikhal. An Andaryan lord, also known as the Lord of the North. Pharikian's premier noble.

Timar Pharikian. The Hierarch, Supreme Ruler of Andaryon.

Torien (Lady). The wife of Lord General Anjer.

Ty Marik. Count of Cardon province under Rykan.

Vanyr. Commander of the Velletian Guard, the Hierarch's personal Guard.

Verris. A commander in Rykan's forces, now deceased.

Xeer. A member of Ky-shan's pirate band.

Realms of the World

First Realm—Endormir

Endormirians are sometimes known as 'Roamerlings' because of their itinerant habits. They are small and slim, dark skinned, with brown or black eyes showing hardly any whites. The Artesan gift runs only through the males, and gifted males always become clan-leaders. As Endomir suffers from severe winter conditions, its people cross the Veils into the other realms for the winter months, where they are well known as traders.

Second Realm—Sinnia

Sinnians are tall and milk-haired, with pale skin. They live in clans and were once nomadic but now live in settlements. All are born able to control their metaforce up to the rank of Adept and are thus considered 'sports'. Their race often produces highly gifted musicians and storytellers.

Third Realm—Relkor

Relkorians are small, fierce and stocky, notorious for raiding the other realms for slaves to work their mines and quarries. Their Artesans, both male and female, invariably become slave-lords.

Fourth Realm—Albia

Albia is the human realm. The Artesan gift runs through both male and female lines, each gender being equal in potential. The craft is currently out of favour due to raiding by both Relkorian and Andaryan Artesans. Albians widely believe that all Artesans use their powers only for gain and control.

Fifth Realm—Andaryon

A warlike race characterised by eyes with slit pupils. They fight constantly amongst themselves, vying for position within the Hierocracy. The Artesan gift passes only through the male line and females play a minor and downtrodden role. Only the most powerful Artesan can become and hold the rank of Hierarch. Their battles for supremacy are governed by strict, ritualistic laws.

Terms

Artesan. A person born with the ability to control metaforce and master the four primal elements.

Brine-rum. Strong liquor, drunk by pirates on Andaryon's eastern seaboard.

Codes of Combat. Strict laws governing any conflict between Andaryan nobles.

Demons. Derogatory term used in Albia to describe those of the Andaryan race.

Earth ball. An explosive sphere of Earth element formed by an Artesan for use as a weapon.

Fellan. A dark, aromatic and bitter beverage brewed from the seeds of the fellan-plant.

Firefield. A barrier formed from the primal element of Fire, through which only Artesans can pass. Firefields formed by those of inferior Artesan rank can easily be destroyed by those of a higher rank.

Firewater. Incredibly strong liquor.

Free traders. Another term for pirate.

Kingsman. Term used to describe members of the High King's fighting forces.

Metaforce (also called **life force**). The force of existence pertaining to all things, both animate and inanimate.

Perdition. A state of non-being for the soul—a place where souls with no ultimate destination reside.

Primal elements. Earth, Water, Fire and Air.

Primal Sacrament. Andaryan name for the Pact, an agreement brokered between Andaryan nobles. Used to settle wars ending in stalemate, it involves the willing suicide of a powerful Artesan.

Portway. Structure formed by an Artesan from a primal element—usually Earth or Water—which gives its creator access through the Veils.

Psyche. An Artesan's unique and personal pattern through which they can manipulate metaforce and channel the primal elements.

Roamerling. Slightly derogatory term for the nomads of Endormir.

Sally port. A small door within a larger fortified barrier, allowing only one person to pass through at a time.

Substrate. The medium in which the primal elements reside, and in which the world and all things have their being.

Tangwyr. Monstrous Andaryan raptor trained to hunt men.

The Pact. Widely believed to have been brokered in Andaryon by an Albian Master-elite, in order to reduce Andaryan raids on Albia. Apparently supported by the current Hierarch.

The Staff. Mysterious and terrible weapon capable of stealing and storing metaforce. Can only be used by Artesans.

The Veils. Misty barriers separating the five Realms of the World. Only Artesans have the power to move through the Veils.

The Void. Dark abyss at the end of life into which all souls pass before reaching their final destination.

The Wheel. Central principle of Albian faith.

Witch. Derogatory term for an Artesan.

Artesan ranks and their attributes

Level one: Apprentice. Person born with the Artesan gift and the ability to influence the first primal element of Earth. Able to hear other Artesans speaking telepathically but unable to initiate such speech.

Level two: Apprentice-elite. Has some skill in influencing their own metaforce. Has attained mastery over the element of Earth. Able to initiate telepathic speech but only with Artesans already known to them. Able to build substrate structures, identify a person by the pattern of their psyche, and counter metaphysical attack to some degree.

Level three: Journeyman. Has mastery over Earth and is able to influence Water. Able to build portways and travel through the Veils. Has some skill in using metaforce for offense. Also able to initiate psyche-overlay and converse telepathically with any other Artesan. Possesses some self-healing potential.

Level four: Adept. Has mastery over both Earth and Water. Able to build more complex substrate structures such as corridors. Able to influence where such structures emerge. Possesses stronger offensive and defensive capabilities. Able to merge psyche fully with other Artesans. Increased healing abilities.

Level five: Adept-elite. Has mastery over Earth and Water and is able to influence Fire. Possesses great healing powers which can even aid the ungifted (with their permission). Able to initiate powersinks and merges of psyche. Able to construct such structures as Firefields.

Level six: Master. Has mastery over Earth, Water and Fire. Able to control the power of an inferior Artesan against their will. Control over personal metaforce now almost total. Possesses incredible healing powers.

Level seven: Master-elite. Has mastery over Earth, Water and Fire and is able to influence Air, the most capricious primal element. Able to absorb a lesser or even equal-ranked Artesan's power and metaforce provided some link or permission (however tenuous) can be found.

Level eight: Senior Master. Has complete mastery over all four primal elements. Is able to absorb another Artesan's power by force, even sometimes without a link. Possesses a high degree of metaphysical (and usually spiritual) strength.

Level nine: Supreme Master. It has never been fully established whether this rank actually exists. Supreme Masters are supposedly able to influence Spirit - largely regarded as the mythical 'fifth element.' Ancient texts refer only to the possibility; no mention has ever been found of a being attaining Supreme Masterhood.

Sport or lay-Artesan. Freaks of nature, sports are thought to be able to control their own metaforce from birth, to whatever level of strength they inherently possess. As they receive no training their working is often undetectable. They are also believed to be able to 'hear' the thoughts of those around them; gifted or ungifted, and directly, not through the substrate.

Cas Peace

Cas Peace was born and brought up in the lovely county of Hampshire, in the UK, where she still lives. On leaving school, she trained for two years before qualifying as a teacher of equitation. During this time she also learned to carriage-drive. She spent thirteen years in the British Civil Service before moving to Rome, where she and her husband, Dave, lived for three years. They return whenever they can.

As well as her love of horses, Cas is mad about dogs, especially Lurchers. She enjoys dog agility training and currently owns two rescue Lurchers, Milly and Milo. Cas loves country walks, working in stained glass, and folk singing. She is currently working on writing and recording songs for each of her fantasy books. For King's Champion there is "The Ballad of Tallimore," which is mentioned in Chapter 19, and appears as a paraphrased verse in Chapter 23. All Cas's book songs can be found at and downloaded from her website, see below.

Cas has also written a nonfiction book, "For the Love of Daisy," which tells the life story of her beautiful Dalmatian. Details and other information can be found on her website, www.caspeace.com.

Artesans of Albia

Book One: *King's Envoy*

Book Two: *King's Champion*

Book Three: *King's Artesan*

If you enjoyed this first trilogy,

watch out for the next one:

Circle of Conspiracy,

coming soon!